GU01044387

'A Drug on the Market' first published in *Dark Terrors 6,*
edited by Stephen Jones and David Sutton, 2002.

'Tomorrow Town' first published at SciFi.com,
edited by Ellen Datlow, 2000.

'The Original Dr Shade' first published in *Interzone,*
edited by David Pringle, 1990.

'Famous Monsters' first published in *Interzone,*
edited by David Pringle, 1988.

'Organ Donors' first published in *Darklands 2,*
edited by Nicholas Royle, 1992.

'Going to Series' first published in *Dark Terrors 5,*
edited by Stephen Jones and David Sutton, 2000.

'Angel Down Sussex' first published in *Interzone,*
edited by David Pringle, 1999.

'Dead Travel Fast' first published in *Unforgivable Stories,*
by Kim Newman, 2000.

'Amerikanski Dead at the Moscow Morgue' first published in *999:*
New Stories of Horror and Suspense,
edited by Al Sarrantonio, 1999.

'The Big Fish' first published in *Interzone,*
edited by David Pringle, 1993.

DEAD

TRAVEL

FAST

105 West 73rd Street
New York, NY 10023
www.dinoship.com

0-9728585-3-9

DEAD

TRAVEL

FAST

Stories by Kim Newman

FOR ELLEN DATLOW

NOTE ON THE TITLE

In *Dracula*, Bram Stoker has a walk-on character mutter 'denn die Todten reiten schnell', which Jonathan Harker recognises as a quotation from Ludwig Berger's poem 'Lenore' (1773). Stoker/Harker slightly fudges the English translation as 'for the dead travel fast' – it should be 'for the dead ride fast'. He uses the same line in 'Dracula's Guest', where it appears (in Russian) on a tomb.

I remember a lurid paperback being passed around school in 1972 called *For the Dead Travel Fast*, by someone named Richard Tate (who turns out to be Anthony Masters) and a net trawl reveals that Gregory Nicoll used 'For the Dead Travel Fast' as a short story title.

Stoker didn't seem sure what the quotation actually meant, and neither am I.

K.N.

INTRODUCTION

The afterwords to the stories collected here have already tipped the word length of this book well over the agreed 100,000 – so I don't intend to detain you long in this general introduction.

When bookshops (bookstores in America) had horror sections, that's where my novels tended to be put. I've written a lot about monsters – including a run of vampire novels (the *Anno Dracula* series). Though I also write science fiction (*The Night Mayor*), fantasy (as by Jack Yeovil) and literary experiment (*Life's Lottery*). And even my monster books have elements of s-f, mystery, satire, romance, thriller, historical speculation, pop culture metafiction and whatever else I feel like it. That's probably an excuse for the catch-all nature of the stories in this book, which range quite widely in setting, subject and voice. Not that I'm one of those writers who distances himself from category – as in 'it may be called *Werewolf Cheerleaders*, but it's about *relationships*'. As Jack Yeovil, I once wrote a book called *Orgy of the Blood Parasites*, and, as Kim Newman, I'm working on one called *An English Ghost Story*, so clearly I'm interested in and proud of work that covers the entire spectrum of a form I'll happily label horror.

If there's a unifying trend in this particular batch of my stories, it might be bleed-over from my other job as a critic. I'm a regular film reviewer for *Empire* and *Sight and Sound* in the UK (plus many other print and broadcast markets) and have written or edited several non-fiction books (*Nightmare Movies, Apocalypse Movies*), mostly about the movies but sprawling over into television, the pulps, genre literature, politics, pop music, comics and other good, fun stuff. As every creative writing teacher will tell you, write what you know. Arthur C. Clarke writes about satellites and John Grisham writes about lawyers because in their other careers they think a lot about space technology and the law, and — big revelation! — *thinking* is where ideas come from. I think a lot about the subjects listed above, and often my fictions come from sparks struck while paying attention to the media.

The equivalence of criticism and vampirism is probably too obvious to be worth elucidating — though I recommend Conor McPherson's play/monologue *St. Nicholas*, which drills into that particular nerve. *Anno Dracula* is literally a vampire novel, in that it fastens on another novel and bleeds it, feeds off it, transforms it and perhaps kills it or perhaps makes it immortal. Most of these stories scratch similar sores.

— Kim Newman, London, February 2004

DEAD

TRAVEL

FAST

A DRUG

ON THE MARKET

Had my first London enterprise met with a lesser success, Leo Dare would not have invited me to join the *consortium*; and had it met with a greater, I should not have accepted his invitation.

However, response to the patent Galvanic Girdle, an electrical aid to weight reduction, merely shaded towards the positive end of indifference. After the craze for such sparking yet health-giving devices in my own native United States, this came as a disappointment. My British partners in the endeavour preferred to make known the virtues of the marvelous modern invention through public demonstration, with testimonials from newly-slender 'Yankee' worthies, rather than incur the apparent expense of taking advertising space by the yard in the illustrated press. This was a sorry mistake: our initial penuriousness served to alienate the proprietors of those organs. The 'papers took to running news items about the nasty shocks suffered by galvanised ladies of a certain age through overuse or misapplication of our battery-belt. In brief, the Fourth Estate was set against us rather than in our corner. The grand adventure of 'slenderness – through electro-cution!' – the slogan was my own contribution to the enterprise – was frankly sluggish and slowing to a halt. I foresaw a lengthy struggle towards profitability, with the prospect of a smash always a shadow to the promise of rich dividends. I was not looking to get out – the example of New York proved that the trick could be done, and the odd singed spinster would be easy to set aside with a proper advertising campaign – but when the third post of a Tuesday brought a card from Leo Dare, requesting my presence at the birth of a *consortium*, my interest was pricked.

The public does not know his name, but Leo Dare is an Alexander of the market-place, a hero and an example among the enterprising. Unlike many of his apparent peers, he endows no museums or galleries, seeks no title or honour and erects no statues to himself. He is not caricatured in *Punch*, quoted in sermons or travestied in the works of lady novelists. He has simply made, risked, lost and regained fortunes beyond human understanding. In '82, Leo Dare cornered quap — an unpleasantly textured, slightly luminescent, West African mud which is the world's major source of elements vital to the manufacture of filaments essential in the (then-uninvented) incandescent lamp. Great quantities of the radio-active stuff sat in warehouse bins for years, as rivals joked that the sharp fellow had been blunted at last. A succession of night-watchmen succumbed to mystery ailments, giving rise to legends of 'the curse of the voo-doo' and of witch-doctors conjuring doom for those who stole 'the sacred dirt'. Then, thanks to Mr Thomas Alva Edison, control of quap became very desirable indeed and Leo Dare, clearly the reverse of cursed, cashed out in style. In '91, he introduced pneumatic bicycle tires and obliterated overnight the market for solid rubber. Not only do pneumatic tires offer a more pleasant, less guts-scrambling bicycling experience but they are prone to puncture and wearing-out, necessitating frequent purchase of replacements and creating an ancillary demand for repair equipment, patches and pumps – in all of which our Alexander naturally took an interest.

The particular genius of Leo Dare, that quality which those 'in the know' aptly call 'Dare-ing', is not in discovery or invention — for canny minds are at his beck and call to handle those tasks — but in the conversion through enterprise of intellect into affluence. The old saw has it that if 'you build a better mouse-trap, the world will beat a path to your door.' In these distracting times, the world has other things on its mind than keeping apace with the latest rodent-apprehension patents, and any major advance in the field has to be brought forcibly to its attention. Even then, Better Mouse Trap must compete with inferior snares that have an established following, or lobby successfully for a Royal Seal of Approval, or are simply blessed with a more 'catching' name. Better Mouse Trap, Ltd. will find itself in the care of the receivers if its finely manufactured products are placed in stores beside a less worthy effort retailing at 2d cheaper under the name of Best Mouse Trap. Leo Dare could make a fine old go of Better Mouse Trap, but if he had the rights to Worse Mouse Trap, he would represent it as Best Mouse Trap of All, emblazon the box with a two-coloured illustration of an evil-looking mouse surprised by a guillotine, undercut Best Mouse Trap by ½d and put both his competitors out of business within the year. Snap! Snap! Snap! That is Leo Dare.

———

'This is Mr William Quinn,' said Leo Dare, introducing me to the three gentlemen and one lady cosied in armchairs and on a sofa in a private room above a fashionable restaurant in Piccadilly. 'As you can tell from the stripe of Billy's suit, he's one of our Transatlantic cousins. A veritable wild red indian among us. He'll be looking after our advertising.'

From the looks on the faces of those assembled, I did not impress them overmuch. As a member of a comparatively new-fangled profession, I was accustomed to glances of suspicion from those whose business forefathers had managed perfectly well in a slower, smaller world without stooping to plaster their names on the sides of London omnibuses. Come to that, they had managed quite well enough without omnibibuses. Our host, who had no such delusions, spoke as if I was already aboard the *consortium*.

It is a peculiarity of Leo Dare that he has no premises of his own. Concerns in which he takes a controlling interest might lease or purchase offices, factories, yards, warehouses, firms of carters and distributors, even railroad trains and cars. He himself resides in hotel suites and has, as the courts would say, no fixed address. It is his practice to engage rooms temporarily for specific purposes. This well-appointed salon, with waiters and attendants firmly shut outside, was the destined birthplace of our fresh venture.

Leo Dare is one of those fellows you can't help looking at, but would be hard-put to describe. In middle years, trim, of average stature, clean-shaven, sly-eyed, impeccably dressed but not ostentatious, he has that sense of command one finds in the best, if least-decorated, generals and statesmen. He alone was standing, back to a fireplace in which a genial blaze burned, one hand behind him, one holding a small glass of what I took to be port.

'Quinn, meet the rest of the *consortium*,' said Leo Dare. 'This is Enid, Lady Knowe, the philanthropist. You'll have heard of her many charitable activities, and of course be familiar with her family name. Her late father was Knowe's Black Biscuits.'

'"An Ounce of Charcoal is a Pound of Comfort",' I quoted.

Lady Knowe, a thin-faced young woman dressed like an eighty-year-old widow, winced. I tumbled at once that she didn't care to be reminded that the funds for her philanthropy came from a species of peaty-looking (and -tasting) edible brick. Knowe's Blacks were dreaded by children entrusted to nannies who believed (or maliciously pretended to believe) their consumption was good for their digestion.

'Sir Marmaduke Collynge, the distinguished parliamentarian ...'

A beef-cheeked man in clothes too small for him, Sir Marmaduke seemed to be swelling all through our meeting, indeed all through our acquaintance, as if the room were far too hot for him and he had just enjoyed an enormous meal unaugmented by Knowe's Black Biscuits. He grunted a cheery greeting.

'Hugo Varrable, our research chemist ...'

A young fellow of about my age, with long hair, a horse face and stained hands, Dr Varrable sat with a leather satchel on his lap. The chemist prized his satchel, which was stuffed to bulging with what I assumed were formulae and vials of experimental compounds.

'And Richard Enfield, administrator of the estate of the late lawyer, Gabriel Utterson.'

A well-dressed gadabout, no longer young, Mr Enfield had the high colour of a man who has spent as little time in his rainy, foggy homeland as possible. He gave a noncommittal, very English wave.

'Does the name "Utterson" mean anything to you, Quinn?' Leo Dare asked.

I confessed that it did not. Leo Dare seemed pleased.

'What about the name of Jekyll? Dr Henry Jekyll?'

'Or Hyde?' suggested Varrable, glumly.

Of course I knew the story. A few seasons back, even the New York 'papers were full of little else.

'Dr Jekyll was the scientifical fellow who brewed the potion that turned him into another man entirely,' I said. 'The dreadful murderer, Edward Hyde.'

'Capital. You did follow the story.'

I shrugged.

'But, Quinn, did you *believe*? Do you credit that a dried-out elderly stick might, by the consumption of a chemical elixir, be transmogrified into a thriving young buck? That he might undergo a radical metamorphosis of mind and body, shucking off the respectable front of Jekyll to indulge in the licentiousness of Hyde?'

I laughed, a little nervously. My humour was not shared by anyone in the room.

'Well, Quinn. Speak up.'

'Mr Dare, I read the published accounts of the strange case of Dr Jekyll and Mr Hyde. I even saw the Mansfield company's stage dramatisation in New York, with startling theatre trickery. Knowing something of the workings of the newspaper business, I have assumed the matter blown up out of all proportion. Surely, this Jekyll simply took a drug that unseated his wits and used disguise to live a double life. He cheated the gallows by suicide, I believe.'

'They were two men,' said Mr Enfield. 'I knew them both.'

'I bow to personal experience,' I said, still not fathoming the import of all this.

'Do you not see the opportunity created by our control of the

Jekyll estate and by the notoriety of his case?'

'You know that I do not. But I have a strong suspicion that you do. You, after all, are Leo Dare and I am someone else. It's your business to see overlooked opportunities.'

'Spoken like a true ad. man, Quinn. Just the right tone of flattery and familiarity. You'll "fit in" all right, I can avow to that.'

I was still no wiser.

'How would you react if I were to tell you that we had, working from the fragmentary papers left behind by the late Dr Jekyll, reconstructed the formula of his potion? That our clever Dr Varrable has reproduced the impurity of salts that was the key, one might also say *secret*, ingredient of Jekyll's elixir of transformation and is at present applying his talents to a system whereby we might compound that miraculous brew in bulk? That our *consortium* has sole license for the manufacture, distribution and sale of the "Jekyll Tonic"?'

Quiet hung in the room. I was aware of the crackling of the fire.

'Surely,' I ventured, 'Britain has a surfeit of murderers as it is? The *Police Gazette* is full of 'em.'

Leo Dare looked a little disappointed. 'The murderousness of Hyde did not emerge for some months, remember. Initially, the experiment was a remarkable success. Jekyll became a new man, a younger, fitter, more *vital* man. Can you not see the possibilities?'

I began to smile. 'In bottles,' I said. 'Lined up on a druggist's shelf. What do you call them here? Chemist's shops. Little blue bottles, with bright yellow labels.'

'I see you understand well enough,' said Leo Dare, approving.

'The formula must be highly diluted,' said Varrable. 'Maybe one-tenth the strength of that Jekyll used, with water ...'

'*Coloured* water,' I put in.

'... added to minimise the unpleasant side-effects. I say, Quinn, why *coloured*?'

'So it doesn't *look* like water. Otherwise, suspicious folk think that's all it is. I served a rough apprenticeship in a medicine show out West. The marks, ah, the customers, ignore the testimonials and the kootch dances. They open their wallets for the stuff that has the prettiest colour.'

'Well, I never.'

'Look to your own medicine cabinet at home. You're an educated man, and I'll wager you purchased your salves and cure-alls on the same basis.'

'We've decided to call it a "tonic",' said Leo Dare.

I thought for a moment, then agreed with him. 'The biggest hurdle will be the public perception of our product as the stuff of melodrama and murder. The name should not have associations with magic or alchemy, as would be the case with "miracle elixir" or "potion". A "tonic" is something we all might have at home without becoming bloodthirsty monsters.'

'From hence forth, the word "monster" is barred among us,' decreed Leo Dare.

Mr Enfield looked down into his empty glass.

'I concur. Though, for a tiny fraction of our customership, the attraction will all be wrapped up in the business of Jekyll and Hyde. Some souls have a temptation to sample the dark depths. We should be aware of that and fashion strategies to pull in that segment without alienating the greater public, whose interest will be chiefly, ah, cosmetic. Everyone above a certain age wishes to look younger, to feel younger.'

'Indeed. And we offer a tonic that will let them *be* younger.'

'We should be cautious, Mr Dare,' said Varrable. 'The formula must be carefully tested. Its effects are, as yet, unpredictable.'

'Indeed. Indeed. But it is also vital, Dr Varrable, that we consider the practicalities. I have asked Quinn to apply his wits to matters outside your laboratory. Many considerations must be made before Jekyll Tonic can be presented to the public.'

'What of the legalities?' I asked. 'Aren't there stringent rules and regulations? Government boards about medicines and poisons?'

'There certainly are, and Sir Marmaduke sits on them all.'

Sir Marmaduke grunted again and made a speech.

'It is not the place of this house to stand in the way of progress, sirrah. The law should not interpose itself between a thing that is desired and the people who desire it. That has always been my philosophy and it should be ever the philosophy of this government. If Jekyll Tonic, this wondrous boon to all humanity, were to be denied us because of the sorry fate of one researcher, where would frivolous, anti-medicinal legislation cease? Would sufferers from toothache be prevented from seeking the solace of such perfectly harmless, widely-used balms as laudanum, cocaine and heroin? I pity anyone who persists in needless pain because the dusty senior fatheads of the medical profession, who earned their doctorates in the days of body-snatching and leeches, insist on tying every new discovery up in committees of inquiry into the committees of inquiry, of over-regulating and hamstringing our valiant and clear-sighted experimental pioneers.

'The present manufacturers have taken to heart the lesson of Dr Jekyll, and have gone to great lengths to remove from his formula the impurities that robbed him of his mind even as it gave him strength of body and constitution. Jekyll Tonic is a different matter now that it has been improved and perfected. Its effects are purely beneficial, purely physical. I myself shall ensure that all the members of my household take one tablespoonful of Jekyll Tonic daily and am confident that there will be no ill-effects. This parliament must declare for Jekyll Tonic, and *decisively*, lest the health of the nation be sapped, and our overseas competitors draw ahead.'

Mr Enfield clapped satirically. Sir Marmaduke bowed gravely to him.

'Think of the enormous benefit it will be for the poor,' said Lady Knowe. 'Always think of the poor.'

'Jekyll Tonic will retail at threepence, but we intend to put out an *extremely* diluted version in a smaller bottle at a halfpenny a bottle,' said Leo Dare.

'For paupers and children,' explained Sir Marmaduke.

I began to do summations in my head. Leo Dare gave figures.

'A farthing for the bottle, the cork and the gummed label; a quarter-farthing for the tonic itself ...'

'That little?'

'In bulk, yes. I have cornered the uncommon elements. The rest is just water and sugar for the taste.'

'More than twopence halfpenny sheer profit?'

'We expect demand to be enormous, Quinn. Especially after you have worked your own brand of alchemy.'

This put galvanic girdles in the ashcan.

'One thing,' I said. 'What does the tonic actually *do*?'

'I suppose someone had to ask that question, Quinn. What does the Jekyll Tonic actually *do*? Let us try an experiment.'

He raised the glass of what I had taken for port, looked at the clear pink-orange fluid, touched the rim to his lower lip, then inclined his head backwards. He took in the glassful at a gulp and swallowed it at once.

Shadows crept across his face.

But it was only the firelight.

'Most refreshing. I can assure you, as I'll be willing to attest before lawyers, that I feel enormously invigorated and that my senses are sharper by several degrees of magnitude. The outward effect made famous by Dr Jekyll is only notable after a *course* of tonics, and then only in the cases of those who most desire a change of appearance. I myself am happy with the way I look.'

I understood perfectly. I had been in the snake-oil business before.

But never with the Jekyll name.

I foresaw rooms full of gold, profits pouring in like cataracts, fortunes made for all of us.

———

Varrable's "laboratory" was a former stables in Shoreditch. Leo Dare had lately purchased Mercury Carriages, a hansom cab concern, not in order to run the operation (whose slogan was an uninspiring 'Fleet and Economical') but to close it down. A sudden surge in demand for quality horsemeat in Northern France made it more profitable to despatch Dobbin to the knackers than to retain the nag in harness.

Leo Dare had come to an arrangement with several long-established businesses with a combined interest in the hackney carriage trade (their more pleasing slogan, 'Hansom is as Hansom Does!'), pledging to eliminate a rogue firm given to undercutting the fares of bigger rivals in return for a substantial honorarium and a percentage of increased profits over a period of five years. Had the cab combine turned him away, he would doubtless have reduced Mercury fares to a laughable minimum and brought about a complete catastrophe in the carriage business, taking his profit from subsidiary concerns. The Mercury premises were at his disposal, and now served as a convenient head-quarters for the developmental work of the Jekyll Tonic *consortium*.

Our research was carried out in such secrecy that no sign outside the works marked our presence. On this first visit, I found the address only by the sheerest chance. I noticed a thin crowd of shifty-looking fellows in heavy coats and scarves loitering on a corner. From the long buggy-whips several of them were toting, I gathered that these were freshly unemployed cabbies, mindlessly haunting their former base of operations. Mercury Carriages had tended to draw their drivers from a pool of swarthy immigrants from the Mediterranean countries, and so I noted not a few fezzes among the traditional flat caps. A couple of big bruisers in billycock hats guarded the stable doors, with cudgels to hand, as a precaution against an invasion of these disgruntled cast-offs.

My own carriage, a sleek four-horse job retained permanently at my disposal by Leo Dare through another clause in his agreement with the cab trust, drew up outside the stables, exciting mutters of discontent from the corner louts. I got out, told the liveried coachman to await my convenience, and presented my credentials to the bruiser who looked most capable of coherent thought.

'Yer on the list, Mr Quinn,' I was told.

A regular-sized door cut into the large stable doors was hauled open and I stepped into a doubly-malodorous place. Doubly, for its former usage was memorialised by the trodden-in dung of equines (currently gracing the plates of provincial French gourmands, I trusted), while its current occupation was most pungently signalled by the stench of chemical processes. I wrapped a handkerchief around my nose and mouth, which gave me the look of a desperado robbing a stage-coach. My eyes still watered.

If you think of a laboratory, you doubtless form a mental picture of tables supporting contraptions of glass tubes, beakers and retorts, with flames at strategic places. Coloured liquids bubble and ferment, while strange heavy smoke pours from funnel-shaped tube-mouths. Perhaps one wall is given over to cages for the animals – rats, rabbits, monkeys – used in experimentation, and in a corner is an arrangement of galvanic batteries, bottles of acid, switches, levers and metallic spheres a-crackle with the blue-ish light of harnessed lightning.

This was a former stables. With open barrels of smelly gloop.

Hugo Varrable, in a much-stained apron and shirtsleeves, stirred a vat with a long stick. He wore a canvas bucket on his head. It looked like a giant dirty thumb stuck out of his collar, with an isinglass face-plate for a nail.

'It's all done, Billy,' said Varrable, voice a mumble inside the bucket. He turned from the vat to pick up a stoppered flask of the now-familiar fluid. 'Come on through.'

He led me out of the stables into a courtyard where the fleet of Mercury cabs, stripped of brass fittings and iron wheelrims, sat decaying slowly to firewood. Leo Dare would profit from that come winter.

'Have our volunteers appeared?' I asked.

Varrable took off his bucket and coughed. 'Some of them.'

'Only some?'

Varrable shrugged. 'The Jekyll name may have given one or two second thoughts about participating in the experiment.'

'Indeed.'

Awaiting us in what had once been the common-room of the cabbies were three lank-haired, languid individuals, students who fancied themselves ornaments to the aesthetic movement. One of the species was a young woman, though she wore the same cut of velvet breeches and jacket as her fellows. They had been exchanging bored, nasal witticisms. At our entrance, they perked up. Beneath their habitual posing, they were skittish. All considered, apprehension was understandable.

'This won't do, Doc,' I said, alarming our volunteers. 'The effect of the Tonic we want to push the most is rejuvenation. These exquisites are sickeningly youthful enough as it is.'

'There are other effects, measurable upon all subjects.'

'Yes, yes. But our "selling point" is the youth angle. Are you telling me you could find no elderly or infirm person willing to take part in the testing of our medical miracle?'

'We put the word out at an art school. All the patent medicine concerns do the same.'

'There's your problem, Doc. However, it's easily set right. If you'll excuse me for a moment.'

I stepped out of the common room and went round to the main gates. The bruisers let me pass and I crossed the road. The loitering ex-cabbies edged away from me with suspicion. Among the Turkish brigands and Greek cutthroats, I found several English individuals of advanced age, faces weathered from exposure to the elements, backs and limbs bent by years spent hunched at the top of a cab, breath wheezy from breathing in gallons of London pea-soup.

'Who among you would care to earn a shilling?' I asked.

———

Varrable worked the results up into a learned paper no one actually read. Leo Dare arranged for its publication in an academic journal whose name eventually lent weight to our campaign. When *The Lancet*, alarmed by the spectres of Jekyll and Hyde, ran an editorial against us, thunderous voices among the medical profession – not to mention Sir Marmaduke Collynge – were raised against the brand of irresponsible trade journalism that inveighs against a perfectly legal product, which has yet to be judged either way by the final arbiters of such matters. 'The public shall make up its own mind,' said Sir

Marmaduke, at every opportunity, 'for it always does, the average fellow being far more astute than your addle-brained quack, consumed with envy of the achievements of younger, more free-thinking men.'

As the brewing and refining continued in Shoreditch, Leo Dare took the elementary precaution of establishing, through Lady Knowe, a philanthropic trust to dispense grants supporting avenues of medical inquiry whose pursuit was blocked by the hidebound bodies responsible for the allocation of funds at the country's major universities, medical schools and teaching hospitals. This enabled many a hobbyhorse to be ridden and pet project to be nurtured, doubtless contributing (in the long run) to the health of the nation and the wealth of scientific knowledge. A correlation of this generosity was that researchers who benefited from the foundation's beneficence were predisposed to uphold the reputation of the late Dr Henry Jekyll on the public podium and give testimony that his work, though unfortunately applied in the first instance, was perfectly sound. These worthies tended to have passionate beliefs in the benefits of naturism, monkey glands, cosmetic amputation, the consumption of one's own water, phrenology, galvanic stimulation (our old friend), vegetarianism and other medical tangentia. However, their M.D.s were every jot as legit. as those of the head surgeon at Barts or the Queen's own physician, and the public (perhaps regrettably) tends to think one doctor as good as another when reading a testimonial.

Having observed the experiment first hand, I did not quite become a fanatic believer in Jekyll Tonic. However, I had to concede that it was a very superior species of snake oil.

For a start, its effects were immediate and visible.

Our would-be poets and unemployed cabbies did not transform into a pack of Neanderthal men and take to battering their fellows with makeshift clubs, but several evinced genuine transformations of feature and form. A very bald fellow instantly sprouted flowing locks that were the envy of the decadents in the room, suggesting we could market the Tonic as a hair restorer (always a popular line). Arthritic fists, all knuckles from a lifetime of gripping reins, opened into strong, young hands. A shy stammerer among the students was suddenly able to pour forth a flood of impromptu rhyming and would not shut up for two days, when the effect suddenly (and mercifully, for his circle) wore off. Another poet, an avowed anarchist and shamer of convention, rushed from the stables, eluding our guards, hacking at his hair with a pen-knife. He was later found to have taken a position as a junior clerk with a respectable firm of solicitors, which he quit suddenly as his old personality resurfaced.

Varrable remained concerned that the effects of the tonic were essentially unpredictable, as proved by further experimentation with a range of volunteers from wider strata of society. We thought we should have to pay substantial 'hush money' to a curate who sampled Jekyll Tonic and passed through a bizarre hermaphrodite stage to emerge (briefly) as a woman of exceedingly low character with an unhealthy interest in the gallants of Britannia's Navy. Leo Dare overruled our request for cash, predicting (correctly) that the cleric in question would rather bribe us to keep from his Bishop any word of the Portsmouth adventures of his female alter ego.

None of our volunteers killed anyone, which was a great relief.

Only the anarchist and the curate vowed never to repeat the experience. I had a sense that the cleric came reluctantly to the decision and would eventually alter it, perhaps making surreptitious purchase of the Tonic once it was generally available and indulging in its use only after taking precautions in the name of discretion. The others returned, bringing with them sundry family-members and friends. They all clamoured for the Tonic in a manner that suggested Leo Dare had another 'winner' on his hands.

The Hon. Hilary Belligo, the stammering aesthete, splutteringly conveyed to us that he would be prepared to forego the shilling remuneration we offered for participation in the experiment and would meet any price we suggested if an inexhaustible supply of the Tonic were made available to him.

Varrable and I independently liquidated all our other holdings and ploughed our money into the *consortium* stock issue. The next day, before any public announcement had been made, the value of our shares tripled.

I drew the line at sampling the formula myself. If called, I was only too happy to swallow a few ounces of coloured water – doubtless the same recipe Leo Dare had theatrically quaffed at our first meeting – and declare myself satisfyingly rejuvenated.

Varrable formed a theory that the effect of the Tonic was to reshape each individual into the person they secretly wanted to be. The ageing, stuffy Jekyll had become the young libertine Hyde; but, as the name suggests, the violent thug had always been 'hiding' inside the respectable man. Sometimes, as perhaps with Jekyll and certainly with our anarchist and our curate, the transformations proved a shock to the subjects because the Tonic was no respecter of hypocrisy. It acted on secret wishes, some concealed even from those who harboured them. Many were unaware of the fierceness that burned in their breasts, the *need* to be somebody else. My own reluctance to take the Tonic came from an unanswered question: I thought that I was perfectly happy to be myself, but what if I were wrong? What if some notion I couldn't consciously recall was stuck there? As a lad, I wanted to be a pirate when I grew up. Would a course of Jekyll Tonic have made me grow an eye-patch and a pegleg? Might I not have come to myself, like that sore curate in a Portsmouth grog-house, to find I had taken the Queen's shilling and was miles out to sea on a ship of the line?

'Our stock issue is closed,' announced Leo Dare. 'Those not aboard by now have missed the omnibus.'

The *consortium* was dining out, no longer in a private room.

Now, part of the game was to be seen, to be envied and admired, to cut a dash before those who matter. We had taken a table at Kettner's and were very visible. Leo Dare had insisted Varrable and myself be taken to Sir Marmaduke's tailor and outfitted in a manner befitting 'men on the rise'. Suits of American cut would not do.

Envious glances were tossed at us. The *maître d' hôtel* presented a succession of inscribed cards from plutocrats and captains of industry. Leo Dare glanced at any message before smiling noncommittally across the room and not extending invitations to our table. The cards from journalists and editors were handed to me, those from churchmen and society leaders to Lady Knowe, those from scientists (who would a month ago not have cared to recognise his name) to Varrable. Between us, we had enough cards for a deck – we could have played whist with them, to show our indifference to those outside the *consortium*.

'I'm no longer at home to fools clamouring for an inside chance at a few shares,' chuckled Sir Marmaduke, mouth full of well-chewed beefsteak. 'Barely a month past, I offered the bunch of 'em a chance to buy in. To a man, they said I was cracked, sirrah, cracked.'

We all laughed, heartily. Even Lady Knowe, whose mode of dress dropped a decade each time we convened. She still wore black, but her gown was less widow's weed than dark blossom.

Leo Dare, whom no one had ever seen eat, oversaw our gustatory indulgences and, begging permission from Lady Knowe, lit up a black *Cubano* cigar. He exhaled clouds that seemed to take sculptural shape before dissipating.

'Our conquest of the market has been so complete,' he said, 'that the "smart money" has stayed away. Some call us a "bubble", you know. They predict a "smash"! Soon, they'll learn that the old certainties have gone. In the coming age, men – and women, Lady Enid – such as we shall set the pace, make the decisions, reap the profits. The Twentieth Century shall belong to us.'

When Nietzsche writes of an "Overman", the philosopher means Leo Dare.

'So we are smarter than "the smart money",' I said.

In my mind, I held the picture of Hilary Belligo, trying to get out the words, the light of inspiration dying in his eyes, to be rekindled as a physical and mental *need* far stronger than any poetic impulse would ever be.

'There'll be no limit to the demand for the Tonic,' said Varrable. 'We could ask five pounds a thimble, and some would pay it.'

I thought of the Hon. Hilary. Varrable was right.

'Let us not be over-greedy,' said Leo Dare, which made Mr Enfield giggle. As usual, the controller of the Utterson-Jekyll estate was slightly soused.

'Think of the poor,' said Lady Knowe, sipping champagne. 'The *poor* poor.'

A card was delivered to her, not from a churchman, but from a golden-haired Guardsman. She giggled at the inscription and placed it separately from the others. I wondered if she'd been at the Jekyll. Samples were already in circulation among the *consortium*.

'I have been reconsidering the matter of price,' said Leo Dare. 'I don't think sixpence a bottle is unreasonable. Any objections?'

Heads shaken all around the table.

'Passed,' said the entrepreneur. 'Now, let us drink to the memory of the late Dr Henry Jekyll, without whom, *et cetera et cetera* ...'

'*Et cetera et cetera*,' we chanted, raising glasses.

———

Varrable and newly-hired assistants continued the course of volunteer tests, making slight refinements to the formula, and the *consortium* stock continued to gain value by the proverbial leaps and bounds. Shoreditch's first telephonic lines were strung, with matching sets of the apparatus installed in my sanctum, once the snug nest of the proprietor of Mercury Carriages, and Varrable's command post above the factory floor. Varrable became addicted to the gadget, 'ringing up' on it several times a day to pass trivial messages, though a perfectly adequate speaking tube between our offices was left over from the Mercury days.

As my role in the enterprise became paramount, I closeted myself with secretaries to take dictation, commercial artists to work up sketches and a few trusted experts to bounce ideas against. For weeks, we "brain-stormed".

A Marvel of the Modern Age!

Ladies – Make of Yourself What You Will!!!

Release the Young Man Inside You!

A Kitten Can Be a Tiger!

Transformed and Improved!! Transmogrified and Reborn!!

It has always been a credo of mine that an advertisement cannot have too many exclamation points.

We bought space on public hoardings and in the press, and sent sandwich-men out onto the streets. We put up posters on the platforms of the London Underground Railway and inside the trains themselves, where passengers had no choice but to look at them. We were plastered on the sides of 'buses, in the windows of chemists' shops and on any walls that happened to be bare before our trusty regiment of boys with paste-pots passed by. Striking illustrations, engraved by the best men in the business, were augmented by 'unsolicited' testimony from our volunteers, much the best of it genuinely unsolicited. I decided to keep the Hon. Hilary in the background, for he was now almost permanently in his secondary personality and the quality of his rhyming, while undoubtedly visionary, was of a nature to prove alarming rather than reassuring. Varrable insisted we keep supplying our initial volunteers with the Tonic so he could study the effects of repeated use. He also asked for more bruisers at the laboratory, to guard against possible riots from the much-swelled cabbie crowd. It seemed our people couldn't get enough of the Jekyll. Varrable tried to water the formula down, to make its effects less immediate and lasting.

Some use could be made of the statements of cabbies and longhairs, but willing participants were also found among the better classes. We prominently displayed sworn testimonials from gracious ladies, leading churchmen, military officers and, inevitably, Sir Marmaduke Collynge. I interviewed all manner of folk who had sampled the Tonic, helping them set down in appropriate words the benefits they genuinely felt had accrued to them. Major General Cogstaff-Blyth, "the Hector of Maiwand", was quoted as saying 'with this spiffing stuff in him, your British soldier shall never lose another battle!' I had the Maj.-Gen. put on his best medals and troop down to Speakers' Corner to harangue passersby with the merits of Jekyll Tonic, and lobby for a bulk purchase of the wonder fluid by the War Office.

In any enterprise, only so much can be done by buying space to hawk your wares. True success can only be achieved if the press find themselves so harried by the interest of their readership that they are obliged – nay, *forced* – to augment paid advertising by running stories that pass as unbiased journalism but which essentially serve to boost your reputation. To reach this point, you have to worm your way into the public mind by fair means or foul. Firstly, I provided the lyrics for an entire song-book of ditties which were set to tunes by a couple of tame music students willing to work in lucrative anonymity. The theory was that one at least of our songs was bound to catch the nation's fancy. Certainly, for a time, "Changing for the Better (Through a Course of Jekyll Tonic)" was heard on every street-corner – Leo Dare magnanimously promised me a fifty per-cent cut of the song-sheet income – and hardly less success was met by "An Inspirational Transformational Super-Sensational Stuff" and "You've Got to Be a Jekyll Tonic Girl (to Get the Boy You Want)".

The greatest success of this campaign was, I venture to say, the affair of the Jekyll Joke.

It took no little negotiation and expense to arrange for the "patter comic" Harry "Brass" Button to conclude his turn at the Tivoli Music Hall with an apparent ad. lib. remark of my own coinage. 'With Jekyll Tonic I feel like a New Man,' said Button, then adding with an indescribable leer, '... luckily, the wife does too!' The results were startling to the performer as anyone else. Not only was Button's "punch-line" greeted nightly with gales of laughter but also applause that lasted for minutes, delaying the first act curtain. The audience could only be quieted if he agreed to give the "Jekyll Joke" over again, as much as seven times. Attendances were up and expectant patrons turned away in crowds. A sticker across the posters outside the hall announced 'the "Jekyll Joke" *will* be told'. Eventually, new posters were put up claiming the Tivoli as 'home of the hilarious "Jekyll Joke"'.

Harry Button, whose check suit and mobile eyebrows had been rather falling from favour, was precipitously elevated to the top of the bill, displacing an entire family of acrobatical contortionists and an opera singer who had conducted a famous *amour* with a Ruthenian Prince. Button only sampled the Tonic once that I heard of. He wept for six hours, then swore off it for life. But he told and retold the Jekyll Joke. I don't doubt that, though his top-of-the-bill days are now but a memory, he still tells it at the drop of a hat. Certainly, he truly believes his was the brain that conceived the marvellous line and he'll try to thrash anyone who says different.

Some fellows entirely unconnected with the *consortium* whipped up a song that Button refused to include in his act on the grounds that it was an affront to the dignity of what had now become a much-loved, therefore *respectable*, music hall institution. However, every other comic in London sang 'Have You Heard the Jekyll Joke?/It'll make you laugh until you choke!/Have You Heard the Jekyll Joke?/Old Brass Button is the funniest bloke!' In the Strand, whenever Harry Button was about, children chanted the chorus, especially the repeated refrain 'now tell us another one, Brass!'

With the departure of Mr Richard Mansfield from the London stage, we commissioned our own dramatisation of *The Strange Case of Dr Jekyll and Mr Hyde*, emphasising the positive aspects of the trans-formation and omitting any mention of the late Sir Danvers Carewe. After all, Edward Hyde never came to trial and so was not proved a murderer in any court of law. Our lawyers sent reminders of this fact to any who tried to publish or stage the hitherto-accepted version of the story. On behalf of the Jekyll Estate, Mr Enfield accepted a great many grudging retractions and apologies. Several times in the play, our Dr Jekyll took a swig of his formula and approvingly exclaimed 'it's a tonic!'

All this, it should be remembered, was well before the Tonic was available in stores. By the time we were ready to begin manufacture and distribution, the *consortium* had gathered again and concluded that 6d was far too meagre a price to ask for such a highly-demanded and beneficial commodity. Lady Knowe bleated a little about pricing the

Tonic out of the reach of the poor, but we decided that — though the Jekyll Tonic was of such incalculable good to the public that it must in effect be declared priceless — we would settle upon the trivial sum of 1s a bottle, in order to effect the greatest possible distribution of the wondrous blessing we were about to grant humankind in general.

'A shilling is little enough to pay,' said Leo Dare.

————

I was mentally formulating an alliterative sentence employing the words 'modern', 'marvel' and 'miracle' in some fresh order when a discreet rap at the door disturbed my process of thought.

'Go away,' I shouted at the Porlockian person. 'It can wait.'

The office door opened a crack and an unfamiliar individual peeked around, holding up something shiny.

'Generally, that's not the case, sir.'

The newcomer was a shabby little man with a London accent. I pegged his section of the market at once – clerk or undermanager, with a little education but no elocution, the son of someone who worked with his hands, the father of someone who'd 'do better'. He would be most susceptible to advertisements that linked the product with easy living, good breeding and "class". A life lived with unformed needs and aspirations, and thus an ideal customer. He'd be looking for something but not know what it was. Enter: the Jekyll Tonic.

'Inspector Mist, sir,' he announced, 'from Scotland Yard.'

I gave him another look. He had a bloodhound's big wet nose and a drooping moustache that covered his mouth entirely. His hat was a year or so past style and his topcoat was too heavy for him, as if the pockets were full of handcuffs for felons, packets of plaster of paris for footprints and magnifying lenses for clues.

'Come in, Inspector. You're Sheriff of these parts?'

'You would be the American, sir. Mister …'

'Quinn.'

'That's the name.'

'How can I help you?'

'Rather delicate matter, sir. Are you acquainted with ...' he consulted a note-pad ... 'a Mr Belligo?'

'What has the Hon. Hilary been up to now? Subversive publications with obscene illustrations?'

'Misappropriation of stock is mentioned, sir. In short, theft.'

'I was under the impression that he was of independent means.'

'Ran through 'em, sir. Looked around. Found another source of readies. Only it wasn't exactly his to tap.'

'Lock the villain away, then. I imagine he'll find an eager audience for his verses in one of your excellent prisons.'

'Have to catch him first, sir.'

'He's not around here.'

'Didn't say he was. Only, it seems you have something the absconder needs. A tonic, I believe. Likely he'll come nosing about.'

The policeman picked up a bottle from my desk.

'Is this it? Jekyll Tonic?'

'No,' I said. 'Just a sample of the bottle. The bottle is important, you know. The comforting size, the colour, the quality of the wax around the stopper, the adhesive label.'

'Looks like a bottle to me.'

'Very perceptive, Inspector.'

'That's as well, then. If Mr Belligo pops up ...'

'I'll send a lad to the Yard.'

'We'd be grateful, Mr Quinn.'

'There is a flaw to your trap, though. At the moment, Jekyll Tonic is a *rara avis*, obtainable only from our experimental laboratories, downstairs in this very building. As of,' I consulted my new gold watch, 'as of eight o'clock tomorrow morning, it will be on sale all across London, then the country. You might have to post a man at every chemist's shop in the nation.'

The bloodhound face drooped.

———

My first thought upon arriving fresh and early in Shoreditch to see a line of policemen outside the factory was that one of our devoted test-subjects had done himself or someone else injury while in the grips of Jekyll Tonic fever. The fellow who would now have to be known as the Dis. Hon. Hilary Belligo sprang naturally to mind. It turned out that Leo Dare had merely suggested it would be sensible to take precautions against rioters. I looked about for the dogged Inspector Mist. If present, he was in one of those impenetrable Scotland Yard disguises.

We understood that the chemist's shops and apothecary's dispensaries which would be our main retail outlets would abide by no decree we might make that the Tonic should be withheld from sale until a certain standardised time. I knew enough about storekeepers to guess they would agree to all our terms and then sell the stuff as soon as they got it, probably knocking a penny off the shilling to undercut the fellow across the street.

So, it was to be a free-for-all.

At eight o'clock, the old stable gates opened and carts trundled out, laden with straw-packed crates of clinking bottles. Each cart was manned by a former Mercury cabbie (retained at a generous two-thirds of his previous wage) and a bare-knuckles boxer with a handy shillaleigh. The purpose of the latter individuals was not so much to prevent any attempts at seizure of the Tonic supply as to suggest to the world at large that the product was so desirable such attempts were highly likely.

Because it seemed expected of us, we put up a stall outside the laboratory, manned by several smart young women recruited from the chorus of the Tivoli, all neat in abbreviated sailor suits and hats with pom-poms. Harry Button had asked an outrageous fee to act as shill at the stall, so we had declined his services. I noticed that the comic had turned up for the historic moment anyway, a little surprised that the eager public were clamouring not for his Joke but for the inspiration of same, the Tonic itself. The first Jekyll Tonic offered for sale direct from the factory was available at an introductory price of 9d. Our shutters went up simultaneous with the emergence of the carts.

We were all there. Leo Dare hung rather in the background, calmly puffing one of his cigars. In press photographs taken that morning, as so often in Kodaks of the *entrepreneur* and Overman, Leo Dare's face is indistinct, masked by frozen shrouds of smoke. Sir Marmaduke and Lady Knowe made speeches, drowned out by the Babel of eager customers beseeching the attention of our becoming sales assistants. Varrable, emerged again from his bucket, still fussed about the vats, already concerned with brewing up tomorrow's batch of Tonic.

I found myself in a corner of the stable-yard with Mr Enfield.

He drew a draught from a hip-flask and offered it to me.

'Is that …?'

'Not on your nellie,' he said.

I took a swallow. Strong whiskey.

'I saw Hyde trample the little girl,' he said. 'Worst thing I ever did see. The look on his face.'

'Monstrous? Evil?'

'No. It was like he was walking over more pavement. As if no one else mattered at all. He was scared all right, when the mob had his collar, scared for himself. A shirty little bastard he was, whining and indignant, with clothes too big for him. That was what was inside Jekyll.'

The first customers were swigging from their own bottles. On labels they hadn't read, we had printed a warning advising that the daily dose should not exceed a spoonful taken in a mug of water. It was not our fault some patrons were too excited to read and regard these instructions.

'The formula was lost,' I said to Mr Enfield. 'Even Jekyll couldn't recreate it. You could have kept it that way. If you were really worried, you could have suppressed the Tonic, stopped this even before it started.'

Mr Enfield looked at me. He took another drink.

'You really don't know Leo Dare, do you?

At that moment, I was distracted.

In the street, ten or fifteen new devotees of the Jekyll Tonic were changing. It was like a Court of Miracles from *Notre Dame de Paris* crossed with the news of the Relief of Mafeking. Crutches thrown away! Speaking in tongues! Vigorous embraces! Cries for more, more, more! Supply at the stall was exhausted, and the sales girls apologised. Banknotes were waved in fists. Coins were thrown. One girl nearly had her eye put out by a flung florin.

The police moved in, augmenting our bare-knuckle men.

I saw the most beautiful woman I ever beheld in my life, a slim blonde angel wrapped in the voluminous garments of a much, much larger lady. She threw away a veiled hat, to unloose a stream of glamorous golden hair. She took my arm and looked at me with unutterably lovely eyes.

'The children call me "pig-face",' she said, wondering.

I did not understand.

'A mirror,' she said. 'Have you a mirror?'

I patted my pockets though I knew I did not have a glass about me. At my shrug of apology, she left me – a slave to her memory – to ask another bystander.

Beyond the crowd, I saw Varrable having heated words with Leo Dare. The chemist listened, arms folded, as Leo Dare stabbed the air with a cigar to emphasise points.

The transformed angel found a mirror and was stunned by her new face, a female Narcissus absolutely smitten with herself.

The mirror was passed around. Our customers beheld their fresh selves. I heard a scream from one, who covered his head with his jacket and plunged alarmingly through the crowd. He was soon forgotten. Others danced on the cobbles, leapt up and down with abandon, shouted 'look at me!', performed feats of strength such as lifting a grown man up in each hand, turning cartwheels. A ragged choir lit into "An Inspirational Transformational Super-Sensational Stuff".

Word escaped that I was connected with the *consortium*, and I was hugged and kissed. I trapped light-fingers reaching for my wallet and watch, and kicked away a junior ruffian who scurried off with good humour to ply his trade elsewhere.

Leo Dare and Varrable caught the ear of Sir Marmaduke. He stood up on a platform by the stall.

'Friends, friends,' announced Sir Marmaduke, booming at the crowd with a voice proved in parliamentary debate. 'Owing to the unprecedented demand, a fresh batch of the wonder Tonic is being brewed up even as we speak. It will take some hours for the complex scientifical processes necessary in its manufacture to be brought to complete fruition, but on behalf of the Jekyll Tonic *consortium* we pledge that the demand shall be met even if it means working our factory round the clock. The Jekyll will be on sale again by twelve noon, this we guarantee.'

'Maybe they still got some at Filkins the Chemist, down the road,' suggested someone.

Half the crowd dashed off.

They soon came back. It had been the same at Filkins the Chemist, and at shops all over London.

The Jekyll Tonic had not so much arrived as exploded.

————

The 'papers were full of it. Questions were asked in the house (and answered at length by a personage familiar to us all). More vats were bought and more fellows engaged to stir the compounds. Our credit was accepted by suppliers of equipment and chemicals. Carts continued to trundle out three times a day, laden with cases of the Jekyll Tonic. The former stables grew more crowded and we had to lease larger premises adjoining the original site. In addition to the vat-stirrers, we had (after unfortunate incidents) to engage more bruisers to watch that the workers didn't siphon off or sample the raw Tonic. Then we had to take on ex-soldiers and former policemen to crack down on the bruisers.

It turned out that there had been a deal of pilferage, and 'super-strength' Jekyll Tonic was being made available to the criminal classes of Whitechapel, Limehouse and Wapping. Inspector Mist snuffled around again, with reports of running battles in the streets between Irish and Hebrew bully-boys with illicit Jekyll interests and the Chinese tongs who found patronage of their opium dens drastically reduced. Leo Dare was not overly concerned, assuring us all that this had been accounted for in his calculations. It would only serve to sharpen the appetite for our legitimate Tonic. All considered, that a street brawler of previously average reputation could see off a dozen Chinamen though one of the celestials had embedded a hatchet in his skull was as fine a testimony for us as any recommendation from a Bishop or Baronet. We did, however, bring swift and merciless court actions against competitors who ventured to sell coloured tincture of laudanum as 'Jeckell Tonik' or 'Jickle Juice'. I made sure to add to all our posters the rubric 'accept no imitations, swallow no substitute ... there is only one original Jekyll Tonic!'

Borrowing against my stock, I removed myself from lodgings in Lewisham to a house in Kensington. Suddenly equipped with (or weighed down by) the trappings of a man of stature. I had to beseech from Sir Marmaduke and Lady Knowe information about how best to employ a household's worth of bowers and scrapers. It took me a disastrous week to learn that the finest servants were not necessarily the most unctuously deferential butlers or the prettiest, cheekiest maids but rather the faintly drab individuals who actually took the bother to do the work they were paid for. I received so many invitations that I had to engage a secretary with a type-writer to respond to them all. I did not let it go to my head. It was all very well to be popular and sought-after, but it was what was on deposit at Coutt's that counted.

Varrable, the last man I should have thought likely to gain a reputation as a rakehell, was seen about town with, in succession, a chorus girl with a dimple, a Drury Lane ornament whose beauty had prompted several duels in Paris, the wealthy young widow of a lately-deceased African millionaire and the youngest daughter of a Duke. Sir Marmaduke was offered a cabinet position, but declined on the grounds that his business interests engaged too much of his time for him to be concerned with the minutiae of canals and waterways. Lady Knowe took tea with the Prince and Princess of Wales, dressed in white for the first time in her life in honour of the occasion. Her philanthropic concerns became extremely fashionable, and many distinguished names were added to her roster of charitable souls. Mr Enfield sold all his stock (mostly, through third parties, to me) and departed for the South Seas, still muttering doom under his breath. He was fleeing from a fortune, but would not be reasoned with and if profit was to be had from his squeamishness I saw no reason why I should not be the one to scoop it.

For me personally, Jekyll Tonic was Inspirational, Transformational and Super-Sensational. And I did not even taste the stuff.

At some point in any venture, my job changes from 'starting up' to 'looking after'. Once the train is up to full steam, it needs a steady hand on the throttle and a good eye on the track ahead. There is no time to relax, to sit back and let the coffers fill. Each day brought a thousand questions from the press, from tradesmen, from the factory. My secretary wore out her type-writer, and a new, improved model had to be purchased. I arranged tours of inspection, interviews with various members of the *consortium* (never Leo Dare, of course), supervised the design of new and improved labels for the bottles. I no longer had a fresh canvas: the name of Jekyll Tonic was known, and had to be protected rather than bruited about. That was the chief reason for seeing off the Jickle and Jeckell jokesters.

All at once, we were the *only* Tonic. Bovril was forgotten, even when advertised by an admirable image of a cow being strapped into an electric chair. Carter's little liver pills piled up unsold in the stores. Dentists reported that even heroin, miracle drug of the decade, was sorely out of fashion. Sufferers from all maladies and pains demanded to go 'on the Jekyll' and would accept no substitutes.

———

By now, a week into the reign of the Tonic, I was surprised by nothing. Approaching Varrable's office early in the morning, I passed a lady who had just emerged from our chemist's sanctum. Though her hair and costume were in disarray, I recognised Mrs Mary Biddlesham, a supporter of Lady Knowe's latest endeavour, to ship supplies of the Jekyll overseas to missionaries in order to coax out the decent Christian lurking within every benighted heathen. Mrs Biddlesham repaired her clothing in a manner that led me to form a conclusion as to the activities with which she had been engaged overnight. She did not meet my eye or answer my good-day.

I found Varrable fussing with his cravat, admiring himself in the cheval glass, and in good spirits.

'You are a wonder,' I said.

Varrable smiled and paraphrased one of my slogans. 'Inside every kitten, there's a tiger!'

I shrugged.

'With claws, Billy,' he assured me. 'I have the scratches to prove it.'

A divan had been installed in Varrable's office, as an aid to abstract thought. Its cushions were on the floor and I gathered that little in the abstract had transpired on the previous evening.

The remains of a late supper stood on a side-table.

I picked up an empty glass, and sniffed the dregs.

Varrable raised a decanter.

'It looks like port, remember,' he said.

'Doc, you've become a blackguard.'

'Have I not? I don't know about the average advertising man, but the average research chemist isn't thought of as a "catch" by the ladies. It's something to do with the penury and long hours, of course, but the reason most often given is the *smell*. At school, they call chemistry "stinks". It stays with you for life. Not so stinky now, of course.'

He sniffed his newly-manicured nails.

'I don't go near the vats any more,' he said. 'We have low people for that.'

'So this is your secret?'

'It's all our secret, isn't it? I confess I've been conducting my own course of private experiments. I should write it up, I suppose. "The

Effects of Dr Henry Jekyll's Transformational Formula Upon the Fairer Sex, as Observed First-Hand by Dr Hugo Varrable, with Fifteen Water-Colour Plates and Extensive Footnotes." At first, I propose a toast and we both "take a Jekyll", only mine is coloured water. An observer has to be distanced. I admit that I do tend to intervene, possibly affecting the outcome of the experiments. A certain, ah, *class* of female is excited by the prospect, and will probably deliver the desired results with a placebo of coloured water. But my interests in that sort ran dry some time ago. Their inner selves are too close to the skin. No, to demonstrate the truly miraculous effects of the Tonic, I have to seek not Rosie O'Grady but the Colonel's Lady. In this case, the Commodore's Lady.'

'What if they're like us, Doc? What if they don't want to find out what's inside or know already? A lot of people are still afraid of the Jekyll.'

Varrable laughed.

'Don't I know it, Billy! Mrs Biddlesham, for one. In her case, I simply gave her an *aperitif* with the complements of your Hibernian friend, Mr Michael Finn.'

'The results?'

'Most satisfactory. I'm not the only researcher in this field. A great many gentlemen have been purchasing the Tonic not for themselves, but for ladies of their glancing acquaintance. Sir Marmaduke insists his household take a tablespoon a day. He lines up his maidservants like sailors being given the rum ration. And he's been rejuvenating himself with regular doses. I understand a few women of dubious character or attractions have ventured their own experiments along these lines. I couldn't approve of that, of course.'

I was not, of course, shocked. But I did perceive a flutter of danger.

'When your, ah, lady-friends, come to themselves, how do they feel?'

'Delighted and rotten all at the same time, I should imagine. I've never really asked. Do you think I should make inquiries? Do a "follow-up" study?'

I thought a moment. There would be complaints. It was but a matter of time before some soiled dove took the matter to the police.

No lady of good name would want this to come out in the courts, but eventually some tart with nothing to lose would try it on. And I would not have wanted to be in Varrable's expensive new shoes if word of last night's experiment were to reach Commodore Biddlesham, whose expertise with both cutlass and revolver could be attested to by not a few deceased Shanghai river pirates.

'You still don't use the Jekyll?' I asked. 'I mean, Doc, this is *you*?'

He looked surprised at the question, but insisted he'd never touched a drop.

Still, even without drinking it, the Tonic had brought out something inside him that would never go back in hiding.

'Tonight, a fresh direction,' he said, sliding on his smart new jacket. 'I am entertaining the Flavering Sisters, Flora and Belinda. Their father, the Earl of Roscommon, sits on the board of the University of ... well, you know who he is. A year ago, Billy, I was discharged from the faculty. Merely for pursuing a line of inquiry involving the effects of caustic solutions upon the mammalian eye. A petition was got up about vivisection and a to-do burst in the 'papers. My name was "Mudd", like your countryman, Dr Samuel Mudd. Now, it might as well be "Rose", for it seems that with the Jekyll Tonic millions pouring in I smell a lot sweeter. This is the Strange Case of Dr Varrable ... and Mr Rose.'

'Flora and Belinda,' I mused. 'With which delightful young lady do you intend to experiment?'

Varrable fixed a fresh-cut rose to his lapel, and sniffed it.

'You misjudge me. Why choose only one?'

––––––––––

'You've complicated our lives at the Yard, sir. And no mistake.'

Inspector Mist had become a frequent visitor to Shoreditch.

Given that, with the Jekyll craze, all I saw were smiling faces, hungry eyes, beautiful women, happy bankers, deferential servants and ecstatic *consortium* comrades, the presence of the Inspector, who trudged about under a perpetual black cloud, was almost a refreshing change. In a world of sunshine and champagne, he brought his own little patch of gloom and weak tea.

'One swig and you change face, body, height, everything. Don't match a description. Don't look like your picture in the *Police Gazette*.'

'You mean the Threadneedle Street bandits?'

'Indeed. A touch of your "Wild Wicked West" in staid old foggy London. There were heart attacks, you know.'

'So I read.'

A small band of habitual crooks, minor rogues who had never done anything worse than lift a purse or knock over a coster-monger, had staged a raid on the Bank of England after the manner of Jesse James. They careened up Threadneedle Street on horses and in a carriage, discharged revolvers at random over the heads of shocked crowds and dashed into the august financial establishment, demanding that cash and bullion be handed over. Before setting out on this exploit, each of the gang had drained a bottle of Jekyll to become another person entirely. It was popularly supposed that the transformed criminals were ape-faced, spider-fingered, devil-horned, cyclops-eyed sub-human fiends. The *Pall Mall Gazette*, perhaps inevitably, had referred to the miscreants as 'a pack of Hydes'. I had already dashed off a telegram to the editor threatening withdrawal of advertising unless a balanced retraction appeared within the week.

'Suppose it's a mercy your average villain is so thick-headed,' said the Inspector. 'This mob had spent all their lives dreaming about robbing the Bank of England. It was the Land of Cockaigne to them, sir. They thought of a golden temple. Heaps of bank-notes and piles of silver sovereigns lying around for the taking. Then they crashed in and discovered it was bank like any other, only snootier. Vaults and strong-boxes, inaccessible to the raiders. When we caught up with them, they had less loot to hand than you'd expect from a provincial post office job. All themselves again, they were, blinking and surprised. Hadn't taken elementary precautions. Got 'em by the mud on their boots. And the blood on their coats.'

Two bank employees had been 'pistol-whipped'. One seemed likely to die.

'Still, a question is answered. One left over from the Hyde business.'

'What question, Inspector?'

'It's like this, sir. We knew what happened when Jekyll drank. He became Hyde. But, even without the potion, there are Hydes in the world. See 'em every day. Not a few on the Force, in fact. Now we know what happens when Hyde drinks. It doesn't make him cleverer, which is a terror and yet a mercy. A terror because all trace of scruple, even that which rises from fear of being caught, evaporates like dew in the morning. But a mercy because your Hyde is a stupid crook. And stupid crooks are easy to catch. But not all villains are idiots, Mr Quinn. Jekyll was a villain, after all. He was different from Hyde, not separate. What mightn't happen if a clever villain drinks your Tonic. What then, sir?'

I had the uncomfortable sensation that I was being judged.

'It's just patent medicine, Inspector,' I said. 'It doesn't really *do* anything, except in the imagination. Oh, it's dramatic, all right. Makes people pull faces. But it wears off in a tick, and you're back for another bottle. There's nothing inherently Evil about the stuff. Have you tried it?'

'Yes sir. Have you?'

Not loitering for an answer, Mist left.

———

Jekyll Tonic had been on sale for two weeks. I was returning to Kensington just after dawn. The sun was up but the thin fog had yet to dissipate. This was not the fabled pea-souper I'd heard about back in the States, just wispy yellowish stuff that hung in the air like the colour-swirls in a glass marble. I trailed my stylish new cane through some strands, setting them in motion like phantom streamers.

I was still a little "tight" from last night's celebration, hosted after the show at the Tivoli by Harry "Brass" Button, in honour of the success of our venture. The entire company of the music hall had been in attendance, and most of the finest, most fashionable in the city. Not to mention the Flavering Sisters — quite the Jekyll Fiends these days, with happy results for Varrable that he was generous enough to share with his comrades in the *consortium*. Even Lady Knowe's besotted Guardsman intended took notice. Of our principles, only Leo Dare — who never appeared at parties of any kind — was absent. I took this up with Sir Marmaduke, who mused that our colossus of finance must be at bottom 'a sad, lonely sort of chap', allowing that he was enviably single-minded in the pursuit of cold wealth but that he lived the life of a monk, in his cell-like hotel suites, reading only ledgers, measuring his life's worth only in bank deposits. 'What's the point of it all if you can't drown yourself in it, sirrah?' Sir Marmaduke then took his table-spoonful of Tonic and joined with the ladies of the chorus and several ladies of distinction, including Lady Knowe and Mrs Biddlesham, in an enthusiastic performance of the can-can, lately the sensation of Paris.

I rounded the corner and observed an orderly commotion.

A crowd was gathered outside my house. Not a mob, but men in black coats and bowler hats, celluloid collars shiny, paper clutched in their hands. My first thought was that they were newspaper reporters. Was the Threadneedle Street Gang at large again?

'It's 'im,' someone shouted, and they all turned.

They rushed at me, thrusting out wax-sealed envelopes, ribbon-tied scrolls and telegrams. I was briefly in fear for my person, but to a man they handed over documents, raised hats politely, bade me good-morning and departed. I was left alone outside my house, hands full of paper. I stuffed as much as I could into my pockets.

My front door opened and my butler emerged, silverware stuck out of his coat-pockets and a crystal punchbowl (full of pocket-watches, snuff-boxes and other portable items of value) in his embrace. He was followed by Cook and two maids, hefting between them a polished mahogany dining table with the linen still on, bumping alarmingly against the door-frame and scraping spiked railings as they came down my front steps.

The butler saw me and did his best to bow without dropping anything.

'In lieu of wages, Mr Quinn. Please accept my regret that we are unable to continue in your employ.'

Lucy, the 'tweeny', sniffled a bit.

I was too astonished to say anything.

'If you would stand aside, sir,' said my former butler. 'So we might pass.'

I did as he suggested and found myself holding the door open to effect the removal of my former dining table. Lucy, eyes downcast, muttered something about it being 'a dreadful shame, sir'. I watched my entire staff struggle down the road, like a Whitechapel family doing a midnight flit.

I did not have time to examine all the papers in my pockets before the bailiffs showed up.

Within the hour, I realised that I did not have so much as a Knowe's Black Biscuit to my name.

————

The Shoreditch facilities were besieged, but not by customers. That would come later. Creditors barred the gates, so that we could not even supply our own stall with the Tonic, let alone distribute as normal. I saw my secretary sprinting off into the fog, cased type-writer on her back like a snail's shell.

Varrable was on the 'phone, needlessly cranking the handle faster as his sentences sped up, hair awry. I gathered that he was talking with his stockbroker. A Flavering girl was perched on the divan, dead flowers in her hair like Ophelia, shivering as if in a rainstorm. Her colour was off, as if she were coming down with the 'flu.

Windows smashed somewhere.

'Sell some *consortium* stock,' Varrable shouted. 'Use the funds to cover … what funds? Why, that stock is worth fifty times what we ploughed into it. A hundred.'

Varrable went white. He replaced the telephonic apparatus in its cradle.

'Billy,' he said, voice hollow. 'I could do with a tonic.'

The Flavering girl obediently sorted through empty bottles.

'Not *that* tonic,' Varrable said, with utter disgust. 'There's brandy around somewhere.'

I found the decanter and poured a generous measure. Varrable snatched the glass from me and raised it to his mouth. Then he gasped in horror and set the glass down.

'Billy, you nearly ... No, the real brandy. It's in the desk.'

I found a bottle and filled two more glasses.

Varrable and I both shocked ourselves with drink. The brandy hit the last of the Tivoli champagne, but did no good.

'Just before close of trade yesterday,' Varrable explained, 'a vast amount of *consortium* stock went on sale. It went in small lots, to dozens, *hundreds* of buyers. There's been clamour for the issue for months, but it's simply not been available. When it was "up for grabs", there was what my man called a "feeding frenzy". A share worth fifty pounds yesterday isn't worth five shillings this morning. And won't be worth fivepence tomorrow.'

'Dare-ing,' I said.

Varrable nodded, swallowing more brandy. 'He sold at fifty pounds, Billy. Without telling us. We're all ruined, you know. Except *him*.'

I could not quite conceive of it.

'There's still the business,' I said, 'the Tonic. Money is pouring in. Buck up, Doc. We can cover debts in a day, costs in a week, and be in profit again by the end of the month.'

Varrable shook his head.

'Jekyll Tonic sells at a loss. Even at a shilling.'

This was news.

'Oh, in the long run, costs would have come down,' said Varrable, bitterly. 'But there is not going to be a "long run". There were unforeseen expenses in development, you see. The original estimates were optimistic. We were moving too swiftly to revise them.'

I understood. A harvest had been reaped, profit had been made. Leo Dare had taken his money out and moved on.

'I borrowed against the stock,' I admitted.

'So did I,' said Varrable.

My pockets were still stuffed with writs of foreclosure, bills suddenly come due, summonses to court, notices of lien, announcements of garnishee and other such waste paper.

A quiet knock came at the door. A doggy head poked around.

'I realise this is an inconvenient time for you both,' said Inspector Mist, 'but I am afraid I must ask you to accompany me to the Yard.'

The thing of it is that if Jekyll Tonic had not worked, Leo Dare would have stayed in it longer. If it were just the coloured water he himself was prepared to drink, the horse might have been ridden for years. Then, there might have been enough gravy to keep us all fat. But, as Varrable had always said, the effects were dramatic but unpredictable, and that made the venture a long-term risk.

The Threadneedle Street raiders inspired similar crimes, no more successful but equally as spectacular. Veiled ladies brought suit against the likes of Dr Hugo Varrable for artificial exploitation of affections, which had in more than one case led to Consequences. Every murderer and knock-down man in the land was purported to be under the influence of the Jekyll, though it is my belief that as many heroic rescues from burning buildings or sinking barges were carried out by persons temporarily not themselves as were homicidal rampages or outrages to the public decency. All manner of folk disclaimed responsibility for reprehensible actions by blaming the Tonic. Sermons were preached against Jekyll Tonic, and editorials – in the very same 'papers that had boosted us – were written in thunderous condemnation. Lawsuits beyond number were laid against the *consortium*, which no longer included Leo Dare. The simple duns for unpaid bills took precedence, driving us to bankruptcy. The criminal and frivolous matters dragged on, though many were dropped when it became apparent that the coffers were empty and that no financial settlement would be arrived at. A tearful Harry Button was booed off stage before he could give his infamous Joke, and shortly thereafter found himself bought out of his contract and booted into the street by the management. Temperance organisations shifted the focus of their attention from the demon alcohol to the impious Jekyll Tonic.

Sir Marmaduke and Lady Knowe made numberless attempts to get in touch with Leo Dare, but I recalled those cards he had made a pack of and ignored in Kettner's and did not waste my efforts. A man with no fixed address finds it easy not to be at home to the most persistent callers. At length, both worthies departed from the stage in no more dignified a manner than "Brass" Button. Sir Marmaduke, sadly, retained a gold-thread curtain cord from the fixtures transported away by the bailiffs and hanged himself in his empty Belgravia town house. Lady Knowe, perhaps surprisingly, married her Guardsman. The couple decamped for a posting in Calcutta, where she devoted her energies to improving the moral health of Her Majesty's troops by campaigning against boy-brothels.

The formula remained ours alone, our sole asset, but many competitors were working to reproduce its effects. A Royal Commission was established, and with uncharacteristic swiftness, made all such research illegal unless conducted under government supervision. I suspected some in Pall Mall still maintained Major General Cogstaff-Blyth's notions of a regiment of Hydes trampling over the Kaiser's borders, chewing through *pickelhaubes* with apelike fangs and rending Uhlans limb from limb. Regulations closed around the Jekyll. An amendment to the Dangerous Drugs Acts insisted that the Tonic now could not be sold unless a customer signed the Poisons Book and waited until the signature was verified. By that time, it was a moot point since there was no Jekyll to be had anywhere. Our Shoreditch factory ceased manufacture when the stock crashed, and supplies dried up within the morning.

Varrable and I spent some nights enjoying the hospitality of one of Her Majesty's police stations, mostly through the good graces of Inspector Mist, who realised we had nowhere else to go and no funds to procure lodgings. A great many lines of inquiry were being pursued and we were told not to leave London. Questions would doubtless be asked of us on a great many natters, but no criminal charges were forthcoming as yet.

We trudged, cabless, to Shoreditch.

———

The factory, thoroughly looted, was abandoned. Our bruisers, our pretty sales-girls, our secretaries, our vat-stirrers, were all flown. And the fittings and furnishings with them. Even the prized telephones.

'What if he didn't drink coloured water that time?' said Varrable, with his now-habitual look of wide-eyed frenzy. 'I'd brewed up the first test batch. It could have been the real Tonic. He could have *changed*?'

'Leo Dare has no Hyde side,' I said. 'He was always himself.'

Varrable admitted it, smashing a beaker too cracked to steal.

We were in the stables, where vats stood overturned and empty, the flagstones stained with chemicals. The stinks still clung to the place. The gates had been torn down and taken away.

'Look,' said Varrable, 'the cabbies are back.'

Opposite the factory was a knot of loitering fellows, despondent and jittery, as I remembered them.

'I imagine not a few of our employees will be joining them,' I said. 'It was all over too swiftly for them to draw more than a week's wages.'

'It's breathtaking, Billy. He sucked all the money out, like you'd suck the juice from an orange, then tossed away the pith and peel. No one else saw anything from the Jekyll bubble.'

The loiterers formed a deputation and crossed the road. They marched into the factory.

'This might be it, Doc. Prepare to repel boarders.'

'They don't look angry.'

'Looks can be deceiving.'

In the gloom, we were surrounded. I made out fallen faces, worn clothing, postures of desolation and resentment.

'D–d–d–d–octor V–V–V–Varr …' stammered one of the louts.

From his shabby clothes and battered face, it would have been impossible to recognise the exquisite aesthete but the voice was unmistakable. The Hon. Hilary Belligo.

'Is there anything left over?' asked one of Hilary's fellows.

I shook my head. 'We are at a financial embarrassment,' I said. 'All in the same boat.'

'N-n-n-not m-*money*!'

'Tonic.'

I remembered a happier day and Varrable's declaration that the likes of Hilary Belligo would be happy to pay five pounds a thimble for the Jekyll. I wished I had a crate of Tonic in a safe store somewhere, but it was all gone. Shipped out and drunk. There wasn't a bottle left on a shelf in London. When supplies stopped coming from the factory, devotees haunted the most out-of-the-way shops and tracked down every last drop. There had been fearful brawls before the counters to get hold of it, as devotees paid whatever canny chemists asked. Even Jickle Juice and Jeckell Tonik, supposedly withdrawn from sale, was snapped up and drunk down. Fools had forked over ten guineas for empty Tonic bottles refilled with Thameswater.

I shrugged, showing empty hands.

'I might know where some Tonic remains,' said Varrable, smoothing his hair with stained hands. 'But we'll need to see, ah, *expenses* up front.'

The desperate souls all had money about them. Not much, and not in good condition – torn bank-notes, filthy coins, bloody sovereigns. I cupped my hands, and they were filled.

'Be here tomorrow, at ten,' said Varrable. 'And keep it quiet.'

They scurried away, possessed with a strange excitement, a promise that took the edge of sufferings.

'*Have* we a secret reserve, Doc?'

Varrable shook his head, disarranging his hair again. 'No, but I still have the formula,' tapping his temple. 'Some of the ingredients must remain here. Few would want to loot chemicals. I can brew up Jekyll in the laboratory, rougher than the stuff we bottled but stronger as well.'

'The demand is still there.'

I knew Hilary Belligo's crew would ignore Varrable's order to keep quiet. By tomorrow, word would be out. In two short weeks, a great many people had become used to a spoonful of Jekyll every day. The business was gone, the *consortium* collapsed, but that didn't mean the *need* had evaporated.

'It'll be illegal,' I ventured. 'Under the Dangerous Drugs Act.'

'All the better,' Varrable snorted. 'We can ask for a higher price. That lot'll slit their grannies' throats for a drop of the Jekyll. And we're sole suppliers, Billy. Do you understand?'

Varrable was as possessed as the Hon. Hilary. With another kind of need.

Leo Dare had passed from the story. He left us all with new needs, but also new opportunities.

'I understand. You're the chemist, I'm the salesman. We'll need a place to work. Several, to keep on the move. Mist won't just forget us, and he's no fool. We can no longer afford fixed addresses. We'll need folk for the distribution, lads to stand on street-corners, fellows to sit in taverns. Servants, perhaps, to get to the customers with the folding money. We'll need places to hide the profits. Not under mattresses, in investments. Respectable, above-board. We'll have to see off the opium tongs. Maybe those East End roughs are still interested in the Jekyll trade. We could pitch in with them. The law of the land will not be with us, just the law of the market. We'll need new names.'

'I have mine. Harold Rose.'

'And I'm Billy Brass. Do you know, ah, Harold, I think that this way we shall wind up richer than before.'

I had the strangest impression that Leo Dare was smiling down upon me.

And so your friends Dr Rose and Mr Brass embarked upon a new venture.

This is my second stab at a sequel to Robert Louis Stevenson's Strange Case of Dr Jekyll and Mr Hyde; *the first was 'Further Developments* in the *Strange Case of Dr Jekyll and Mr Hyde'*, published in *Maxim Jakubowski's* Chronicles of Crime. *That took a very different tack in imagining what might have happened after the events of Stevenson's story than 'A Drug on the Market'. Dr Jekyll also appears briefly in my novel* Anno Dracula. *Obviously, the original lingers in the memory, sparking ideas that need to be written up. I even liked the film of Valerie Martin's brilliant novel* Mary Reilly, *though I think Eddie Murphy should be prohibited by law from making another* Nutty Professor *sequel.*

Of all the founding texts of the horror/monster/gothic genre, Stevenson's novella strikes me as being the best all-round piece of writing. While Frankenstein *and* Dracula *are big, sprawling books full of flaws and hasty patches, careless of characterisation, choked by plot,* Strange Case *is put together, as Stephen King once noted, like a Swiss watch, without a wasted word, cliché character or dull paragraph. Mr Hyde is one of the genre's most vividly-imagined monsters: not the lusty caveman of most film versions but a shrunken, frightened, bullying, vicious little man who never picks on anyone his own size. In this piece, I was also influenced by H.G. Wells's* Tono-Bungay, *which has a terrific section about a voyage to corner quap (a wonderful word Wells seems to have invented and which I hope comes back into circulation) and is an early fulmination against the advertising industry. Though it doesn't play with the original text in the way* Anno Dracula *does, 'A Drug on the Market' does take a similar line: extrapolating from a story about individual monstrousness to imagine its effects if spread to a wider society that is Victorian London but also our own world a century on.*

TOMORROW

TOWN

*T*his way to the Yeer 2000.

The message, in Helvetia typeface, was repeated on arrow-shaped signs.

'That'll be us, Vanessa,' said Richard Jeperson, striding along the platform in the indicated direction, toting his shoulder-slung hold-all. He tried to feel as if he were about to time-travel from 1971 to the future, though in practice he was just changing trains.

Vanessa was distracted by one of the arrow-signs, fresh face arranged into a comely frown. Richard's associate was a tall redhead in hot-pants, halter top, beret and stack-heeled go-go boots — all blinding white, as if fresh from the machine in a soap-powder advert. She drew unconcealed attention from late-morning passengers milling about the railway station. Then again, in his lime dayglo blazer edged with gold braid and salmon-pink bell-bottom trousers, so did he. Here in Preston, the fashion watchword, for the eighteenth consecutive season, was 'drab'.

'It's misspelled,' said Vanessa. 'Y Double-E R.'

'No, it's F O N E T I K,' he corrected. 'Within the next thirty years, English spelling will be rationalised.'

'You reckon?' She pouted, sceptically.

'Not my theory,' he said, stroking his mandarin moustaches. 'I assume the lingo will muddle along with magical illogic as it has since "the Yeer Dot". But orthographic reform is a tenet of Tomorrow Town.'

'Alliteration. Very Century 21.'

They had travelled up from London, sharing a rattly first-class carriage and a welcome magnum of Bollinger with a liberal Bishop on a lecture tour billed as 'Peace and the Pill' and a working-class playwright revisiting his slag-heap roots. To continue their journey, Richard and Vanessa had to change at Preston.

The arrows led to a guarded gate. The guard wore a British Rail uniform in shiny black plastic with silver highlights. His oversized cap had a chemical lighting element in the brim.

'You need special tickets, Ms and Mm,' said the guard.

'Mm,' said Vanessa, amused.

'Ms,' Richard buzzed at her.

He searched through his pockets, finally turning up the special tickets. They were strips of foil, like ironed-flat chocolate bar wrappers with punched-out hole patterns. The guard carefully posted the tickets into a slot in a metal box. Gears whirred and lights flashed. The gate came apart and sank into the ground. Richard let Vanessa step through the access first. She seemed to float off, arms out for balance.

'Best not to be left behind, Mm,' said the guard.

'Mm,' said Richard, agreeing.

He stepped onto the special platform. Beneath his rubber-soled winkle-pickers, a knitted chain-mail surface moved on large rollers. It creaked and rippled, but gave a smooth ride.

'I wonder how it manages corners,' Vanessa said.

The moving platform conveyed them towards a giant silver bullet. The train of the future hummed slightly, at rest on a single gleaming rail which was raised ten feet above the gravel railbed by chromed tubular trestles. A hatchway was open, lowered to form a ramp.

Richard and Vanessa clambered through the hatch and found themselves in a space little roomier than an Apollo capsule. They half-sat, half-lay in over-padded seats which wobbled on gyro-gimbals. Safety straps automatically snaked across them and drew tight.

'Not sure I'll ever get used to this,' said Richard. A strap across his forehead noosed his long, tangled hair, and he had to free a hand to fix it.

Vanessa wriggled to get comfortable, doing a near-horizontal dance as the straps adjusted to her.

With a hiss the ramp raised and became a hatch-cover, then sealed shut. The capsule-cum-carriage had seat-berths for eight, but today they were the only passengers.

A mechanical voice counted down from ten.

'Richard, that's a Dalek,' said Vanessa, giggling.

As if offended, the voice stuttered on five, like a record stuck in a groove, then hopped to three.

At zero, they heard a rush of rocketry and the monorail moved off. Richard tensed against the expected g-force slam, but it didn't come. Through thick-glassed slit windows, he saw green countryside passing by at about 25 miles per hour. They might have been on a leisurely cycle to the village pub rather than taking the fast train to the future.

'So this is the transport of tomorrow?' said Vanessa.

'A best-guess design,' explained Richard. 'That's the point of Tomorrow Town. To experiment with the lives we'll all be living at the turn of the century.'

'No teleportation then?'

'Don't be silly. Matter transmission is a fantasy. This is a reasonable extrapolation from present-day or in-development technology. The Foundation is rigorous about probabilities. Everything in Tomorrow Town is viable.'

The community was funded partially by government research grants and partially by private sources. It was projected that it would soon be a profitable concern, with monies pouring in from scientific wonders developed by the visioneers of the new technomeritocracy. The Foundation, which had proposed the 'Town of 2000' experiment, was a think tank, an academic-industrial coalition dedicated to applying to present-day life lessons learned from contemplating the likely future. Tomorrow Town's two-thousand odd citizen-volunteers ('zenvols') were boffins, engineers, social visionaries, health-food cranks and science fiction fans.

Three years ago, when the town was given its charter by the Wilson government, there had been a white heat of publicity: television programmes hosted by James Burke and Raymond Baxter, picture features in all the Sunday colour supplements, a novelty single ('Take Me to Tomorrow' by Big Thinks and the BBC Radiophonic Workshop) which peaked at Number 2 (prevented from being Top of the Pops by The Crazy World of Arthur Brown's 'Fire'), a line of 'futopian fashions' from Carnaby Street, a heated debate in the letter columns of *New Scientist* between Arthur C. Clarke (pro), Auberon Waugh (anti) and J.G. Ballard (hard to tell). Then the brouhaha died down and Tomorrow Town was left to get on by itself, mostly forgotten. Until the murder of Varno Zhoule.

Richard Jeperson, agent of the Diogenes Club — least-known branch of the United Kingdom's intelligence and investigative services — was detailed to look into the supposedly open-and-shut case and report back to the current Prime Minister on the advisability of maintaining government support for Tomorrow Town.

He had given Vanessa the barest facts.

'What does the murder weapon of the future turn out to be?' she asked. 'Laser-beam? Poisoned moon-rock?'

'No, the proverbial blunt instrument. Letting the side down, really. Anyone who murders the co-founder of Tomorrow Town should have the decency to stick to the spirit of the game. I doubt if it's much comfort to the deceased, but the offending bludgeon was vaguely futurist, a stylised steel rocketship with a heavy stone base.'

'No home should be without one.'

'It was a Hugo Award, the highest honour the science fiction field can bestow. Zhoule won his murder weapon for Best Novelette of 1958, with the oft-anthologised "Court Martian".'

'Are we then to be the police of the future? Do we get to design our own uniforms?'

'We're here because Tomorrow Town has no police force as such. It is a fundamental of the social design that there will be no crime by the year 2000.'

'Ooops.'

'This is a utopian vision, Vanessa. No money to steal. No inequality to foster resentment. All disputes arbitrated with unquestionable fairness. All zenvols constantly monitored for emotional instability.'

'Maybe being "constantly monitored" leads to "emotional instability". Not to mention being called a "zenvol".'

'You'll have to mention that to Big Thinks.'

'Is he the boss-man among equals?'

Richard chuckled. 'He's an it. A computer. A very large computer.'

Vanessa snapped her fingers.

'Ah-ha. There's your culprit. In every sci-fi film I've ever seen, the computer goes power mad and starts killing people off. Big Thinks probably wants to take over the world.'

'The late Mm Zhoule would cringe to hear you say that, Vanessa. He'd never have deigned to use such a hackneyed, unlikely premise in a story. A computer is just a heuristic abacus. Big Thinks can beat you at chess, solve logic problems, cut a pop record and make the monorail run on time, but it hasn't got sentience, a personality, a motive or, most importantly, arms. You might as well suspect the fridge-freezer or the pop-up toaster.'

'If you knew my pop-up toaster better, you'd feel differently. It sits there, shining sneakily, plotting perfidy. The jug-kettle is in on it too. There's a conspiracy of contraptions.'

'Now you're being silly.'

'Trust me, Richard, it'll be the Brain Machine. Make sure to check its alibi.'

'I'll bear that in mind.'

––––––

They first saw Tomorrow Town from across the Yorkshire Dales, nestled in lush green and slate grey. The complex was a large-scale version of the sort of back garden space station that might have been put together by a talented child inspired by Gerry Anderson and instructed by Valerie Singleton, using egg boxes, toilet roll tubes, the innards of a broken wireless, pipe-cleaners and a lot of silver spray-paint.

Hexagonal geodesic domes clustered in the landscape, a central space covered by a giant canopy that looked like an especially aerodynamic silver circus tent. Metallised roadways wound between trees and lakes, connecting the domes. The light traffic consisted mostly of electric golf-carts and one-person hovercraft. A single hardy zenvol was struggling along on what looked like a failed flying bicycle from 1895 but was actually a moped powered by wing-like solar panels. It was raining gently, but the town seemed shielded by a half-bubble climate control barrier that shimmered in mid-air.

A pylon held up three sun-shaped globes on a triangle frame. They radiated light and, Richard suspected, heat. Where light fell, the greenery was noticeably greener and thicker.

The monorail stopped outside the bubble, and settled a little clunkily.

'You may now change apparel,' rasped the machine voice.

A compartment opened and clothes slid out on racks. The safety straps released them from their seats.

Richard thought for a moment that the train had calculated from his long hair that he was a Ms rather than a Mm, then realised the garment on offer was unisex: a lightweight jump-suit of semi-opaque polythene, with silver epaulettes, pockets, knee- and elbow-patches and modesty strips around the chest and hips. The dangling legs ended in floppy-looking plastic boots, the sleeves in surgeon's gloves.

'Was that "may" a "must"?' asked Vanessa.

'Best to go along with native customs,' said Richard.

He turned his back like a gentleman and undressed carefully, folding and putting away his clothes. Then he took the jump-suit from the rack and stepped into it, wiggling his feet down into the boots and fingers into the gloves. A seam from crotch to neck sealed with velcro strips, but he was left with an enormous swathe of polythene sprouting from his left hip like a bridal train.

'Like this,' said Vanessa, who had worked it out.

The swathe went over the right shoulder in a toga arrangement, passing under an epaulette, clipping on in a couple of places, and falling like a waist-length cape.

She had also found a pad of controls in the left epaulette, which activated drawstrings and pleats that adjusted the garment to suit individual body type. They both had to fiddle to get the suits to cope with their above-average height, then loosen and tighten various sections as required. Even after every possible button had been twisted every possible way, Richard wore one sleeve tight as sausage skin while the other was loose and wrinkled as a burst balloon.

'Maybe it's a futopian fashion,' suggested Vanessa, who — of course — looked spectacular, shown off to advantage by the modesty strips. 'All the dashing zenvols are wearing the one-loose-one-tight look this new century.'

'Or maybe it's just aggravated crackpottery.'

She laughed.

The monorail judged they had used up their changing time, and lurched off again.

———

The receiving area was as white and clean as a bathroom display at the Belgian Ideal Home Exhibition. A deputation of zenvols, all dressed alike, none with mismatched sleeves, waited on the platform. Synthesised Bach played gently and the artificial breeze was mildly perfumed.

'Mm Richard, Ms Vanessa,' said a white-haired zenvol, 'welcome to Tomorrow Town.'

A short oriental girl repeated his words in sign-language.

'Are you Georgie Gewell?' Richard asked.

'Jor-G,' said the zenvol, then spelled it out.

'My condolences,' Richard said, shaking the man's hand. Through two squeaking layers of latex, he had the impression of sweaty palm. 'I understand you and Varno Zhoule were old friends.'

'Var-Z is a tragic loss. A great visioneer.'

The oriental girl mimed sadness. Other zenvols hung their heads.

'Jesu, Joy of Man's Desiring' segued into the 'Dead March' from Saul. Was the musak keyed in somehow to the emotional state of any given assembly?

'We, ah, founded the Foundation together.'

Back in the 1950s, Varno Zhoule had written many articles and stories for science fiction magazines, offering futuristic solutions to contemporary problems, preaching the gospel of better living through logic and technology. He had predicted decimal currency and the vertical take-off aeroplane. Georgie Gewell was an award-winning editor and critic. He had championed Zhoule's work, then raised finance to apply his solutions to the real world. Richard understood the seed money for the Foundation came from a patent the pair held on a kind of battery-powered circular slide rule that was faster and more accurate than any other portable calculating device.

Gewell was as tall as Richard, with milk-fair skin and close-cropped snow-white hair. He had deep smile and frown lines and a soft, girlish mouth. He was steadily leaking tears, not from grief but from thick, obvious reactalite contact lenses that were currently smudged to the darker end of their spectrum.

The other zenvols were an assorted mix, despite their identical outfits. Most of the men were short and tubby, the women lithe and fit — which was either Big Thinks's recipe for perfect population balance or some visioneer's idea of a good time for a tall, thin fellow. Everyone had hair cut short, which made both Richard and Vanessa obvious outsiders. None of the men wore facial hair except a red-faced chap who opted for the Puritan beard-without-a-moustache arrangement.

Gewell introduced the delegation. The oriental girl was Moana, whom Gewell described as 'town speaker', though she continued to communicate only by signing. The beardie was Mal-K, the 'senior medico' who had presided over the autopsy, matched some bloody fingerprints and seemed a bit put out to be taken away from his auto-mated clinic for this ceremonial affair. Other significant zenvols: Jess-F, 'arbitrage input tech', a hard-faced blonde girl who interfaced with

Big Thinks when it came to programming dispute decisions, and thus was the nearest thing Tomorrow Town had to a human representative of the legal system — though she was more clerk of the court than investigating officer; Zootie, a fat little 'agri-terrain rearrangement tech' with a bad cold for which he kept apologising, who turned out to have discovered the body by the hydroponics vats and was oddly impressed and uncomfortable in this group as if he weren't quite on a level of equality with Gewell and the rest; and 'vocabulary administrator' Sue-2, whom Gewell introduced as 'sadly, the motive', the image of a penitent young lady who 'would never do it again'.

Richard mentally marked them all down.

'You'll want to visit the scene of the crime?' suggested Gewell. 'Interrogate the culprit? We have Buster in a secure store-room. It had to be especially prepared. There are no lockable doors in Tomorrow Town.'

'He's nailed in,' said Jess-F. 'With rations and a potty.'

'Very sensible,' commented Richard.

'We can prise the door open now you're here,' said Gewell.

Richard thought a moment.

'If you'll forgive me, Mr Jep — ah, Mm Richard,' said Mal-K, 'I'd like to get back to my work. I've a batch of anti-virus cooking.'

The medico kept his distance from Zootie. Did he think a streaming nose reflected badly on the health of the future? Or was the artificial breeze liable to spread sniffles around the whole community in minutes?

'I don't see any reason to detain you Mm Mal-K,' said Richard. 'Vanessa might pop over later. My associate is interested in the work you're doing here. New cures for new diseases. She'd love to squint into a microscope at your anti-virus.'

Vanessa nodded with convincing enthusiasm.

'Mal-K's door is always open,' said Gewell.

The medico sloped off without comment.

'Should we crack out the crowbar, then?' prompted Gewell.

The co-founder seemed keen on getting on with this: to him,

murder came as an embarrassment and an interruption. It wasn't an uncommon reaction. Richard judged Gewell just wanted all this over with so he could get on with things, even though the victim was one of his oldest friends and the crime demonstrated a major flaw in the social design of Tomorrow Town. If someone battered Vanessa to death, he didn't think he'd be so intent on putting it behind him — but he was famous for being sensitive. Indeed, it was why he was so useful to the Diogenes Club.

'I think as long as our putative culprit is safely nailed away, we can afford to take our time, get a feel for the place and the set-up. It's how I like to work, Mm Gewell. To me, understanding why is much more important than knowing who or how.'

'I should think the why was obvious,' said Gewell looking at Sue-2, eyes visibly darkening.

She looked down.

'The arbitration went against Buster, and he couldn't accept it,' said Jess-F. 'Though it was in his initial contract that he abide by Big Thinks decisions. It happens sometimes. Not often.'

'An arbitration in a matter of the heart? Interesting. Just the sort of thing that comes in a box marked "motive" and tied with pink string. Thank you so much for mentioning it early in the case. Before we continue the sleuthing, perhaps we could have lunch. Vanessa and I have travelled a long way, with no sustenance beyond British Rail sandwiches and a beverage of our own supply. Let's break bread together, and you can tell me more about your fascinating experiment.'

'Communal meals are at fixed times,' said Gewell. 'The next is not until six.'

'I make it about six o'clock,' said Richard, though his watch-face was blurred by the sleeve-glove.

'It's only f-five by our clock,' said Sue-2. 'We're on two daily cycles of ten kronons. Each kronon runs a hundred sentikronons.'

'In your time, a kronon is 72 minutes,' explained Gewell. 'Our six is your . . .'

Vanessa did the calculation and beat the slide-rule designer, 'twelve minutes past seven.'

'That's about it.'

Richard waved away the objection.

'I'm sure a snack can be rustled up. Where do you take these communal meals?'

Moana signalled a direction and set off. Richard was happy to follow, and the others came too.

———

The dining area was in the central plaza, under the pylon and the three globes, with zinc-and-chrome sheet-and-tube tables and benches. It was warm under the globes, almost Caribbean, and some zenvols wore poker-players' eyeshades. In the artificially balmy climate, plastic garments tended to get sticky inside, which made for creaky shiftings-in-seats.

An abstract ornamental fountain gushed nutrient-enriched, slightly carbonated, heavily-fluoridized water. Gewell had Moana fetch a couple of jugs for the table, while the meek Sue-2 hustled off to persuade 'sustenance preparation' techs to break their schedule to feed the visitors. Vanessa cocked an eyebrow at this division of labour, and Richard remembered Zhoule and Gewell had been planning this futopia since the 1950s, well before the publication of *The Female Eunuch*. Even Jess-F, whom Richard had pegged as the toughest zenvol he had yet met, broke out the metallised glass tumblers from a dispenser by the fountain, while Gewell and the sniffling Zootie sat at their ease at table.

'Is that the building where Big Thinks lives?' asked Vanessa.

Gewell swivelled to look. Vanessa meant an imposing structure, rather like a giant art deco refrigerator decorated with Mondrian squares in a rough schematic of a human face. Uniformly-dressed zenvols came and went through airlock doors that opened and closed with hisses of decontaminant.

Gewell grinned, impishly.

'Ms Vanessa, that building *is* Big Thinks.'

Richard whistled.

'Bee-Tee didn't used to be that size,' said Jess-F. 'Var-Z kept insisting we add units. More and more complicated questions need more and more space. Soon, we'll have to expand further.'

'It doesn't show any telltale signs of megalomania?' asked Vanessa. 'Never programs Wagner for eight straight hours and chortles over maps of the world.'

Jess-F didn't look as if she thought that was funny.

'Bee-Tee is a machine, Ms.'

Sue-2 came back with food. Coloured pills that looked like smarties but tasted like chalk.

'All the nutrition you need is here,' said Gewell, 'in the water and the capsules. For us, mealtimes are mostly ceremonial, for debate and reflection. Var-Z said that some of his best ideas popped into his head while he was chatting idly after a satisfying pill.'

Richard didn't doubt it. He also still felt hungry.

'Talking of things popping into Zhoule's head,' he said. 'What's the story on Buster of the bloody fingerprints?'

Jess-F looked at Sue-2, as if expecting to be contradicted, then carried on.

'Big Thinks assessed the dispute situation, and arbitrated it best for the community if Sue-2 were to be pair-bonded with Var-Z rather than Buster.'

'Buster was your old boyfriend?' Vanessa asked Sue-2.

'He is my husband,' she said.

'On the outside, in the past,' put in Jess-F. 'Here, we don't always acknowledge arbitrary pair-bondings. Mostly, they serve a useful purpose and continue. In this instance, the dispute was more complicated.'

'Big Thinks arbitrated against the arbitrary?,' mused Richard. 'I suppose no one would be surprised at that.'

He looked from face to face and fixed on Sue-2, then asked: 'Did you leave Buster for Mm Zhoule?'

Sue-2 looked for a cue, but none came.

'It was best for the town, for the experiment,' she said.

'What was it for you? For your husband?'

'Buster had been regraded. From "zenvol" to "zenpass". He could-n't vote.'

Richard looked to Jess-F for explication. He noticed Gewell had to give her a teary wink from almost-black eyes before she would say anything more.

'We have very few citizen-passengers,' she said. 'It's not a punish-ment category.'

'Kind of you to clarify that,' said Richard. 'I might have made a misconclusion otherwise. You say zenpasses have no vote?'

'It's not so dreadful,' said Gewell, sipping nutrient. 'On the outside, in the past, suffrage is restricted by age, sanity, residence and so on. Here, in our technomeritocracy, to register for a vote — which gives you a voice in every significant decision — you have to demonstrate your applied intelligence.'

'An IQ test?'

'Not a quotient, Mm Richard. Anyone can have that. The vital factor is application. Bee-Tee tests for that. There's no personality or human tangle involved. Surely, it's only fair that the most useful should have the most say?'

'I have a vote,' said Zootie, proud. 'Earned by applied intelligence.'

'Indeed he does,' said Gewell, smiling.

'And Mm Jor-G has fifteen votes. Because he applies his intelli-gence more often than I do.'

Everyone looked at Zootie with different types of amazement.

'It's only fair,' said Zootie, content despite a nose-trickle, washing down another purple pill.

Richard wondered whether the agri-terrain rearrangement tech was hovering near regrading as a zenpass.

Richard addressed Sue-2. 'What does your husband do?'

'He's a history teacher.'

'An educationalist. Very valuable.'

Gewell looked as if his pill was sour. 'Your present is our

past, Mm Richard. Buster's discipline is surplus.'

'Doesn't the future grow out of the past? To know where you're going you must know where you've been.'

'Var-Z believes in a radical break.'

'But Var-Z is in the past too.'

'Indeed. Regrettable. But we must think of the future.'

'It's where we're going to spend the rest of our lives,' said Zootie.

'That's very clever,' said Vanessa.

Zootie wiped his nose and puffed up a bit.

'I think we should hand Buster over to you,' said Gewell. 'To be taken outside to face the justice of the past. Var-Z left work undone that we must continue.'

'Not just yet,' said Richard. 'This sad business raises questions about Tomorrow Town. I have to look beyond the simple crime before I make my report. I'm sure you understand and will extend full coop- eration.'

No one said anything, but they all constructed smiles.

'You must be economically self-supporting by now,' continued Richard, 'what with the research and invention you've been applying intelligence to. If the Prime Minister withdrew government subsidies, you'd probably be better off. Free of the apron strings, as it were. Still, the extra cash must come in handy for something, even if you don't use money in this town.'

Gewell wiped his eyes and kept smiling.

Richard could really do with a steak and kidney pie and chips, washed down with beer. Even a Kit-Kat would have been welcome.

'Have you a guest apartment we could use?'

Gewell's smile turned real. 'Sadly, we're at maximum optimal zenvol residency. No excess space wastage in the living quarters.'

'No spare beds,' clarified Zootie.

'Then we'll have to take the one living space we know to be free.'

Gewell's brow furrowed like a rucked-up rug.

'Zhoule's quarters,' Richard explained. 'We'll set up camp there. Sue-2, you must know the way. Since there are no locks we won't need keys to get in. Zenvols, it's been fascinating. I look forward to seeing you tomorrow.'

Richard and Vanessa stood up, and Sue-2 followed suit.

Gewell and Jess-F glared. Moana waved bye-bye.

––––––––

'What are you looking for?' Vanessa asked. 'Monitoring devices.'

'No,' said Richard, unsealing another compartment, 'they're in the light fittings and the communicator screen, and seem to have been disabled. By Zhoule or his murderer, presumably.'

There was a constant hum of gadgetry in the walls and from behind white-fronted compartments. The ceiling was composed of translucent panels, above which glowed a steady light.

The communicator screen was dusty. Beneath the on-off switch, volume and brightness knobs and channel selector was a telephone dial, with the Tomorrow Town alphabet (no Q or X). Richard had tried to call London but a recorded voice over a cartoon smiley face told him that visiphones only worked within the town limits. Use of the telephone line to the outside had to be approved by vote of zenvol visioneers.

In a compartment, he found a gadget whose purpose was a mystery. It had dials, a trumpet and three black rubber nipples.

'I'm just assuming, Vanessa, that the co-founder of Tomorrow Town might allow himself to sample the forbidden past in ways denied the simple zenvol or despised zenpass.'

'You mean?'

'He might have real food stashed somewhere.'

Vanessa started opening compartments too.

It took a full hour to search the five rooms of Zhoule's bungalow. They discovered a complete run of *Town Magazeen*, a microfilm publication with all text in fonetik, and a library of 1950s science fiction magazines, lurid covers mostly promising Varno Zhoule stories as back-up to Asimov or Heinlein.

They found many compartments stuffed with ring-bound notebooks which dated back twenty years. Richard flicked through a couple, noting Zhoule had either been using fonetik since the early 50s or was such a bad speller that his editors must have been driven to despair. Most of the entries were single sentences, story ideas, possible inventions or prophecies. *Tunel under Irish See. Rokit to Sun to harvest heet. Big lift to awbit. Stoopids not allowd to breed. Holes in heds for plugs.*

Vanessa found a display case, full of plaques and awards in the shapes of spirals or robots.

'Is this the murder weapon?' Vanessa asked, indicating a needle-shaped rocket. 'Looks too clean.'

'I believe Zhoule was a multiple Hugo-winner. See, this is Best Short Story 1957, for "Vesta Interests". The blunt instrument was . . .'

Vanessa picked up a chunk of ceramic and read the plaque, 'Best Novelette 1958.' It was a near-duplicate of the base of the other award.

'You can see where the rocketship was fixed. It must have broken when the award was lifted in anger.'

'Cold blood, Vanessa. The body and the Hugo were found elsewhere. No blood traces in these quarters. Let's keep looking for a pork pie.'

Vanessa opened a floor-level compartment and out crawled a matt-black robot spider the size of an armoured go-kart. The fearsome thing brandished death-implements that, upon closer examination, turned out to be a vacuum cleaner proboscis and limbs tipped with chamois, damp squeegee and a brush.

'Oh, how useful,' said Vanessa.

Then the spider squirted hot water at her and crackled. Electrical circuits burned out behind its photo-eyes. The proboscis coughed black soot.

'Or maybe not.'

'"I have seen the future, and it works",' quoted Richard. 'Lincoln Steffens, on the Soviet Union, 1919.'

'"What's to become of my bit of washing when there's no washing to do",' quoted Vanessa. 'The old woman in *The Man in the White Suit*, on technological progress, 1951.'

'You suspect the diabolical Big Thinks sent this cleaning robot to murder Varno Zhoule? A Frankensteinian rebellion against the Master-Creator?'

'If Bee-Tee is so clever, I doubt it'd use this arachnoid doodad as an assassin. The thing can't even beat as it sweeps as it cleans, let alone carry out a devilish murder plan. Besides, to use the blunt instrument, it would have to climb a wall and I reckon this can't even manage stairs.'

Richard poked the carapace of the machine, which wriggled and lost a couple of limbs.

'Are you still hungry?'

'Famished.'

'Yet we've had enough nourishment to keep body and spirit together for the ten long kronons that remain until breakfast time.'

'I'll ask medico Mal-K if he sees many cases of rickets and scurvy in futopia.'

'You do that.'

Richard tried to feel sorry for the spider, but it was just a gadget. It was impossible to invest it with a personality.

Vanessa was thinking.

'Wasn't the idea that Tomorrow Town would pour forth 21st Century solutions to our drab old 1970s problems?'

Richard answered her. 'That's what Mr Wilson thought he was signing up for.'

'So why aren't Mrs Mopp Spiders on sale in the Charing Cross Road?'

'It doesn't seem to work all that well.'

'Lot of that about, Mm Richard. A monorail that would lose a race with Stephenson's Rocket. Technomeroticratic *droit de seigneur*. Concentrated foods astronauts wouldn't eat. Robots less functional than the wind-up ones my nephew Paulie uses to conquer the playground. And I've seen the odd hovercraft up on blocks with "Owt of Awder" signs. Not to mention Buster the Basher, living incarnation of a society out of joint.'

'Good points all,' he said. 'And I'll answer them as soon as I solve another mystery.'

'What's that?'

'What are we supposed to sleep on?'

Around the rooms were large soft white cubes which distantly resembled furniture but could as easily be tofu chunks for the giants who would evolve by the turn of the millennium. By collecting enough cubes into a windowless room where the lighting panels were more subdued, Richard and Vanessa were able to put together a bed-shape. However, when Richard took an experimental lie-down on the jigsaw-puzzle affair, an odd cube squirted out of place and fell through the gap. The floor was covered with warm fleshy plastic substance that was peculiarly unpleasant to the touch.

None of the many compartment-cupboards in the bungalow contained anything resembling 20th Century pillows or bedding. Heating elements in the floor turned up as the evening wore on, adjusting the internal temperature of the room to the point where their all-over condoms were extremely uncomfortable. Escaping from the Tomorrow Town costumes was much harder than getting into them.

It occurred to Richard and Vanessa at the same time that these spacesuits would make going to the lavatory awkward, though they reasoned an all-pill diet would minimise the wasteful toilet breaks required in the past. Eventually, with some co-operation, they got free and placed the suits on hangers in a glass-fronted cupboard which, when closed, filled with coloured steam. 'Dekontaminashun Kompleet,' flashed a sign as the cabinet cracked open and spilled liquid residue. The floor was discoloured where this had happened before.

Having more or less puzzled out how the bedroom worked, they set about tackling the bathroom, which seemed to be equipped with a dental torture chamber and a wide variety of exotic marital aids. By the time they were done playing with it all, incidentally washing and cleaning their teeth, it was past ten midnight and the lights turned off automatically.

'Nighty-night,' said Richard.

'Don't let the robot bugs bite,' said Vanessa.

———

He woke up, alert. She woke with him.

'What's the matter? A noise?'

'No,' he said. 'No noise.'

'Ah.'

The Tomorrow Town hum, gadgets in the walls, was silenced. The bungalow was technologically dead. He reached out and touched the floor. It was cooling.

Silently, they got off the bed.

The room was dark, but they knew where the door — a sliding screen — was and took up positions either side of it.

The door had opened by touching a pad. Now the power was off, they were shut in (a flaw in the no-locks policy), though Richard heard a winding creak as the door lurched open an inch. There was some sort of clockwork back-up system.

A gloved hand reached into the room. It held an implement consisting of a plastic handle, two long thin metal rods, and a battery pack. A blue arc buzzed between the rods, suggesting lethal charge.

Vanessa took the wrist, careful not to touch the rods, and gave a good yank. The killing-prod, or whatever it was, was dropped and discharged against the floor, leaving a blackened patch and a nasty smell.

Surprised, the intruder stumbled against the door.

As far as Richard could make out in the minimal light, the figure wore the usual Tomorrow Town suit. An addition was an opaque black egg-shaped helmet with a silver strip around the eyes which he took to be a one-way mirror. A faint red radiance suggested some sort of infra-red see-in-the-dark device.

Vanessa, who had put on a floral bikini as sleepwear, kicked the egghead in the chest, which clanged. She hopped back.

'It's armoured,' she said.

'All who defy Buster must die,' rasped a speaker in the helmet.

Vanessa kicked again, at the shins, cutting the egghead down.

'All who defy Buster must die,' squeaked the speaker, sped-up. 'All who de . . . de . . . de . . . de . . .'

The recorded message was stuck.

The egghead clambered upright.

'Is there is a person in there?' Vanessa asked.

'One way to find out,' said Richard.

He hammered the egghead with a bed-cube, but it was too soft to dent the helmet. The intruder lunged and caught him in a plastic-and-metal grasp.

'Get him off me,' he said, kicking. Unarmoured, he was at a disadvantage.

Vanessa nipped into the en-suite bathroom and came back with a gadget on a length of metal hose. They had decided it was probably a water-pick for those hard-to-clean crannies. She stabbed the end of the device at the egghead's neck, puncturing the plastic seal just below the chin-rim of the helmet, and turned the nozzle on. The tappet-key snapped off in her fingers and a high-pressure stream that could have drilled through cheddar cheese spurted into the suit.

Gallons of water inflated the egghead's garment. The suit self-sealed around the puncture and expanded, arms and legs forced out in an X. Richard felt the water-pressure swelling his captor's chest and arms. He wriggled and got free.

'All who defy Buster . . .'

Circuits burned out, and leaks sprouted at all the seams. Even through the silver strip, Richard made out the water rising.

There was a commotion in the next room.

Lights came on. The hum was back.

It occurred to Richard that he had opted to sleep in the buff and might not be in a decorous state to receive visitors. Then again, in the future taboos against social nudity were likely to evaporate.

Georgie Gewell, the ever-present Moana and Jess-F, who had another of the zapper-prod devices, stood just inside the doorway.

There was a long pause. This was not what anyone had expected.

'Buster has escaped,' said Gewell. 'We thought you might be in danger. He's beyond all reason.'

'If he was a danger to us, he isn't any longer,' said Vanessa.

'If this is him,' Richard said. 'He was invoking the name.'

The egghead was on the floor, spouting torrents, super-inflated like the Michelin Man after a three-day egg-eating contest.

Vanessa kicked the helmet. It obligingly repeated 'All who defy Buster must die.'

The egghead waved hands like fat starfish, thumbing towards the helmet, which was sturdier than the rest of the suit and not leaking.

'Anybody know how to get this thing off?' asked Richard

The egghead writhed and was still.

'Might be a bit on the late side.'

Gewell and Jess-F looked at each other. Moana took action and pushed into the room. She knelt and worked a few buttons around the chinrim of the helmet. The egghead cracked along a hitherto-unsuspected crooked seam and came apart in a gush of water.

'That's not Buster,' said Vanessa. 'It's Mal-K, the medico.'

'And he's drowned,' concluded Richard.

––––––––––

'A useful rule of thumb in open-and-shut cases,' announced Richard, 'is that when someone tries to murder any investigating officers, the case isn't as open-and-shut as it might at first have seemed.'

He had put on a quilted double-breasted floor-length jade green dressing gown with a Blakeian red dragon picked out on the chest in sequins.

'When the would-be murderer is one of the major proponents of the open-and-shut theory,' he continued, 'it's a dead cert that an injustice is in the process of being perpetrated. Ergo, the errant Buster is innocent and someone else murdered Mm Zhoule with a Hugo award.'

'Perhaps there was a misunderstanding,' said Gewell.

Richard and Vanessa looked at him.

'How so?' Richard asked.

Wheels worked behind Gewell's eyes, which were amber now.

'Mm Mal-K might have heard of Buster's escape and come here to protect you from him. In the dark and confusion, you mistook his attempted rescue as an attack.'

'And tragedy followed,' completed Jess-F.

Moana weighed invisible balls and looked noncommittal.

It was sixty-eight past six o'kronon. The body had been removed and they were in Zhoule's front room. Since all the cubes were in the bedroom and wet through, everyone had to sit on the body-temperature floor. Vanessa perched decorously, see-through peignoir over her bikini, on the dead robot spider. Richard stood, as if lecturing.

'Mm Jor-G, you were an editor once,' he said. 'If a story were submitted in which a hero wanted to protect innocent parties from a rampaging killer, would you have allowed the author to have the hero get into a disguise, turn off all the lights and creep into the bedroom with a lethal weapon?'

'Um, I might. I edited science fiction magazines. Science fiction is about ideas. No matter what those New Wavers say. In s-f, characters might do anything.'

'What about "All who defy Buster must die"?' said Vanessa.

'A warning?' Gewell ventured, feebly.

'Oh, give up,' said Jess-F. 'Mal-K was a bad 'un. It's been obvious for desiyears. All those speeches about "expanding the remit of the social experiment" and "assuming pole position in the larger technomeritocracy". He was in a position to doctor his own records, to cover up instability. He was also the one who matched Buster's fingerprints to the murder weapon. Mm and Ms, congratulations, you've caught the killer.'

'Open-and-shut-and-open-and-shut?' suggested Richard.

Moana gave the thumbs-up.

'I'm going to need help to convince myself of this,' said Richard. 'I've decided to call on mighty deductive brainpower to get to the bottom of the mystery.'

'More yesterday men?' said Jess-F, appalled.

'Interesting term. You've been careful not to use it before now. Is that what you call us? No, I don't intend to summon any more plods from the outside.'

Gewell couldn't suppress his surge of relief.

'I've decided to apply the techniques of tomorrow to these crimes of the future. Jess-F, I'll need your help. Let's take this puzzle to Big Thinks, and see how your mighty computer does.'

Shutters came down behind Jess-F's eyes.

'Computer time is precious,' said Gewell.

'So is human life,' answered Richard.

———

The inside of the building, the insides of Big Thinks, was the messiest area Richard had seen in Tomorrow Town. Banks of metal cabinets fronted with reels of tape were connected by a spaghetti tangle of wires that wound throughout the building like coloured plastic ivy. Some cabinets had their fronts off, showing masses of circuit-boards, valves and transistors. Surprisingly, the workings of the master brain seemed held together with a great deal of sellotape, string and blu-tak. Richard recognised some components well in advance of any on the market, and others that might date back to Marconi or Babbage.

'We've been making adjustments,' said Jess-F.

She shifted a cardboard box full of plastic shapes from a swivel chair and let him sit at a desk piled with wired-together television sets. To one side was a paper-towel dispenser which coughed out a steady roll of graph-paper with lines squiggled on it.

He didn't know which knobs to twiddle.

'Ms Jess-F, could you show me how a typical dispute arbitration is made. Say, the triangle of Zhoule, Buster and Sue-2.'

'That documentation might be hard to find.'

'In this futopia of efficiency? I doubt it.'

Jess-F nodded to Moana, who scurried off to root through large bins full of scrunched and torn paper.

Vanessa was with Gewell and Zootie, taking a tour of the hydroponics zone, which was where the body of Varno Zhoule had been
found. The official story was that Buster (now, Mal-K) had gone to
Zhoule's bungalow to kill him but found him not at home. He had
taken the Hugo from its display case and searched out the victim-to-
be, found him contemplating the green gunk that was made into his
favourite pills, and did the deed then and there. It didn't take a
computer to decide it was more likely that Zhoule had been killed
where the weapon was handy for an annoyed impulse-assassin to reach
for, then hovercrafted along with the murder weapon to a public place
so some uninvolved zenvol clot could find him. But why ferry the
body all that way, with the added risk of being caught?

'Tell you what, Ms Jess-F, let's try BeeTee out on a hypothetical
dispute? Put in the set-up of *Hamlet*, and see what the computer thinks
would be best for Denmark.'

'Big Thinks is not a toy, Mm.'

Moana came back waving some sheaves of paper.

Richard looked over it. Jess-F ground her teeth.

Though the top sheet was headed 'Input tek: Buster Munro', this
was not the triangle dispute documentation. Richard scrolled through
the linked print-out. He saw maps of Northern Europe, lists of names
and dates, depositions in non-phonetic English, German and Danish,
and enough footnotes for a good-sized doctoral thesis. In fact, that was
exactly what this was.

'I'm not the first to think of running a hypothetical dispute past
the mighty computer,' said Richard. 'The much-maligned Buster got
there before me.'

'And wound up recategorised as a zenpass,' said Jess-F.

'He tried to get an answer to the Schleswig-Holstein Question,
didn't he? Lord Palmerston said only three men in Europe got to the
bottom of it — one who forgot, one who died and one who went
mad. It was an insanely complicated argument between Denmark and
Germany, over the governance of a couple of border provinces. Buster

put the question to Big Thinks as if it were a contemporary dispute, just to see how the computer would have resolved it. What did it suggest, nuclear attack? Is that why all the redecoration? Buster's puzzle blew all the fuses.'

Richard found the last page.

The words 'forgot died mad' were repeated over and over, in very faint ink. Then some mathematical formulae. Then the printer equivalent of scribble.

'This makes no sense.'

He showed it to Jess-F, hoping she could interpret it. He really would have liked Big Thinks to have got to the bottom of the tussle that defeated Bismarck and Metternich and spat out a blindingly simple answer everyone should have seen all along.

'No,' she admitted. 'It makes no sense at all.'

Moana shrugged.

Richard felt a rush of sympathy for Jess-F. This was painful for her.

'BeeTee can't do it,' said Richard. 'The machine can do sums very fast, but nothing else?'

Jess-F was almost at the point of tears.

'That's not true,' she said, with tattered pride. 'Big Thinks is the most advanced computer in the world. It can solve any logic problem. Give it the data, and it can deliver accurate weather forecasts, arrange schedules to optimise efficiency of any number of tasks . . .'

'But throw the illogical at it, and BeeTee just has a good cry.'

'It's a machine. It can't cry.'

'Or arbitrate love affairs.'

Jess-F was in a corner.

'It's not fair,' she said, quietly. 'It's not BeeTee's fault. It's not my fault. They knew the operational parameters. They just kept insisting it tackle areas outside its remit, extending, tampering, overburdening. My techs have been working all the hours of the day . . .'

'Kronons, surely?'

'. . . all the bloody kronons of the day, just trying to get Big Thinks working again. Even after all this, the ridiculous demands keep coming through. Big Thinks, Big Thinks, will I be pretty, will I be rich? Big Thinks, Big Thinks, is there life on other planets?'

Jess-F put her hands over her face.

'"They"? Who are "they"?'

'All of them,' Jess-F sobbed. 'Across all disciplines.'

'Who especially?'

'Who else? Varno Zhoule.'

'Not any more?'

'No.'

She looked out from behind her hands, horrified.

'It wasn't me,' she said.

'I know. You're left-handed. Wrong wound pattern. One more question: what did the late Mm Mal-K want from Big Thinks?'

Jess-F gave out an appalled sigh.

'Now, he was cracked. He kept putting in these convoluted specific questions. In the end, they were all about taking over the country. He wanted to run the whole of the United Kingdom like Tomorrow Town.'

'The day after tomorrow, the world?'

'He kept putting in plans and strategies for infiltrating vital industries and dedicating them to the cause. He didn't have an army, but he believed Big Thinks could get all the computers in the country on his side. Most of the zenvols thought he was a dreamer, spinning out a best-case scenario at the meetings. But he meant it. He wanted to found a large-scale Technomeritocracy.'

'With himself as Beloved Leader?'

'No, that's how mad he was. He wanted Big Thinks to run everything. He was hoping to put BeeTee in charge and let the future happen.'

'That's why he wanted Vanessa and me out of the story. We were a threat to his funding. Without the subsidies, the plug is pulled.'

'One thing BeeTee can do is keep track of figures. As a community, Tomorrow Town is in the red. Enormously.'

'There's no money here, though.'

'Of course not. We've spent it. And spent money we don't have. The next monorail from Preston is liable to be crowded with dunning bailiffs.'

Richard thought about it. He was rather saddened by the truth. It would have been nice if the future worked. He wondered if Lincoln Steffens had any second thoughts during the Moscow purge trials?

'What threat was Zhoule to Mal-K?' he asked.

Jess-F frowned. 'That's the oddest thing. Zhoule was the one who really encouraged Mal-K to work on his coup plans. He did see himself as, what did you call it, "Beloved Leader". All his stories were about intellectual supermen taking charge of the world and sorting things out. If anything, he was the visioneer of the tomorrow take-over. And he'd have jumped anything in skirts if femzens wore skirts here.'

Richard remembered the quivering Sue-2.

'So we're back to Buster in the conservatory with the Hugo award?'

'I've always said it was him,' said Jess-F. 'You can't blame him, but he did it.'

'We shall see.'

Sirens sounded. Moana put her fingers in her ears. Jess-F looked even more stricken.

'That's not a good sign, is it?'

———

The communal meal area outside Big Thinks swarmed with plastic-caped zenvols, looking up and pointing, panicking and screaming. The three light-heat globes, Tomorrow Town's suns, shone whiter and radiated hotter. Richard looked at the backs of his hands. They were tanning almost as quickly as an instant photograph develops.

'The fool,' said Jess-F. 'He's tampered with the master controls. Buster will kill us all. It's the only thing he has left.'

Zenvols piled into the communally-owned electric carts parked in a rank to one side of the square. When they proved too heavy for the vehicles, they started throwing each other off. Holes melted in the canopy above the globes. Sizzling drips of molten plastic fell onto screaming tomorrow townies.

The sirens shrilled, urging everyone to panic.

Richard saw Vanessa through the throng.

She was with Zootie. No Gewell.

A one-man hovercraft, burdened with six clinging zenvols, chugged past inch by inch, outpaced by someone on an old-fashioned, non-solar-powered bicycle.

'If the elements reach critical,' said Jess-F, 'Tomorrow Town will blow up.'

A bannerlike strip of paper curled out of a slit in the front of Big Thinks.

'Your computer wants to say goodbye,' said Richard.

SURKIT BRAKER No. 15.

'Not much of a farewell.'

Zootie walked between falling drips to the central column, which supported the three globes. He opened a hatch and pulled a switch. The artificial suns went out. Real sunlight came through the holes in the canopy.

'Now that's what computers can do,' said Jess-F, elated. 'Execute protocols. If this happens, then that order must be given.'

The zenvol seemed happier about her computer now.

Richard was grateful for a ditch-digger who could read.

———————

'This is where the body was?' he asked Zootie. They were by swimming-pool sized tanks of green gunk, dotted with yellow and brown patches since the interruption of the light-source. 'Bit of a haul from Zhoule's place.'

'The body was carried here?' asked Vanessa.

'Not just the body. The murder weapon too. Who lives in that bungalow?'

On a small hill was a bungalow not quite as spacious as Zhoule's, one of the mass of hutches placed between the silver pathways, with a crown of solar panels on the flat roof, and a dish antennae.

'Mm Jor-G,' said Moana.

'So you do speak?'

She nodded her head and smiled.

————

Gewell sat on an off-white cube in the gloom. The stored power was running down. Only filtered sunlight got through to his main room. He looked as if his backbone had been removed. All the substance of his face had fallen to his jowls.

Richard looked at him.

'Nice try with the globes. Should have remembered the circuit-breaker, though. Only diabolical masterminds construct their private estates with in-built self-destruct systems. In the future, as in the past, it's unlikely that town halls will have bombs in the basement ready to go off in the event that the outgoing Mayor wants to take the whole community with him rather than hand over the chain of office.'

Gewell didn't say anything.

Vanessa went straight to a shelf and picked up the only award in the display. It was another Hugo.

'Best Fan Editor 1958,' she read from the plaque.

The rocketship came away from its base.

'You killed him here,' said Richard, 'broke your own Hugo, left the bloody rocketship with the body outside. Then, when you'd calmed down a bit, you remembered Zhoule had won the same award. Several, in fact. You sneaked over to his bungalow — no locks, how convenient — and broke one of his Hugos, taking the rocket to complete yours. You made it look as if he were killed with his own award, and you were out of the loop. If only you'd got round to developing the glue of the future and fixed the thing properly, it wouldn't be so obvious. It's plain that though you've devoted your life to planning out the details of the future, your one essay in the fine art of murder was a rushed botch-up job done on the spur of the moment. You haven't really improved on Cain. At least, Mm Mal-

K made the effort with the space-suit and the zapper-prod.'

'Mm Jor-G,' said Jess-F, '*why*?'

Good question, Richard thought.

After a long pause, Gewell gathered himself and said 'Varno was destroying Tomorrow Town. He had so many . . . so many *ideas*. Every morning, before breakfast, he had four or five. All the time, constantly. Radio transmitters the size of a pinhead. Cheap infinite energy from tapping the planet's core. Solar-powered personal flying machines. Robots to do everything. Robots to make robots to do everything. An operation to extend human lifespan threefold. Rules and regulations about who was fit to have and raise children, with gonad-block implants to enforce them. Hats that collect the electrical energy of the brain and use it to power a personal headlamp. Non-stop, unrelenting, unstoppable. Ideas, ideas, ideas . . .'

Richard was frankly astonished by the man's vehemence. 'Isn't that what you wanted?'

'But Varno did the easy bit. Once he'd tossed out an idea, it was up to *me* to make it work. Me or Big Thinks or some other plodding zenvol. And nine out of ten of the ideas didn't work, couldn't ever work. And it was always our fault for not making them work, never his for foisting them off on us. This town would be perfect if it hadn't been for his ideas. And his bloody dreadful spelling. Back in the 50s, who do you think tidied all his stories up so they were publishable? Muggins Gewell. He couldn't write a sentence that scanned, and rather than learn how he decreed the language should be changed. Not just the spelling, he had a plan to go through the dictionary crossing out all the words that were no longer needed, then make it a crime to teach them to children. It was something to do with his old public school. He said he wanted to make gerunds extinct within a generation. But he had these wonderful, wonderful, ghastly, terrible ideas. It'd have made you sick.'

'And the medico who wanted to rule the world?'

'Him too. He had ideas.'

Gewell was pleading now, hands fists around imaginary bludgeons. 'If only I could have had ideas,' he said. 'They'd have been good ones.'

Richard wondered how they were going to lock Gewell up until the police came.

————

The monorail was out of commission. Most things were. Some zenvols, like Jess-F, were relieved not to have to pretend that everything worked perfectly. They had desiyears — months, dammit! — of complaining bottled up inside, and were pouring it all out to each other in one big whine-in under the dead light-heat globes.

Richard and Vanessa looked across the Dales. A small vehicle was puttering along a winding, illogical lane that had been laid out not by a computer but by wandering sheep. It wasn't the police, though they were on the way.

'Who do you think this is?' asked Vanessa.

'It'll be Buster. He's bringing the outside to Tomorrow Town. He always was a yesterday man at heart.'

A car-horn honked.

Zenvols, some already changed out of their plastic suits, paid attention. Sue-2 was excited, hopeful, fearful. She clung to Moana, who smiled and waved.

Someone cheered. Others joined.

'What is he driving?' asked Vanessa 'It looks like a relic from the past.'

'For these people, it's deliverance,' said Richard. 'It's a fish 'n' chip van.'

On its first publication (for the SciFi.com website), I prepared a set of hyperlink annotations to explain certain Britishisms for American net-surfers, and also to embed the story in various criss-crossing series I've been playing with in recent years. Here they are, for the puzzled.

Since the Year [Yeer] Dot: since time immemorial.

A Dalek. Trundling cyborg giant pepperpot featured in the long-running BBC-TV science-fiction programme Doctor Who, *introduced in 1963. The Daleks' distinctive mechanical voices were much-imitated by British children in the 1960s. Their catch-phrase: 'ex-ter-min-ate!'*

The Wilson Government. Harold Wilson was Labour Prime Minister of Great Britain from 1964 to 1970 and again from 1974 to 1976. A Maigret-like pipe-smoking, raincoated figure, he famously boasted of 'the white heat of technology' when summing up British contributions to futuristic projects like the Concorde. At the time of this story, he had been succeeded by the Tory Edward Heath, a laughing yachtsman.

James Burke and Raymond Baxter. The hosts in the 1960s of BBC-TV's long-running Tomorrow's World, *a magazine programme covering the worlds of invention and technology. They were also anchors for UK TV coverage of the moon landings.*

The Sunday colour supplements. A UK publishing phenomenon of the 1960s, magazines included with Sunday newspapers. The pioneering rivals were The Sunday Times *and* The Observer.

The BBC Radiophonic Workshop. The corporation's sound effects department, responsible for Dalek voices and the Doctor Who *theme. Their consultants included Pink Floyd and Michael Moorcock.*

The Crazy World of Arthur Brown. 'I am the God of Hell Fire,' rants Arthur on his single 'Fire', which was Number One in the UK charts in 1968. An influence on Iron Maiden and other pioneer Heavy Metal groups, Arthur was also a devoted surrealist-cum-Satanist. He never had another hit, but is still gigging.

New Scientist. UK weekly magazine, scientific sister publication to the left-leaning political journal New Statesman.

Arthur C. Clarke. Now Sir Arthur C. Clarke, author of Childhood's End, *screenwriter of* 2001: A Space Odyssey, *writer on scientific topics and Sri Lankan resident. Known in the UK as host of* Arthur C. Clarke's Mysterious World, *a TV series about Fortean phenomena that is twenty years on the template for much X-Files-ish fringe documentary programming.*

Auberon Waugh. Crusty conservative commentator, son of Evelyn Waugh, author of satirical novels. In the 1960s, his waspish journalism was most often found in The Spectator *and the* Daily Telegraph.

J.G. Ballard. Major British novelist, a key influence in the so-called New Wave of British s-f in the 1960s and 70s, now better known for more or less mainstream work that is weirder than most genre stuff.

Varno Zhoule. British s-f author, most prolific in the 1950s, when he published almost exclusively in American magazines. His only novel, The Stars in Their Traces, *is a fix-up of stories first seen in* Astounding. *His 'Court Martian' was dramatised on the UK TV series* Out of the Unknown *in 1963.*

The Diogenes Club. First mentioned by Sir Arthur Conan Doyle in 'The Greek Interpreter' and revealed as a government agency by Billy Wilder and I.A.L. Diamond in The Private Life of Sherlock Holmes, *the Diogenes Club has employed various investigators of the odd and paranormal for over a century. Richard Jeperson and Vanessa have also appeared in 'End of the Pier Show' (Dark of the Night), 'You Don't Have to Be Mad . . .' (White of the Moon), 'The Biafran Bank Manager' (Dark Detectives), 'Egyptian Avenue' (Embrace the Mutation) and 'Swellhead' (Night Visions 11). I first played around with my version of this institution in* Anno Dracula, *set in an alternate timeline, but have enjoyed visiting the place in various stories set in various time periods – most elaborately, the cycle that makes up 'Seven Stars' (which can be found in Stephen Jones's* Dark Detectives *on my UK collection* Seven Stars) *but also one-offs like 'Angel Down, Sussex' (later in this collection).*

Gerry Anderson. TV producer famous in collaboration with his wife Sylvia, for 1960s technophilic puppet shows Fireball XL-5, Stingray, Thunderbirds *and* Captain Scarlet and the Mysterons. *His 1970s live-action* Space 1999 *has not achieved the lasting place in UK pop culture attained by the 'supermarionation' shows.*

Valerie Singleton. Presenter of the BBC-TV children's magazine programme Blue Peter. *Well-spoken and auntie-like, she famously showed kids how to make things out of household oddments without ever mentioning a brand-name (a co-host who once said 'Biro' instead of 'ball-point pen' was nearly fired).*

Smarties. Chocolate discs inside shells of various colours, available from Rowntree & Company in cardboard tubes. Still a staple 'sweet' (ie: candy) in the UK; similar to M&Ms.

Kit-Kat. A chocolate bar.

The Tomorrow Town Alphabet. Q and X are replaced by KW and KS; the vestigial C exists only in CH and is otherwise replaced by K or S. Eg: THE KWIK BROWN FOKS JUMPED OVER THE LAYZEE DOG.

The Man in the White Suit. *Film directed by Alexander Mackendrick, starring Alec Guinness. An inventor develops a fabric that never wears out or gets dirty, and the clothing industry tries to keep it off the market.*

Can't even beat as it sweeps as it cleans. The UK slogan for Hoover vacuum cleaners in the 1970s was 'it beats as it sweeps as it cleans'.

Michelin Man. Cheery advertising mascot of the tire company, he consists of white bloated tires.

The Schleswig-Holstein Question. Bane of any schoolboy studying O level European history in 1975. It's a key plot point in George Macdonald Fraser's novel Royal Flash.

Muggins: a sap, a patsy.

THE ORIGINAL
DR SHADE

Like a shark breaking inky waters, the big black car surfaced out of the night, its searchlight headlamps freezing the Bolsheviks *en tableau* as they huddled over their dynamite. Cohen, their vile leader, tried to control his raging emotions, realising that yet again his schemings to bring about the ruination of the British Empire were undone. Borzoff, his hands shaking uncontrollably, fell to his ragged-trousered knees and tried one last prayer to the God whose icons he had spat upon that day in the mother country when he had taken his rifle butt to the princess' eggshell-delicate skull. Petrofsky drooled into his stringy beard, his one diseased eye shrinking in the light like a slug exposed to salt, and uselessly thumb-cocked his revolver.

The canvas top of the Rolls Royce 'Shadowshark' raised like a hawk's eyelid, and a dark shape seemed to grow out of the driver's seat, cloak billowing in the strong wind, twin moons reflected in the insectlike dark goggles, wide-brimmed hat at a jaunty angle.

Petrofsky raised his shaking pistol, and slammed back against the iron globe of the chemical tank, cut down by another silent dart from the doctor's famous airgun. In the distance, the conspirators could hear police sirens, but they knew they would not be taken into custody. The shadowman would not allow them to live out the night to further sully the green and fruitful soil of sacred England with their foul presence.

As the doctor advanced, the headlamps threw his expanding shadow on the Bolsheviks.

Israel Cohen, the Mad Genius of the Revolution, trembled, his flabby chins slapping against his chest, sweat pouring from his ape-like forehead down his protruberant nose to his fleshy, sensual lips. He raised a ham-sized fist against the doctor, sneering insane defiance to the last:

'Curse you, Shade!'

Rex Cash, Dr Shade Vs the Dynamite Boys (1936)

————

They ate an expensively minimalist meal at Alastair Little's in Frith Street, and Basil Crosbie, Leech's Art Editor, picked up the bill with his company card. Throughout, Tamara, his agent, kept reminding Crosbie of the *Eagle* awards Greg had picked up for *Fat Chance*, not mentioning that that was two years ago. As with most restaurants, there was nowhere that could safely accomodate his yardsquare artwork folder, and he was worried the sample strips would get scrunched or warped. He would have brought copies, but wanted to put himself over as sharply as possible. Besides, the ink wasn't dry on the pieces he had finished this morning. As usual, there hadn't been time to cover himself.

Whenever there was dead air in the conversation, Tamara filled it with more selected highlights from Greg's career. Greg guessed she had invited herself to this lunch to keep him under control. She remembered, but was carefully avoiding mention of, his scratchy beginnings in the '70s—spiky strips and singletons for punk fanzines like *Sheep Worrying, Brainrape* and *Kill Your Pet Puppy*—and knew exactly how he felt about the Derek Leech organisation. She probably thought he was going to turn up in a ripped rubbish bag, with lots of black eyeliner and safety-pins through his earlobes, then go for Crosbie with a screwdriver. Actually, while the Sex Pistols were swearing on live television and gobbing at gigs, he had been a neatly-dressed, normal-haired art student. It was only at the easel, where he used to assemble police brutality collages with ransom note captions, that he had embodied the spirit of '77.

If Tamara would shut up, he thought he could get on with Crosbie. Greg knew the man had started out on the *Eagle*, and filled in on *Garth* once in a while. He had been a genuine minor talent in his day. Still, he worked for Leech, and if there was one artefact that summed up everything Greg loathed about Britain under late Thatcherism, it was Leech's *Daily Comet*. The paper was known for its Boobs 'n' Pubes, its multi-million Giveaway Grids, its unflinching support of the diamond-hard right, its lawsuit-fuelled muckraking, and prose that read like a football hooligan's attempt to imitate the *Janet and John* books. It was Britain's fastest-growing newspaper, and the hub of a communications empire that was putting Leech in the Murdoch-Maxwell bracket. In Madame Tussaud's last annual poll, the statue of Derek Leech had ranked eighth on the Most Admired list, between Gorbachev and Prince Charles, and second on the Most Hated and Feared chart, after Margaret Thatcher but before Adolf Hitler, Colonel Quadaffi, Count Dracula and the Yorkshire Ripper.

Crosbie didn't start talking business until eyedropper-sized cups of coffee arrived. With the plates taken away, the Art Editor opened his folder on the table, and brought out a neatly paperclipped set of notes. Tamara was still picking at her fruit salad, five pieces of pale apple and/or pear floating in a steel bowl of water with a solitary grape. She and Crosbie had been drinking dry white wine with the meal, but Greg stuck to mineral water. The gritty coffee gave him quite a punch, and he felt his heart tighten like an angry fist. Since *Fat Chance*, he hadn't done anything notable. This was an important meeting for him. Tamara might not dump him if it didn't come out right, but she might shift him from her A-list to her B-list.

'As you probably know,' Crosbie began, 'Leech United Kingdom is expanding at the moment. I don't know if you keep up with the trades, but Derek has recently bought up the rights to a lot of defunct titles with a view to relaunch. It's a lot easier to sell something familiar than something new. Just now, Derek's special baby is the *Evening Argus*.'

'The Brighton paper?' Greg asked.

'No, a national. It folded in 1953, but it was very big from the '20s through to the War. Lord Badgerfield ran it.'

'I have heard of it,' Greg said. 'It's always an *Argus* headline in those old films about Dunkirk.'

'That's right. The paper had what they used to call "a good War". Churchill called it "the voice of true democracy". Like Churchill, it was never quite the same after the War . . . but now, what with the interest in the 50th anniversary of the Battle of Britain and all that, we think the time is right to bring it back. It'll be nostalgia, but it'll be new too . . .'

'Gasmasks and rationing and the spirit of the Blitz, eh?'

'That sort of thing. It'll come out in the Autumn, and we'll build up to it with a massive campaign. "The voice is back." We'll cut from this ovaltine-type '40s look to an aggressive '90s feel, yuppies on carphones, designer style, full-colour pages. It'll be a harder newspaper than the *Comet*, but it'll still be a Leech UK product, populist and commercial. We aim to be the turn-of-the-century newspaper.'

'And you want a cartoonist?'

Crosbie smiled. 'I liked your *Fat Chance* work a lot, Greg. The script was a bit manky for my taste, but you draw with clean lines, good solid blocks of black. Your private eye was a thug, but he looked like a real strip hero. There was a bit of *Jeff Hawke* there. It was just what we want for the *Argus*, the feel of the past but the content of the present.'

'So you'll be wanting Greg to do a *Fat Chance* strip for the new paper?'

Greg had made the connection, and was cracking a smile.

'No, Tamara, that's not what he wants. I've remembered the other thing I know about the *Argus*. I should have recognised the name straight off. It's a by-word . . .'

Crosbie cut in, 'that's right. The *Mirror* had *Jane* and *Garth*, but the Argus had . . .'

Greg was actually excited. He thought he had grown up, but there was still a pulp heart in him. As a child, he had pored through second- and third-hand books and magazines. Before *Brainrape* and *Fat Chance* and *PC Rozzerblade*, he had tried to draw his other heroes: Bulldog Drummond, the Saint, Sexton Blake, Biggles, and . . .

'Dr Shade.'

———

'You may haff caught me, *Herr Doktor Schatten*, but ze glory off ze Sird Reich vill roll over zis passetic country like a tchugger- naucht. I die for ze greater glory off Tchermany, off ze Nazi party and off Adolf Hitler . . .'

'That's where you're wrong, Von Spielsdorf. I wouldn't dirty my hands by killing you, even if it is what you so richly deserve.'

'Ain't we gonna ice the lousy stinkin' rat, Doc?' asked Hank the Yank. The American loomed over the German mastermind, a snub-nosed automatic in his meaty fist.

'Yours is a young country, Henry,' said Dr Shade gently, laying a black-gloved hand of restraint upon his comrade's arm. 'That's not how we do things in England. Von Spielsdorf here may be shot as a spy, but that decision is not ours to make. We have courts and laws and justice. That's what this whole war's about, my friend. The right of the people to have courts and laws and justice. Even you, Von Spielsdorf. We're fighting for your rights too.'

'Pah, decadent *Englische schweinhund!*'

Hank tapped the German on the forehead with his pistol-grip, and the saboteur sat down suddenly, his eyes rolling upwards.

'That showed him, eh, Doc?'

Dr Shade's thin, normally inexpressive lips, curled in a slight smile. 'Indubitably, Henry. Indubitably.'

Rex Cash, "The Fiend of the Fifth Column",
Dr Shade Monthly No 111, (May, 1943)

———

The heart of Leech UK was a chrome and glass pyramid in London docklands, squatting by the Thames like a recently-arrived flying saucer. Greg felt a little queasy as the minicab they had sent for him slipped through the pickets. It was a chilly Spring day, and there weren't many of them about. Crosbie had warned him of 'the Union Luddites' and their stance against the new technology that enabled Leech to put out the *Comet* and its other papers with a bare minimum of production staff. Greg hoped none of the placard-carriers would recognise him. Last year, there had been quite a bit of violence as the pickets, augmented by busloads of radicals as annoyed by Leech's editorials as his industrial relations policies, came up against the police and a contingent of the *Comet*-reading skinheads who were the backbone of Leech's support. Now, the dispute dragged on but was almost forgotten. Leech papers had never mentioned it much, and the rest of the press had fresher strikes, revolutions and outrages to cover.

The minicab drove right into the pyramid, into an enclosed reception area where the vehicle was checked by security guards. Greg was allowed out and issued with a blue day pass that a smiling girl in a smart uniform pinned on his lapel.

Behind her desk were framed colour shots of smiling girls without uniforms, smart or otherwise, their nipples like squashed cherries, their faces cleanly unexpressive. The *Comet* Knock-Outs were supposed to be a national institution. But so, according to the *Comet*, were corporal punishment in schools, capital punishment for supporters of Sinn Fein, and the right to tell lies about the sexual preferences of soap opera performers. Greg wondered what Penny Stamp—Girl Reporter, Dr Shade's sidekick in the old strip, would have made of a *Comet* Knock-Out. Penny had always been rowing with the editor who wanted her to cover fashion shows and garden parties when she would rather be chasing crime scoops for the front page; perhaps her modern equivalent should be a pin-up girl who wants to keep her clothes on and become Roger Cook or Woodward and Bernstein?

He rode up to the 23rd floor, which was where Crosbie had arranged to meet him. The girl downstairs had telephoned up, and her clone was waiting for him in the thickly-carpeted lobby outside the lift. She smiled and escorted him through an open-plan office where telephones and computers were being installed by a cadre of workmen. At the far end were a series of glassed-off cubicles. She eased him into one of these and asked if he wanted tea or coffee. She brought him instant coffee, the granules floating near the bottom of a paper cupful of hot brown water. There was a dummy edition of the *Evening Argus* on the desk. The headline was 'IT'S WAR!' Greg didn't have time to look at it.

Crosbie came in with a tall, slightly stooped man and ordered more coffee. The newcomer was in his '70s but looked fit for his age. He wore comfortable old trousers and a cardigan under a new sports jacket. Greg knew who he was.

'Rex Cash?' he asked, his hand out.

The man's grip was firm. 'One of him,' he said. 'Not the original.'

'This is Harry Lipman, Greg.'

'Harry,' Harry said.

'Greg. Greg Daniels.'

'*Fat Chance?*'

Greg nodded. He was surprised Harry had kept up with the business. He had been retired for a long time, he knew.

'Mr Crosbie told me. I've been looking your stuff out. I don't know much about the drawing side. Words are my line. But you're a talented young man.'

'Thanks.'

'Can we work together?' Harry was being direct. Greg didn't have an answer.

'I hope so.'

'So do I. It's been a long time. I'll need someone to snip the extra words out of the panels.'

Harry Lipman had been Rex Cash from 1939 to 1952, taking over the name from Donald Moncrieff, the creator of Dr Shade. He had filled 58 Dr Shade books with words, 42 novels and 135 short stories, and he had scripted the newspaper strip all the while, juggling storylines. Several of the best-known names in British adventure comics had worked on the Dr Shade strip: Mack Bullivant, who would create *Andy of the Arsenal* for *British Pluck*, Tommy Wrathall, highly regarded for his commando and paratroop stories in Boys' War, and, greatest of all, Frank FitzGerald, who had, for six years, made Dr Shade dark, funny and almost magical. They were all dead now. Harry was the last survivor of those days. And so the *Argus* was calling in Greg to fill the footprints.

'Harry has been working up some storylines,' said Crosbie. 'I'll leave you to talk them through. If you need more coffee, give Nicola a buzz. I'll be back in a few hours to see how you're doing.'

Crosbie left. Harry and Greg looked at each other and, for no reason, started laughing like members of a family sharing a joke they could never explain to an outsider.

'Considering Dr Shade must be about 150 by now,' Harry began, 'I thought we'd start the strip with him trying to get the DHSS to up his heating allowance for the winter . . .'

———

SHADE, DOCTOR Scientific vigilante of mysterious origins, usually hidden behind a cloak and goggle-like dark glasses, although also a master of disguise with many other identities. Operating out of an outwardly dilapidated but inwardly luxurious retreat in London's East End, he employs a group of semi-criminal bully boys in his neverending war against foreign elements importing evil into the heart of the British Empire. Originally introduced (under the name 'Dr Jonathan Shadow') as a minor character in *The Cur of Limehouse* (1929), a novel by Rex Cash (Donald Moncrieff), in which he turns up in the final chapters to help the aristocratic pugilist hero Reggie Brandon defeat the East End opium warlord Baron Quon. The character was so popular with the readers of *Wendover's Magazine*, the monthly publication in which the novel was serialised, that Moncrieff wrote several series of short adventures, later collected in the volumes *Dr Shadow and the Poison Goddess* (1931) and *Dr Shadow's Nigger Trouble* (1932). In 1934, alleging plagiarism of their character, THE SHADOW, Street and Smith threatened to sue Badgerfield, publishers of *Wendover's* and of the collections, and, to appease the American firm, the character was renamed Dr Shade.

A semi-supernatural, ultra-patriotic avenger whose politics would seem to be somewhat to the right of those of Sapper's Bulldog DRUMMOND or the real-life Oswald Mosley (of whom Moncrieff was reputed to be a great admirer), Dr Shade is much given to executing minor villains with his airgun or gruesomely torturing them for information. He appeared in nearly 100 short novels, all credited to Rex Cash, written for *Dr Shade Monthly*, a pulp periodical issued by Badgerfield from 1934 until 1947. The house pseudonym was also used by a few other writers, mostly for back-up stories in the 1930s, when the prolific Moncrieff's inspiration flagged. The character became even more popular when featured in a daily strip in the *Evening Argus*, most famously drawn by Frank FitzGerald, from 1935 to 1952. Moncrieff, after a bitter dispute with Lord Badgerfield, stopped writing Dr Shade in 1939, and the strip was taken over by Harry Lipman, a writer who had done a few Dr Shade stories for the magazine. By the outbreak of war, Lipman had effectively become Rex Cash, and was producing stories and novels for the magazine as well as scripting the strip.

Lipman's Dr Shade is a less frightening figure than Moncrieff's. Although his uniform and gadgets are unchanged, Lipman's hero is an official agent of the British government who refrained from sadistically mistreating his enemies the way Moncrieff's had. It was revealed that Dr Shade is really Dr Jonathan Chambers, an honest and dedicated general practitioner, and the supernatural elements of the strip were toned down. During WW II, Dr Shade's politics changed; as written by Moncrieff, he is an implacable foe of the non-white races and international communism, but Lipman's hero is a straightforward defender of democracy in the face of the Nazi menace. Moncrieff's Moriarty figure, introduced in *Dr Shade and the Whooping Horror* (1934), is Israel Cohen, a stereotypically Jewish master criminal in league with Russian anarchists and Indian Thuggees in a plot to destroy Britain's naval superiority. During the War, Cohen was retired (although he returned in the late 1940s as a comic East End nightclub owner and *friend* of Dr Shade) and the penumbral adventurer, joined by two-fisted American OSS agent Henry Hemingway and peppy girl reporter Penny Stamp, concentrated exclusively on licking Hitler.

Moncrieff's Dr Shade novels include *Dr Shade Vs the Dynamite Boys* (1936), *A Yellow Man's Treachery* (1936), *Dr Shade's Balkan Affair* (1937), *To the Last Drop of Our British Blood* (1937), *The Bulldog Bites Back* (1937), *The International Conspirators* (1938) and *Dr Shade in Suez* (1939), while Lipman's are *Dr Shade's Home Front* (1940), *Underground in France* (1941), *Dr Shade Takes Over* (1943), *Dr Shade in Tokyo* (1945), *Dr Shade Buries the Hatchet* (1948) and *The Piccadilly Gestapo* (1951). The character also featured in films, beginning with *Dr Shade's Phantom Taxi Mystery* (1936; dir. Michael Powell), in which he was played by Raymond Massey, while Francis L. Sullivan was a decidedly non-Semitic Israel Cohen, renamed 'Idris Kobon'. Valentine Dyall took the role in a BBC Radio serial from 1943 to 1946, and Ronald Howard wore the cloak in a 1963 Rediffusion TV serial, *Introducing Dr Shade . . .*, with Elizabeth Shepherd as Penny Stamp and Alfie Bass as Israel Cohen.

See also: Dr Shade's associates: Reggie BRANDON, Lord Highbury and Islington; Henry HEMINGWAY (Hank the Yank); Penny STAMP, Girl Reporter; and his enemies: Israel COHEN, the Mad Genius of the Revolution; ACHMET the Almost-Human; Melchior Umberto GASPARD, Prince of Forgers; Professor IZAN, the Führer's Favourite.

David Pringle,
Imaginary People: A Who's Who of Modern Fictional Characters (1987)

―――――

Greg and Harry Lipman met several times over the next few weeks, mainly away from the Leech building. In Soho pubs and cheap restaurants, they discussed the direction of the new Dr Shade strip.

Greg had liked Harry immediately, and came to admire his still-quick storyteller's mind. He knew he could work with this man. Having taken Dr Shade over from Donald Moncrieff, he didn't have a creator's obsessive attachment to the property, and was open to suggestions that would change the frame of the strip. Harry agreed that there was no point in producing a '40s pastiche. Their Dr Shade had to be different from all the character's previous incarnations, but still maintain some of the continuity. Gradually, their ideas came together.

In keeping with the *Argus'* stated old-but-new approach, they decided to set the strip in the near future. Everybody was already talking about the turn of the century. They would have Dr Shade come out of retirement, disenchanted with the post-war world he fought for back in the old days, and assembling a new team of adventurers to tackle up-to-the-moment villains against a backdrop of urban decay and injustice. Greg suggested pitting the avenging shadowman against rapacious property speculators laying waste to his old East End stamping grounds, a crack cartel posing as a fundamentalist religious sect, corporate despoilers of the environment, or unethical stockbrokers with mafia connections.

'You know,' Harry said one afternoon in The Posts, sipping his pint, 'if Donald were writing these stories, Dr Shade would be on the side of those fellers. He died thinking he'd lost everything and here we are, half a century later, with a country the original Dr Shade would have been proud of.'

Nearby, a bored mid-afternoon drinker, swallows tattooed on his neck, zapped spaceships, his beeping deathrays cutting into the piped jazz. Greg pulled open his bag of salt and vinegar crisps. 'I don't know much about Moncrieff. Even the reference books are pretty sketchy. What was he like?'

'I didn't really know the man, Greg. To him, Lipmans were like Cohens . . . not people you talked to.'

'Was he really a fascist?'

'Oh yes,' Harry's eyes got a little larger. 'Nobody had a shirt blacker than Donald Moncrieff. The whole kit and kaboodle, he had: glassy eyes, toothbrush moustache, thin blond hair. Marched through Brixton with Mosley a couple of times. Smashed up my brother's newsagent's shop, they did. And he went on goodwill jaunts to Spain and Germany. I believe he wrote pamphlets for the British Union of Fascists and he certainly conned poor old Frank into designing a recruiting poster for the Cause.'

'Frank FitzGerald?'

'Yes, your predecessor with the pencils. Frank never forgave Donald for that. During the War, the intelligence people kept interrogating Frank whenever there was a bit of suspected sabotage. You know the line in *Casablanca*? "Round up the usual suspects." Well, Donald put Frank on the list of "usual suspects".'

The space cadet burned out. He swore and thumped the machine as it flashed its 'Game Over' sneer at him.

'Were you brought in specifically to change Dr Shade?'

'Oh yes. Badgerfield was an appeasement man right up until Munich but he was a smart newspaper boy and saw the change in the wind. He dumped a lot of people—not just fascists, lots of pacifists got tarred with the same brush—and about-faced his editorial policy. You'd think he'd overlook the comic strip, but he didn't. He knew it was as much a part of the Argus as the editorial pages and his own "Honest Opinion" column. My orders when I took over were quite blunt. He told me to "de-Nazify" Dr Shade.'

'What happened to Moncrieff?'

'Oh, he sued and sued and sued, but Badgerfield owned the character and could do what he wanted. When the War started, he became very unpopular, of course. He spent some time in one of those holiday camps they set up for Germans and Italians and sympathisers. They didn't have much concrete on him and he came back to London. He wrote some books, I think, but couldn't get them published. I heard he had a stack of Dr Shade stories he was never able to use because only His Lordship had the right to exploit the character. Then, he died . . .'

'He was young, wasn't he?'

'Younger than me. It was the blitz. They tried to say he was waving wrote some books, I think, but couldn't get them published. I heard he had a stack of Dr Shade stories he was never able to use because only His Lordship had the right to exploit the character. Then, he died . . .'

'He was young, wasn't he?'

'Younger than me. It was the blitz. They tried to say he was waving a torch in the blackout for the *lüftwaffe*, but I reckon he was just under the wrong bomb at the wrong time. I saw him near the end and he was pretty cracked. Not at all the privileged smoothie he'd been in the '30s. I didn't like the feller, of course, but you had to feel sorry for him. He thought Hitler was Jesus Christ and the War just drove him off his head. Lots of Englishmen like that, there were. You don't hear much about them these days.'

'I don't know. They all seem to be in parliament now.'

Harry chuckled. 'Too right, but Dr Shade'll see to 'em, you bet, eh?'

They raised their drinks and toasted the avenging shadow, the implacable enemy of injustice, intolerance and ill-will.

———

IN PRAISE OF BRITISH HERO'S

Those of us PROUD TO BE BRITISH know that in this nations HOUR OF DIREST NEED, the True Blue BRITISH HERO'S will appear and STAND TALL TOGETHER to WIPE FROM THE FACE OF THIS FAIR FLOWER OF A LAND those who BESMERCH IT'S PURITY. With the WHITE BRITON'S in danger of drowning under the tidal wave of COLOUREDS, and the dedicated and law-upholding BRITISH POLICE going unarmed against the SEMITEX BOMBS, OOZY MACHINE GUNS and ROCKET LAUNCHERS of the KINK-HAIRED NIGGER'S, MONEY-GRUBBING YIDS, ARSE-BANDIT AIDS-SPREAD-ERS, SLANT-EYED KUNGFU CHINKIE'S, LONG-HAIRED HIPPY RABBLE, LOONY LEFT LESBIONS, and RAGHEADED MUSSULMEN, the time has come for KING ARTHUR to return from under the hill, for the CROSS OF ST GEORGE to fly from the

BROOKE OF SARAWAK to show the coons and gooks and spooks and poofs whats what, for the MURDER of GENERAL GORDON to be avenged with the blood of AY-RAB troublemakers, for DICK TURPIN to rob the JEW-INFESTED coffers of the INVADING IMMIGRANT VERMIN AND FILTH, for DR SHADE to use his airgun on the enemies of WHITE LIBERTY . . .

The time will come soon when all GOOD BRITISH MEN will have to dip their FISTS in PAKKYNIGGERYIDCHINKAY-RAB BLOOD to make clean for the healthy WHITE babies of our women this sacred island. The STINKING SCUM with their DOG-EATING, their DISGUSTING UNCHRISTIAN RITUAL PRACTICES, their PIG-SCREWING, CHILD-RAPING, MARRIAGE-ARRANGING, DISEASE-SPREADING habits will be thrown off the WHITE cliffs of Dover and swept out to sea as we, THE TRUE INHABITANTS OF GREAT BRITAIN, reclame the homes, the jobs, the lands and the women that are ours by DIVINE RIGHT.

KING ARTHUR! ST GEORGE! DR SHADE!

Today, go out and glassbottle a chinkie waiter, rapefuck a stinking coon bitch, piss burning petrol in a pakky newsagent, stick the boot to a raghead, hang a queer, shit in a sinnagog, puke on a lesbion. ITS YOUR LEGAL RIGHT! ITS YOUR DUTY! ITS YOUR DESTINY!

ARTHUR is COMING BACK! DR SHADE WILL RETURN!

Our's is the RIGHT, our's is the GLORY, our's is the ONLY TRUE JUSTICE! We shall PREVALE!

We are the SONS OF DR SHADE!

'Johnny British Man', *Britannia Rules* fanzine,
Issue 37, June 1991.
(Confiscated by police at a South London football fixture.)

Harry had given him a map of the estate, but Greg still got lost. The place was one of those '60s wastelands, concrete slabs now disfigured by layers of spray-painted hatred, odd little depressions clogged with rubbish, more than a few burned-out or derelict houses. There was loud Heavy Metal coming from somewhere, and teenagers hung about in menacing gaggles, looking at him with empty, hostile eyes as they compared tattoos or passed bottles. One group were inhaling something—glue?—from a brown paper bag. He looked at them a moment or two longer than he should have and they stared defiance. A girl whose skin haircut showed the odd bumps of her skull flashed him the V sign.

He kept his eyes on the ground and got more lost. The numbering system of the houses was irregular and contradictory and Greg had to go round in circles for a while. He asked for directions from a pair of henna-redheaded teenage girls sitting on a wall and they just shrugged their shoulders and went back to chewing gum. One of the girls was pregnant, her swollen belly pushing through her torn T-shirt, bursting the buttons of her jeans fly.

Greg was conscious that even his old overcoat was several degrees smarter than the norm in this area and that that might mark him as a mugging target. He also knew he had less than ten pounds on him and that frustrated muggers usually make up the difference between their expectations and their aquisitions with bare-knuckle beatings and loose teeth.

It was a Summer evening and quite warm, but the estate had a chill all of its own. The block-shaped tiers of council flats cast odd shadows that slipped across alleyways in a manner that struck Greg as being subtly wrong, like an illustration where the perspective is off or the light sources contradictory. The graffiti wasn't the '80s hip-hop style he knew from his own area, elaborate signatures to absent works of art, but was bluntly, boldly blatant, embroidered only by the occasional swastika (invariably drawn the wrong way round), football club symbol or Union Jack scratch.

CHELSEA FC FOREVER. KILL THE COONS! NF NOW. GAS THE YIDS! UP THE GUNNERS. FUCK THE IRISH MURDERERS! HELP STAMP OUT AIDS: SHOOT A POOF

TODAY. And the names of bands he had read about in *Searchlight*, the anti-fascist paper: SKREWDRIVER, BRITISH BOYS, WHITE-WASH, CRÜSADERS. There was a song lyric, magic markered on a bus stop in neat primary school writing, 'Jump down, turn around, kick a fucking nigger. Jump down, turn around, kick him in the head. Jump down, turn around, kick a fucking nigger. Jump down, turn around, kick him till he's dead . . .'

You would have thought that the Nazis had won the War and installed a puppet Tory government. The estate could easily be a '30s science-fiction writer's idea of the ghetto of the future, clean-lined and featureless buildings trashed by the bubble-helmeted brownshirts of some interplanetary axis, Jews, blacks and Martians despatched to some concentration camp asteroid. This wasn't the Jubilee Year. Nobody was even angry any more, just numbed with the endless, grinding misery of it all.

Eventually, more or less by wandering at random, he found Harry Lipman's flat. The bell button had been wrenched off, leaving a tuft of multi-coloured wires, and there was a reversed swastika carved into the door. Greg knocked and a light went on in the hall. Harry admitted him into the neat, small flat. Greg realised the place was fortified like a command bunker, a row of locks on the door, multiple catches on the reinforced glass windows, a burglar alarm fixed up on the wall between the gas and electricity meters. Otherwise, it was what he had expected: bookshelves everywhere, including the toilet, and a pleasantly musty clutter.

'I've not had many people here since Becky died'—Greg had known that Harry was a widower—'you must excuse the fearful mess.'

Harry showed Greg through to the kitchen. There was an Amstrad PCW 8256 set up on the small vinyl-topped table, a stack of continuous paper in a tray on the floor feeding the printer. The room smelled slightly of fried food.

'I'm afraid this is where I write. It's the only room with enough natural light for me. Besides, I like to be near the kettle and the Earl Gray.'

'Don't worry about it, Harry. You should see what my studio

looks like. I think it used to be a coal cellar.'

He put down his art folder and Harry made a pot of tea.

'So, how's Dr Shade coming along? I've made some drawings.'

'Swimmingly. I've done a month's worth of scripts, giving us our introductory serial. In the end, I went with the East End story as the strongest to bring the doctor back . . .'

The East End Story was an idea Harry and Greg had developed in which Dr Jonathan Chambers, miraculously not a day older than he was in 1952 when he was last seen (or 1929, come to that), returns from a spell in a Tibetan Monastary (or somewhere) studying the mystic healing arts (or something) to discover that the area where he used to make his home is being taken over by Dominick Dalmas, a sinister tycoon whose sharp-suited thugs are using violence and intimidation to evict the long-time residents, among whom are several of the doctor's old friends. Penelope Stamp, formerly a girl reporter but now a feisty old woman, is head of the Residents' Protection Committee, and she appeals to Chambers to resume his old crime-fighting alias and to investigate Dalmas. At first reluctant, Chambers is convinced by a botched assassination attempt to put on the cloak and goggles, and it emerges that Dalmas is the head of a mysterious secret society whose nefarious schemes would provide limitless future plotlines. Dalmas would be hoping to build up a substantial powerbase in London with the long-term intention of taking over the country, if not the world. Of course, Dr Shade would thwart his plots time and again, although not without a supreme effort.

'Maybe I'm just old, Greg,' Harry said after he had shown him the scripts, 'but this Dr Shade feels different. People said that when I took over from Donald, the strip became more appealing, with more comedy and thrills than horror and violence, but I can't see much to laugh about in this story. It's almost as if someone were trying to force Dr Shade to be Donald's character, by creating a world where his monster vigilante makes more sense than my straight-arrow hero. Everything's turned around.'

'Don't worry about it. Our Dr Shade is still fighting for justice.

He's on the side of Penny Stamp, not Dominick Dalmas.'

'What I want to know is whether he'll be on the side of Derek Leech?'

Greg really hadn't thought of that. The proprietor of the *Argus* would, of course, have the power of veto over the adventures of his cartoon character. He might not care for the direction Greg and Harry wanted to take Dr Shade in.

'Leech is on the side of money. We just have to make the strip so good it sells well, then it won't matter to him what it says.'

'I hope you're right, Greg, I really do. More tea?'

Outside, it got dark, and they worked through the scripts, making minor changes. Beyond the kitchen windows, shadows crept across the tiny garden towards the flat, their fingers reaching slowly for the concrete and tile. There were many small noises in the night, and it would have been easy to mistake the soft hiss of an aerosol paintspray for the popping of a high-powered airgun.

———

AUSSIE SOAP STAR GOT ME ON CRACK: Doomed schoolgirl's story—EXCLUSIVE—begins in the *Comet* today.

THE COMET LAW AND ORDER PULL-OUT. We ask top coppers, MPs, criminals and ordinary people what's to be done about rising crime?

BRIXTON YOBS SLASH WAR HERO PENSIONER: Is the birch the only language they understand? 'Have-a-Go' Tommy Barraclough, 76, thinks so. A special *Comet* poll shows that so do 69% of you readers.

DEREK LEECH TALKS STRAIGHT: Today: IMMIGRATION, CRIME, UNEMPLOYMENT.
'No matter what the whingers and moaners say, the simple fact is that Britain is an island. We are a small country and we only have room for the British. Everybody knows about the chronic housing shortage and

the lack of jobs. The pro-open door partisans can't argue with the facts and figures.

'British citizenship is a privilege not a universal right. This simple man thinks we should start thinking twice before we give it away to any old Tom, Dick or Pandit who comes, turban in hand, to our country, hoping to make a fortune off the dole . . .'

WIN! WIN! WIN! LURVERLY DOSH! THE *COMET* GIVE-AWAY GRID DISHES OUT THREE MILLION KNICKER! THEY SAID WE'D NEVER DO IT, BUT WE DID! MILLIONS MORE IN LURVERLY PRIZES MUST GO!

This is BRANDI ALEXANDER, 17, and she'll be seen without the football scarf in our ADULTS ONLY Sunday edition. BRANDI has just left school. Already, she has landed a part in a film, *Fiona Does the Falklands*. The part may be small, but hers aren't . . .

CATS TORTURED BY CURRYHOUSE KING?: What's really in that vindaloo, Mr Patel?

DID ELVIS DIE OF AIDS?: Our psychic reveals the truth!

GUARDIAN ANGEL KILLINGS CONTINUE: Scotland Yard Insiders Condemn Vigilante Justice.

The bodies of Malcolm Williams, 19, and Barry Tozer, 22, were identified yesterday by the Reverend Kenneth Hood, a spokesman for the West Indian community. The dead men were dumped in an underpass on the South London Attlee Estate. Both were shot at close range with a small-bore gun, execution-style. Inspector Mark Davey of the Metropolitan Police believes that the weapon used might be an airgun. This incident follows the identical killings of five black and Asian youths in recent months.

Williams and Tozer, like the other victims, had extensive police records. Williams served three months in prison last year for breaking and entering, and Tozer had a history of mugging, statutory rape, petty thieving and violence. It is possible that they were killed shortly after committing an assault. A woman's handbag was found nearby, it's contents scattered. Witnesses report that Williams and Tozer left The Flask, their local, when they couldn't pay for more drinks, and yet they had money on them when they were found.

The police are appealing for any witnesses to come forward. In particular, they would like to question the owner of the bag, who might well be able to identify the 'Guardian Angel' executioner. Previous appeals have not produced any useful leads.

A local resident who wishes to remain anonymous told our reporter, 'I hope they never catch the Guardian Angel. There are a lot more nigger b*st*rds with knives out there. I hope the Angel gets them all. Then maybe I can cash my pension at the post-office without fearing for my life.'

Coming Soon: BRITAIN'S NEW-OLD NEWSPAPER. CHURCHILL'S FAVOURITE READING IS BACK. DR SHADE *WILL* RETURN. At last, the EVENING has a HERO.

From the Daily Comet, Monday July the 1st, 1991

Saturday mornings were always quiet at comic conventions. Every time Greg went into the main hall there was a panel. All of them featured three quiet people nodding and chuckling while Neil Gaiman told all the jokes from his works-in-progress. He had heard them all in the bar the night before, and kept leaving for yet another turn around the dealers' room. They had him on a panel in the evening about reviving old characters: they were bringing back Tarzan, Grimly Feendish and Dan Dare, so Dr Shade would be in good company. At the charity auction, his first attempts at designing a new-look Dr Shade had fetched over £50, which must mean something.

He drifted away from the cardboard boxes full of overpriced American comic books in plastic bags to the more eccentric stalls which offered old movie stills, general interest magazines from the '40s and '50s (and, he realised with a chill, the '60s and '70s), odd items like *Stingray* jigsaws (only three pieces missing, £ 12.00) and *Rawhide* boardgames (£ 5.00), and digest-sized pulp magazines.

A dealer recognised him, probably from an earlier con, and said he might have something that would interest him. He had precisely the smugly discreet tone of a pimp. Bending down below his trestle table, which made him breath hard, he reached for a tied bundle of pulps and brought them up.

'You don't see these very often . . .'

Greg looked at the cover of the topmost magazine. *Dr Shade Monthly*. The illustration, a faded FitzGerald, showed the goggled and cloaked doctor struggling with an eight-foot neanderthal in the uniform of an SS officer, while the blonde Penny Stamp, dressed only in flimsy '40s foundation garments and chains, lay helpless on an operating table. INSIDE: "Master of the Mutants" a complete novel by REX CASH. Also, "Flaming Torture", "The Laughter of Dr Shade" and "Hank the Yank and the Hangman of Heidelberg". April, 1945. A Badgerfield Publication.

Greg had asked Harry Lipman to come along to the con but the writer had had a few bad experiences at events like this and said he didn't want to 'mix with the looneys.' He knew Harry didn't have many of the old mags with his stuff in and that he had to buy these for him. Who knows, there might be a few ideas in them that could be re-used.

'Ten quid the lot?'

He handed over two fives and took the bundle, checking the spines to see that the dealer hadn't slipped in some *Reader's Digests* to bulk out the package. No, they were all *Dr Shades*, all from the '40s. He had an urge to sit down and read the lot.

Back in the hall, someone was lecturing an intently interested but pimple-plagued audience about adolescent angst in *The Teen Titans* and *X-Men*, and Greg wondered where he could get a cup of tea or coffee and a biscuit. Neil Gaiman, surrounded by acolytes, grinned at him and waved from across the room, signalling. Greg gestured his thanks. Neil had alerted him to the presence of Hunt Sealey, a British comics entrepreneur he had once taken to court over some financial irregularities. Greg did not want to go through that old argument again. Avoiding the spherical Sealey, he stepped into a darkened room where a handful of white-faced young men with thick glasses were watching a Mexican horror-wrestling movie on a projection video. The tape was a third- or fourth-generation dupe, and the picture looked as if it were being screened at a tropical drive-in during the monsoon.

'Come, Julio,' said a deep American voice dubbed over the lip movements of a swarthy mad doctor, 'help me carry the cadaver of the gorilla to the incinerator.'

Nobody laughed. The video room smelled of stale cigarette smoke and spilled beer. The kids who couldn't afford a room in the hotel crashed out in here, undisturbed by the non-stop Z-movie festival. The only film Greg wanted to see (a French print of Georges Franju's *Les Yeux sans Visage*) was scheduled at the same time as his panel. Typical.

On the assumption that Sealey, who was known for the length of time he could hold a grudge, would be loitering in the hall harassing Neil, Greg sat on a chair and watched the movie. The mad doctor was transplanting gorilla hearts and a monster was terrorising the city, ripping the dresses off hefty *senoritas*. The heroine was a sensitive lady wrestler who wanted to quit the ring because she had put her latest opponent in a coma.

Greg got bored with the autopsy footage and the jumpy images, and looked around to see if anyone he knew was there. The audience were gazing at the screen like communicants at mass, the video mirrored in their spectacles, providing starlike pinpoints in the darkness.

He had been drawing a lot of darkness recently, filling in the shadows around Dr Shade, only the white of his lower face and the highlights of his goggles showing in the night as he stalked Dominick Dalmas through the mean streets of East London. His hand got tired after inking in the solid blacks of the strip. Occasionally you saw Dr Chambers in the daytime, but 95% of the panels were night scenes.

There was a glitch on the videotape and the film vanished for a few seconds, replaced by Nanette Newman waving a bottle of washing-up liquid. Nobody hooted or complained and the mad doctor's gorilla-man came back in an instant. A tomato-like eyeball was fished out, gravyish blood coursing down the contorted face of a bad actor with a worse toupee. Stock music as old as talking pictures thundered on the soundtrack. If it weren't for the violence, this could easily have been made in the '30s, when Donald Moncrieff's Dr Shade was in the hero business, tossing mad scientists out of tenth-storey windows and putting explosive airgun darts into Bolshies and rebellious natives.

Although his eyes were used to the dark, Greg thought he wasn't seeing properly. A corner of the room, behind the video, was as thickly black as any of his panels. To one side of the screen, he could dimly see the walls with their movie posters and fan announcements, a fire extinguisher hung next to a notice. But the other side of the room was just an impenetrable night.

He had a headache and there were dots in front of his eyes. He looked away from the dark corner and back again. It didn't disappear. But it did seem to move, easing itself away from the wall and expanding towards him. A row of seats disappeared. The screen shone brighter, dingy colours becoming as vivid as a comic book cover.

Greg clutched his *Dr Shades*, telling himself this was what came of too much beer, not enough food and too many late nights in the convention bar. Suddenly, it was very hot in the video room, as if the darkness were burning up, suffocating him . . .

A pair of glasses glinted in the dark. There was someone inside the shadow, someone wearing thick sunglasses. No, not glasses. Goggles.

He stood up, knocking his chair over. Somebody grumbled at the noise. On the screen, the Mexico City cops had shot the gorilla man dead and the mad doctor—his father—was being emotional about his loss.

The darkness took manshape, but not mansize. Its shadow head, topped by the shape of a widebrimmed hat, scraped the ceiling, its arms reached from wall to wall.

Only Greg took any notice. Everyone else was upset about the gorilla man and the mad doctor. Somewhere under the goggles, up near the light fixtures, a phantom white nose and chin were forming around the black gash of a humourless mouth.

Greg opened the door and stepped out of the video room, his heart spasming in its cage. Slamming the door on the darkness, he pushed himself into the corridor and collided with a tall, cloaked figure.

Suddenly angry, he was about to lash out verbally when he realised he knew who the man was. The recognition was like a ECT jolt.

He was standing in front of Dr Shade.

––––––––

The Jew fled through the burning city, feeling a clench of dread each time a shadow fell over his heart. There was nowhere he could hide. Not in the underground railway stations that doubled as bomb shelters, not in the sewers with the other rats, not in the cells of the traitor police. The doctor was coming for him, coming to avenge the lies he had told, and there was nothing that could be done.

The all-clear had sounded, the drone of the planes was gone from the sky, and the streets were busy with firemen and panicking Londoners. Their homes were destroyed, their lilywhite lives ground into the mud. The Jew found it in his heart to laugh bitterly as he saw a mother in a nightdress, calling for her children outside the pile of smoking bricks that had been her house. His insidious kind had done their job too well, setting the Aryan races at each other's throats while they plotted with the Soviet Russians and the heathen Chinee to dominate the grim world that would come out of this struggle. Germans dropped bombs on Englishmen, and the Jew smiled.

But, in this moment, he knew that success of the Conspiracy would mean nothing to him. Not while the night still had shadows. Not while there was a Dr Shade . . .

He leaned, exhausted, against a soot-grimed wall. The mark of Dr Shade was on him, a black handprint on his camelhair coat. The doctor's East End associates were dogging him, relaying messages back to their master, driving him away from the light, keeping him running through the night. There was no one to call him 'friend'.

A cloth-capped young man looked into the alley, ice-blue eyes penetrating the dark. He put his thumb and forefinger to his mouth and gave a shrill whistle.

''Ere, mateys, we gots us a Yid! Call fer the doc!'

There was a stampede of heavy boots. Almost reluctant to keep on the move, wishing for it all to be over, the murdering filth shoved himself away from the wall and made a run for the end of the alley. The wall was low, and he hauled himself up it onto a sloping roof. The East End boys were after him, broken bottles and shivs in their hands, but he made it ahead of them. He strode up the tiles, feeling them shift under his feet. Some came loose and fell behind him, into the faces of Shade's men.

Using chimneys to steady himself, the stinking guttershite ran across the rooftops. He had his revolver out, and fired blindly into the darkness behind him, panic tearing him apart from the inside. Then, he came to the end of his run.

He stood calmly, arms folded, his cloak flapping in the breeze, silhouetted sharply against the fiery skyline. The thin lips formed a smile, and the child-raping libellous Israelite scum knew he was justly dead.

'Hello Harry,' said Dr Shade.

Donald Moncrieff, "Dr Shade, Jew Killer" (unpublished, 1942)

————

'Hello, Harry,' said Greg, jiggling the phone in the regulation hopeless attempt to improve a bad connection, 'I thought we'd been cut off . . .'

Harry sounded as if he were in Jakarta, not three stops away on the District Line. 'So there I was, face to goggles with Dr Shade.'

He could make it sound funny now, hours later.

'The guy was on his way to the masquerade. There are always people in weird outfits at these things. He had all the details right, airgun and all.'

Greg had called Harry from his hotel room to tell him about all the excitement the Return of Dr Shade was generating with the fans. Kids whose *parents* hadn't been born when the Argus went out of business were eagerly awaiting the comeback of the cloaked crimefighter.

'Obviously, the doc has percolated into our folk memory, Harry. Or maybe Leech is right. It's just time to have him back.'

His panel had gone well. The questions from the audience had almost all been directed to him, and he had had to field some to the other panelists so as not to hog the whole platform. The fans had been soliciting for information. Yes, Penny Stamp would be back, but she wouldn't be a girl reporter any more. Yes, the doctor's Rolls Royce 'Shadowshark' would be coming out of the garage, with more hidden tricks than ever. Yes, the doctor would be dealing with the contemporary problems of East London. When someone asked if the proprietor of the paper would be exerting any influence over the content of the strip, Greg replied 'well, he hasn't so far,' and got cheers by claiming, 'I don't think Dr Shade is a *Comet* reader, somehow.' Somebody even knew enough to ask him to compare the Donald Moncrieff Rex Cash with the Harry Lipman Rex Cash. He had conveyed best wishes to the con from Harry and praised the writer's still-active imagination.

At the other end of the line, Harry sounded tired. Sometimes, Greg had to remind himself how old the man was. He wondered whether the call had woken him up.

'We've even had some American interest, maybe in republishing the whole thing as a monthly book, staggered behind the newspaper series. I'm having Tamara investigate. She thinks we can do it without tithing off too much of the money to Derek Leech, but rights deals are tricky. Also, Condé Nast, the corporate heirs of Street and Smith, have a long memory and still think Moncrieff ripped off The Shadow in the '30s. Still, it's worth going into.'

Harry tried to sound enthusiastic.

'Are you okay, Harry?'

He said so, but somehow Greg didn't believe him. Greg checked his watch. He had agreed to meet Neil and a few other friends in the bar in ten minutes. He said goodnight to Harry, and hung up.

Wanting to change his panelist's jacket for a drinker's pullover, Greg delved through the suitcase perched on the regulation anonymous armchair. He found the jumper he needed, and transferred his convention badge from lapel to epaulette. Under the suitcase, he found the bundle of *Dr Shade Monthlys* he had bought for Harry. He hadn't mentioned them on the phone.

Harry couldn't have got back to bed yet. He'd barely be in the hall. Greg stabbed the REDIAL button and listened to the clicking of the exchange. Harry's phone rang again.

The shadows in the room seemed longer. When Harry didn't pick up immediately, Greg's first thought was that something was wrong. He imagined coronaries, nasty falls, fainting spells, the infirmities of the aged. The telephone rang. Ten, twenty, thirty times.

Harry couldn't have got back to bed and fallen into a deep sleep in twenty seconds.

You also couldn't get a wrong number on a phone with a REDIAL facility.

The phone was picked up at the other end.

'Hello,' said a female voice, young and hard, 'who's this then?'

'Harry,' Greg said. 'Where's Harry?'

''E's got a bit of a problem, mate,' the girl said. 'But we'll see to 'im.'

Greg was feeling very bad about this. The girl on the phone didn't sound like a concerned neighbour. 'Is Harry ill?'

A pause. Greg imagined silent laughter. There was music in the background. Not Harry Lipman music but tinny Metal, distorted by a cheap boombox and the telephone. Suddenly, Greg was down from his high, the good feeling and the alcohol washed out of his system.

'Hello?'

'Still here,' the girl said.

'Is Harry ill?'

'Well, I'll put it this way,' she said, 'we've sent for the doctor.'

———————

Evidence has come to light linking Derek Leech, the man at the top of the pyramid, with a linked chain of dubious right-wing organisations here and abroad. A source inside the Leech organisation, currently gearing up to launch a new national evening paper, revealed to our reporter, DUNCAN EYLES, that while other press barons diversify into the electronic media and publishing, Derek Leech has his eye on a more direct manner of influencing the shape of the nation.

'Derek has been underwriting the election campaigns of parliamentary candidates in the last few by-elections,' the source told us. 'They mostly lost their deposits. Patrick Massinghame, the Britain First chairman who later rejoined the Tories, was one. The idea was not to take a seat but to use the campaigns to disseminate propaganda. *The Comet* has always been anti-immigration, pro-law-and-order, anti-anything-socialist, pro-hanging-and-flogging, pro-military spending, pro-political-censorship. But the campaigns were able to be rabidly so.'

Leech, who has regularly dismissed similar allegations as 'lunatic conspiracy theories', refused to comment on documents leaked to us which give facts and figures. In addition to funding Patrick Massinghame and others of his political stripe, Leech has contributed heavily to such bizarre causes as the White Freedom Crusade, which channels funds from British and American big business into South Africa, the English Liberation Front, who claim that immigrants from the Indian Sub-Continent and the Caribbean constitute 'an army of occupation' and should be driven out through armed struggle, the Revive Capital Punishment lobby, and even caucasian supremacist thrash metal band Whitewash, whose single 'Blood, Iron and St George' was banned by the BBC and commercial radio stations but still managed to reach Number 5 in the independent charts.

Even more disturbing in the light of these allegations, is the paramilitary nature of the security force Leech is employing to guard the pyramid that is at the heart of his empire. Recruiting directly from right-wing youth gangs, often through advertisements placed in illiterate but suspiciously well produced and printed fanzines distributed at football matches, the Leech organisation has been assembling what can only be described as an army of yobs to break the still-continuing print union pickets in docklands. Our source informs us that the pyramid contains a well-stocked armoury, as if the proprietor of the *Comet* and the forthcoming *Argus* were expecting a siege. Rumour has it that Leech has even invested in a custom-made Rolls Royce featuring such unusual extras as bullet-proof bodywork, James Bond-style concealed rocket launchers, a teargas cannon and bonnet-mounted stilettos.

Derek Leech can afford all the toys he wants. But perhaps it's about time we started to get worried about the games he wants to play . . .

Searchlight, August 1991.

————

The minicab driver wouldn't take him onto the estate no matter what he offered to pay and left him stranded him at the kerb. At night, the place was even less inviting than by day. There were wire-mesh protected lights embedded in concrete walls every so often, but skilled vandals had got through to them. Greg knew that dashing into the dark maze would do no good, and forced himself to study the battered, graffiti-covered map of the estate that stood by the road. He found Harry's house on the map easily. By it, someone had drawn a stickman hanging from a gallows. It was impossible to read a real resemblance into the infants' scrawl of a face, but Greg knew it was supposed to represent Harry.

He walked towards the house, so concerned for Harry Lipman that he forgot to be scared for himself. That was a mistake.

They came from an underpass and surrounded him. He got an impression of Union Jack T-shirts and shaven heads. Studded leather straps wrapped around knuckles. They only seemed to hit him four or five times, but it was enough.

He turned his head with the first blow and felt his nose flatten into his cheek. Blood was seeping out of his instantly swollen nostrils and he was cut inside his mouth. He shook his head, trying to dislodge the pain. They stood back, and watched him yelp blood onto his chest. He was still wearing his convention tag.

Then one of them came in close, breathed foully in his face, and put a knee into his groin. He sagged, crying out, and felt his knees going. They kicked his legs, and he was on the ground. His ribs hurt.

'Come on, P,' one of them said, "e's 'ad 'is. Let's scarper.'

'Nahh,' said a girl—the one he had talked to on the telephone?—as she stepped forwards, "es not properly done yet.'

Greg pressed his nostrils together to stanch the blood and realised his nose wasn't broken. There was a lump rising on his cheek, though. He looked into the girl's face.

She was young, maybe fifteen or sixteen, and there was blonde fur on her skull. Her head was lumpy and the skinhead cut made her child's face seem small, as if painted on an easter egg. He had seen her the last time he was here. She wore Britannia earrings, and had a rare right-way-round swastika tattooed in blue on her temple.

'Come on, . . .'

P smiled at him and licked her lips like a cat. 'Do you need telling any more, Mr Artist?'

The others were bunched behind her. She was small and wiry, but they were like hulks in the shadows.

'Do you get the picture?'

Greg nodded. Anything, just so long as they let him alone. He had to get to Harry.

'Good. Draw well, 'cause we'll be watching over you.'

Lights came on in a house opposite and he got a clearer look at their faces. Apart from P, they weren't kids. They were in the full skin-head gear, but on them it looked like a disguise. There were muffled voices from the house, and the lights went off again.

'Kick 'im, Penelope,' said someone.

P smiled again. 'Nahh, Bazzo. 'E knows what's what, now. We don't want to hurt 'im. 'E's important. Ain't ya, Mr Artist?'

Greg was standing up again. There was nothing broken inside his head, but he was still jarred. His teeth hurt and he spat out a mouthful of blood.

'Dirty beast.'

His vision was wobbling. P was double-exposed, a bubble fringe shimmering around her outline.

'Goodnight,' said P. 'Be good.'

Then they were gone, leaving only shadows behind them. Greg ran across the walkway, vinegar-stained pages of the *Comet* swirling about his ankles. Harry's front door was hanging open, the chain broken, and the hallway was lit up.

Greg found him in his kitchen, lying on the floor, his word processor slowly pouring a long manuscript onto him. The machine rasped as it printed out.

He helped Harry sit up, and got him a teacup of water from the tap. They hadn't hurt him too badly, although there was a bruise on his forehead. Harry was badly shaken. Greg had never seen him without his teeth in and he was drooling like a baby, unconsciously wiping his mouth on his cardigan sleeve. He was trying to talk but couldn't get the words out.

The phone was ripped out of the wall. The printer was scratching Greg's nerves. He sat at the desk and tried to work out how to shut it off without losing anything. He wasn't familiar with this model.

Then he looked at the continuous paper. It was printing out a draft of the first month of new Dr Shade scripts. Greg couldn't help but read what was coming out of the machine.

It wasn't what he had been working on. It wasn't even in script form. But Harry had written it and he would be expected to draw it.

Unable to control his shaking, Greg read on.

'I'm sorry,' said Harry. 'It was Him. They brought Him here. He was here before Donald started writing Him. He'll always be here.'

Greg turned to look at the old man. Harry was standing over him, laying a hand on his shoulder. Greg shook his head and Harry sadly nodded.

'It's true. We've always known, really.'

Beyond Harry was his hallway. Beyond that, the open door allowed Greg to see into the night. The shadowman was out there, laughing . . .

. . . the laughter faded into the noise of the printer.

Greg read on.

————

He thought for a moment before selecting the face he would wear tonight. The Chambers identity was wearing thin, limiting him too much. These were troubled times and stricter methods were required. He considered all the people he had been, listed the names, paged through their faces.

Sitting behind the desk at the tip of the glass and steel pyramid, he felt the thrill of power. Out there in the night cowered the crack dealers and the anarchists, the blacks and the yellows, the traitors and the slackers. Tonight they would know he was back.

The press baron was a useful face. It had helped him gain a purchase on these new times, given him a perspective on the sorry state of the nation.

He thought of the true patriots who had been rejected. Oswald Mosley, Unity Mitford, William Joyce, Donald Moncrieff. And the false creatures who had succeeded them. This time, things would be different. There would be no bowing to foreign interests.

He fastened his cloak at his throat, and peeled off the latest mask. Smiling at the thin-lipped reflection in the dark mirror of the glass, he pulled on the goggles.

The private lift was ready to take him to the Shadowshark. He holstered his trusty airgun.

Plunging towards his destiny, he exulted in the thrill of the chase. He was back.

Accept no pale imitations. Avoid the lesser men, the men of wavering resolves, of dangerous weaknesses.

He was the original.

Rex Cash, "The Return of Dr Shade" (1991)

————

Greg was at his easel, drawing. There was nothing else he could do. No matter how much he hated the commission, he had to splash the black ink, had to fill out the sketches. It was all he had left of himself. In the panel, Dr Shade was breaking up a meeting of the conspirators. African communists were infiltrating London, foully plotting to sabotage British business by blowing up the stock exchange. But the doctor would stop them. Greg filled in the thick lips of Papa Dominick, the voodoo commissar, and tried to get the fear in the villain's eyes as the shadowman raised his airgun.

'Did you hear,' P said, 'they're giving me a chance to write for the Argus. The Stamp of Truth, they'll call my column. I can write about music or politics or fashion or anything. I'll be a proper little girl reporter.'

Crosbie told him Derek Leech was delighted at the way the strip was going. Dr Shade was really taking off. There was Dr Shade graffiti all over town, and he had started seeing youths with Dr Shade goggles tattooed around their eyes. A comics reviewer who had acclaimed *Fat Chance* as a masterpiece described the strip as 'racist drivel.' He hadn't been invited to any conventions recently, and a lot of his old friends would cross the street to avoid him. Greg's telephone rang rarely, now. It was always Crosbie. To his surprise, Tamara had cut herself out of the 10% after the first week of the *Argus* and told him to find other representation. He never heard from Harry, just received the scripts by special messenger. Greg could imagine the writer disconsolately tapping out stories in Donald Moncrieff's style at his Amstrad. He knew exactly how the other man felt.

He had the radio on. There riots were still flaring up. The police were concerned by a rash of airgun killings but didn't seem to be doing much about them. It appeared that the victims were mainly rabble-rousing ringleaders, although not a few West Indian and Asian community figures had been killed or wounded. Kenneth Hood, a popular vicar, had tried to calm down the rioters and been shot in the head. He wasn't expected to live and two policemen plus seven 'rioters' had died in the violent outburst that followed the attempt on his life. Greg imagined the shadowman on the rooftops, taking aim, hat pulled low, cloak streaming like demon wings.

Greg drew the Shadowshark, sliding through the city night, hurling aside the petrol-bomb-throwing minions of Papa Dominick. 'The sun has shone for too long on the open schemes of the traitors,' Harry had written, 'but night must fall . . . and with the night comes Shade.'

Early on, Greg had tried to leave the city but they were waiting for him at the station. The girl called P and some of the others. They had escorted him home. They called themselves Shadeheads now, and wore hats and cloaks like the doctor, tattered black over torn T-shirts, drainpipe jeans and steel-toed Doc Martens.

P was with him most of the time now. At first, she had just been in the corner of his vision, watching over him. Finally, he'd given in and called her over. Now, she was in the flat, making her calls to the doctor, preparing his meals, warming his single bed. They'd pushed him enough and now he had to be reassured, cajoled. He worked better that way.

Derek Leech was on the radio now, defending the record of his security staff during the riots. He had pitched in to help the police, using his news helicopters to direct the action and sending his people into the fighting like troops. The police were obviously not happy, but public opinion was forcing them to accept the tycoon's assistance. Leech made a remark about 'the spirit of Dr Shade' and Greg's hand jumped, squirting ink across the paper.

'Careful, careful,' said P, dipping in with a tissue and delicately wiping away the blot, saving the artwork. Her hair was growing out. She'd never be a *Comet* Knock-Out but she was turning into a surprisingly housewifely, almost maternal, girl. In the end, Shadeheads believed a woman's place was with her her legs spread and her hands in dishwater.

In the final panel, Dr Shade was standing over his vanquished enemies, holding up his fist in a defiant salute. White fire was reflected in his goggles.

The news was over, and the new Crüsaders single came on. 'There'll Always Be an England.' It was climbing the charts.

Greg looked out of the window. He imagined fires on the horizon.

He took a finer pen and bent to do some detail work. He wished he had held out longer. He wished he'd taken more than one beating. Sometimes, he told himself he was doing it for Harry, to protect the old man. But that was bullshit. They hadn't been Reggie Barton and Hank Hemingway. Imaginative torture hadn't been necessary and they hadn't sworn never to give in, never the break down, never to knuckle under. A few plain old thumps and the promise of a few more had been enough. Plus more money a month than either of them had earned in any given three years of their career.

Next week, the doctor would execute Papa Dominick. Then, he would do something about the strikers, the scroungers, the slackers, the scum . . .

A shadow fell over the easel, cloak spreading around it. Greg turned to look up at the goggled face of his true master.

Dr Shade was pleased with him.

This seems to strike chords with readers interested in the history of the hero pulps and with those who share the concerns of Searchlight *(a real and sadly necessary publication, by the way). Derek Leech, who debuts here, has become a recurring character; he turns up again in this collection in* 'Organ Donors', *emerging as a major character (along with his Dr Shade aspect) in my novel* The Quorum. *Set slightly in the (then) future, the story demonstrates my usual ineptitude with short-term prophecy. Its '80s images now seem almost quaint. Like my novel* Bad Dreams, *also written in one decade and published in the next, 'Dr Shade' can charitably be construed as set in an alternate world where Margaret Thatcher remained in power into the '90s and the economic bubble took a little longer to burst. I wish I could say that things were worse on street-level in the story than in the real world. British fascist parties have been popping up again and there are UK newspapers with barely veiled racist editorial policies, though these days they tend to target 'asylum-seekers' and Islam groups rather than the Afro-Caribbean or Sub-Continental 'immigrants' picked on in the '70s and '80s.*

The Ripping Yarns bookshop in North London specialises in out-of-print adventure and detective stories. Browsing there, I once found (but didn't buy) a book whose blunt title reminds you how much standards have changed in society and popular fiction. It was called Dead Nigger. *In 'Dr Shade', I hoped to affirm that, before WW II, Britain had two traditions we usually associate with other countries: the (mainly) nice thing was a black-masked heroic adventure pulpery paralleling the American adventures of The Shadow and Batman; the (totally) nasty thing was a ground-roots fascist movement not entirely unlike those of Germany or Italy. As Neil Gaiman, who cameos here, once said: America really does have a tradition of masked vigilantes who go out by night to defend their vision of society and they do have names ominously like the Justice League of America. Before 'Dr Shade' appeared, I cleared personal appearances. David Pringle, who later invoked Dr Shade in an ad for Imaginary People, wound up first publishing the story (in* Interzone), *and Neil Gaiman later had me pick the film program for his serial killers' convention in* Sandman, *then had me guest appear in the comic itself ('Calliope', #17).*

At the time, I was pleased with the catchy name I gave my monster hero. Recently, I read in Jim Harmon's Radio Mystery and Adventure *(1992) that there was an* original Original Dr Shade, *the hunchbacked villain of the 1946-54 radio serial* Sky King. *Sheldon Lewis played 'Doc' Shade in* The Sky Rider, *a 1928 Western starring Champion the Dog. And, yes, I have heard of DC Comics' characters the Shade and Shade the Changing Man. Another Doctor Shade showed up as a villain-ness, played by Juliet Landau in the Whoopi Goldberg/talking dinosaur comedy* Theodore Rex – *which in 1995 became the most expensive film ever made to go straight to video.*

FAMOUS
MONSTERS

You know, I wouldn't be doing this picture if it wasn't for Chaney Junior's liver. They said it was a heart attack, but anyone who knew Lon knows better. Doing all these interviews with the old-timers, you must have heard the stories. They don't tell the half of it. I didn't get to work with Lon till well past his prime. Past my prime too, come to that. It was some Abbott and Costello piece of shit in the fifties. Already, he looked less human than I do. Wattles, gut, nose, the whole fright mask. And the stink. Hell, but he was a good old bastard. Him and me and Brod Crawford used to hit all the bars on the Strip Friday and Saturday nights. We used to scare up a commotion, I can tell you. I guess we were a disgrace. I quit all that after I got a tentacle shortened in a brawl with some hophead beatniks over on Hollywood Boulevard. I leaked ichor all over Arthur Kennedy's star. That's all gone now, anyway. There aren't any bars left I can use. It's not that they won't serve me—the Second War of the Worlds was, like, twenty-five years ago now, and that's all forgotten—but no one stocks the stuff any more. It's easy enough to get. Abattoirs sell off their leavings for five cents a gallon. But this California heat makes it go rancid and rubbery inside a day.

Anyway, just before Lon conked out—halfway through a bottle of Wild Turkey, natch—he signed up with Al to do this picture. It was called *The Mutilation Machine* back then. It's *Blood of the Cannibal Creature* now. Al will change it. He always does. The footage with Scott

Brady and the bike gang is from some dodo Al never got finished in the sixties. *Something a-Go-Go*, that's it. Lousy title. *Cycle Sadists a-Go-Go*. It must be great being a film historian, huh? What with all this confusion and crapola. Do you know how they were paying Lon? Bottles. When Al wanted him to walk across a room in a scene, he'd have the assistant director hold up a bottle of hooch off-camera and shake it. Lon would careen across the set, knocking things and people over, and go for the booze, and Al would get his shot. I don't suppose I'm all that much better off. One of the backers is a wholesale butcher, and he's kicking in my fee in pig blood. I know you think that sounds disgusting, but don't knock it until you've tried it.

For a while, it looked like Lon would last out the picture. Al got the scene where he's supposed to pull this kootch-kootch dancer's guts out. He was playing Groton the Mad Zombie, by the way. So it's not Chekhov. Al has already cut the scene together. Okay, so there's some scratching on the neg. Al can fix it. He's going to put on some more scratches, and make them look like sparks flying out of Lon. Groton is supposed to be electric. Or atomic. One or the other. The girl keeps laughing while Lon gets his mitts inside her sweater, but they can dub some screams in, and music and growling and it'll be okay. At least, it'll be as okay as anything ever is in Al's movies. Did you catch *Five Bloody Graves*? It was a piece of shit. After this, he wants to do a picture with Georgina Spelvin and The Ritz Brothers called *The Fucking Stewardesses*. You can bet he'll change *that* title.

But one scene is all there is of Lon. So, when he buys the farm Al calls me up. I don't have an agent any more, although I used to be with the William Morris crowd. I do all my deals myself. I couldn't do a *worse* job than some of the people in this business. I used to be handled by a guy called Dickie Nixon, a real sleazo scumbag. He was the one who landed me in *Orbit Jocks*, and screwed me out of my TV residuals. Anyway, I know Al. I worked for him once before, on *Johnny Blood Rides Roughshod*. That was the horror western that was supposed to put James Dean back on the top. What a joke. The fat freak kept falling off his horse. It turned out to be a piece of shit. Al and me worked something out on this one, and so here I am in Bronson Caverns again, playing Groton the Mad Zombie. They've rewritten the script so I can be Lon in all the early scenes. I know it sounds ridiculous, what with the shape and everything. But, hell, I can cram myself into a pair and a half of jeans and a double-size poncho. In the new script, my character is a Martian—I mean, I can't play an Eskimo, can I?—but when John Carradine zaps me with the Mutilation Machine I turn into a human being. Well, into Groton the Mad Zombie. It's the most challenging part that's come my way in years, even if the film is going to be a total piece of shit. I'm hoping my performance will be a tribute to Lon. I've got the voice down. 'George, lookit duh rabbits, George.' Now, I'm working on the walk. That's difficult. You people walk all weird. No matter how long I hang around you, I still can't figure out how you manage with just the two legs.

I'm an American citizen, by the way. I was hatched in Los Angeles. Put it down to the Melting Pot. Mom flopped down in the twenties, when the Old World political situation started going to hell. She'd been through WWI and couldn't face that again. It's in the culture, I guess. When your head of government is called the High War Victor you know you're in trouble. I'm not that way. I'm mellow. A typical native Californian, like my twenty-eight brood siblings. I'm the only one of us left now. The rest all died off or went back to the skies. I can't let go. It's showbiz, you know. It's in the ichor. You must understand that if you do all these interviews. What do you call it, oral history? It's important, I suppose. Someone should take all this down before we all die out. Did you get to Rathbone? There was a guy with some stories. I never got on with him though, despite all those pictures we did together. He lost some relatives in the First War of the Worlds, and never got around to accepting that not all non-terrestrials were vicious thugs.

I suppose you'll want to know how I got into the movies? Well, I'm that one in a million who started as an extra. It was in the late thirties, when I'd barely brushed the eggshell out of my slime. Four bucks a day just for hanging around cardboard nightclubs or walking up and down that street where the buildings are just frontages. In *Swing Time*,

I'm in the background when Fred and Ginger do their 'Pick Yourself Up' routine. They were swell, although Rogers put my name down on some list of communist sympathisers in the fifties and I nearly had to go before HUAC. Do I look like a commie? Hell, how many other Americans can blush red, white and blue?

I didn't stay an extra long. I suppose I'm noticeable. There were very few of us in Hollywood, and so I started getting bit parts. Typically, I'd be a heavy in a saloon fight, or an underworld hanger-on. If you catch *The Roaring Twenties* on a re-run, look out for me during the massacre in the Italian restaurant. Cagney gets me in the back. It's one of my best deaths. I've always been good at dying.

My big break came when 20th Century-Fox did the Willie K'ssth films. Remember? Rathbone played Inspector Willie K'ssth of the Selenite Police Force. *Willie K'ssth Takes Over, Willie K'ssth and the Co-Eds, Willie K'ssth On Broadway*, and so on. There were more than twenty of them. I was Jimbo, Willie's big, dumb Martian sidekick. I did all the comedy relief scenes—going into a tentacle-flapping fright in haunted houses, getting hit on the head and seeing animated stars in fight sequences. The films don't play much now, because of the Selenite pressure groups. They hate the idea of a human actor in the role. And when Earl Derr Biggers was writing the books in the twenties, the Grand Lunar had them banned on the Moon. I don't see what they were bothered about. Willie always spots the killer and comes out on top. He usually gets to make a bunch of human beings look ridiculous as well. In not one of the books or movies did Jimbo ever guess who the murderer was, even when it was blatantly obvious. And it usually was. For a while, I was typed as the dumb, scared Martie. Some of my siblings said I was projecting a negative image of the race, but there was a Depression on and I was the only one of the brood in regular work. I've got nothing against Selenites, by the way, although the Grand Lunar has always had a rotten Sapient Rights record. It's no wonder so many of them headed for the Earth.

After the New York Singe, I was quickly dropped from the series. We were half-way through *Willie K'ssth On Coney Island* when the studio quietly pulled my contract. They rewrote Jimbo as a black chauffeur called Wilbur Wolverhampton and got Stepin Fetchit to do the role. They still put out the film under its original title, even though there wasn't a Coney Island any more. I'd have sued, but there was a wave of virulent Anti-Martian feeling sweeping the country. That was understandable, I guess. I had relatives in New York, too. Suddenly, forty years of cultural exchange was out of the porthole and we were back to interspecial hatred. Nobody cared that Mom was a refugee from High War Victor Uszthay in the first place, and that since his purges most of her brood siblings were clogging up the canals. I was pulled out of my apartment by the Beverly Hills cops and roughed up in a basement. They really did use rubber hoses. I'll never forget that. I ended up in an internment camp, and the studio annexed my earnings. The hate mail was really nasty. We were out in the desert, which wasn't so bad. I guess we're built for deserts. But at night people in hoods would come and have bonfires just outside the perimeter. They burned scarecrows made to look like Martians and chanted lots of blood and guts slogans. That was disturbing. And the guards were a bit free with the cattle prods. It was a shameful chapter in the planet's history, but no one's researched it properly yet. The last interview I did was with some Martian-American professor doing a thesis on Roosevelt's treatment of so-called 'enemy aliens'. He was practically a hatchling, and didn't really understand what we had to go through. I bet his thesis will be a piece of shit. There were rumours about this camp in Nevada where the guards stood back and let a mob raze the place to the ground with the Marties still in it. And who knows what happened in Europe and Asia?

Then the cylinders started falling, and the war effort got going. Uszthay must have been a bigger fool than we took him for. With Mars' limited resources, he couldn't possibly keep the attack going for more than six months. And Earth had cavorite, while he was still using 19th Century rocket cannons. Do you know how many cylinders just landed in the sea and dsunk? So, Roosevelt got together with the world leaders in Iceland—Hitler, Stalin, Oswald Cabal—and they geared up for Earth's counter-invasion. Finally, I got all the hassles with my citizenship sorted out, and the authorities reluctantly admitted I had as much right to be called an American as any other second generation immigrant. I had to carry a wad of documentation the size of a phone book, but I could walk the streets freely. Of course, if I did I was still likely to get stoned. I did most of my travelling in a curtained car. According to what was left of my contract, I owed 20th a couple of movies. I assumed they'd pay me off and I'd wind up in an armaments factory, but no, as soon as I was on the lot I was handed a stack of scripts. Suddenly, everyone was making war pictures.

The first was *Mars Force*, which I did for Howard Hawks. I was loaned to Warners for that. It was supposed to be a true story. I don't know if you remember, but the week after the Singe a handful of foolhardy volunteers climbed into their Cavor Balls and buzzed the red planet. They didn't do much damage, but it was Earth's first retaliative strike. In the movie, they were after the factories where the elements for the heat rays were being synthesised. In real life, they just flattened a couple of retirement nests and got rayed down. In *Mars Force*, I played the tyrannical Security Victor at the factories. I spent most of the film gloating over a crystalscope, looking at stock footage of the smoking plains where New York used to be. I also got to drool over a skinny terrestrial missionary, snivel in fear as the brave Earthmen flew over in their Christmas tree ornaments and be machine-gunned to death by John Garfield. It was typical propaganda shit, but it was a pretty good picture. It stands up a lot better than most of the other things I did back then.

I was typecast for the rest of the war. I've raped more nurses than any actor alive—although what I was supposed to see in you sandpaper-skinned bipeds is beyond me. And I did a lot of plotting, scheming, saluting, backstabbing, bombing, blasting, cackling, betraying, sneering and strutting. I saw more action than Patton and Rommel put together, and without ever stepping off the backlots. The furthest I ever went for a battle was Griffith Park. I had a whole set of shiny, slimy uniforms. I played every rank we had going. In *Heat Ray!*,

Kim Newman

I even got to play Uszthay, although that's like asking Mickey Mouse to play John the Baptist. I soon lost count of the number of times I had to swear to crush the puny planet Earth in my lesser tentacles. I got killed a lot. I was shot by Errol Flynn in *Desperate Journey*, bombed by Spencer Tracy in *Thirty Seconds Over Krba-Gnsk*, and John Wayne got me in *Soaring Tigers, The Sands of Grlshnk* and *The Fighting Seabees*. In *Lunaria*, Bogart plugs me as I reach for the crystalphone on the launch-field. Remember that one? Everyone says it's a classic. It got the Academy Award that year. Claude Rains asks Bogart why he came to Lunaria, and Bogart says he came for the atmosphere. 'But there's no atmosphere on the Moon,' says Rains. 'I was misinformed.' I wanted the role of the freedom fighter who floats off to Earth with Ingrid Bergman at the end, but Jack Warner chickened out of depicting a sympathetic Martie and they made the character into a Selenite. Paul Henried could never keep his antennae straight. I had to make do with being another Inferior War Victor. No one believed there were any Anti-Uszthay Martians. That's typical earthbound thinking.

Then the war ended, and suddenly there were no more Martian roles. In fact, suddenly there were no more Martians period. The allies did a pretty fair job of depopulating the old planet. Since then, we've been a dying race. We're feeble, really. Every time the 'flu goes round, I have to go to funerals. There was a rash of anti-war movies. There always is after the zapping is over. Remember *A Walk in the Dust* or *Terrestrial Invaders*? I didn't get work in those. All you ever saw of the Martian troops were bodies. There were plenty of newsreel scenes of big-eyed orphans waving their tentacles at the camera in front of the sludging ruins of their nests. Those movies didn't do any business. The whole solar system was tired of war. They started making musicals. I can't do what you people call dancing, so those were lean years. I did a bit of investing, and set up my own business. I thought I'd hit on the ideal combination. I opened a Martian bar and a kosher butcher's shop back-to-back. The Jews got the meat, and the Marties got the drain-ings. It was a good idea, and we did okay until the riots. I lost everything then, and went back to acting.

I did some dinner theatre. Small roles. I thought my best performance was as Dr Chasuble in *The Importance of Being Earnest*, but there weren't many managements willing to cast me in spite, rather than because of, my race. I tried to get the backing to put on *Othello* in modern dress with the Moor as a Martian, but no one was interested. When Stanley Kramer bought up *Worlds Apart*, the hot best-seller about the persecution of Martians on Earth, I put in a bid for the lead, but Stanley had to say no. By then, I was too associated with the stereotype Jimbo Martie. He said audiences wouldn't take me seriously. Maybe he was right, but I'd have liked to take a shot at it. As you must know, Ptyehshdneh got the part and went onto be the first nonterrestrial to walk off with the Best Actor statuette on Oscar night. I'm not bitter, but I can't help thinking that my career in the last twenty years would have been very different if Kramer had taken the chance. Ptyeh' is such a *pretty* Martie, if you know what I mean. Not much slime on his hide.

Of course, Willie K'ssth came back on television in the early 50s. They made twenty-six half-hour episodes with Tom Conway under the beak and me back as dumb Jimbo. The series is still in syndication on graveyard shift TV. I get fan mail from nostalgia-buff insomniacs and night watchmen all over the country. It's nice to know people notice you. I saw one of those episodes recently. It was a piece of shit. But at the time it was a job right? It didn't last long, and I was more or less on the skids for a couple of years. I was on relief between guest spots. I'm in a classic *Sergeant Bilko*, where they're trying to make a movie about the canal Bilko is supposed to have taken in the war. Doberman wins a Dream Date With a Movie Star in a contest and all the platoon try to get the ticket off him. Finally, Bilko gets the ticket and turns up at the Hollywood nightspot, and I turn out to be the Dream Date Star. Phil Silvers has a terrific talent, and it was nice just to be funny for a change. We worked out a good little routine with the drinks and the cocktail umbrellas. I'd like to have done more comedy, but when you've got tentacles producers don't think you can milk a laugh. I popped out of a box on *Laugh-In* once.

The sixties were rough, I guess. I had a little bit of a drink problem, but you must have heard about that. You've done your research, right? Well, skipping the messy parts of the story, I ended up in jail. It was only a couple of cows all told, but I exsanguinated them all right. No excuses. Inside, I got involved in the protest movement. I was in with lots of draft evaders. They gave me some LSD, and I wound up signing a lot of petitions and, outside, going on plenty of marches. Hell, everybody now thinks the War on Mercury was a waste of time, but the planet was gung-ho about it back then. Those little jelly-breathers never did anyone any harm, but you'd creamed one planet and got a taste for it. That's what I think. I did a bit of organizational work for the Aliens' League, and spoke on campuses. I was on President Kissinger's enemies list. I'm still proud of that.

I had a few film roles while all this was going on. Nothing spectacular, but I kept my face on the screen. I was the priest in *The Miracle of Mare Nostrum*, Elvis' partner in the spear-fishing business in *She Ain't Human*, and Doris Day's old boyfriend in *With Six You Get Eggroll*. The films were mostly pieces of shit. I'm unbilled in a couple of Sinatra-Martin movies because I knocked around with the Rat Pack for a couple of summers before I got politics. I get a tentacle down Angie Dickinson's *decolleté* in *Ocean's 11*. I know you're going to ask me about *Orbit Jocks*. I was just naive. Again, no excuses. When I shot my scenes, I thought it was a documentary. They had a whole fake script and everything. I took the job because of the trip to Mars. I'd never been before, and I wanted to discover my roots. I stood in front of landmarks reading out stuff about history. Then the producers spliced in all the hardcore stuff later. I don't know if you've seen the film, but the Martian in all the sex scenes is not me. It's hard to tell with a steel cowl, but he's got all his tentacles.

I'm not retired. I won't retire until they plough me under. But I'm being more selective. I'll take a picture if I can pal around with any of the other old-timers. I was in something called *Vampire Coyotes* last year, with Leslie Howard, Jean Harlow and Sidney Greenstreet. I don't mind working on low-budget horror movies. It's more like the old days. The big studios these days are just cranking out bland television crap. I was asked to be a guest villain on *Columbo*, but I turned it down and they got Robert Culp instead. I went to a science fiction film convention last year. Forrest J Ackerman interviewed me on stage. He's a great guy. When I finally turn tentacles-up, I'm having it in my will that I be stuffed and put in his basement with the Creature From the Black Lagoon and all that other neat stuff. Lon would have gone for that too, but humans are prejudiced against auto-icons. It's a pity. I hope Forry can make do with just Lon's liver. It was the heart and soul of the man anyway.

After this, I've got a three-picture deal with Al. That's not as big a thing as it sounds, since he'll shoot them simultaneously. *Blood of the Brain Eaters, Jessie's Girls* and *Martian Exorcist*. Then, I might go to the Philippines and make this movie they want me to do with Nancy Kwan. Okay, so it'll be a piece of shit . . .

If I had it all over again, do you know what? I'd do everything different. For a start, I'd take dancing lessons

When I wrote this, I thought nobody would be interested enough in film arcana to publish it. But after David Pringle put it in Interzone, *it was the first piece of mine to be picked (by Gardner Dozois) for a* Year's Best *anthology. I originally hesitated because 'Famous Monsters' is not a story but a monologue (if really suicidal, I'd have gone the Robert Browning route and done the whole thing in verse); its (selective) acceptance has encouraged me to play faster and looser with the forms and content of what I write. This may not entirely be a good thing. I read Howard Waldrop's 'Night of the Cooters' and 'The Passing of the Western' after writing 'Famous Monsters'; a good thing since 'Cooters' tackles related subject matter while 'Western' has a similar solution to the problem of telling its story. H.G. Wells is, of course, one of my major influences, witness the cameos for a Martian War Machine and Dr Moreau in my novels* Jago *and* Anno Dracula. *This was one of my first attempts to come to terms with his legacy. Intended as a 'fun' piece, there is (as usual) a seam of seri-ousness in the rescrambling of actual attitudes in Hollywood and Society at Large to various types of differentness, ranging from the patronising to the hysterical. I wondered how it felt to be Peter Lorre or Conrad Veidt, escaping Hitler only to wind up wearing Nazi uniforms in war movies. Also, it struck me as an interesting omission, in* War of the Worlds *and most subsequent alien invasion stories, that writers rarely speculate on what would happen* after *the bug-eyed monsters had been defeated.*

ORGAN

DONORS

She came out of the lift into Reception and heard there'd been another accident outside. Beyond sepia-tinted doors, a crowd gathered. People kneeled, as if pressing someone to the pavement. Heidi was phoning an ambulance. A man crouched over the fallen person, white shirt stained red, head shaking angrily. The picture was silent, a gentle whir of air conditioning like the flicker of a projector. Sally walked to the doors, calmly hugging file folders to her chest. She looked through heavy brown glass.

Without shock, she knew it was Connor. She could only see feet, still kicking in the gutter. White trainers with shrieking purple-and-yellow laces. His furry legs were bare. Tight black cycle shorts ripped up a seam, showing a thin triangle of untanned skin.

A gulp of thought came: at least their where-are-we-going? lunch was off. She choked back relief, tried to unthink it to limbo. Then craziness kicked in. She dropped her folders and waded through paper, pushing apart the doors. Outside in Soho Square, noise fell on her like a flock of pigeons. Everyone shouted, called, talked. A siren whined rhythmically.

A dozen yards away, a van was on its side, a dazed and bloody man being pulled free. The bicycle was a tangle of metal and rubber. In the broken frame, she saw, squashed, the yellow plastic drinks container she'd bought him. A satchel of video tapes lay in the gutter.

'Connor,' she said, '*Connor!*'

'Don't look, love,' someone said, extending an arm across her chest.

People shifted out of her way, parting like stage curtains. Heat burst in her head, violet flashes dotted her vision. Her ankles and knees ceased to work. The ground shifted like a funhouse ride. Connor's head was a lumpy smear on the pavement, tire track of patterned blood streaking away. She was limp, held up by others. Her head lolled and she saw angry blue sky. Buildings all around were skyscrapers. She was at the bottom of a concrete canyon. Darkness poured in.

————

At her first interview, Tiny Chiselhurst had been chuffed by her *curriculum vitae*. Like everyone for the last twelve years, he didn't expect a private investigator to look like her. She told him yes, she still had her license, and no, she didn't own a gun. Not any more.

Her independence was a Recession casualty. She wound up the Sally Rhodes Agency and escaped with no major debts, but there was still the mortgage. None of the big security/investigation firms were hiring, so she was forced to find another job her experience qualified her for. Being a researcher was essentially what she was used to: phoning strangers, asking questions, rushing about in heavy traffic, rummaging through microfiche. There were even seductive improvements: working in television, she could rush about in minicabs and retire her much-worn bus-train-tube pass.

On her first day, she was ushered into the open-plan *Survival Kit* office and given a desk behind one of the strange fluted columns that wound their way up through the Mythwrhn Building. Her work station was next to April Treece, an untidy but well-spoken redhead.

'Don't be surprised if you find miniature bottles in the drawers,' April told her. 'The previous tenant went alky.'

Sally had little to move in. No photographs, no toys, no gun. Just a large desk diary and a contacts book. Her mother had given her a Filofax once, but it was somewhere at home unused.

'Welcome to the TV Trenches,' April said, lighting the next cigarette from the dog-end of the last, 'the business that chews you up and spits you out.'

'Why work here, then?'

'Glamour, dahling,' she said, scattering ash over the nest of post-it notes around her terminal. The other woman was a year or so younger than Sally, in her early thirties. She wore a crushed black velvet hat with a silver arrow pin.

'They put all the new bugs next to me. Like an initiation.'

Their desks were in a kind of recess off the main office, with no window. Sally hadn't yet worked out the building. It seemed a fusion of post-modern neo-brutalism and art deco chintz. In Reception, there was a plaque honouring an award won by Constant Drache for the design. She suspected that, after a while, the place would make her head ache.

'Need protection?' April said, opening the cavernous bottom drawer of her desk. 'We did an item last series and were deluged with samples. Have some Chums.'

She dumped a large carton of condoms on Sally's desk. Under cellophane, Derek Leech, multi-media magnate, was on the pack, safe sex instructions in a speech balloon issuing from his grin.

'Careful,' she warned. 'They rip if you get too excited. We had the brand thoroughly road-tested. The office toy boy was sore for months.'

Sally looked at the carton, unsure how to react. Naturally that was when Tiny Chiselhurst dropped by to welcome her to the team.

————

She woke up on a couch in Reception. She saw the painted ceiling, a graffiti nightmare of surreal squiggles and souls in torment. Then she saw April.

'Bender tried loosening your clothes,' she said, referring to the notorious office lech, 'but I stopped him before he got too far.'

April's eye-liner had run but she'd stopped crying.

Sally sat up, swallowing a spasm. Her stomach heaved but settled.

April hugged her, quickly, then let her go.

'Do you want a cab? To go home?'

She shook her head. She buttoned up her cardigan and waited for a tidal wave of grief-pain-horror. Nothing hit. She stood, April with her. She looked around Reception. Plants spilled out of the lead rhomboid arrangement that passed as a pot. Framed photographs of Tiny and the other presenters, marked with the logos of their programs, were arranged behind Heidi's desk.

'Sal?'

She felt fine. The buzz of worry-irritation which usually cluttered her head was washed away. All morning, she'd been picking through viewing statistics. Her impending Connor discussion prevented concentration; she'd had to go through the stats too many times, filling her mind with useless figures.

She remembered everything but didn't feel it. She might have had total amnesia and instantly relearned every detail about her life. Her memory was all there but didn't necessarily have anything to do with her.

'Connor is dead?' She had to ask.

With a nod, April confirmed it. 'Tiny says so long as you're back to work tomorrow afternoon for the off-line, you're free.'

'I don't need time away,' she said.

April was startled. 'Are you sure? You've had a shock, lovie, you're entitled to be a zombie.'

Sally shook her head, certain. 'Maybe later.'

———

Although April introduced Connor as the 'office toy boy', it was a joke. He was tall, twenty-one, and trying to earn enough as a bike messenger to go back to college. Like everyone (except Sally), he wanted a career in television. Zipping in and out of Soho gridlock biking memos, sandwiches, video-tape and mysterious parcels between production companies was his way of starting at the bottom. He was one of the lean young people in bright lycra who congregated in Soho

Square, ever alert for a walkie-talkie call. He was freelance but Mythwrhn was his major employer. There were a lot like him.

Sally first slept with him on a Friday night, after a party to mark the first transmission of the series. It had been a long time for her and she was flattered by his enthusiasm. Besides he was kind of fun.

As he poked about her flat early next morning like a dog marking territory, she wondered if she'd made a mistake. She hid under the duvet as he wandered, unselfconsciously and interestingly naked, in and out of the room, chattering at her. He said he was 'looking for clues'. April had told everyone Sally used to be a private eye, and the Philippa Marlowe jokes were wearing thin.

She checked the bedside clock and saw it was before seven. Also on the table was the carton of Chums, one corner wrenched open. They'd come in handy after all. It'd have been hard to get aroused if she'd thought of Derek Leech leering off the pack at her. She turned the pack, putting Leech's face to the wall.

Connor jumped on her bed, eager to get to it again but she had to get up to pee. As she left the bedroom, she realised he must be looking at her as she had looked at him. Last night, it had been dark. Putting on a dressing gown would kill the moment, so she went nude into the bathroom. After relieving herself, she looked in the long mirror and wasn't too disappointed. When she was Connor's age, she'd been almost chubby; with the years, she'd exercised and worried away the roundness. April said she envied Sally her cheekbones.

When she got back to the bedroom, Connor had already fit another condom over his swelling penis.

'I started without you,' he said.

———

Tiny told her she didn't have to come to that week's production meeting, but didn't mean it. Sally was still waiting to wake up an emotional basket case but it hadn't happened yet. She slept through the alarm more often and had stomach troubles, as if suffering from persistent jet-lag, but her thoughts were clear. She even dealt with mental time-bombs like the travelling toothbrush left in her bathroom. Perhaps after all these years, she was used to weirdness. Maybe she couldn't survive without a stream of the unexpected, the tragic, the grotesque.

Networked on ITV at eight on Friday evenings, *Survival Kit* was an aggressive consumer show, proposing that life in the late twentieth century was frighteningly random and unspeakably dangerous. Tiny Chiselhurst was at once editor and presenter, and the show, in its fifth season, was the cash-cow that kept Mythwrhn Productions, a reasonably-successful independent, listed as rising. This series, Sally had helped Tiny, whose sarky humour was what kept viewers watching, expose a crooked modelling agency run on white slavery lines. Now she was switched to something that had little to do with the show itself and so was primarily an ornament at these meetings, called upon to report privately afterwards.

Tiny sat in the best chair at the round table as researchers, assistants, producers, directors and minions found places. He seemed to be made entirely of old orange corduroy, with a shaggy seventies mop and moustache. The meeting room was a windowless inner sanctum, eternally lit by grey lights, a crossbreed of padded cell and A-Bomb shelter. After reviewing last week's program, doling out few complements and making Lydia Marks cry again, Tiny asked for updates on items-in-progress. Useless Bruce, fill-in presenter and on-screen reporter, coughed up botulism stats. Tiny told him to keep on the trail. The item hadn't yet taken shape but was promising. What that meant, Sally knew, was that no sexy case—a ten-year-old permanently disabled by fish fingers, say—had come to light. When there was a pathetic human face to go with the story, the item would go ahead.

Finally there was the slot when people were supposed to come up with ideas. This was where performance could be best monitored, since ideas were the currency of television. She'd begun to realise actual execution of an item could be completely botched; what Tiny remembered was who had the idea in the first place. Useless Bruce was well known for ideas that never quite worked.

'I was talking to a bloke at a launch the other night,' said April.

Someone said something funny, and she stared them silent. 'He turned out to be a corporate psychiatrist at one of the investment banks, talks people out of jumping off the top floor when they lose a couple of million quid. Anyway, he mentioned this thing, "Sick Building Syndrome", which sounded worth a think.'

Tiny gave her the nod and April gathered notes from a folder.

'There are companies which suffer from problems no one can explain. Lots of days lost due to illness, way above the norm. Also, a high turn-over of staff, nervous breakdowns, personal problems, *sturfe* like that. Even suicides, murders. Other companies in exactly the same business with exactly the same pressures breeze through with *pas de* hassles. It might be down to the buildings they work in, a quirk of architecture that traps ill feelings. You know, bad vibrations.'

Sally noticed Tiny was counterfeiting interest. For some reason, he was against April's idea. But he let her speak.

'If we found one of these places, it might make an item.'

'It's very visual, Ape,' said Bender, an associate producer, enthusiasm blooming. 'We could dress it up with *Poltergeist* effects. Merchant bank built over a plague pit, maybe.'

Tiny shook his head. This was the man who'd stayed up all night with a camera crew waiting for the UFOs to make corn circles.

'No,' he said. 'I don't think that suits us.'

'Completely over-the-top,' Bender said, enthusiasm vanishing. 'We're a serious program.'

'Thank you, April,' Tiny said. 'But Bender has a point. Maybe last series, we could have done this paranormal hoo-hah . . .'

'This isn't a spook story,' she protested. 'It's psychology.'

Tiny waved his hand, brushing the idea away. 'Remember the big picture. With the franchise bid, we mustn't do anything to make the ITC look askance. It's up to us to demonstrate that we pass the quality threshold.'

April sat back, bundling now-useless notes. Sally was used to this: it was all down to Tiny and he could be as capricious as any Roman Emperor at the games.

Roger the Replacement, one of the directors, had noticed a dry piece in the *Financial Times* about a travel firm considered a bad investment, which suggested further digging might turn up something filmable. British holidaymakers sent to unbuilt hotels in war zones. Tiny gave him a thumbs-up, and, since April wasn't doing anything, assigned her to work the idea. The meeting was wound up.

In the Ladies, Sally found April gripping a sink with both hands, staring down at the plug, muttering 'I hate him I hate him I hate him hate hate hate hate'.

———

After her exercise class, they had *al fresco* lunch in Soho Square. In summer, it was a huge picnic area; now, in early autumn, office workers—publishing, film, television, advertising—melted away, leaving the square to tramps and runners. He had sandwiches while she dipped Kettle Chips into cottage cheese and pineapple. Connor always pushed his idea that *Survival Kit* do a week-in-the-life-of-a-wino item, unsubtly pressuring Sally to take it into a production meeting. She'd tried to tell him it'd been done before but his excitement always prevailed. Today he pointed out the 'characters' who pan-handled in Soho, explaining their fierce territoriality.

'You don't notice til you're on the streets, Sal. It's a parallel world.'

On a bench nearby sat two men of roughly the same age, a pony-tail in a Gaultier suit and a crusty with filth-locks and biro tattoos. Each pretended the other didn't exist.

'It's a pyramid. At the bottom, people get crushed.'

He was right but it wasn't *Kit*. Besides, she was irritated: was he interested in her mainly as a conduit to the inner circle? With one of his lightning subject-shifts, Connor made a grab, sticking his ribena-sweetened tongue down her throat. His walkie-talkie chirruped and he broke off the kiss. It was just past two and lunch hour was officially over. He frowned as a voice coughed in his ear.

'It's for you,' he said.

Knowing there'd be trouble, she took the receiver. Tiny had been after her to use a portable phone. She was summoned to the Penthouse. Mairi, Tiny's p.a., conveyed the message. Tiny wanted to chat. Sally assumed she was going to be fired and dutifully trudged across the square to Mythwrhn.

She stabbed the top button and the lift jerked up through the building. Tiny had a suite of offices on the top floor which she hadn't visited since her interview. Mairi met her at the lift and offered her decaf, which she refused. She wondered if the girl disapproved of her and Connor. She had the idea it wasn't done to dally out of your age range or income bracket. At least, not if you were a woman. All the young middle-age male production staff had permanent lusts for the fresh-from-school female secretaries, runners and receptionists.

Tiny's all-glass office was a frozen womb. He sat behind his desk, leaning back. She noticed again the figurine on its stand: a bird-headed, winged woman, throat open in a silent screech. It was an old piece, but not as old as some.

'Know what that is?' Tiny asked rhetorically, prepared to explain and demonstrate his erudition.

'It's the Mythwrhn,' she pre-empted. 'An ancient bird goddess-demon, probably Ugric. Something between a harpy and an angel.'

Tiny was astonished. 'You're the first person who came in here knowing that . . .'

'I had an interesting career.'

'You must tell me about it sometime.'

'I must.'

The last time she'd seen a statuette of the Mythwrhn, she'd been on a nasty case involving black magic and death. It had been one of her few exciting involvements, although the excitement was not something she wished to repeat.

Without being asked, she took a seat. Apart from Tiny's puffily upholstered black leather egg-shape, all the chairs in the office were peculiar assemblages of chrome tubing and squeaky rubber. As Tiny made cat's cradles with his fingers, she was certain he'd fire her.

'I've been thinking about you, Sally,' he said. 'You're an asset but I'm not sure how well-placed you are.'

Her three-month trial wasn't even up, so she wasn't on a contract yet. No redundancy payment. At least the dole office was within walking distance of the flat. The poll tax would be a problem, but she should qualify for housing benefit.

'Your experience is unique.'

Tiny's confrontational, foot-in-the-door interviews with dodgy characters put him in more danger in any one series of *Survival Kit* than she had been in all her years of tracing the heirs of intestate decedents, finding lost cats and body-guarding custody case kids. But he was still impressed by a real life private dick. April said the term was sexist and called her a private clit.

'You know about the franchise auction?'

The independent television franchises, which granted a right to broadcast to the companies that made up the ITV network, were being renegotiated. There was currently much scurrying and scheming in the industry as everyone had to justify their existence or give way to someone else. There was controversy over the system, with criticism of the government decision that franchises be awarded to the highest bidder. The Independent Television Commission, the body with power of life and death over the network, had belatedly instituted a policy of partially assessing bids for quality of service rather than just totting up figures. In the run-up to the auction, battles raged up and down the country, with regional companies assailed by challengers. More money than anyone could believe was being poured into the franchise wars. A worry had been raised that the winners were likely to have spent so much on their bids they'd have nothing left over to spend on the actual programs.

'Mythwrhn is throwing in its hat,' Tiny said.

For an independent production company, no matter how financially solid, to launch a franchise bid on its own would be like Lichtenstein declaring war on Switzerland.

'We'll be the most visible element of a consortium. Polymer

Records have kicked in, and Mausoleum Films.'

Both were like Mythwrhn, small but successful. Polymer used to be an indie label and now had the corner on the heavier metallurgists, notably the 'underground' cult band Loud Shit. Mausoleum distributed French art and American splatter; they were known for the *Where the Bodies Are Buried* series, although Sally knew they'd funelled some of their video profits into British film production, yielding several high profile movies she, along with vast numbers of other people, hadn't wanted to see.

'Deep pockets,' she commented, 'but not deep enough.'

Tiny snapped all his fingers. 'Very sharp, Sally. We have major financial backing, from a multi-media conglomerate who, for reasons of its own, can't be that open about their support. I'm talking newspapers, films and satellite.'

That narrowed it down considerably. To a face the size of a condom packet, in fact.

'We're contesting London, which puts us up against GLT. So it's not going to be a walk-over.'

Greater London Television was one of the keystones of the ITV net, long-established monolith with three shows in the ratings Top Ten, two quizzes and a soap. In television terms, it was, like its audience, middle-aged verging on early retirement. Mythwrhn had a younger demographic.

'I'd like you to be part of the bid,' Tiny said.

She was surprised. 'I'm not a programmer or an accountant.'

'Your special talents can be useful. We'll need a deal of specialised research. In wrapping our package, it'd be handy to have access to certain information. We need to know GLT's weaknesses to help us place our shots.'

This sounded very like industrial espionage. As a field, IE never appealed to Sally. Too much involved affording the client 'plausible deniability' and being paid off to sit out jail sentences.

'You'll keep your desk and your official credit on *Kit* but we'll gradually divert you to the real work. Interested?'

Thinking of the Muswell Hill DSS, she nodded. Tiny grinned wide and extended a hand, but was distracted by a ringing telephone. It was a red contraption aside from his three normal phones, suggesting a hot-line to the Kremlin or the Batcave.

Tiny scooped up the receiver, and said 'Derek, good to hear from you . . .'

———————

'Since the franchise *schmeer*,' April said, a drip of mayonnaise on her chin, 'the whole building has gone batty.'

Sally ate her half-bap in silence. She wasn't the only one diverted from usual duties and hustled off to secret meetings.

'They should put valium dispensers in the loos.'

When the consortium announced their intention to contest London, GLT replied by issuing a complacent press release. Ronnie Shand, host of GLT's 'whacky' girls' bowling quiz *Up Your Alley*, made a joke about Tiny's ego in his weekly monologue. High-level execs were heaping public praise on programs made by their direst enemies. The dirty tricks had started when GLT, alone of the ITV net, pre-empted *Survival Kit* for a Royal Family special. As payback, Tiny had ordered Weepy Lydia to inflate a tedious offshore trust story involving several GLT board members into a majorly juicy scandal item. In the mean time, the best he could do was give five pounds to any office minion who called up the ITV duty officer and logged a complaint about a GLT show. It had the feel of a phoney war.

'Bender's wife chucked him out again last night,' April said. 'Found him writing silly letters to Pomme.'

Pomme was an eighteen-year-old p.a. who looked like a cross between Princess Diana and Julia Roberts. If it weren't for her Liza Doolittle accent, she'd have been easy to hate.

'He kipped in the basement of the building, blind drunk. Must have walked into a wall by the look of his face. I hope he keeps the scars.'

Six months before Sally joined the company, when April was

young and naive, she had slept with Bender. It hadn't done either of them any good.

'Are you all right?'

People kept asking her that. Sally nodded vigorously. April touched her cheek, as if it'd enable her to take Sally's emotional temperature.

The funeral had been yesterday. Sally had sent a floral tribute but thought it best not to go. Connor's friends would think she was his aunt or someone. She had never met his parents and didn't especially want to.

From the sandwich shop, Sally saw the square. A knot of messengers hung about the gazebo, all in lycra shorts and squiggly T-shirts. Sprawled on benches, they let long legs dangle as they worked pain out of their knees. Some, unlike Connor, had helmets like plastic colanders. Staff at Charing Cross Hospital had a nickname for Central London cycle messengers: organ donors. Scrapes and spills were an inevitable part of accelerated lives. And so was human wastage. Ironically Connor had carried an donor card: he was buried without corneas and one kidney.

'Come on,' said April, looking at her pink plastic watch, 'back to the front . . .'

If she had doubts about the identity of the consortium's financial backer, they were dispelled by the front page of the *Comet*, tabloid flagship of Derek Leech's media empire. Ronnie Shand was caught in the glare of flash-bulbs, guiltily emerging from a hotel with a girl in dark glasses. The story, two hundred words of patented *Comet* prose, alleged *Up Your Alley* was fixed. Contestants who put out for Shand (51, married with three children) were far more likely to score a strike and take home a fridge-freezer or a holiday in Barbados. An inset showed Ronnie happy with his family in an obviously posed publicity shot. Inside the paper, the girl, an aspiring model, could be seen without clothes, a sidebar giving details about 'my sizzling nights with TV's family man'. Shand was unavailable for comment but GLT made a statement that *Up Your Alley* would be replaced by repeats of *Benny Hill* while an internal investigation was conducted. Sally wondered whether they'd investigate the allegations or witch-hunt their staff for the traitor who'd tipped off the *Comet*.

Tiny was a bundle of suppressed mirth at their meeting and chuckled to himself as she reported. She'd carried out a thorough, boring check of the finances of GLT's component parts, and discovered profits from hit shows had been severely drained by a couple of disastrous international co-productions, The *Euro-Doctors* and *The Return of Jason King*. The interruption of *Up Your Alley* was a severe embarrassment. GLT must be hurting far more than their bland press releases suggested.

'If it comes to it, we can outspend the bastards,' Tiny said. 'We'll have to make sacrifices. Congratulations, Sally. I judge you well.'

There was something seductive about covert work. Setting aside moral qualms about the franchise system and relegating to a deep basement any idea of serving the viewing public, she could look at the situation and see any number of moves which would be to Mythwrhn's advantage. Taken as a game, it was compulsive. It being television, it was easy to believe no real people at all were affected by any action she might suggest or take.

'I've been looking at *Cowley Mansions*,' she said, referring to GLT's long-running thrice-weekly soap set in a Brixton block of flats. It was said GLT wouldn't lose their franchise because John Major didn't want to go down in history as the Prime Minister who took away the *Mansions*.

Tiny showed interest.

'I've not got paper back-up but I heard a whisper that GLT took a second mortgage to finance *The Euro-Doctors* and put the *Mansions* on the block.'

'Explain.'

'To sucker in the Italians and the French, GLT threw in foreign rights to the *Mansions* with the deal. Also a significant slice of the domestic ad revenues for a fixed period.'

Tiny whistled.

'As you know, TéVéZé, the French co-producer, went bust at the beginning of the year and was picked up for a song by a British-based concern which turns out to be a subsidiary of Derek Leech Enterprises.'

Tiny sat up.

'If I were, say, Derek Leech, and I wanted to gain control of the *Mansions*, I think I could do it by upping my holdings in an Italian cable channel by only two percent, and by buying, through a third party, the studio and editing facilities GLT have currently put on the market to get fast cash. Years ago, in one of those grand tax write-off gestures, slices of the *Mansions* pie were given in name to those GLT sub-divisions and when they separate from the parent company, the slices go too. Then, all I'd have to do to get a majority ownership would be to approach the production team and the cast and offer to triple salaries in exchange for their continued attachment. I might have to change the name of the program slightly, say by officially calling it *The Mansions*, to get round GLT's underlying rights.'

Tiny pulled open a drawer and took out a neat bundle of fifty-pound notes. He tossed it across his broad desk and it slid into Sally's lap.

'Buy yourself a frock,' he said.

In the lift, there was something wrong with a connection. The light-strip buzzed and flickered. Sally had a satisfaction high but also an undertone of nervous guilt. It was as if she had just taken part in a blood initiation and was now expected to serve forever the purpose of Kali the Destroyer.

———

As usual, there was nothing on television. She flicked through the four terrestrial channels: Noel Edmonds, tadpole documentary, *Benny Hill* (ha ha), putting-up-a-shelf. Like all Mythwrhn employees, she'd been fixed up with a dish gratis as a frill of the alliance with Derek Leech, so she zapped through an additional seven Cloud 9 satellite channels: bad new film, bad old film, Russian soccer, softcore in

German, car ad, Chums commercial disguised as an AIDS documentary, shopping. After heating risotto, she might watch a *Rockford Files* from the stash she'd taped five years ago. James Garner was the only TV private eye she had time for: the fed-up expression he had whenever anyone got him in trouble was the keynote of her entire life.

The telephone rang. She scooped up the remote, pressing it between shoulder and ear as she manoeuvered around her tiny kitchen.

'Sally Rhodes,' she said. 'No divorce work.'

'Ah, um,' said a tiny voice, 'Miss, um, Ms, Rhodes. This is Eric Glover . . . Connor's Dad.'

She paused in mid-pour and set down the packet of spicy rice.

'Mr Glover, hello,' she said. 'I'm sorry I couldn't make . . .'

There was an embarassed (embarassing) pause.

'No, that's all right. Thank you for the flowers. They were lovely. I knew you were Connor's friend. He said things about you.'

She had no response.

'It's about the accident,' Eric Glover said. 'You were a witness?'

'No, I was there after.' When he was dead.

'There's a fuss about the insurance.'

'Oh.'

'They can't seem to find the van driver. Or the van.'

'It was overturned, a write-off. The police must have details.'

'Seems there was a mix-up.'

'It was just a delivery van. Sliding doors. I don't know the make.'

She tried to rerun the picture in her mind. She could see the dazed driver crawling out of the door, helped by a young man with a shaved head.

'I didn't suppose you'd know, but I had to ask.'

'Of course. If I remember . . .'

'No worry.'

There had been a logo on the side of the van. On the door.

'Good-bye now, and thanks again.'

Eric Glover hung up.

It had been a Mythwrhn logo, a prettified bird-woman. Or something similar. She was sure. The driver had been a stranger, but the van was one of the company's small fleet.

Weird. Nobody had mentioned it.

Water boiled over in the rice pan. Sally struggled with the knob of the gas cooker, turning the flame down.

———

A couple of calls confirmed what Eric Glover told her. It was most likely the van driver would be taken to Charing Cross, where Connor was declared dead, but the hospital had no record of his admission. It was difficult to find one nameless patient in any day's intake, but the nurse she spoke to remembered Connor without recalling anyone brought in at the same time. Sally had only seen the man for a moment: white male, thirties-forties, stocky-tubby, blood on his face. The production manager said none of the vans had been out that day and, yes, they were all garaged where they were supposed to be, and why are you interested? As she made more calls, checking possible hospitals and trying to find a policeman who'd filed an accident report, she fiddled with a loose strand of cardigan wool, resisting the temptation to tug hard and unravel the whole sleeve.

April had dumped her bag and coat on her chair but was not at her desk. That left Sally alone in her alcove, picking at threads when she should be following through the leads Tiny had given her. She had a stack of individual folders containing neatly-typed allegations and bundles of photocopied 'evidence', all suggesting chinks in the Great Wall of GLT. The presenter of a holiday morning kid's show might have a conviction under another name for 'fondling' little girls. A hairy-chested supporting actor on *The Euro-Doctors*, considered to have 'spin-off potential' even after the failure of the parent series, was allegedly a major player in the Madrid gay bondage scene. And, sacrilegiously, it was suggested the producer of a largely unwatched motoring program had orchestrated a write-in campaign to save it from cancellation. In case Sally wondered where these tid-bits came from, she'd already found an overlooked sticker with the DLE logo and a 'please return to the files of the *Comet*' message; checking other files, she found dust-and-fluff-covered gluey circles that showed where similar stickers had been peeled off. So, apart from everything else, she was in charge of Tiny's Dirty Tricks Department. She wondered if G. Gordon Liddy had got sick to his stomach. This morning, she had thrown up last night's risotto. She should have learned to cook.

Bender popped his head into the alcove. When he saw only her, his face fell.

'Have you seen Ape?'

'She was here,' Sally told him. 'She must be in the building.'

Bender looked as if he'd pulled a couple of consecutive twenty-four hour shifts.

'No matter,' he said, obviously lying. 'This is for her.'

He gave her a file, which she found room for on her desk.

'She's not really supposed to have this, so don't leave it lying around. Give it to her personally.'

Bender, a tall man, never looked a woman in the face. His eyeline was always directed at her chest. In an awkward pause, Sally arranged her cardigan around her neck to cover any exposed skin. The associate producer was a balding schoolboy.

'We were all sorry about, um, you know . . .'

Sally thanked him, throat suddenly warm. She didn't know why Bender was loitering. Had April taken up with him again? Considering the vehemence of her comments, it was not likely. Or maybe it was.

'If you see . . . when you see Ape, tell her . . .'

There was definitely something weird going down. Bender really looked bad. His usual toadying smoothness was worn away. He had an angry red mark on his ring-finger. It had probably had to be sawn free, and serve him right.

'Tell her to return the files a.s.a.p. It's important.'

When he left, she decided to try work therapy. A minion named Roebuck was reputedly interested in being bribed to let Mythwrhn peek at GLT's post-franchise proposals. He'd contacted Tiny and it was down to her to check his standing. Being suspicious, she guessed Roebuck was her opposite number in GLT's Spook Dept trying to slip the consortium dud information. She only had a name and she wanted an employment history. There were several people she could phone and—since everyone in television had at some point worked for, or at least applied to work for, everyone else—her first obvious choice was Mythwrhn's own personnel manager. If he had Roebuck's c.v. on file, it might have clues as to his contacts or loyalties.

As she bent over in her chair to reach her internal directory from her bottom drawer, her stomach heaved. Gulping back sick, she hurried to the Ladies.

———

One loo was occupied but the other was free. Apart from a mid-morning cup of tea, there was nothing to come up but clear fluid. It wasn't much of a spasm and settled down almost immediately. She washed her face clean and started to rebuild her make-up. The lighting in the Ladies was subdued and the decor was ugly, walls covered in wavy lumps like an ice cave. She supposed it had been designed to prevent loitering.

Pomme came in for a pee. She greeted Sally cheerfully, and, after a quick and painless tinkle, chatted as she made a kiss-mouth and retouched her lips.

'That bleedin' door is stuck again,' Pomme said, nodding at the occupied stall. 'Or someone has been in there for a two hour crap.'

Sally looked at the shut door. There was no gap at the bottom to show feet.

'Have you noticed how that happens in this building?' Pomme said. 'Doors lock when you ain't lookin', or come unlocked. The lifts have lay-overs in the Twilight Zone. Even them security keys don't work most of the time. Must be bleedin' haunted.'

The p.a. left, her face requiring considerably less help than Sally's. Finally, Sally was satisfied. She put her make-up things back in her bag.

Turning to leave, she heard a muttering.

'Hello,' she asked the closed door.

There was a fumbling and the 'occupied' flag changed. The door pulled inwards.

'April,' she said, looking.

The woman lolled on the closed toilet, eyes fluttering. She'd had a bad nosebleed and her man's dress shirt was bloodied. The bottom half of her face was caked with dried blood and flecked with white powder. Sally hadn't known she did coke. Or that things could get so bad with a supposedly 'fun' drug. April tried to speak but could only gargle. She pinched her nose and winced, snorting blood.

Sally wondered if she should get two tampons from the dispenser and shove them up April's nose. Instead, she wet a paper towel and tried to clean April's face. Her friend was as compliant as an exhausted three-year-old. Most of the blood was sticky on the floor of the stall.

'Pressure,' April said, over and over, repeating the word like a mantra. 'Pressure, pressure, pressure . . .'

Sally wondered how she was going to get April out of the building and home without anyone noticing. She told April to stay while she went and got her coat and bag. When she came back, April was standing and almost coherent.

'Sal,' she said, smiling as if she hadn't seen her for days, 'things are just fine up here. Except for . . .'

Sally tried to put April's hat on her, but she wasn't comfortable and kept tilting it different ways, examining herself in the mirror. Her shoulders heaved as if she alone could hear music and wanted to dance. Sally settled the coat around April's shoulders and steered her out of the loo.

The lift was on the floor, so she was able to get April straight in. If she could get her down to Reception and out into the square and find a cab, she could say April was taken ill. A nasty gynaecological problem would go unquestioned. Those were mysteries men didn't want to penetrate.

She stabbed the ground floor button and the doors closed. If they got quickly past Heidi, she could limit the damage. But the lift was going up, she realised. To the Penthouse. April was almost writhing now, and chanting 'pressure, pressure, pressure' until the word lost all meaning.

She slipped an arm around April's waist and tried to hold her still. April laughed as if tickled and a half-moustache of blood dribbled from one nostril. The doors parted and Tiny got in. He was hunched over in an unfamiliar position of subservience, grinning with desperate sincerity as he looked up to his companion. The other man, a human reptile of indeterminate age and indistinct features, was someone Sally recognised from the front of a condom packet.

'Sally, April,' Tiny said, so overwhelmed by his master's presence that he didn't notice their state, 'have you met Derek?'

Sally prayed to be teleported to Japan. The magnate, who kept going in and out of focus as if it were unwise to look at him with the naked eye, smiled a barracuda smile that seemed to fill the lift. She'd always thought of Derek Leech as a James Bond villain, with a high-tech hide-out in an extinct volcano and a missile silo concealed beneath his glass pyramid HQ in London Docklands. A human spider at the heart of a multi-media web, he sucked unimaginable monies from the millions who bought his papers, watched his television, made love with his protection, voted for his bought-and-paid-for politicians. But in person, he was just another well-groomed suit.

Leech nodded at them. Sally tried a weak smile, and April, snorting back blood and residual traces of nose powder, radiated warmth and love before fainting. She slithered through Sally's grasp and collapsed on the floor, knees bunched up against her breasts.

'That's happened before,' Leech said. 'Embarassing, really.'

————

Three days into April's 'leave', Bender went up to the Penthouse while Tiny was out recording an interview about the franchise bid. After voiding his bowels on Tiny's granite-slab desk-top and hurling the Mythwrhn statuette through the picture window, he crawled out through shattered glass and stood on the narrow sill while a crowd gathered below. Then, flapping his arms like the failed Wright Brother, he tried to fly over Soho Square. Ten yards from the persistent smear that marked the site of Connor's death, Bender fell to asphalt, neck broken.

It had not been unexpected, somehow. Sally noticed people were marginally less shocked and surprised by Bender than they'd been by Connor. The office had a wartime feel; the troops kept their heads down and tried not to know too much about their comrades. Everyone secretly looked for jobs somewhere else.

Roger the Replacement went into hospital after a severe angina attack. He was thirty-eight. While he was away, his wife came to clear out his things and told Sally that he now planned to take a year off to consider his career options.

'What's the point,' the woman said. 'If he's dead, he can't spend it.'

'True,' she conceded.

Tiny took to wandering around chewing his moustache, checking and double-checking everyone's work. Still wrapped up 101% in the franchise bid, he suddenly became acutely aware that Mythwrhn's current product would influence the ITC decision. The consequences of being blamed for failure would be unthinkable. Off to one side on 'other projects', she was spared the worst but the *Survival Kit* team suffered badly from the sudden attack of caution. Items toiled on for months were suddenly dropped, wasting hundreds of hours; others, rejected out of hand, were re-activated, forcing researchers to redo work that had been binned. In one case, the company was brought very close to Lawsuit County as a hastily slapped-together exposé of dangerous toys named a blatantly innocent designer rather than the shoddy manufacturer.

'I blame Derek Leech,' Useless Bruce said out loud in the meeting room as they waited for an unconscionably late Tiny.

'Shush,' Lydia Marks said, 'this place is probably bugged.'

'Tiny's completely hung up on the bid and Kit is suffering. Plus

Leech has this Mephistopheles effect, you know. I swear reality bends wherever he stands.'

There were mumbles of agreement, including Sally's. There was something else she blamed Derek Leech for, considering the reputation of his products. She thought she was pregnant.

———

First, her doctor congratulated her in the spirit of female solidarity; then, interpreting her blank expression, she dug out a leaflet and said that at Sally's advanced age, she could probably justify an abortion on health grounds. So it was official: thirty-five was 'advanced'. Also, Sally was unmistakably 'with child'. She wondered if her mother would be pleased. And whether she could stand another upheaval.

There wasn't time to talk with Dr Frazier, since she had to rush from the Women's Clinic to a meet with the GLT Deep Throat. Miraculously, Nick Roebuck seemed to be a genuine defector. He wanted old-fashioned money and a shot at a position with the consortium if and when they took over the franchise. Someone reputedly sharp who knew GLT from the inside was convinced enough the consortium were going to win to gamble his career on it. That should be good news for Mythwrhn.

In the cab, Sally held her belly as if she had a stomach ache, trying to feel the alien lodged in her. A tiny Connor, perhaps, dribbled through a ruptured Chum? Or a little Sally, worm-shaped but an incipient woman? Half the time she thought her body had betrayed her; then she was almost won round by the possibilities. All her contemporaries who were going to have babies had already done so. She'd be the last of her generation to give in.

Roebuck had arranged to meet her at a sawdust-on-the-floor pub in Islington, well off the media beat. The cab cruised Upper Street, looking for the sign.

Sally had seen hard-edged women turn mushy-gooey upon producing a baby. She wondered if she'd ever even met a child she liked, let alone whether she was a fit mother. She corrected herself: fit single mother. Christ, should she even tell Connor's parents? There was some of their son left after all. Did she want to invite those strangers into her life, give them a part of her baby?

The cab drew up outside the pub and she paid the driver. Inside, a few glum men were absorbed in their pints. It was mid-afternoon and beer was half-price to the unwaged. She supposed they called it 'the miserable hour'. A country and western song on the juke-box proclaimed 'If They Didn't Have Pussy, There'd Be a Bounty on Their Pelts'.

She spotted Roebuck at once, at a corner table. Shiny of suit and face, scalp red and glistening under thin strands of cross-combed blond hair. Apart from the barmaid, Sally was the only woman in the pub. She let Roebuck buy her a Perrier (until she decided what to do about the baby, she was off the gin) and listened to him gibber inconsequentially as he fiddled with the satchel he'd brought the papers in. He was nervous to the point of terror, as if he expected GLT shock troops in black balaclavas to burst in and execute him.

'May I?' she said, reaching for the goods. 'Just a taste.'

Roebuck looked appalled.

'It could be old copies of the *Independent*,' she explained.

Reluctantly, he handed over. The satchel was almost a schoolkid's accessory, not at all like the slimly imposing briefcases common in the business.

'I trust this'll go in my favour,' Roebuck said.

'I'm sure the consortium will do well by you.'

She looked at a few sheets. There were authentic audience figures, with alarmed notes scrawled in the margins. A couple of thick documents marked 'HIGHLY CONFIDENTIAL' outlined proposed changes in GLT production and transmission schedules. Without a close examination, she guessed the purpose was to cut short term production costs to cover the losses GLT would sustain ponying up for a winning bid. She was almost satisfied to find a confidential memo from the board, insisting the company try to buy back its squandered percentages of *Cowley Mansions* before a raider took over completely.

'This seems to be in order,' she said.

Roebuck nodded, face burning. Palpable desperation sweated off the man. He gripped the table to prevent his hands shaking. Sally wondered how low the consortium's unseen campaign would get. Roebuck had looked around throughout the meeting, as if searching for a familiar face.

'It'll stop now,' he said. 'Won't it?'

'I don't know what you mean.'

Disgust bulged through fear for a moment and he got up, barging out of the pub, leaving her with the satchel. A couple of others left almost immediately.

She gathered the papers. She'd win untold brownie points for this coup, but didn't know how much of it was her doing. As she left, she noticed an almost-full pint abandoned on a table by the door. The man who'd sat there had struck her as familiar. Broad, undistinguished, in overalls. With a spine-scrape of fear, she wondered if he might be the van driver.

Out in the street, she couldn't see Roebuck or the nondescript drinker who could have been following him. So much to think about. She looked for another cab.

————

A man in a suit was dismantling April's desk, sorting through every scrap of paper and odd object in its tardis drawers. April had a system whereby every unwanted freebie and done-with document was shoved into a drawer until it disappeared. Tiny was either overseeing the job or ordered to be present at the dissection. The suit worked like a callous surgeon, calmly incising closed envelopes and packets. Sally wondered if he were from the drug squad.

'This is Mr Quilbert,' Tiny said, 'our new security manager.'

Quilbert smiled and shook her hand limply. She instantly pegged him as a cuckoo slipped into the Mythwrhn nest by Derek Leech. He had one of those close-to-the-skull haircuts that disguise premature baldness with designer style.

'We've lost an important file,' Tiny said. 'Bender might have given it to April.'

'I didn't think they were talking,' she said. 'Well, not recently.'

'Nothing scary,' Quilbert said, 'just stats about the building. There was a security survey in there.'

'We can get a copy from the consultants,' Tiny said, 'but it'd be embarassing.'

Quilbert slit open a packet and slid out a pornographic magazine in Hungarian.

'That's from one of last year's items,' Tiny said. Quilbert smiled tightly and dumped it on the pile.

'Have you tried asking April?' she suggested.

'A bit tricky,' Tiny said. 'She's had a relapse. They've had to put her under restraint.'

She took the file, which she'd sincerely forgotten about, home, hoping it might help her understand the tangle of mysteries. Besides, an evening poring through arcane security lore seemed more comfortable than an evening phoning her mother and announcing a compromised 'blessed event'.

There was a new security guard, in a black one-piece bodysuit, installed in Reception, presumably on Quilbert's orders. She was sure his X-Ray vision would perceive the documents she was smuggling out but he was too busy trying to cosy up to Heidi. That hardly suggested fearsome efficiency.

She made herself tea and sat on her sofa, television on but with the sound down. The file Bender had given her for April was tied with red ribbon. She let it lie a moment and drank her tea. On the screen, an interracial couple argued their way to a cliffhanging climax on *Cowley Mansions*. The soap's storylines had become increasingly bizarre: Peter, the gay yuppie, was discovered to be 'pregnant', a long-unborn twin developing inside his abdomen; Joko, the cool black wastrel, was revealed to be a white boy with permanently dyed skin, hiding out; and Ell Crenshaw, the cockney matriarch who ruled the top floor, spontaneously combusted the week the actress demanded a vast salary hike. Either the writers saw a Leech take-over as inevitable and were devaluing the property before the new landlord arrived, or GLT had ordered audience-grabbing sensationalism in the run-up to the auction.

After the soap came a commercial for the serialisition of Josef Mengele's Auschwitz diaries in the *Argus*, Leech's heavy paper. Then a caring, sensitive ad for Chums.

Sally undid the ribbon and didn't find a security survey. The first item was familiar: a glossy Mythwrhn press release, dated three years ago, about the redesign of their Soho Square premises. She paged through and found quotes from critics praising the features of the building that now drove people mad. The brochure also profiled Constant Drache, the award-winning architect entrusted with the commission. He'd been an unknown until Derek Leech chose him to construct the DLE pyramid, the black glass creation that now domonated Docklands. In a broody shot, Drache posed in black like the lead singer of a Goth group. A wedge of gibberish about his intentions with the building was printed white on black. It was silly, considering that a lot of Drache's 'severe edges' were now best known for ripping the clothes of passing people, but hardly worth Quilbert's search-and-destroy mission. Drache referred to buildings as 'devices', insisting each have its own purpose and be designed to concentrate 'human energies' towards the fulfilment of that purpose. Cathedrals, for instance, were designed to concentrate prayer upwards. Sally wondered what low ceilings and floor-level lighting were supposed to concentrate you towards, and, before she could stop herself, guessed Bender had probably worked it out.

She zapped to the Leech channel and found a scary scene from one of the *Where the Bodies Are Buried* sequels. A teenager screamed silently as Hackwill, the monster, slashed him with a cake-slice.

Under the brochure was a clipped-together batch of articles from a psychology journal. April hadn't abandoned her 'sick building syndrome' idea, or at least had got Bender to retrieve materials from the files before Tiny pulled the plug. Sally skimmed until her head hurt with jargon. Respectable psychology segued into the *Fortean Times* and even weirder quarters. She found pieces, with significant passages underlined in violet, on 'curses' and 'hauntings'.

The television monster laughed loud enough to be heard even with the sound down. The camera pulled back from a graveyard through which a girl was running to reveal that the tilted tombstones constituted a giant face.

The last items were thin strips of word-processed news copy. A fine print tag at the bottom of each page identified the copy as having been generated for the *Comet*. Sally guessed that for a tabloid these pieces would constitute a heavyweight Sunday section article. She read them through, recognising the style and concerns of the Leech press. Dated a year ago, the article a celebrated major police infiltration a nest of Satanic Child-Abusers. Naming a few names, the piece was about decadent high society types turning to black magic to advance themselves. A 23-year-old stockbroker was purported to have made a million on Market Tips From Hell. A top model, who'd doubtless have posed nude for the illo, claimed drinking goat blood landed her international assignments.

It was typical *Comet* drivel but had never appeared in the paper. Each strip of prose was individually stamped in red with a large 'NO' design that contained, in tiny letters, the initials 'DL'. She supposed this was Leech's personal veto. Why hadn't the piece appeared? It seemed a natural for the *Comet*. So, most likely, Leech had an interest in its suppression. She read everything through again and found it. The reference in the copy was to the '£3.5 million modern home' which was the gathering point for the cult. In the margin, in faded pencil that looked as if it had been almost rubbed out, were the words 'Drache Retreat'.

———

'Where's the goon?' Sally asked Heidi. The security man wasn't at his post.

'Caught his hand in the lift,' the receptionist said. 'Dozens of little bones broken.'

Sally raised an eyebrow. A workman was examining the lift door, screw-drivers laid out on a dustcloth like surgical instruments.

'There was blood all over the floor. Disgusting.'

Carefully, she climbed the stairs, trying keep her elbows away from Drache's 'severe edges'. If the architect had chosen to inset razor-blades into all the walls, the effect might have been more obvious.

The *Survival Kit* offices were depopulated. Pomme told her every-one was off with a bout of the 'flu. Pomme's perfect complexion was marred by eruptions.

'Bleedin' worry, I reckon,' she said, scratching her blood-dotted chin.

April's desk had been put together again but was stripped clean. There was a padded envelope on Sally's desk, with her name printed on it. She opened it and found a bundle of £20 notes. There was no 'compliments' slip.

She took a giant-size bag of Kettle Chips out of her case and, after a furtive glance-around, ate them rapidly, one by one. She was eating for two. The cash was for Roebuck's papers, she understood. A bonus, blood money.

She had just scrunched up the crisp packet and buried it in her waste-bin when Pomme slid her head into the alcove.

'Remember Streaky?' she said, referring to the office cat who'd disappeared three months ago.

Sally nodded.

'The lift-repair man just found the bones at the bottom of the shaft. Ugh.'

————

All the black magicians she knew were dead, which was not some-thing she usually found upsetting. She couldn't ask anyone to explain things to her. Nevertheless, she thought she'd worked it out.

It was possible to climb past the Penthouse and get onto the roof. The original idea had been to make it a party area but Drache insisted on a rubbery-leathery species of covering that made the slight slope dangerously slippery.

Sally sat carefully and looked out at Soho Square, thinking. Her hair was riffled by the slight breeze. She wished she had more crisps. Down in the world, the organ donors were waiting to be sent out. Today, things had ground to a halt in the business. It was an Armistice, a pause before the *putsch* of the franchise auction. Thousands would go under the mud in that armageddon, leaving the map of Media London dotted with crushed corpses.

It was almost peaceful. Above the building, she felt a calm which was elusive inside it. The knot of worry which she'd got used to eased away.

'Chim-chim-a-nee,' she hummed. 'Chim-chim-a-nee, chim-chim-cha-roo . . .'

She decided she'd have her baby. And she'd leave Mythwrhn. There, two decisions and her life was solved.

Hours might have passed. The sun came out from behind a cloud and the roof heated. Should she give her blood bonus away? She'd been taking tainted money so long, she might as well keep this too. Soon she'd have to buy cribs and baby-clothes and nappies. Leech's money was no worse than anyone else's.

A few of the rubberised tiles nearby had been dislodged, and a dull metal was exposed. Beneath was a thick layer of lead, its surface covered in apparently-functionless runes. She assumed they were symbolic. She picked free a few further tiles, disclosing more and more lead plates, all etched with hieroglyphs, incantations, invocations.

It confirmed what she had guessed. A cathedral was designed to direct upwards; the Mythwrhn Building was designed to capture and contain. It psychic terms, it was earthed. She hoped she wasn't succumbing to the New Age now life was developing inside her. But for the past few months, she had worked among enough negative energy to blacken anybody's crystal.

Kim Newman

No wonder everyone in Mythwrhn was miserable. They were supposed to be. Misery was the cake, she supposed; all the blood was icing. Drache's Design must extend under the pavement into the street, to catch the drippings from Connor. If Bender had jumped from the roof rather than the Penthouse, would he have escaped?

The Device worked like a scale. All the misery weighed one pan down, thrusting the other upwards. She could guess who would be sitting on the other pan. And what the uplift was for.

Under her crossed legs, the building thrummed with pent-up unhappiness. She was above it all. At once, she was centered. In her condition, she had power.

———

Over the years, she'd collected a library, mainly by ordering from the Amok Bookstore in Los Angeles, which was dedicated to 'extremes of information in print'. She skipped past William B. Moran's *Covert Surveillance and Electronic Penetration*, G.B. Clark's *How to Get Lost and Start All Over Again* and Colonel Rex Applegate's *Kill or Get Killed: For Police and the Military, Last Word on Mob Control*, paused for an amused flick through one of John Minner's seven-volume *How to Kill* series, then selected Kurt Saxon's *The Poor Man's James Bond*.

Saxon, an extreme right-winger and authority on explosives, had authored a guide for the defence of the USA in the event of a Russian invasion, compiling information on sabotage, home-made weaponry and sundry guerilla tactics. Although Saxon declared himself 'very pro-establishment and pro-law enforcement' and that he would 'not knowingly sell his more sensitive books to any left-wing group or individual', given the ever-decreasing likelihood of a Soviet invasion, the only conceivable purpose of his work was as a manual for the criminal.

Along with more conservative texts—Seymour Lecker's *Deadly Brew: Advanced Improvised Explosives*, the CIA's *Field Expedient Methods for Explosives Preparations*—Saxon's book gave Sally a wide variety of recipes to consider. She made a shopping list and went out to the chemist's, a DIY shop, a tobacconist's, Sainsbury's and Rumbelow's to buy the easily-available ingredients she now knew how to convert into a functioning infernal device. The most hard-to-obtain items were the steel buckets in which she wanted to place her home-made bombs, to direct the blasts upwards. Everyone had plastic these days.

She was in her kitchen, attempting to distil a quantity of picric acid from ten bottles of aspirin, when her mother telephoned to see how she was getting on.

'I'm cooking, Mum.'

'That's nice, dear. Having a guest for dinner?'

'No, just practicing.'

––––––––

'What's in the buckets?' Heidi asked.

'Live crabs,' she claimed. 'We're doing an item on the crooked pet racket.'

'Ugh.'

'You're telling me.'

The security guard was back at his post, hand mittened with plaster. Sally held up a bucket and he avoided looking into it.

'Careful,' she warned, 'the little bastards don't half nip.'

She was nodded through. On her lunch-hour she went back to Muswell Hill to fetch the other two buckets from her flat and went through the whole thing again.

That afternoon, there was enough blast-power under her desk to raise the roof. She hoped.

––––––––

There was a confab going on up in the Penthouse, a long-term post-franchise planning session. Sally would have to wait until everyone left. The idea of detonating some of the consortium along with the building was tempting, but she was more likely to get away with what she intended if no one was hurt. If the roof was blown off the Device, the energy should dissipate. She couldn't bring Connor or Bender back or restore April's mind or Pomme's complexion but she could spoil the nasty little scheme.

As the afternoon dragged on, she pretended to work. She ate three packets of Kettle Chips, shuffled papers around on the desk, phoned people back. She guessed this would be her last day. It'd be a shame to do without the leaving party and the whip-round present. She'd probably have qualified for paid maternity leave, too. Actually, she'd be lucky to stay out of jail.

She had the idea, however, that Leech would not want her talking too much about the motive for her terrorist atrocity. A *Comet* think piece about how pregnancy drives women up the walls wouldn't serve to explain away her loud resignation notice.

The few *Kit* staff around drifted off about tea-time. Pomme invited her out for a drink but Sally said she wanted to get something finished before leaving.

'You look a bit peaky, Sal,' Pomme said. 'You should get a good night's kip.'

Sally agreed.

'You've been driven to smoking?'

There was a packet of cigarettes on her desk. Sally coughed and smiled.

'Your face looks better, Pomme.'

'Fuckin' tell me about it, Sal.'

The girl shrugged and left. Sally realised she'd miss some of the others. Even Useless Bruce. She'd never worked much with people before, and there were nice things about it. From now on, she'd be alone again. Perhaps she would re-start the Agency.

Alone in the office as it got dark outside, she ate more crisps, made herself tea and sat at her desk with a new-bought occult paperback. She gathered the building was a magical pressure cooker and the accumulation of 'melancholy humours' was a species of sacrifice, a way of getting someone else to pay your infernal dues. It was capitalist black magic, getting minions to pay for the spell in suffering while the conjurers got ahead on other people's sweat. Obviously, some people would do anything to get a television franchise. Since catching on, she had been noticing more and more things about the Mythwrhn Building: symbols worked into the design like the hidden cows and lions in a 'How Many Animals Can You See in This Picture?' puzzle; spikes and hooks deliberately placed to be hostile to living inhabitants; numerical patterns in steps, windows and corners.

Sally divided the cigarettes into five sets of three. Pinching off the filters, she connected each of the sets into six-inch-long tubes, securing the joins with extra layers of roll-up paper. Then she dripped lighter fluid, letting the flammable liquid seep through the tobacco cores. One test fuse she stood up in a lump of blu-tak and lit. It took over five minutes to burn down completely. Long enough.

At eight o'clock, she put an internal call up to the Penthouse and let it ring. After an age, Tiny's answering machine cut in asking her to leave a message. She double-checked by opening a window in the office and leaning out as far as possible into the well, looking up. No light spilled out of the Penthouse.

The lift was still out of order, so she had to take the works up the stairs. First she went up and circumvented the suite's personal alarm. With some deft fiddling and her electronic key, she got the doors open. The Penthouse was dark and empty. It took three quick trips to get everything into Tiny's office and she arranged it all on his desk, working by the streetlight.

She felt ill. Since realising what was going on, she'd been more sensitive to the gloom trapped within the walls of the Mythwrhn Building. It was a miasma. The water in the pipes smelled like blood.

Had Bender been trying to break the Device when he smashed the windows? If so, he'd made a mistake.

There was a hatch directly above the desk, just where it was indicated on the plans she'd borrowed. Above would be a crawlspace under the lead shield. She put a chair and the now-untenanted statuette stand on the desk, making a rough arrangement of steps, and climbed up to the ceiling. A good thump dislodged the hatch and she stuck her head into smelly dark.

She'd assumed this was where all the energies would gather. The cavity didn't feel any worse than the rest of the building and she had a moment of doubt. Was this really crazy?

After ferrying up the four buckets and the other stuff, she jammed through into the crawlspace. Here she could turn on the bicycle lamp Connor had left in her flat. She shone the beam around. She almost expected to find screaming skeletons and the remains of blood sacrifices, but the cavity was surprisingly clean. Meccano struts shored up the lead shield and criss-crossed the plastered ceiling. There was a slope to the roof, so the crawlspace grew from a two-foot height at the street edge of the building to four feet at the rear. If she placed her buckets near the rear end, the blast should neatly slide off the lead shield and dump it into the square. With luck, not on the heads of innocent passersby.

She crawled carefully but still opened her palm on a protruding nail. The floor was studded with spikes, either one of Drache's devilish frills or a defensive feature. Crouching at the rear of the building, she pushed up, testing the shield. It was unresisting. Prominent bolts were spaced around the walls. With a monkey-wrench, she loosened as many as she could reach. She banged her elbows constantly and skinned her right knuckles. Her hair was stuck to her face by sweat. This was not usually prescribed for expectant mothers.

With enough bolts loosened, she tried to push the shield again. It creaked alarmingly and shifted. Sally found she was shaking. She thought she could almost dislodge the lead without the bombs. But it was best to be safe.

She'd hoped the joists would be wooden, so she could screw in hooks to hang the buckets from. However, the metal struts came equipped with handy holes, so she was able to rig up the hanging bombs with stout wire. In each bucket of packed-down goo, she'd used Sexton's recommended dosage for disabling a Russian tank. She stuck the long cigarettes in each bucket and flicked a flame from her disposable lighter.

Once the fuses were burning, she intended to get down to her desk and alert the skeleton overnight staff. She'd say she'd seen smoke pouring down the stairs. With five minutes, she should be able to evacuate the building.

She lit the four cigarettes and wriggled back towards the hatch. Down in the Penthouse, lights came on and voices exclaimed surprise. Knowing she was dead, she dangled her legs through the hatch and dropped into the office.

———

'What, no Leech?' she said.

Tiny was between the others, shaking and pale. The Device had been eating at him as much as his employees. Sally guessed he was only in the consortium as a judas goat.

Quilbert was in charge, Drache was along for the ride, and the non-descript man holding Tiny up was the muscle. He was also the van-driver who'd knocked down Connor and the balls-squeezer who'd pressured Roebuck. He looked more like a plumber than Satan's Hit Man.

'Ms Rhodes, what are you doing?' Quilbert asked.

'Raising the roof.'

Tiny shook his head and sagged into his chair. Drache strode around the office, examining his handiwork. He had a black leather trenchcoat and showy wings of hair like horns.

'The stand should be here,' he said, pointing to the dust-free spot where it had stood. 'For the proper balance. Everything is supposed to be exact. How often have I told you, the patterns are all-important?'

Quilbert nodded to the muscle, who clambered onto the desk and stuck his head into the crawlspace.

'Smells like she's been smoking,' he said.

'It's a secret,' she said. 'I quit but backslid. I have to take extreme measures to cover up.'

'I think I can see . . . *buckets*?'

Quilbert looked at Sally as if trying to read her mind. 'What have you done?'

'I've forestalled the Device,' she said. 'It was all wasted.'

Quilbert's clear blue eyes were unreadable.

'Only an innocent can intervene,' Drache said pompously. 'You've taken blooded coin.'

'He's right,' Quilbert said. 'You don't understand at all. Everything has been pre-arranged.'

'Not everything,' she said. 'I'm going to have a baby.'

Drache looked stricken but Quilbert and Tiny didn't get it. She susposed they found it all as hard to believe as she did.

'There's something burning,' a voice mumbled from above. 'In the buckets . . .'

Drache flew around in a cold rage.

'If she's carrying a child, she's washed clean,' he said, urgently. 'It'll upset the balances.'

'What have you done?' Quilbert asked.

Sally smiled. 'Wouldn't you like to know?'

'Put out the fires,' Quilbert shouted up, 'at once!'

She should tell them not to tamper with the buckets in case the burning fuses fell. For the sake of her child, she couldn't die.

'Careful,' she said . . .

The ceiling burst and a billow of flame shot into the office, flattening everyone. A dead human shape thumped onto the desk, covered in burning jelly. Sally's ears were hammered by the blast. The stench of evaporating goo was incredible. Metal wrenched and complained. Hot rivets rained onto the fitted carpet. She heard screaming. A raft of steel and plaster bore down on Quilbert and Tiny. The windows had blown out, and the air was full of flying shards, glinting and scratching. She felt a growing power deep inside her and knew she would survive.

The cloud of flame burned away almost instantly, leaving little fires all around. Drache stumbled, a bloody hand stuck to half his face, and sank to his knees, shrieking. Sally was flat on her back, looking up at the ceiling. She saw night sky and felt the updraft as the accumulated misery of months escaped to the Heavens like prayers.

———

They kept her in hospital for weeks. Not the same one as Drache and Quilbert, who were private, and certainly not in the department that had received the still officially unidentified van-driver. She only had superficial injuries, but in her condition the doctors wanted to be careful with her.

She read the media pages every day, following the ripples. In the week before the auction, the consortium fell apart. Mausoleum Pictures, wildly over-extended, went bust, bringing down yet another fifth of the British Film Industry. Tiny promised *Survival Kit* would be back as soon as he was walking, but he'd have to recruit a substantially new staff since almost everyone who had worked in the now-roofless Mythwrhn Building was seeking employment elsewhere. Most wanted to escape from television altogether and find honest work.

The police had interviewed her extensively but she plead amnesia, pretending to be confused about what had happened just before the 'accident'. No charges against her were even suggested. Mythwrhn even continued to pay her salary even though she'd given notice. After the baby, she would not be returning.

Derek Leech, never officially involved in the consortium, said nothing and his media juggernaut rolled on unhindered by its lack of a controlling interest in a franchise. GLT, somewhat surprised, scaled down their bid and fought off a feeble challenge at auction time, promising to deliver to the British Public the same tried-and-tested program formulae in ever-increasing doses. On *Cowley Mansions*, Peter the gay yuppie had a son-brother and, salary dispute over, the ghost of Ell Crenshaw possessed her long-lost sister.

Apart from the van-driver and Drache, who lost an eye, nobody had really been punished. But none of them benefited from the Device either. All the gathered misery was loose in the world.

The day before she was due out, April and Pomme visited. April was taking it 'one day at a time' and Pomme had discovered a miracle cure. They brought a card signed by everybody on *Survival Kit* except Tiny.

The women cooed over Sally's swollen stomach and she managed not to be sickened. She felt like a balloon with a head and legs and nothing she owned, except her nightie, fit any more.

She told them she'd have to sell the flat and get a bigger one or a small house. She'd need more living space. That, she had learned, was important.

'Organ Donors' is a curtain-raiser to my novel The Quorum, *in which Sally Rhodes has another go-round with Derek Leech and the concept of 'capitalist black magic' is further explored. It was written for Nicholas Royle's* Darklands 2, *a collection of modern, British, 'quiet' horror. Though all the companies and individuals involved are fictional, the ITV franchise auction actually happens every decade or so, with various farcical results (Andrew Davidson's* Under the Hammer *is a good, funny history of the 1991 event) not all that removed from my dark version.*

GOING

TO SERIES

EMO

From: Tiny Chiselhurst, producer/creator

To: April Treece, junior researcher.

Re: Untiled Docusoap/Gameshow Pilot

Here's the final draft of the flyer. Every word approved by Dr Wendel and Miss Lark as calculated to reach the cross-section of personality types we need.

EVERYDAY MEGASTARS WANTED

Is this you? 18-45, sexy, extrovert, killer body, unconventional, tagged 'difficult' by lesser mortals, ambitious, unattached, competitive, 'bonkers', up for anything? Apply: Mythwrhn Productions, Box 101, Leech Pyramid Plaza, London Docklands.

As a classified ad, this is to go into the following periodicals: *Big Bazookas*, the *Sunday Comet*, the *Nazi Atrocities* part-work, *Young Offender*, *Pop Hitz* and *Shy Girl Monthly*. As a flyer, it is to be distributed via inner-city clubs, comic shops, student union buildings, social security offices and police stations. We agree that we should target especially the waiting rooms of probation officers and court-approved psycho-therapists, the business places of drugs and weapons dealers, abortion and v.d. clinics, all-night casualty wards, Young Conservative meetings, and pubs that cater to the motorcycle, rugby football, slag-on-the-pull and stockbroking communities. Word from the top of the Pyramid is that Cloud 9 (Derek Leech!) is really hyped on this project, so let's get things moving.

————

[NB: THIS IS FOR SENDING TO THE APPLICANTS ONLY, AND SHOULD UNDER NO CIRCUMSTANCES BE CONFUSED WITH THE REAL SERIES PROPOSAL, WHICH IS AVAILABLE ON AN EYES ONLY NEED-TO-KNOW BASIS TO SECURITY-CLEARED INSIDERS AT MYTHWRHN AND CLOUD 9 — TINY]

SERIES PROPOSAL

This seven-part (initial run) series combines three of the most popular (and, let's face it, economical) TV formats of the last ten years: fly-on-the-wall docusoap, slags-on-holiday mock doc and sci-fi/adventure gameshow. A group of charismatic, sexy young chicks and chaps, strangers to each other, are brought together in a luxurious, Bond-style environment (country estate, mountaintop hunting lodge, beach house) and have to spend a week together. Cut off from civilisation, the contestants (subjects, stars?) are in contact with a host — we think we can get US smartmouth obonxio-comic Barry Gatlin, but other options are Ruby Wax or someone off *Star Trek* — who communicates via video-link each evening and sets tasks and competitions, which range from puzzle-solving exercises through treasure hunting on the grounds of the luxury retreat and harmless combat games to how-low-can-you-go? gross-out or endurance dares. Meanwhile, the stars are on camera day and night; we trust that days of strenuous competition will be followed by evenings of unwinding in wild, entertaining and provocative manners. Over the course of the week, we will see how each contestant scores, in every imaginable way.

Tiny Chiselhurst, Creator and Owner

Dear Potential Megastar,

Thank you for your interest. Please fill in the attached form and return it to me at Mythwrhn Productions.

This isn't an exam: the answers you give aren't right or wrong, but will help us determine whether you are the type of person for our show. Don't think too hard or try to give answers you think we want. Be yourself.

All forms are confidential.

Best wishes,

April Treece, Researcher

ARE YOU A MEGASTAR?

1: Please write your name, age, contact details, next of kin, and rough annual income.

2: Sex?
    . . . male.
    . . . female.
    . . . yes, please!
    . . . don't know.

3: How many jobs have you had since leaving school?

4: Do you feel yourself to be . . .
    . . . attractive to the opposite sex.
    . . . unattractive to the opposite sex.
    . . . attractive to the same sex.

... horny.

... a love god/goddess in the flesh.

5: How many sex partners have you had per year, on average, since the age of twelve?

6: Do you feel yourself to be ...

... more intelligent than the average.

... less intelligent than the average.

... of average intelligence.

... too intelligent to be measured by this stupid question.

... a real Brainiac.

... a spoon.

7: If attacked in your home, what household items would you use to defend yourself.

8: Which of these describes you?

... a conformist.

... a maverick.

... a team-player.

... scary.

... a tosser.

... a leader.

... a nurturer.

... a bitch.

... the best there is at what you do.

... a disappointment.

9: Have you ever broken a law and not been caught? If so, please give details.

10: Would you be willing to do severe harm to ...

... an enemy soldier on a battlefield.

   . . . a violent criminal threatening your mother.

   . . . a member of parliament.

   . . . a spastic.

   . . . your mother.

   . . . a wounded animal.

   . . . a stranger.

   . . . no one at all, under any circumstances.

   . . . a television personality.

   . . . a former boy or girlfriend who treated you badly.

11: Would you have sex with someone unappealing just because they were famous, notorious, physically unusual, or on television? If you have, please give details.

12: When Bambi's mother was shot, what was your reaction?

   . . . it was very tragic and sad.

   . . . the bitch got what she deserved.

   . . . venison pies, yum!

   . . . Bambi ought to avenge his family.

   . . . Who's Bambi?

13: Have you ever written an anonymous letter or made a prank phone call? If so, please give details.

14: When you broke up with your last boy or girlfriend, was it . . .

   . . . just one of those things.

   . . . all for the best, really.

   . . . your fault.

   . . . their fault.

   . . . a prelude to revenge.

   . . . one more fucking thing on your plate.

   . . . never had a boy or girlfriend, and don't much like the sound of it.

15: Would you play a computer game called *Dunblane Massacre*?

16: Have you ever . . .

  . . . performed in a karaoke pub.

  . . . had sex with two or more partners simultaneously.

  . . . experienced memory loss after alcohol or drug intake.

  . . . been on television.

  . . . considered joining the armed forces.

  . . . had sex in a public place.

  . . . used terms of racial ('nigger', 'chink') or sexual ('cunt', 'queer') abuse in general conversation.

  . . . deliberately botched a job interview?

  . . . stalked a celebrity.

  . . . got your own back on someone who had done you a wrong.

17: Which of the Spice Girls would you most like to rape?

18: Do you believe in . . .

  . . . UFO abductions.

  . . . Our Lord, Jesus Christ.

  . . . other people's pain.

  . . . microwaves.

  . . . ghosts.

  . . . an eye for an eye.

  . . . Swedish Sin.

  . . . yourself.

  . . . turning the other cheek.

  . . . capital punishment.

19: When was the last time you were really happy? Please give details. If never, please give details.

20: Could you take a week off from your life/work/family to star in a television series? Please answer honestly, to save time later.

———

PRODUCTION SUB-MEETING, No. 19

PRESENT, for MYTHWRHN PRODUCTIONS: April Treece (Featured Researcher), Claire Bates (Minion), Davinda Paquignet (Recording Angel).

BATES:	Can I just say, off the record, how much I *hate* this proposal.
TREECE:	Get in the queue, Claire. Tiny's got this bonnet bee that they love it at the top of the Pyramid. It's all the things Derek Leech, our ultimate lord and master at Cloud 9 Television, is supposed to be keen on. Cheap, crass, cruel and compulsive.
BATES:	And crap!
TREECE:	You might say that. I couldn't possibly comment.
BATES:	Dav, stop writing this down!
PAQUIGNET:	Sorry, force of habit.
BATES:	Ape, have you sorted through the completed forms?
TREECE:	God, yes.
BATES:	Where did we find these sickos?
TREECE:	Milling about in general population.
BATES:	"Which of the Spice Girls would you most like to rape?" What sort of question is that? A bit sex-specific, surely.
TREECE:	The responses are 75 per-cent male.
BATES:	Sur-prise.
TREECE:	So far as we can tell. Those who ticked 'yes, please' for 'sex?' are sometimes hard to work out. And those are our pass applicants.
BATES:	They'll be men. Or really dim tarts.
TREECE:	A frightening number of women responded. Some skipped the Spice question. Some didn't. A few nominated male equivalents. You wouldn't think

anyone could have those fantasies about Frank Dobson or . . .

BATES: Ugh! Don't say any more! I don't want to know!

PAQUIGNET: I didn't think it was possible to have the amount of sex most of these people say they have.

TREECE: Not if you work in television, it isn't.

BATES: Too bloody right.

TREECE: Dr Wendel says to divide that answer by ten to get a proper figure. Except for the ones who claim to be virgins. Half of them aren't lying.

PAQUIGNET: What about the lad who gave names and addresses? Are we supposed to phone the victims up to check him out?

TREECE: No wonder he can't keep a steady girlfriend.

BATES: If you had a party, would you want any of these people to come?

TREECE: God, no. But this is Tiny's baby, and we have to carry it to term, no matter how we feel. Look, Claire, it's a looney idea and even Derek Leech wouldn't seriously consider putting it out. We're more likely to see live bullfighting on British TV than this horror, so we won't get hurt. Let's go as far with it as we have to before Tiny, inevitably, changes his mind.

BATES: I don't want my name on any of the documentation, or a credit on any proposal or pilot. I'm serious. I don't want a paper trail connecting me to this . . . this atrocity. Dav, stop bloody writing!

———————

Dear Loser

Thank you for your interest. Unfortunately, you are not the person we — or anyone else — are looking for at this time.

We wish you joy in your continued obscurity.

Sincerely,

April Treece, Rejecter-in-Chief

—————

MEMO

From: April Treece, senior researcher.
To: Tiny Chiselhurst, producer/creator
Re: Horrible People Pilot

We sent out entry forms to the first 5,000 people who responded to the ad or the flyer and got 2,389 completed returns. I passed on the 968 papers with 'yes, please!' ticked for Question Two — the famous 'trigger signal' — to Dr Wendel and Miss Lark, who have evaluated them all and selected 178 'possibles'. I'm astonished not only at the number of people out there who have sent anonymous letters but are proud enough of the fact to boast about it at enormous length, continuing onto the other side of the paper, to strangers. As requested, I've sent a curt rejection letter to all 178 and ignored the rest.

I still don't believe this is going to fly, or that even Cloud 9 will broadcast it if it does. That said, reading over the completed forms, I'm starting to understand why audiences might actually enjoy watching the show. Are real people really this awful? The runners have stuck up their favourite forms on the message board. At the moment, the champion is the Sporty Spice fan who would see off an attacker by taking a mouthful of bleach and offering a blow-job, though my clear winner is the 'nurturer' guy or girl (ambiguous name and no helpful answer to Q2) who claims to have shagged seven of Dr Who's companions (not including K-9, I trust). Do we have a title yet?

—————

MEMO

From: Tiny Chiselhurst, producer/creator
To: April Treece, chief researcher.
Re: Bedlam Unplugged

Any of the 'possibles' who get back to us to complain about the 'Dear Loser' letters should be invited for interview. Please note whether applicants complain via e-mail, telephone or the post, and pass print-outs, recordings and photocopies to Dr Wendel and Miss Lark. Anyone not classed as a 'possible' who complains we haven't got back to them should also be considered for interview if the complaint shows the proper character type. Taking the usual wastage into account, we only need a dozen or so strong candidates.

I know the troops have their doubts about this, Ape, but I've got a gut feeling that it is going to be a winner! At present, Cloud 9 inclining towards a neutral title like *A Week Off* or *Microcosm*, though I'm all for something as blunt as *It's Madhouse!* or *The Pit* and cleverclogs Bender has voted for *The Raft of the Medusa*. How does one go about offering someone a blow-job if one has a mouthful of bleach? Sign language. And if you threw a brick in the Soho House, you'd be lucky to hit someone who *hadn't* shagged seven of Dr Who's companions. Onwards and upwards!

INTERVIEW TRANSCRIPT, NO. 17.

APPLICANT: Harry 'Donger' Bennett, 32.
FOR MYTHWRHN: Tiny Chiselhurst, Dr Vernon Wendel, Myra Lark, April Treece.

LARK:	Harry . . .
BENNETT:	Everyone calls me 'Donger'. Ever since school.
LARK:	Ah, Donger . . . first, we must apologise for the mix-up with the letter.

BENNETT: So you should. Nearly missed your chance there, didn't you?

LARK: Indeed.

BENNETT: But I like your whole approach, really. 'Dear Loser'. No poncing about there. Puts the losers right in their place. The real losers. I like to see that.

LARK: You describe yourself as competitive?

BENNETT: No. I would describe myself as a winner. It's just a fact of life. Ever since school.

LARK: You did well in school?

BENNETT: Too right. Fighting them off, I was. Had half the Sixth Form, and a couple of the younger teachers. The beginning of a great career.

LARK: And academically?

BENNETT: Rugby, football, basketball. Everything. Except cricket. That's for poofs.

LARK: You don't like, uh, homosexuals?

BENNETT: Show me a bloke who says he does and I'll show you a poof. It's not a natural thing, is it? Whatever they say these days.

LARK: You've never been married?

BENNETT: I've been engaged a couple of times, if that's what it takes to get the cork to pop.

LARK: It's important that you be unattached, for the show. Do you have a girlfriend?

BENNETT: A couple, actually. But no one I can't chuck if something tasty comes along.

LARK: You understand, then, that there's a certain standard of, ah, wildness expected on shows like this.

BENNETT: I've seen my share. Holidays in the sun. Drunken tarts gagging for it. Is this like that?

LARK: There's an element of that format, but there's also a game aspect, a competitive streak. Physical competition.

BENNETT: *Blind Date meets Gladiators?*

LARK: You might say that. You look as if you could look after yourself.

BENNETT: I've had my share of scrapes. I come out on top. By any means necessary, if you know what I mean and I think you do.

LARK: You work for an estate agent?

BENNETT: I work *as* an estate agent. It's just what I do in the days. History is made at night.

LARK: Do you like your job?

BENNETT: I like helping people. Setting families on the road to home-ownership.

LARK: Really. Really?

BENNETT: Well, no. You're sharp. That's what we're supposed to say. I like the push and the commission. There are so many ways to make something work to your advantage. That side of it is fun, but there's always a problem with the pillocks.

LARK: The pillocks?

BENNETT: Buyers, sellers, the lot of them. Pillocks. Always pulling out at the last minute, or screaming that they've been rooked, that they weren't told something it was their business to find out. You know the sort. Pillocks.

CHISELHURST: Donger, do you find April attractive?

BENNETT: Phwoarr!

TREECE: Really, Tiny.

BENNETT: No, fair question. You look very good for your age, Miss Treece. April. Smart. Good clothes. I like that. Not like some of the shag-slags. Some women put on a suit and look dikey, but not you.

CHISELHURST: If Dr Wendel came at you in a pub with a knife, could you take him?

BENNETT: No offence, but yes.

WENDEL: You might be surprised.

BENNETT: Like I said, I'm a winner. If he had a knife and I didn't, I'd bottle him. End of story. It's not even that he's older and smaller, but it's that he hasn't got the heart. Most people haven't. Too squeamish.

CHISELHURST: Thank you, Harry . . . ah, Donger. We'll be in touch.

BENNETT: Have I passed? Is there anyone behind the mirror?

CHISELHURST: We have enjoyed this interview.

BENNETT: I'm in, aren't I? I bloody knew it. You won't regret this. You need me. I'm a natural for your show, what's it called?

TREECE: Provisionally, *It's a Madhouse!* It may change.

BENNETT: *It's a Madhouse!*, yeah. I like that. Anything can happen in the next half hour. Anything.

CHISELHURST: April will show you out, ah, 'Donger'.

BENNETT: Excellent. I'll be back. Ka-poww!

———

INTERVIEW TRANSCRIPT, NO. 34.

APPLICANT: Shona Murtaugh, 24
FOR MYTHWRHN: Tiny Chiselhurst, Dr Vernon Wendel, Myra Lark, April Treece.

WENDEL: So, Shona . . .

MURTAUGH: [high-pitched giggles]

WENDEL: I beg your pardon.

MURTAUGH: 'So, Shona'. Sounds funny like that. [high-pitched giggles] Are you all right? Look like you've swallowed a lemon, you do.

WENDEL: It'll pass.

MURTAUGH: [high-pitched giggles]
[noise of glasses and bottles rattling on table]

WENDEL: I beg your pardon.

MURTAUGH: You're funny, you are. You've got to have a laugh, haven't you, though. [high-pitched giggles]

WENDEL: It's not actually a physiological necessity, but there may be some psychological explanation.

MURTAUGH: You what? You talk mental, you do. [high-pitched giggles]

CHISELHURST: We were interested in your sexual history.

MURTAUGH: [extremely high-pitched giggles]

CHISELHURST: Well, Shona, we were. You seem to have been an unusually busy girl.

MURTAUGH: I just like ... [high-pitched giggles]

WENDEL: We're not here to judge you.

MURTAUGH: Yes, you are. To see if I'm right for your show. [noise of bracelets clattering]

WENDEL: Well, of course, in that sense, you're right.

MURTAUGH: You should watch what you say. People might think you were taking liberties. People might not like that. People might not like that at all, thank you very much indeed. I should cocoa. [thump on table]

WENDEL: I apologise.

MURTAUGH: So you should, so you should. [high-pitched giggles] I can't help it. It's your face. You look like a bearded collie. I think I'll wet my knickers. I'm mad, me. You must think I'm dreadful. Sorry. [faint grinding of teeth]

LARK: Others have noted the, ah, resemblance between Dr Wendel and a dog.

MURTAUGH: [high-pitched giggles] I'll do myself an injury at this rate. You're a funny mob, aren't you. Not outright funny like Jim Davidson, but it's the way you say things, all sly and clever but with hidden meanings. It's all there, isn't it? You must have enough cleverness to get to the moon in this room, eh? All to get to the bottom of me. It don't seem right.

	I should be trying to get to the bottom of you.
TREECE:	You're not working at the moment.
MURTAUGH:	I was sacked from my last place, at the DSS. Went from one side of the counter to the other. Something will come along. It always does. I'm good at getting jobs, not so good at keeping them. [high-pitched giggles] This is like a job interview, isn't it?
WENDEL:	There are simlarities. But there are differences.
MURTAUGH:	That sounds cryptic. [high-pitched giggles] So, do I get it?
CHISELHURST:	You're short-listed, certainly.
MURTAUGH:	[high-pitched giggles]
CHISELHURST:	April will show you out.
MURTAUGH:	Ta ta for now.
	[noise of leaving]
TREECE:	What was that girl on? Laughing gas?
LARK:	Every time she went off, I felt it in my fillings. It's quite extraordinary.
TREECE:	All the dogs in the area have gone mad.
CHISELHURST:	I think she's a natural for *It's a Madhouse!*.
TREECE:	You can't put Shona on television, Tiny. There'd be bomb threats.
CHISELHURST:	Ape, that girl is a star. Her funeral will be bigger than Diana's.

———

EXTRACT FROM INTERVIEW TRANSCRIPT, NO. 41.

APPLICANT: Martin Leigh, 39
FOR MYTHWRHN: Tiny Chiselhurst, Dr Vernon Wendel, Myra Lark, April Treece.

LEIGH:	Prison's not so bad, once you've made your mark. You just have to let them know where you are on the

totem pole. You pick out some old villain, some big nob from years ago who still thinks he's got it, and you take him apart. Mark his face, put him in the infirmary, get the boot in. Then you take what was his, make it yours. Earn some respect. You can come out ahead, if you've got good currency. Fags and smack, mostly, but you can build an empire on a good source of chocolate.

TREECE: You have a lot of tattoos.

LEIGH: More than you can see. Turns you on, does it? All the birds like ink. And, inside, some of the fellers. You'd think it'd make a difference, but after a while. Well, one hole's as good as another.

WENDEL: And so, how long were you a warder?

LEIGH: About five years. After the Paras and the SAS wouldn't have me, it seemed a decent option. You wouldn't think the Paras and the SAS would be soft, would you? I've had ex-Paras on my block and made them whine and beg. Shows you how much tests and interviews count for anything.

––––––––

EXTRACT FROM INTERVIEW TRANSCRIPT, NO. 72.

APPLICANT: Andrea D'Arbanvilliers-Holmes, 19
FOR MYTHWRHN: Tiny Chiselhurst, Dr Vernon Wendel, Myra Lark, April Treece.

LARK: What are you looking for in a
                             man, Andrea?

D'ARBANVILLIERS-HOLMES: Good shoes are a sign.

LARK: Of what?

D'ARBANVILLIERS-HOLMES: Status, you might call it. There are
                             other giveaways. Like, if he has a

good post code but only owns a
flat. I mean, if he hasn't got enough
to buy a house by now, things are
hardly likely to get better.

LARK: Do you believe in romance?

D'ARBANVILLIERS-HOLMES: Yes, of course. But it's easy to
come by, isn't it. There are always
blokes falling over their willies to
get to you. After a while, you have
to impose stricter criteria. It's not
money in and of itself, it's the
things that come with it.

LARK: Do you believe in marriage?

D'ARBANVILLIERS-HOLMES: Absolutely. That's why I'm so
careful about who I get married
to. And about who I hop into bed
with. It can't be just anybody,
you know.

TREECE: Andrea, why do you want to
be on television?

D'ARBANVILLIERS-HOLMES: Well, it's advertising, isn't it?
I hope to make an impression on
the right people.

EXTRACT FROM INTERVIEW TRANSCRIPT, NO. 108.

APPLICANT: Donovan Wyke, 27
FOR MYTHWRHN: Tiny Chiselhurst, Dr Vernon Wendel, Myra
Lark, April Treece.

WENDEL: I put it to you, Donovan, that you are a habitual
fantasist, a chancer who drifts through life dreaming
of the big scores but inevitably botches even the

petty scams, a bloodsucker who has exploited and betrayed every human connection you have ever made, a man unable to understand even the concepts of honour and fidelity, a compulsive liar with no conscience about wild promises made and broken, a congenital screw-up who is lucky not to have been knifed in an alley or wound up living on the streets begging for spare change to feed your crack habit.

WYKE: Well, I suppose if you were being hardcore about it, but there are explanations.

CHISELHURST: Welcome to *It's a Madhouse!*, Donny.

WYKE: You won't regret this. I can promise you that.

EXTRACT FROM INTERVIEW TRANSCRIPT, NO. 125.

APPLICANT: Petra Kidner, 22
FOR MYTHWRHN: Tiny Chiselhurst, Dr Vernon Wendel, Myra Lark, April Treece.

KIDNER: There's just something sexy about fire. I feel it in my clit, in my nipples, in the scar tissue on my inner thigh and upper back. I love everything about fire. The smoke, the flames, the heat, the crackle. Every month, I take off my eyebrows. See. The pain is there, a part of it, but very minor. I just like to see things burn.

LARK: Things?

KIDNER: Things, *mostly*. But there's nothing like it, you know. The smell, the texture, the taste. Burning flesh. It gets to me. Does that make me weird? I'm not, you know. I like a cup of tea and *EastEnders* and always send my Mum a box of chocs on Mother's Day.

Kim Newman

	Some girls love one particular pop group or a particular type of bloke. With me, it's different. It's fire.
LARK:	So what is your favourite pop song?
KIDNER:	[laughs] What else? Jose Feliciano, 'Come on Baby, Light My Fire'.

———

EXTRACT FROM INTERVIEW TRANSCRIPT, NO. 128.

APPLICANT: Joshua Brew, 22
FOR MYTHWRHN: Tiny Chiselhurst, Dr Vernon Wendel, Myra
Lark, April Treece.

CHISELHURST:	You complained that we hadn't responded to your entry form?
BREW:	IT'S NOT *RIGHT* THAT PEOPLE SHOULD BE TREATED THAT WAY.
CHISELHURST:	We explained that your form was lost in the post.
BREW:	YES, I ACCEPT THAT *NOW*.
CHISELHURST:	But when you phoned the duty officer, you made quite an impression. That's a distinctive voice you've got there.
BREW:	WHEN YOU'RE USED TO PREACHING THE *WORD OF OUR LORD JESUS CHRIST* AT *HEATHEN POP FESTIVALS*, YOU NEED A BIT OF *LUNG POWER*. I DO BREATHING *EXERCISES*.
CHISELHURST:	You'll forgive me for saying this, but you don't seem like the normal type of young person we've been seeing for this show.
BREW:	JUST BECAUSE I'M A *CHRISTIAN* DOESN'T MEAN I DON'T LIKE A '*GOOD TIME*' AS MUCH AS THE NEXT YOUTH. I OWN MANY *CLIFF RICHARD* COMPACT DISCS.

	I CAN JIVE WITH THE BEST OF THEM. SOME OF OUR *CHRISTIAN YOUTH MOVEMENT* EVENINGS ARE EVERY BIT AS *WILD* AS A RAVE. WE PLAY CHARADES AND DRINK *CIDER*.
TREECE:	Kickin'.
BREW:	OH YES. BUT MY MAIN INTEREST IS BATTLING *THE DEVIL* WHEREVER I FIND HIS *EVIL WORKS*. I WON'T TOLERATE *SATAN* IN ANY OF HIS MANY FORMS. THAT I CAN *GUARANTEE*.

MEMO

From: April Treece, production associate.

To: Tiny Chiselhurst, producer/creator

Re: *It's a Madhouse!*

Disaster! Donger Bennett, our prize plonker, the man we most want to see on *It's a Madhouse!*, has found 'true lurve' and wants to back out. Apparently, there's someone out there blind stupid enough to marry him. One Maxine Evenson, another estate agent. They'll probably breed! It's too horrible! We have a contract, we could sue, but that could lead to publicity, which might lead to Derek the Antichrist having us killed. NB: that last bit was a joke! Please advise.

MEMO

From: Tiny Chiselhurst, producer/creator

To: April Treece, assistant producer.

Re: *It's a Madhouse!*

Make an appointment for a house viewing with Miss Evenson, and claim to be Donger's last fiancée — I know that's going to be disgusting for you, but maximum brownie points are involved — with only her best interests at heart. Play her a snippet of the initial interview tape, to wit:

LARK: You've never been married?

BENNETT: I've been engaged a couple of times, if that's
          what it takes to get the cork to pop.

Then present her with the background check dossier we assembled before offering him the contract. You might highlight in pink the more significant sentences. Tell her you had the dossier done when he proposed, like a survey before buying a house. If she's another bloody estate agent, she'll understand. If this is handled quickly, the crisis will fizzle. Trust me.

MEMO

From: April Treece, co-associate producer.

To: Tiny Chiselhurst, producer/creator

Re: *It's a Madhouse!*

Maxine Evenson is out of Donger Bennett's life, lucky girl. On my own initiative, I ordered Claire to call on the Donger for a follow-up interview, which means we owe her hazard pay. While fighting him off and, we trust, not lying back and thinking of television, she let him see suitably cropped and doctored photographs of Andrea Double-Barrel, Miss Giggly and Petra the Pyro. Donger is extremely keen to climb back into the Madhouse. It's my hope he gets on especially well with Martin 'Lockdown' Leigh.

PRODUCTION MEETING, No. 54

PRESENT, for MYTHWRHN PRODUCTIONS: Tiny Chiselhurst (Producer), Phil Bender (Director), Barry Gatlin (Presenter), Constant Drache (Designer), April Treece (Production Assistant),

Claire Bates (Researcher), Davinda Paquignet (Researcher).
PRESENT, for CLOUD 9 TELEVISION: Derek Leech (Supremo),
Heather Wilding (Executive Expediter), Basil Quilbert (Security)

CHISELHURST: You've all seen the highlights reel we put together
of the video interviews. Incidentally, you'll notice
we got coverage of the room from three angles.
The traditional behind-the-mirror shot was
augmented by prototypes of the secret cams we'll
be using for *Madhouse!* None of the interviewees
spotted either gadget, and here we had to install the
equipment in an existing environment rather than
being able to dress the set from the ground up as we
will on location.

WILDING: One is in the light fitting. As for the other, I give up.

CHISELHURST: Behind the fire regulations notice.

WILDING: You're recording now?

CHISELHURST: No. Davinda is taking minutes.

WILDING: Derek?

LEECH: That is acceptable.

CHISELHURST: So, how did you all like the tape? Do you see the
potential.

GATLIN: MY FAVOURITE IS THE *CHRISTIAN!*

PAQUIGNET: Ouch, my ears!

WILDING: We see potential, Tiny. The tape represents your
best prospects for *Madhouse*?

CHISELHURST: We have a couple in back-up, but yes. Dr Wendel?

WENDEL: It's not just a matter of getting the right people,
but of getting the right mix. They can't all be too
samey. There has to be a demographic spread of
class, age and sex types among the subjects.

WILDING: But, ugh, no oldies, right? This is yoof you're
giving us.

WENDEL: No one over thirty-five, indeed. And eighty

	per-cent under twenty-five. We built that early into the parameters of the experiment.
WILDING:	Experiment?
CHISELHURST:	It's how Biffo the Boffin thinks. Heth, believe me, this is Light Entertainment, not Heavy Educational.
WILDING:	Educational worries me. It's a zapper prod. And so, frankly, are a lot of these people. Where did you get them?
CHISELHURST:	They're real people, Heth. They came in of their own accord.
WILDING:	You must have recruited the prison guard . . . what was his name?
TREECE:	Martin Leigh. Lockdown Leigh.
WILDING:	Yeah, him. He's a Central Casting Psycho.
CHISELHURST:	He's our borderline choice, actually. Miss Lark thinks he's a bit obvious. Those tattoos might scare off some of the others too early.
LEECH:	I like Leigh. He'll be a leader. For a while.
CHISELHURST:	My thoughts exactly, Derek. He's a star in the making.
BATES:	The one I hate most is Arabella Thingy-Thingy. The gold-digging posh bird.
BENDER:	She's my favourite. That voice. It's not on a level with the LOUD CHRISTIAN or Miss Giggle, but there's something awful about it. Almost Thatchery.
GATLIN:	Looks like a horse, though. I don't want to fuck her.
BENDER:	Enough people will. You're a Yank, Barry. You don't understand this nanny thing we Brits have.
GATLIN:	I don't want to fuck her. But I do want to hit her.
BATES:	Is that how you divide them. Into ones you want to, uh, have sex with, and ones you want to hit?
GATLIN:	Them? People in general?
BATES:	Contestants, participants, subjects, victims, whatever we call them.

GATLIN: It's a fair enough system. Now, the Flame-On Chick. I definitely want to fuck her. I could light her fire, baby-cakes. You can take that to the bank and cash it!

TREECE: You're a sick man!

GATLIN: That's why you hired me, cherry-bee. You ain't gonna get Alastair Cooke to present *It's a Madhouse!*

TREECE: There's still Craig Charles.

GATLIN: [laughs] Get the fuck outta here!

CHISELHURST: We're off-topic, space kiddettes. Back to our mad people, please.

PAQUIGNET: I don't think they're mad.

CHISELHURST: What do you mean, Davinda?

PAQUIGNET: They're just . . . ordinary. Even the pyromaniac girl. I don't see them as any worse than the people I meet in clubs every night of the week.

WENDEL: Miss Paquignet, you are a junior assistant minion, I am a senior forensic psychologist. I assure you every one of these subjects is suffering from a severe, probably incurable personality disorder.

LEECH: Incurable?

WENDEL: By conventional means.

CHISELHURST: It's possible that *Madhouse!* will have some therapeutic effect.

WILDING: Oh, give us a break, Tiny. This is docusoap shit, not *On the Psychiatrist's Couch.* If we even thought you were sneaking something with content past us, you'd be off the air faster than a Girl Guides *Tribute to Gary Glitter* concert. We're not funding this for therapy. The point is that the people you've selected don't *deserve* help. Right?

TREECE: I certainly don't want to see 'Donger' Bennett get in touch with his inner self and accept it.

BATES/PAQUIGNET: Donger the Plonker!

TREECE: He made a big impression on the girls in the office.

WILDING: And our office too. And we only saw the tape.

TREECE: You should meet him in person, get the full-strength Donger. Someone must have died and made him Bumgroper General. And he has this . . . smell. I think he uses rhino semen as an aftershave.

BATES: If nothing else, *Madhouse!* is the show that will tell the world Donger Bennetts are no longer acceptable.

GATLIN: So, none of you wanted to fuck him?

BATES/PAQUIGNET/TREECE:[retching noises]

GATLIN: Just asking, kittens. I thought he made some solid points, myself.

TREECE: [laughs] Are you sure you don't want to be a contestant rather than the presenter?

GATLIN: [laughs and shivers] No way, Ape.

WILDING: As ever, we're concerned with costs. How have you been coming along with the location?

CHISELHURST: That's Constant's department. Care to report?

DRACHE: Clearly we need isolation, and also a certain ambience of luxury. There's a lifestyle element to the series, a subliminal trace of *Fantasy Island* or the 007 films, so we want a touch of class to set off the anticipated behaviour of the participants. First, we looked for country houses within the United Kingdom, but that proved impractical. Besides the liabilities of renting somewhere we all expect to sustain quite a bit of damage during the recording, our mainland is too small, too crowded. There's nowhere, even in the wilds of Scotland, more than half a day's hike from civilisation. It's important that the players not have the option of just quitting and walking off. In the end, we've settled on an island. Several possibilities in British

	waters have come to light, but we favour the Med.
WILDING:	That'll cost.
DRACHE:	Not in the end. We think the climate, the traditional association of the Mediterranean with 'fun in the sun', will significantly add to the show's appeal. Never make the mistake of underestimating the fuck factor.
BENDER:	*Baywatch* was a joke in the States, but a huge ratings hit here. That's not all down to tits. If you live in Bolton and it's drizzling over the gas-works, you want to switch on the telly and see sun-drenched beaches, azure seas, drinks with a mess of fruit in them and skimpy bathing suits. It's a can't-miss proposition.
CHISELHURST:	And international waters will help with some of the legalities. That's always been a concern for Cloud 9, I know.
LEECH:	It makes sense.
WILDING:	Then it'll be authorised. But we've worked with you before, Constant. I want no overruns on this. Don't kit the set up with so much fucking decor that the animals get lost. This is a people programme, remember.
DRACHE:	We have definite ideas on the look of the show.
TREECE:	Abstract sculptures. Lots of sharp metal edges. Heavy candlesticks. Agricultural implements as ornaments.
CHISELHURST:	You see the possibilities, Derek.
WILDING:	No need to spell it out, Tiny. Now, our other concern. Clearly, we're in a cutthroat business and the competition can't get wind of this. The format'd be too easy to clone.
CHISELHURST:	We're already thinking of licensing it to the States. Look how *Who Wants to Be a Millionaire?* took off.

	And it's a natural for the Japanese market.
WILDING:	Our main concern isn't plagiarism, though. It's backlash. You all know Mr Quilbert?
CHISELHURST:	Basil, hi.
WILDING:	He'll be heading up our security operation. As of now, he owns you. Understand.
QUILBERT:	Good morning, Mr Chiselhurst, Miss Treece. And those I haven't met. We'll have one-to-one sessions scheduled soon. It is a condition of the involvement of Cloud 9 in this project that all matters concerning security be channelled through me. There will be no exceptions. We have prepared acceptable cover stories as to the nature of the programme, based on the mock proposal you sent out to the applicants, and these will be leaked steadily to the trades. We're building the cover stories around Mr Gatlin's track record in extreme stand-up and the well-established 'adventure game' style of show. The truly radical nature of *It's a Madhouse!* should not become evident until we are ready to broadcast. I have prepared various strategies for dealing with the cries for suppression we envison as inevitable. Cloud 9 will preface the premiere with a week of anti-censorship programming, with our tame 'intellectuals' debating the less coherent and attractive members of various censorious or regulatory bodies. The purpose of this is to defang those most likely to object to a show which we consider will have the widest possible audience. If columnists have just spent an hour on Cloud 9 crying for freedom of speech and expression, they can hardly turn round and say we should not broadcast a show they consider to be objectionable. We used this basic strategy very successfully last year

with the launch of the Lolita Channel and a variant
is currently in play to pave the way for our
24-hour War and Gore strand.

CHISELHURST: So, I take it, you're giving us a go. Derek?

WILDING: Cloud 9 will take *Madhouse!* to series. Make us
television history, Tiny.

THE FINAL SELECTION

Harry Bennett

Joshua Brew

Andrea D'Arbanvilliers-Holmes

Petra Kidner

Martin Leigh

Shona Murtaugh

Donovan Wyke

NOTES, by MYRA LARK

The optimum number of participants was set at seven early in the
planning stages. An odd number ensures that, in the event of faction-
alisation, there will be an uneven split, with shifting loyalties or
connections making for an unstable, potentially eventful series of relationship storms. In the event of heterosexual liaisons forming, one of
the men will be left out. The most obvious candidate would be Mr
Brew, because of his religious persuasions. More interesting from our
purposes would be Mr Bennett, whose self-image is constructed
entirely around his ability to coerce sex from females. It has been a
subject for concern that Mr Leigh is too obviously dominant among
the group, being habitually used to attaining his personal objectives
through violence, but Dr Wendel and I have conferred and we see
avenues around this 'problem'. If a blunt solution is required, Mr Leigh
could be handicapped in some manner and forced to a great extent to

rely on the goodwill of the others for his continued comfort. A subtler way out would be to arrange matters so that, from the outset, Mr Wyke is in a more commanding position. His record suggests that he can for a short while at least project the image of a confident, born leader.

After running simulations and role-play scenarios with fully-briefed substitutes, these eventualties occur in every single variation of the basic situation.

a) After three days, multiple sexual exchanges will have taken place. There will also have been betrayals, extensive verbal and minor physical abuse and the development of very deep, though shifting, attachments and dislikes within the group.

b) At the six-day stage, a danger point is reached as the group turn against the experiment. We believe they will make an effort to destroy all recording devices in sight, and repeat our suggestion that these be dummies. Some of the 'hidden' cameras should be easily discoverable and disablable too. It is vital that we keep the subjects' attentions on each other and not foster a group paranoia directed at external bodies (eg: the production company), so we must insert into the scenario the idea that one or more of the subjects are in fact 'plants' working for us. You will recall that an early stage of development, we rejected the idea of actually having a 'mole' in the group as unnecessary and unsatisfying. We believe these subjects are capable of creating and starring in their own paranoia/entertainment scenario with very little help from us.

c) Once the imaginary 'plants' have been dealt with, the programme will continue as before. Food, sexual favours, soft drugs and basic services will become currency. It is to be stressed that we should not go out of our way to make things difficult for the subjects — by withdrawing or tampering with the food supply, for instance — since the purpose of the show is to let them be themselves. Their own personality types are what is at issue here, are the factors that will make them stars. We have every confidence in them.

d) Most of the variables become extreme on the eighth day, when the subjects realise the experiment is not limited to the week they thought they had committed themselves to. Then, the communications from Mr Gatlin should become more cryptic or mocking, playing on the knowledge of the survivor personalities we have gained in the course of the first week. It is possible that the group will forge together to attempt escape, but the inherent instabilities of the personality mix make this a highly unlikely and unworkable venture.

NB: Our amended psych profiles and the medical details of the subjects are attached. Note especially Mr Bennett's asthma, Miss Kidner's understandable high degree of tolerance for searing pain and Mr Wyke's clinical sociopathy.

MEMO

From: Tiny Chiselhurst, producer/creator
To: April Treece, co-associate producer.
Re: *It's a Madhouse!*

We have our madhouse! It's three miles or so from St. Helena, and we've bought it outright so it's our own country (what should we call it?) and we can write the law-book. It was a refuge for the idle rich in the 1920s, and comes complete with a villa Drache is having restored to its original condition at great expense to Cloud 9. From the snaps I've seen, it's very Agatha Christie. The hidden cams are being installed as I write. We're taking advantage of the restoration to build a lot of versatility into the cams. There will be no blind spots on this island, though the stars will be told that there is one room set aside for privacy. Naturally, that's where we expect a great deal of the action to take place, so it's bugged from here to there and gone.

Just in case our stars take too long to find out about each other, we're planting scrapbooks about each of them in the villa library. For the first week, Barry will transmit instructions nightly via a two-way TV hook-up to set out games and contests we've designed to be uneven and unfair, to sow discontent among the stars, and string them along the game aspect. Dr Wendel and Miss Lark disagree about when or if they will tumble to the 'real' nature of the show, but both are sure it won't come until well after we have got the good stuff going. I sense Satellite Awards in the making.

MEMO

From: April Treece, associate producer.
To: Tiny Chiselhurst, producer/creator
Re: *It's a Madhouse!*

Mr Q reports Shona Murtaugh is really Judy Burke, a freelance journalist for *Scam* magazine. The bitch is undercover doing an exposé on rigged docusoaps. She must be imagining headlines along the lines of TV TEAM FORCED ME TO HAVE SEX WITH PLONKER.

MEMO

From: Tiny Chiselhurst, producer/creator
To: April Treece, co-executive producer.
Re: *It's a Madhouse!*

Shona or Judy? It doesn't matter. What I want to know is whether the meltdown giggle is real or fake?

MEMO

From: April Treece, executive producer.
To: Tiny Chiselhurst, producer/creator
Re: *It's a Madhouse!*

The shriek is real. I've got that from three sources. Probably why she got the assignment. No one can stand to have her in the office.

––––––––

MEMO

From: Tiny Chiselhurst, producer/creator
To: April Treece, co-producer.
Re: *It's a Madhouse!*

If the giggle's real, the girl's in. Have Mr Q disable any mobile phone or computer up-link she might contrive to get to our island (that goes for the others too, BTW). Miss Lark considers someone genuinely hiding her name will be a shoo-in to get tagged as the 'plant'. If the scenario runs as expected, I doubt Judy the Journo will ever file copy.

––––––––

REQUEST FORM No. 69

Re: *It's a Madhouse!*
From: Constant Drache, Production Designer
To: April Treece, producer

It is vital that my team be supplied with the following as soon as possible.

1: A set of Sabatier kitchen knives. The sharpest in the world, and the most stylish. The full set runs to eighty-five pieces, and includes special blades for paring apricots, shelling crabs, etc.
2: Traditional tools for the shed. Nothing electric or rubber-gripped, just plain old wooden-handled hammers, screwdrivers, saws, awls and axes. I want that rough, honest-work, *Waltons* feel for this location.
3: Matches (books, boxes, art deco containers), cigarette lighters, flints, candles, magnifying glasses, tapers. Every room, almost every surface, will be fully equipped with little temptations. Also: fire-lighters, paraffin, brandy.
4: Paintings. We're concealing the video com-link behind a print of Edvard

Munch's *The Scream*. It's a cliché touch, perhaps, but effective. Miss Lark and Dr Wendel have come up with a list of artworks appropriate for every participant, and we can make sure their rooms are designed to reflect, intensify or provoke their particular quirks. Bennett's room, for instance, will be furnished with erotic prints of male nudes.

5: Ill-hanging doors. The villa is being refitted from the ground up. It is appropriate, given the title and the intent of the show, that none of the doors or windows be fitted properly. Every angle will be a few degrees out of right, every oblong almost imperceptibly a parallelogram. The house is almost an eighth player in our game, and it gets billing on the title so I'm sure even the tightwads at the top of the Pyramid will be pleased to allow the expenditure.

MEMO

From: April Treece, meister producer.
To: Claire Bates, senior researcher.
Re: *It's a Madhouse!*

Much as I like the idea of Donger Bennett being woken up at three in the morning every night by an hour of Barry White played full blast through the speakers in his room, I think you're missing the point. *Madhouse!* is not about what we do to them, but what they do to each other. Ideally, we should be able to sit back and let them get on with it. That was what all the psycho-babble was about, to harp on Dr Wendel's favourite tune, 'to get the right mix of personalities'. However, thanks very much for the contribution: Tiny does see potential in the music. What we've decided to do is, in effect, put JOSHUA BREW in charge of the entertainment. The CD library will be equipped with every recording Cliff ever made and the player will be set up so that it can only sound out full blast and in every room in the house plus outside speakers that cover the whole island. If JOSHUA wants to listen to his favourite God Bothering chart-topper, then the rest of them have to as well. That should be an interesting frill, and comes out of the personality mix rather than being imposed on it.

———————

PRODUCTION SUB-MEETING, No. 109

PRESENT, for MYTHWRHN PRODUCTIONS: April Treece (Next to God), Claire Bates (Senior Researcher), Davinda Paquignet (Researcher).

PAQUIGNET: So, Ape, who's your fave?

TREECE: Fabu fave or urgh fave?

PAQUIGNET: Fabu, first.

TREECE: Weirdly, it's Petra the Pyro.

BATES: Me too.

PAQUIGNET: Why?

BATES: She's the human one. If it weren't for her kink, she'd be just like us. I hope she comes out of it.

TREECE: So do I. She should be the one who surprises the others. I'm betting on her as the star-in-the-making. She could have a scourge-of-God thing going for her.

PAQUIGNET: And as for the urgh fave? Donger Bennett?

TREECE: At first, but after a while he just gets to seem sad. Probably something about his childhood.

BATES: That's just a strategy, Ape. Donger Bennett is filth in a human skin, a dinosaur penis dragging a walnut brain around.

TREECE: Claire, you *didn't* . . .

BATES: Give me a break, Ape. I'm not that desperate to rise in the industry.

PAQUIGNET: Easy for you to say. You're out of minion class now, darling.

TREECE: I'm with Claire now. It's Andrea I hate most. I remember girls like her from school. Always taking things away from you.

BATES: I've switched too. The real monster is Wyke. The more they dig into his past, the worse he gets. Lark says he's the true sociopath in the pack. Do you know he ran a bogus charity marathon for Eritrea? Organised it, rather. Couldn't run for a bus, if you ask me. And he's the one who picked up the initial flyer in the v.d. clinic.

TREECE: No, that was Leigh. Wyke came from the Young Conservatives. He's never voted in his life, because he doesn't like to give a fixed address. He was buttering up some Andrea clone, trying to get her to invest in a bogus Internet service for dimbo debs. Bastard.

PAQUIGNET: Petra the Pyro is coming for them all, retribution with a flick-lighter.

BATES: Ape, would you watch this show?

TREECE: I don't want to think about that. In the end, I don't think I could resist it. You're still an anti, though?

BATES: No. I cracked when you sent me after Donger. I hate myself for this, but I wouldn't miss it for the world.

PAQUIGNET: It's going to be very popular. I think we're all going to do very well out of it.

TREECE: So, Claire, do you want to change your mind about the credit? After the Donger Affair, Tiny said you could go from Senior Researcher to Junior Producer if you want. It's a Hell of a way to get it, but . . .

BATES: Ape, I'll take it. Where do I sign, and in what?

CONTINUITY ANNOUNCER SCRIPT, CLOUD 9 TELEVISION.

Seven very special people. One very unusual house. An island paradise.
What happens?
You can find out *tonight*, exclusively on Cloud 9 TV, the Derek

Leech Channel. To subscribe to this pay-per-view premiere, call our numbers now!

The show everyone will be talking about tomorrow!

It's people. It's real. It's raw. It's struggle. It's surprise. It's life. It's Something Else.

It's a Madhouse!

Coming up next . . .

This was a story someone *was going to write eventually, just as* My Little Eye *(which covers a related set of phenomena from a different perspective) is a film* someone *(director Marc Evans, as it happens) was going to make. It's worth mentioning that, like Evans, I got the piece down* before *the UK and US TV success of* Big Brother *and* Survivor *led to the whole 'reality TV' boom that is just about burning out now. I had vaguely heard of the European original version of* Big Brother, *but the actual models for* It's a Madhouse! *were even cheesier cable shows like* The Villa – *or, rather, my imagined versions of them from reading TV listings and catching a few trailers. To this day, I've never sat down and watched one of the things since I devote the bulk of my leisure time to reading Proust in the original, listening to Mahler and watching only Iranian films. Of course, now the reality boom has run its course, we can expect a lot more stories and films along these lines. I think I realised this at the time of writing, which is why I chose to concentrate on the behind-the-scenes folk. All the other versions will tell you what happened on the show itself.*

'Going to Series' is also, of course, a sequel to 'Organ Donors'; I was trying to bring Derek Leech's media empire up to date, and fit him into a new political landscape. I did a couple of days work as an expert on the gothic (well, sort of) on Regency House Party, *a genteel if still weird Channel 4 UK docusoap (modern folk have to live in a* Pride and Prejudice *house for a summer and make suitable matches). The experience, both backstage and in front of the cameras, struck me as like living in the Village from* The Prisoner. *I showed this story to the production team and they endorsed its surprising accuracy. I remember one behind-the-scenes person telling me he was amazed that one of the contestants (subjects? victims?) had got through the psych profiling since he was visibly close to cracking up.*

ANGEL DOWN,

SUSSEX

Too Late in the Year, Surely, for Wasps'

The Reverend Mr Bartholomew Haskins, rector of Angel Down, paused by the open gate of Angel Field. His boots sank a little into the frost-crusted mud. Icewater trickled in his veins. He was momentarily unable to move. From somewhere close by came the unmistakable, horrid buzz of a cloud of insects.

It was too late in the year, surely, for wasps. But his ears were attuned to such sounds. Since childhood, he'd been struck with a horror of insects. Jane, his sister, had died in infancy of an allergic reaction to wasp stings. It was thought likely that he might share her acute sensitivity to their venom, but the reason for his persistent fear — as for so much else in his life — was that it was his stick, poked into a pulpy nest, which had stirred the insects to fury. As a boy, he had prayed to Jane for forgiveness as often as he prayed to Our Lord. As a man, he laboured still under the burden of a guilt beyond assuaging.

'Bart,' prompted Sam Farrar, the farmer, 'what is it?'

'Nothing,' he lied.

At the far end of Angel Field was a copse, four elms growing so close together by a shallow pond their roots and branches were knotted. A flock of sheep were kept here. As Sam hauled his gate shut behind them, Haskins noticed the sheep forming a clump, as if eager to gather around their owner. There were white humps in the rest of the field, nearer the copse. They didn't move. Wasps did swarm over them.

Hideous, dreadful creatures.

Haskins forced himself to venture into Angel Field, following the farmer. He kept his arms stiffly by his side and walked straight-legged, wary of exciting a stray monster into sudden, furious hostility.

'Never seen anything like this, Bart,' said Sam. 'In fifty year on the land.'

The farmer waded through his flock and knelt by one of the humps, waving the wasps away with a casual, ungloved hand. The scene swam before Haskins's eyes. A filthy insect crawled on Sam's hand and Haskins's stomach knotted with panic.

He overcame his dread with a supreme effort and joined his friend. The hump was a dead sheep. Sam picked up the animal's woolly head and turned its face to the sunlight.

The animal had been savagely mutilated. Its skull was exposed on one side. The upper lip, cheek and one side of the nose were torn away as if by shrapnel.

'I think it's been done with acid.'

'Should you be touching it, then?'

'Good point.'

Sam dropped the beast's head. The seams in his face deepened as he frowned.

'The others are the same. Strange swirls etched into their hides. Look.'

There were rune-like patches on the dead sheep. They might have been left by a weapon or branding iron. The skin and flesh was stripped off or eaten away.

'My Dad'd never keep beasts in Angel Field. Not after the trouble with my Aunt Rose. That was in '72, afore I was born. You know that story, of course. Was kept from me for a long time. This is where it happened.'

The wasps had come back. Haskins couldn't think.

'Always been something off about Angel Field. Were standing stones here once, like at Stonehenge but smaller. After Rose, Grandad had 'em all pulled down and smashed to bits. There was a fuss and a protest, but it's Farrar land. Nothing busybodies from Up London could do about it.'

Grassy depressions, in a circle, showed where the stones had stood for thousands of years. The dead sheep were within the area that had once been bounded by the ring.

It seemed to Haskins that the insects were all inside the circle too, gathering. Not just wasps, but flies, bees, hornets, ants, beetles. Wings sawed the air, so swiftly they blurred. Mouth-parts stitched, stingers dripped, feelers whipped, legs scissored. A chitinous cacophony.

Bartholomew Haskins was terrified, and ashamed of his fear. Soon, Sam would notice. But at the moment, the farmer was too puzzled and annoyed by what had befallen his sheep.

'I tell you, Bart, I don't know whether to call the vet or the constable.'

'This isn't natural,' Haskins said. 'Someone did this.'

'Hard to picture, Bart. But I think you're right.'

Sam stood up and looked away, at his surviving sheep. None bore any unusual mark, or seemed ailing. But they were spooked. It was in their infrequent bleating. If even the sheep felt it, there must be something here.

Haskins looked about, gauging the positions of the missing stones. The dead sheep were arranged in a smaller circle within the larger, spaced nearly evenly. And at the centre was another bundle, humped differently.

'What's this, Sam?'

The farmer came over.

'Not one of mine,' he said.

The bundle was under a hide of some sort. Insects clung to it like a ghastly shroud. They moved, as if the thing were alive. Haskins struggled to keep his gorge down.

The hide undulated and a great cloud of wasps rose into the air in a spiral. Haskins swallowed a scream.

'It's moving.'

The hide flipped back at the edge and a small hand groped out.

'Good God,' Sam swore.

Haskins knelt down and tore away the hide. It proved to be a tartan blanket, crusted with mud and glittering with shed bug scales..

Large, shining eyes caught the sun like a cat's. The creature gave out a keening shriek that scraped nerves. There was something of the insect in the screech, and something human. For a moment, Haskins thought he was hearing Jane again, in her dying agony.

The creature was a muddy child. A little girl, of perhaps eight. She was curled up like a buried mummy, and brown all over, clothes as much as her face and limbs. Her feet were bare, and her hair was drawn back with a silvery ribbon.

She blinked in the light, still screeching.

Haskins patted the girl, trying to soothe her. She hissed at him, showing bright, sharp, white teeth. He didn't recognise her, but there was something familiar in her face, in the set of her eyes and the shape of her mouth.

She hesitated, like a snake about to strike, then clung to him, sharp fingers latched onto his coat, face pressed to his chest. Her screech was muffled, but continued.

Haskins looked over the girl's shoulder at Sam Farrar. He was bewildered and agoggle. In his face, Haskins saw an echo of the girl's features, even her astonished expression.

It couldn't be . . .

. . . but it was. Missing for over fifty years and returned exactly as she had been when taken.

This was Rose Farrar.

'Beyond the Veil'

'There is one who would speak with you, Catriona Kaye,' intoned Mademoiselle Astarte. 'One who has passed beyond the veil, one who cares for you very much.'

Catriona nodded curtly. The medium's lacquered fingers bit

deeply into her hand. She could smell peppermint on the woman's breath, and gin.

Mademoiselle Astarte wore a black dress, shimmering with beaded fringes. A tiara of peacock feathers gave her the look of an Aztec priestess. A rope of pearls hung flat against her chest and dangled to her navel. As table-rappers went, she was the bee's roller-skates.

She shook her head slightly, eyes shut in concentration. Catriona's hand really hurt now.

'A soldier,' the medium breathed.

The Great War had been done with for seven years. It was a fair bet that anyone of Catriona's age — she was a century baby, born 1900 — consulting a woman in Mademoiselle Astarte's profession would be interested in a soldier. Almost everyone had lost a soldier — a sweetheart, a brother, even a father.

She nodded, noncommittally.

'Yes, a soldier,' the medium confirmed. A lone tear ran neatly through her mascara.

There were others in the room. Mademoiselle didn't have her clients sit about a table. She arranged them on stiff-backed chairs in a rough semi-circle and wandered theatrically among them, seizing with both hands the person to whom the spirit or spirits who spoke through her wished to address themselves.

Everyone was attentive. The medium put on a good show.

Mademoiselle Astarte's mother, a barrel-shaped lady draped in what might once have been a peculiarly ugly set of mid-Victorian curtains, let her fingers play over the keys of an upright piano, tinkling notes at random. It was supposed to suggest the music of the spheres, and put the spirits at ease. Catriona was sure the woman was playing 'Knocked 'Em in the Old Kent Road' very slowly.

Smoke filtered into the room. Not scented like incense, but pleasantly woody. It seemed to come from nowhere. The electric lamps were dimmed with Chinese scarves. A grey haze gathered over the carpet, rising like a tide.

'His passing was sudden,' the medium continued. 'But not painful.

A shock. He hardly knew what had happened to him, was unaware of his condition.'

Also calculated: no upsetting details — choking on gas while gutted on barbed wire, mind smashed by months of bombardment and shot as a coward — and a subtle explanation for why it had taken years for the spirit to come through.

There was a fresh light. It seemed sourceless, but the smoke glowed from within as it gathered into a spiral. A prominent china manufacturer gasped, while his wife's face was wrung with a mix of envy and joy — they had lost a son at Passchendaele.

A figure was forming. A man in uniform, olive drab bleached grey. The cap was distinct, but the face was a blur. Any rank insignia were unreadable.

Catriona's hands were almost bloodless. She had to steel herself to keep from yelping. Mademoiselle Astarte yanked her out of her chair and held tight.

The figure wavered in the smoke.

'He wants you to know . . .'

'. . . that he cares for me very much?'

'Yes. Indeed. It is so.'

Mademoiselle Astarte's rates were fixed. Five pounds for a session. Those whose loved ones 'made contact' were invariably stirred enough to double or triple the fee. The departed never seemed overly keen on communicating with those left behind who happened to be short of money.

Catriona peered at the wavering smoke soldier.

'There's something I don't understand,' she said.

'Yes, child . . .'

Mademoiselle Astarte could only be a year or two older than her.

'My soldier. Edwin.'

'Yes. Edwin. That is the name. I hear it clearly.'

A smile twitched on Catriona's lips.

'Edwin . . . isn't . . . actually *dead*.'

The medium froze. Her nails dug into Catriona's bare arms. Her face was a study in silent fury. Catriona detached Mademoiselle Astarte's hands from her person and stood back.

'The music is to cover the noise of the projection equipment, isn't it?'

Mademoiselle's mother banged the keyboard without interruption. Catriona looked up at the ceiling. The chandelier was an arrangement of mirror pendants clustered around a pinhole aperture.

'There's another one of you in the room upstairs. Cranking the projector. Your father, I would guess. It's remarkable how much more reliable your connection with the spirit world has become since his release from Pentonville.'

She poked her hand into the smoke and wiggled her fingers. Greatcoat buttons were projected onto her hand. The sepia tint was a nice touch.

'You bitch,' Mademoiselle Astarte spat, like a fishwife.

The others in the circle were shocked.

'I really must protest,' began the china manufacturer. His bewildered wife shook her head, still desperate to believe.

'I'm afraid this woman has been rooking you,' Catriona announced. 'She is a clever theatrical performer, and a rather nasty specimen of that unlovely species, the confidence trickster.'

The medium's hands leaped like hawks. Catriona caught her wrists and held the dagger-nails away from her face. Her fringes writhed like the fronds of an angry jellyfish.

'You are a disgrace, Mademoiselle,' she said, coldly. 'And your sham is blown. You would do well to return to the music-halls, where your prestidigitation does no harm.'

She withdrew tactfully from the room. A commotion erupted within, as sitters clamoured for their money back, and Mademoiselle and her mother tried in vain to calm them. The china manufacturer, extremely irate, mentioned the name of a famous firm of solicitors.

In the hallway, Catriona found her good cloth coat and slipped it on over a moderately fringed white dress. It was daringly cut just above the knee, barely covering the rolled tops of her silk stockings. She fixed a cloche hat over her bobbed brown hair, catching sight of her slightly too satisfied little face in the hall mirror. She still had freckles, which made the carefully placed beauty mark a superfluous black dot. Her mouth was nice, though, just the shape for a rich red cupid's bow. She blew a triumphant kiss at herself, and stepped out onto Phene Street.

Her cold anger was subsiding. Charlatanry always infuriated her, especially when combined with cupidity. The field of psychical research would never be taken seriously while the flim-flam merchants were in business, fleecing the grieving and the gullible.

Edwin Winthrop awaited her outside, the Bentley idling at the kerb like a green and brass land-yacht. He sat at the wheel, white scarf flung over his shoulder, a large check cap over his patent-leather hair, warmed not by a voluminous car coat but by a leather flying jacket. The ends of his moustache were almost unnoticeably waxed, and he grinned to see her, satisfied that she had done well at the séance. Her soldier was seven years out of uniform, but still obscurely in the service of his country.

'Hop in, Catty-Kit,' he said. 'You'll want to make a swift get-away, I suspect. Doubtless, the doers of dastardly deeds will have their fur standing on end by now, and be looking to exact a cowardly revenge upon your pretty little person.'

A heavy plant-pot fell from the skies and exploded on the pavement a foot away from her white pumps. It spread shrapnel of well-watered dirt and waxy aspidistra leaves. She glanced up at the town house, noticing the irate old man in an open window, and vaulted into the passenger seat.

'Very neatly done, Cat,' Edwin complimented her.

The car swept away, roaring like a jungle beast. Fearful curses followed. She blushed to hear such language. Edwin sounded the bulb-horn in reply.

She leaned close and kissed his chilled cheek.

'How's the spirit world, my angel?' she asked.

'How would I know?' he shrugged.

'I have it on very good authority that you've taken up residence there.'

'Not yet, old thing. The Hun couldn't get shot of me on the ground or in the air during the late unpleasantness, and seven stripes of foul fellow have missed their chance since the cessation. Edwin Winthrop, Esquire, of Somerset and Bloomsbury, is pretty much determined to stick about on this physical plane for the foreseeable. After all, it's so deuced interesting a sphere. With you about, one wouldn't wish to say farewell to the corporeal just yet.'

They drove through Chelsea, towards St James's Park. It was a bright English autumn day, with red leaves in the street and a cleansing nip in the air.

'What do you make of this?'

One hand on the wheel, he produced a paper from inside his jacket. It was a telegram.

'It's from the Old Man,' he explained.

The message was terse, three words. Angel Down Sussex.

'Is it an event or a place?' she asked.

Edwin laughed, even teeth shining.

'A bit of both, Catty-Kit. A bit of both.'

'In the Strangers Room'

Strictly speaking, the gentle sex were not permitted within the portals of the Diogenes Club. When this was first brought to Winthrop's attention, he had declared his beloved associate to be not a woman but a minx and therefore not subject to the regulation. The Old Man, never unduly deferential to hoary tradition, accepted this and Catriona Kaye was now admitted without question to the Strangers Room. As she breezed into the discreet building in Pall Mall and sat herself daintily down like a deceptively well-behaved schoolgirl, Winthrop derived petty satisfaction from the contained explosions of fury that emanated from behind several raised numbers of *The Times*. He realised that the Old Man shared this tiny pleasure.

Though he had served with the Somerset Light Infantry and the Royal Flying Corps during the Great War, Edwin Winthrop had always been primarily responsible to the Diogenes Club, least-known and most eccentric instrument of the British Government. If anything, peace had meant an increase in his activities on their behalf. The Old Man — Charles Beauregard, Chairman of the Club's Ruling Cabal — had formed a section to look into certain matters no other official body could be seen to take seriously. Winthrop was the leading agent of that special section, and Catriona Kaye, highly unofficially, his most useful aide. Her interest in psychical research, a subject upon which she had written several books, dovetailed usefully with the section's remit, to deal with the apparently inexplicable.

The Old Man joined them in the Strangers Room, signalled an attendant to bring brandy and sat himself down on an upholstered sofa. At seventy-two, his luxurious hair and clipped moustache were snow white but his face was marvellously unlined and his eyes still bright. Beauregard had served with the Diogenes Club for over forty years, since the days when the much-missed Mycroft Holmes chaired the Cabal and the Empire was ceaselessly harried by foreign agents after naval plans.

Beauregard complimented Catriona on her complexion; she smiled and showed her dimple. There was a satirical undercurrent to this exchange, as if all present had to pretend always to be considerably less clever than they were, but were also compelled to communicate on a higher level their genuine acuities. This meant sometimes seeming to take the roles of windy old uncle and winsome young flirt.

'You're our authority on the supernatural, Catriona,' said the Old Man, enunciating all four syllables of the name. 'Does Angel Down mean anything to you?'

'I know of the story,' she replied. 'It was a nine-day wonder, like the *Mary Celeste* or the Angel of Mons. There's a quite bad Victorian book on the affair, Mrs Twemlow's *The Girl Who Went With the Angels*.'

'Yes, our little vanished Rosie Farrar.'

Until today, Winthrop had never heard of Angel Down, Sussex.

'There was a wave of "angelic visitations" in the vicinity of Angel Down in the 1870s,' Catriona continued, showing off rather fetchingly.

'Flying chariots made of stars harnessed together, whooshing through the treetops, leaving burned circles in fields where they touched ground. Dr Martin Hesselius, the distinguished specialist in supernatural affairs, was consulted by the Farrar family and put the business down to a plague of fire elementals. More recently, in an article, Dr Silence, another important researcher in the field, has invoked the Canadian wendigo or wind-walker as an explanation. But in the popular imagination, the visitors have always been angels, though not perhaps the breed we are familiar with from the Bible and Mr Milton. The place name suggests that this rash of events was not unprecedented in the area. Mrs Twemlow unearthed medieval references to miraculous sightings. The visitations revolved around a neolithic circle.'

'And what about the little girl?' Winthrop asked.

'This Rosie Farrar, daughter of a farmer, claimed to have talked with the occupants of these chariots of fire. They were cherubs, she said, about her height, clad in silvery-grey raiment, with large black eyes and no noses to speak of. She was quite a prodigy. One day, she went into Angel Field, where the stones stood, and was transported up into the sky, in the presence of witnesses, and spirited away in a fiery wheel.'

'Never to be seen again?' Winthrop ventured.

'Until yesterday,' the Old Man answered. 'Rose has come back. Or, rather, a child looking exactly as Rose did fifty years ago has come back. In Angel Field.'

'She'd be an old woman by now,' Winthrop said.

'Providing time passes as we understand it in the Realm of the Angels,' said Catriona.

'And where exactly might that be, Cat?'

She poked her tongue out at him, just as the attendant, a fierce-looking ghurka, returned with their brandy. He betrayed no opinion, but she was slightly cowed. Serve her right.

'The local rector made the report. One Bartholomew Haskins. He called the Lord Lieutenant, and the matter was passed on to the Diogenes Club. Now, I'm entrusting it to you.'

'What does this girl have to say for herself?' Catriona asked. 'Does she actually claim to be Rosie Farrar?'

'She hasn't said anything yet. Photographs exist of the real Rose, and our girl is said to resemble them uncannily.'

'Uncannily, eh?' said Winthrop.

'Just so.'

'I should think this'll make for a jolly weekend away from town,' Winthrop told the Old Man. 'Angel Down is near enough to Falmer Field for me to combine an investigation with a couple of sorties in *Katie*.'

Winthrop had kept up his flying since the War, maintaining his own aeroplane, a modified Camel fighter named *Katie*. She was getting to be a bit of an antique paraded next to the latest line in gleaming metal monoplanes, but he trusted her as much as he did Catriona or the Bentley. He knew the kite's moods and foibles, and could depend on her in a pinch. If she could come through the best efforts of the late Baron von Richthofen's Flying Circus, she could survive any peace-time scrape. If he were to tangle with 'chariots of stars', he might have need of the faithful *Katie*.

Catriona was thoughtful. As ever, she saw this less as a jaunt than he did. He needed her to balance him. She had a strong sense of what was significant, and kept him from haring off on wild streaks when he needed to be exercising the old brain-box.

'Has this miraculous reappearance been made public?'

The Old Man's brows knit. 'I'm afraid so. The Brighton *Argus* carried the story this morning, and the afternoon editions of all the dailies have it, in various lights. Haskins knows enough to keep the child away from the press for the moment. But all manner of people are likely to take an interest. You know who I mean. It would be highly convenient if you could come up with some unsensational explanation that will settle the matter before it goes any further.'

Winthrop understood. It was almost certain this business was a misunderstanding or a hoax. If so, it was best it were blown up at once. And, if not, it was sadly best that it be thought so.

'I'll see what I can do, Beauregard.'

'Good man. Now, you children run off and play. And don't come back until you know what little Rosie is up to.'

———

'A Demure Little Thing'

With Sam Farrar queerly reluctant to take his miraculously returned aunt into his house, Haskins had to put the little girl up at the rectory. He wondered, chiding himself for a lack of charity, whether Sam's hesitation was down to the question of the stake in Farrar Farm, if any, to which Rose might be entitled. It was also true that for Sam and Ellen to be presented in late middle age with a child they might be expected to raise as their own would be an upheaval in their settled lives.

The girl had said nothing yet, but sat quietly in an oversized chair in his study, huddled inside one of Haskins's old dressing gowns. Mrs Cully, his housekeeper, had got the poor child out of her filthy clothes and given her a bath. She had wanted to throw away the ruined garments, but Haskins insisted they be kept for expert examination. Much would hinge on those dirty rags. If it could be proven that they were of more recent provenance than 1872, then this was not Rose Farrar.

Haskins sat at his desk, unable to think of his sermon. His glance was continually drawn to the girl. Now she had stopped keening, she seemed a demure little thing. She sat with one leg tucked up under her and the other a-dangle, showing a dainty, uncallused foot. With her face clean and her hair scrubbed — she insisted on having her silver ribbon back — she could have been any well-brought-up child waiting for a story before being packed off to bed.

Telegrams had arrived all morning. And the telephone on his desk had rung more often than in the last six months. He was to expect a pair of investigators from London. Representatives from Lord Northcliffe's *Mail* and Lord Beaverbrook's *Express* had made competing overtures to secure the 'rights' to the story. Many others had shown an interest, from charitable bodies concerned with the welfare of 'a unique orphan' to commercial firms who wished 'the miracle girl' to endorse their soap or tonic. Haskins understood the girl must be shielded from such public scrutiny, at least until the investigators had assessed her case.

One telegram in particular stirred Haskins. A distinguished person offered Rose any service it was within his power to perform. Haskins had replied swiftly, inviting the author-knight to Angel Down. If anyone could get to the bottom of the matter, it would be the literary lion whose sharpness of mind was reputed to be on a par with that of the detective he had made famous and who had worked so tirelessly in his later years to demonstrate the possibility of the miraculous here on Earth.

The girl seemed unaware of Haskins's fascination with her. She was a Victorian parent's idea of perfection — pretty as a picture, quiet as a mouse, poised as a waxwork. Haskins wondered about the resemblance to Sam Farrar. It had seemed so strong in the first light of discovery but was now hard to see.

He got up from his desk, abandoning his much-begun and little-developed sermon, and knelt before the child. He took her small hands, feeling bird-like bones and fragile warmth. This was a real girl, not an apparition. She had been vigorously bathed and spent the night in the guest bedroom. Ghosts did not leave dirty bathwater or crumpled sheets. She had consumed some soup last night and half an apple for breakfast.

Her eyes fixed his and he wanted to ask her questions.

Since she had stopped making her peculiar noise, she had uttered no sound. She seemed to understand what was said to her but was disinclined to answer. She did not even respond to attempted communication via rudimentary sign language or Mrs Cully's baby-talk.

'Rose?' he asked.

There was no flicker in her eyes.

Sam had produced pictures, yellowed poses of the Farrar children from the dawn of photography. One among a frozen gaggle of girls resembled exactly this child. Sam reluctantly confirmed the child in the portrait as his vanished Aunt Rose, the Little Girl Who Went With the Angels.

'What happened to you, Rose?'

According to the stories, she had been swept up to the Heavens in a column of starlight.

Haskins heard a buzzing. There was a wasp in the room!

He held the girl's hands too tightly. Her face contorted in pain. He let go and made an attempt to soothe her, to prevent the return of her screeches.

Her mouth opened, but nothing came out.

The wasp was still here. Haskins was horribly aware of it. His collar was damp and his stomach shifted.

There was more than one.

The buzzing grew louder. Haskins stood up and looked about for the evil black-and-yellow specks.

He looked again at Rose, suddenly afraid for her. The girl's face shifted and she was his sister, Jane.

It was like an injection of wasp venom to the heart.

Her mouth was a round aperture, black inside. The wasp shrill was coming from her.

Haskins was terrified, dragged back to his boyhood, stripped of adult dignities and achievements, confronted with his long-dead victim.

He remembered vividly the worst thing he had ever done. The stick sinking into the nest. His cruel laughter as the cloud swarmed from the sundered ovoid and took flight, whipped away by strong wind.

Jane stood on the chair, dressing gown a heavy monk's robe. She still wore her silver ribbon. She wasn't *exactly* Jane. There was some Rose in her eyes. And a great deal of darkness, of something else.

She reached out to him as if for a cuddle. He fell to his knees, this time in prayer. He tried to close his eyes.

The girl's mouth was huge, a gaping circle. Black apparatus emerged, a needle-tipped proboscis rimmed with whipping feelers. It was an insectile appendage, intricate and hostile, parts grinding together with wicked purpose.

Her eyes were black poached eggs overflowing their sockets, a million facets glinting.

The proboscis touched his throat. A barb of ice pierced his skin. Shock stopped his heart and stilled his lungs, leaving his mind to flutter on for eternal seconds.

———

'A Funny Turn'

Angel Down Rectory was a nice little cottage close by the church, rather like the home Catriona had grown up in. Her kindly father was a clergyman in Somerset, in the village where Edwin's distant father had owned the Manor House without really being Lord of the Manor.

Colonel Winthrop had been literally distant for most of his later life, stationed in India or the Far East after some scandal which was never spoken of in the village. An alienist might put that down as the root of a streak of slyness, of manipulative ruthlessness, that fitted his son for the murkier aspects of his business. Recognising this dark face, fed with blood in the trenches and the skies, as being as much a part of Edwin's personality as his humour, generosity and belief in her, Catriona did her best to shine her light upon it, to keep him fixed on a human scale. The Reverend Kaye mildly disapproved of her spook-chasing and changed the subject whenever anyone asked about his daughter's marriage plans, but was otherwise as stalwart, loyal and loving a parent as she could wish.

They had found the village with ease, homing in on a steeple visible from a considerable distance across the downs. For such a small place, Angel Down was blessed with a large and impressive church, which was in itself suggestive. If a site can boast an ancient stone circle and a long-established Christian church, it is liable to have been a centre of unusual spiritual activity for quite some time.

There was something wrong. She knew it at once. She made no claim to psychic powers, but had learned to be sensitive. She could almost always distinguish between an authentic spectre and a fool in a bedsheet, no matter how much fog and shadow were about. It was a question of reading the tiniest signs, often on an unconscious level.

'Careful, dearest,' she told Edwin, as they got out of the car.

He looked at her quizzically. She couldn't explain her unsettling feeling, but he had been with her in enough bizarre situations to accept her shrug of doubt as a trustworthy sign of danger ahead. He thrust a hand into his coat pocket, taking hold of the revolver he carried when about the business of the Diogenes Club.

She heard something. A sound like an insect, but then again not. It was not within her experience.

Edwin rapped on the door with his knuckles.

A round pink woman let them in. Upon receipt of Edwin's card, the housekeeper — Mrs Cully — told them they were expected and that she would tell the rector of their arrival.

The narrow hallway was likeably cluttered. A stand was overburdened with coats and hats, boots lined up for inspection nearby, umbrellas and sticks ready for selection. A long-case clock ticked slow, steady seconds.

There was no evidence of eccentricity.

Mrs Cully returned, pink gone to grey. Catriona was immediately alert, nerves singing like wires. The woman couldn't speak, but nodded behind her, to the rector's study.

With his revolver, Edwin pushed open the door.

Catriona saw a black-faced man lying on the carpet, eyes staring. His hands were white.

Edwin stepped into the room and Catriona followed. They both knelt by the prone man. He had a shock of red-grey hair and wore a clerical collar, taut as a noose around his swollen throat.

The Reverend Mr Haskins — for this could be none other — was freshly dead. Still warm, he had no pulse, heartbeat or breath. His face was swollen and coal-coloured. His mouth and eyes were fixed open. Even his tongue was black and stiff. Droplets of blood clung to his hard, overripe cheeks.

'Snakebite?' she asked, shuddering.

'Could be, Cat,' he said, standing up.

She was momentarily troubled. Did she hear the soft slither of a dire reptile winding across the carpet? She was not fond of the beasts. A criminal mandarin-sorcerer had once tried to murder Edwin with a black mamba delivered in a Harrod's hamper. She had been unfortunate enough to be sharing a punt with him when the scheme came to hissing light. She had cause to remember that snakes can swim.

'And who have we here?' he asked.

She stood. Edwin had found the girl, sat calmly in an armchair, wearing a man's large dressing gown, leafing through a picture book of wild flowers. The supposed Rose Farrar was a tiny thing, too sharp-featured to be considered pretty but with a striking, triangular face and huge, curious eyes. Her expression was familiar to Catriona. She had seen it on shell-shocked soldiers coming home from a war that would always be fought in their minds.

She wanted to warn Edwin against touching the girl. But that would have been ridiculous.

'Little miss, what happened?' he asked.

The girl looked up from her book. For a moment, she seemed like a shrunken adult. The real Rosie would be almost sixty, Catriona remembered.

'He had a funny turn,' the child said.

That much was obvious.

'Do you have a name, child?' he asked.

'Yes,' she said, disinclined to reveal more.

'And what might it be?' she asked.

The little girl turned to look at her, for the first time, and said, 'Catriona.'

It was a tiny shock.

'I am Catriona,' Catriona said. 'And this is Edwin. You are . . . ?'

She held up her book. On the page was a picture of a wild rose, delicate green watercolour leaves with incarnadine petal splashes.

'Rose,' the girl said.

This was considerably more serious than a hoax. A man was dead. No longer just a puzzle to be unpicked and forgotten, this was a mystery to be solved.

A panicked cough from the doorway drew their attention. It was Mrs Cully, eyes fixed on the ceiling, away from the corpse.

'There's another come visiting,' she said.

Catriona knew they must have been racing newspapermen to get here. There would be reporters all over the village, and soon — when this latest development was out — front-page headlines in all the papers.

'Is it someone from the press?' Edwin asked.

The woman shook her head. A big, elderly man gently stepped around her and into the room. He had a large, bushy moustache and kindly eyes. She knew him at once.

'Sir Arthur,' said Edwin, 'welcome to Angel Down. I wish the circumstances of our meeting had been different.'

'Venomous Lightning'

Winthrop shifted his revolver to his left hand, so he could extend his right arm and shake hands with Sir Arthur Conan Doyle. The author was in his mid-sixties, but his grip was firm. He was an outdoor-looking man, more Watson than Holmes.

'You have me at a disadvantage, sir.'

'I am Edwin Winthrop, of the Diogenes Club.'

'Oh,' said Sir Arthur, momentously, '*them.*'

'Yes, indeed. Water under the bridge, and all that.'

Sir Arthur rumbled. He had clearly not forgotten that the Diogenes Club had once taken such a dim view of his mentioning their name in two pieces placed in the Strand magazine that considerable pressure had been brought to ensure the suppression of further such narratives. While the consulting detective was always slyly pleased that his feats be publicised, his civil servant brother — Beauregard's predecessor — preferred to hide his considerable light under a bushel. Sir Arthur had never revealed the exact nature of the Club and Mycroft's position within it, but he had drawn attention to a man and an institution who would far rather their names were unknown to the general public. No real lasting harm was done, though the leagues who followed Sherlock Holmes were tragically deprived of thrilling accounts of several memorable occasions upon which he had acted as an instrument of his older brother and his country.

'And this is Miss Catriona Kaye,' Winthrop continued.

'I know who she is.'

The sentence was like a slap, but Catriona did not flinch at it.

'This woman,' Sir Arthur said, 'has made it her business to harass those few unselfish souls who can offer humanity the solace it so badly needs. I've had a full account of her unwarranted attack this morning on Mademoiselle Astarte of Chelsea.'

Winthrop remembered Sir Arthur was a committed, not to say credulous, Spiritualist.

'Sir Arthur,' said Catriona, fixing his steely gaze, 'Mademoiselle Astarte is a cruel hoaxer and an extortionist. She does your cause — nay, *our* cause — no credit whatsoever. I too seek only light in the darkness. I should have thought, given your well-known association with the most brilliant deductive mind of the age, you would see my activities as a necessary adjunct to your own.'

She had him there. Sir Arthur was uncomfortable, but too honest a man not to admit Catriona was right. In recent years, he had been several times duped by the extraordinary claims of hoaxers. There was that business with the fairies. He looked around the room, avoiding Catriona's sharp eyes. He saw the body of Mr Haskins. And the girl curled up in the chair.

'Good Lord,' he exclaimed.

'This is exactly the scene we found,' Winthrop said.

'I heard a noise earlier, as we arrived,' Catriona revealed. 'Something like an insect.'

'It seems as if a whole hive of bees has stung him.'

Sir Arthur had trained as a doctor, Winthrop remembered.

'Could it have been poison?' he asked.

'If so, someone's tidied up,' Sir Arthur said, confidently turning the swollen head from side to side. 'No cup or glass with spilled liquid. No half-eaten cake. No dart stuck in the flesh. The face and chest are swollen but not the hands or, I'll wager, the feet. I'd say whatever struck him did so through this wound here, in the throat.'

A florin-sized red hole showed in the greasy black skin.

'It is as if he were struck by venomous lightning.'

Sir Arthur found an orange blanket in a basket by the sofa and spread it over the dead man. The twisted shape was even more ghastly when shrouded.

'The girl says he had a "funny turn",' Winthrop said.

For the first time, Sir Arthur considered the child.

'Is this Rose? Has she spoken?'

The girl said nothing. She was interested in her book again. At her age, she could hardly be expected to be much concerned with grown-up things.

If she was the age she seemed.

Sir Arthur went over to the chair and examined the girl. His hands, steady as a rock when patting down a gruesome corpse, trembled as they neared her hair. He touched fingertips to the silver ribbon that held back her curls, and drew them away as if shocked.

'Child, child,' he said, tears in his eyes, 'what wonders have you seen? What hope can you give us?'

This was not the dispassionate, scientific interrogation Winthrop had planned. He was touched by the old man's naked emotion. Sir Arthur had lost a son in the War, and thereafter turned to Spiritualism for comfort. He betrayed a palpable need for confirmation of his beliefs. Like the detective he had made famous, he needed evidence.

The possible Rose was like a child queen regarding an aged and loyal knight with imperious disdain. Sir Arthur literally knelt at her feet, looking up to her.

'Do you know about the Little People?' she asked.

———

'A Gift From Faerie'

Catriona had been given to understand that Rose did not speak, but she was becoming quite chatty. Sir Arthur quizzed her about 'the Little People', who were beginning to sound more like fairies than cherubs. She wondered if Rose were not one of those children who cut her personality to suit the adult or adults she was with, mischievous with one uncle, modest with the next. The girl was constantly clever, she felt, but otherwise completely mercurial.

It was only a few years since the name of Sir Arthur Conan Doyle, a watchword for good sense to most of Great Britain, had been devalued by the affair of the Cottingley Fairies. Two little girls, not much older than this child, had not only claimed to be in regular communion with the wee folk but produced photographs of them — subsequently shown to be amateur forgeries — which Sir Arthur rashly endorsed as genuine, even to the extent of writing *The Coming of the Fairies*, an inspirational book about the case. Though the hoax had been exploded a dozen times, Sir Arthur stubbornly refused to disbelieve. Catriona sensed the old man's *need* for faith, his devout wish for the magical to penetrate his world and declare itself irrefutably.

'I went away with them,' the girl told them. 'The Little People. I was in their home in the sky. It's inside of a cloud, and like a hollow tree, with criss-cross roots and branches. We could all fly there, or float. There was no up or down. They played with me for ever such a long time. And gave me my ribbon.'

She turned her head, showing the ribbon in her hair. Catriona had noticed it before.

'Rose, may I see your ribbon?' Sir Arthur asked.

Catriona wasn't comfortable with this. Surely something should be done for poor Mr Haskins before the girl was exhaustively interviewed.

Rose took the ribbon out of her hair solemnly and offered it to Sir Arthur.

'Extraordinary,' he said, running it through his fingers. He offered it to Catriona.

She hesitated a moment and accepted the thing.

It was not any fabric she knew. Predominantly silvery, it was imprinted with green shapes, like runes or diagrams. Though warm to the touch, it might be a new type of processed metal. She crumpled the ribbon into a ball, then opened her fist. The thing sprang back into its original shape without a crease.

'You're bleeding,' Edwin said.

The edges were sharp as pampas grass. Without feeling it, she had shallowly grazed herself.

'May I have it again now?' Rose asked.

Catriona returned the ribbon, which the girl carefully wound into her hair. She did not knot it, but *shaped* it, into a coil which held back her curls.

'A gift from faerie,' Sir Arthur mused.

Catriona wasn't sure. Her hand was began to sting. She took a hankie from her reticule and stemmed the trickle of blood from the scratch.

'Rose, my dear,' said Sir Arthur. 'It is now 1925. What year was it when you went away, to play with the Little People? Was it a long time ago? As long ago, ahem, as 1872?'

The girl didn't answer. Her face darkened, as if she were suddenly afraid or unable to do a complicated sum in mental arithmetic.

'Let's play a game?' Edwin suggested, genially. 'What's this?'

He held up a pencil from the rector's desk.

'Pencil,' Rose said, delighted.

'Quite right. And this?'

The letter-opener.

'A thin knife.'

'Very good, Rose. And this?'

He picked the telephone receiver up from its cradle.

'Telly Phone,' the girl said.

Edwin set the receiver down and nodded in muted triumph.

'Alexander Graham Bell,' he said, almost sadly. '1876.'

'She's been back two days, man,' Sir Arthur said, annoyed. He turned to the girl and tried to smile reassuringly. 'Did the rector tell you about the telephone? Did you hear it make a ring-ring noise, see him talk to friends a long way away with it?'

Rose was guarded now. She knew she had been caught out.

If this was a hoax, it was not a simple one. That ribbon was outside nature. And Haskins had died by means unknown.

'Why don't you use that instrument to summon the police?' said Sir Arthur, nodding at the telephone.

'Call the police?' Edwin said. 'Tut-tut, what would Mr Holmes say? This matter displays unusual features which the worthy Sussex constabulary will not be best equipped to deal with.'

'This man should at least have a doctor look at him.'

'He has had one, Sir Arthur. You.'

The author-knight was not happy. And neither was she.

––––––––

'A Changeling'

Winthrop was satisfied that this girl was not the real Rose, and that an imposture was being planned — perhaps as part of a scheme to dupe the farmer, Sam Farrar, out of his property. The Reverend Mr Haskins must have stumbled onto the trick and been done nastily to death. From the look of the rector's throat, something like a poison-tipped spear had been used on him. It remained for the girl to be persuaded to identify the conspirators who had tutored her in imposture. She was too young to be guilty by herself.

'Now, missy, let's talk about this game you've been playing,' he said. 'The dress-up-and-pretend game. Who taught it to you?'

The girl's face was shut. He thought she might try crying. But she was too tough for that. She was like any adult criminal, exposed and sullen, refusing to cooperate, unaffected by remorse.

'It's not that simple, Edwin,' Catriona said. 'The ribbon.'

Winthrop had thought of that. Lightweight metallicised fabrics were being used in aircraft manufacture these days, and that scrap might well be an offcut. It was a strange touch, though.

'There's something else. Look at her.'

He did. She had an ordinary face. There was something about the eyes, though. A violet highlight.

'There are Little People,' she said. 'There are, there are. They are bald, and have eyes like saucers, and no noses. They played with me. For a long time. And they have friends here, on the ground. Undertakers with smoked glasses.'

'What is your name?'

'Rose,' she said, firmly.

Was she trying to get back to the story she had been taught? Or had she been hypnotised into believing what she was saying?

Suddenly, he saw what Catriona meant.

The girl's face had changed, not just its expression but its shape. Her nose was rounder, her chin less sharp, her cheekbones gone. Her mouth had been thin, showing sharp teeth; now she had classic bee-stung lips, like Catriona's. Her curls were tighter, like little corkscrews.

He stood back from her, worried by what he had seen. He glanced at the rector's body, covered with its orange blanket. It was not possible, surely, that this child . . .

. . . this angel?

'What is it, man? What is it?'

Sir Arthur was agitated, impatient at being left out. He must feel it humiliating not to have spotted the clue. Of course, he had come into it later and not seen the girl as she was when Winthrop and Catriona had arrived. It seemed now that her face had always been changing, subtly.

'Consider her face,' Winthrop said.

'Yes.'

'It changes.'

The violet highlights were green now.

Sir Arthur gasped.

The girl looked older, twelve or thirteen. Her feet and ankles showed under the dressing gown. Her shoulders filled the garment out more. Her face was thinner again, eyes almost almond.

'This is not the girl who was taken away,' Sir Arthur said. 'She is one of them, a Changeling.'

For the first time, Winthrop rather agreed with him.

'There are bad fairies,' Sir Arthur said. 'Who steal away children and leave one of their own in the crib.'

Winthrop knew the folk-tales. He wasn't satisfied of their literal truth, but he realised in a flash that this girl might be an instance of whatever phenomenon gave rise to the stories in the first place.

You didn't have to believe in fairies to know the world was stranger than imagined.

'Who are you, Rose?' Catriona asked, gently.

She knelt before the girl, as Sir Arthur had done, looking up into her shifting face.

Winthrop couldn't help but notice that the girl's body had become more womanly inside the dressing gown. Her hair straightened and grew longer. Her eyebrows were thinner and arched.

'Rose?'

Catriona reached out.

The girl's face screwed up and she hissed, viciously. She opened her mouth, wider than she should have been able to. Her incisors were needle-fangs. She hissed again, flicking a long, fork-tipped tongue.

A spray of venom scattered at Catriona's face.

'Cruel Cunning'

The shock was so great she almost froze, but Catriona flung her hand in front of her eyes. The girl's sizzling spit stung the back of her hand. She wiped it instinctively on the carpet, scraping her skin raw. She had an idea the stuff was deadly.

The girl was out of her chair and towering above her now, shoulders and hips swaying, no longer entirely human. Her skin was greenish, scaled. Her eyes were red-green, with triangular pupils. Catriona thought she might even have nictitating membranes.

Catriona remembered the slither of the mamba.

She was frozen with utter panic, and a tiny voice inside nagged her for being weak.

Edwin siezed the letter opener — the thin knife — from the desk and stabbed at the snake girl.

A black-thorned green hand took his wrist and bent it backwards. He dropped his weapon. Her hissing face closed in on his throat.

Catriona's panic snapped. She stuck her foot between the girl's ankles and scythed her legs out from under her.

They all fell in a tangle.

Rose broke free of them, leaving the dressing gown in a muddle on the floor.

She stood naked by Sir Arthur, body scaled and shimmering, as beautiful as horrid. She was striped in many shades of green, brown, yellow, red and black. She had the beginnings of a tail. Her hair was flat against her neck and shoulders, flaring like a cobra's hood. Her nose and ears were slits, frilled inside with red cilia.

Catriona and Edwin tried to get up, but were in each other's way.

Rose smiled, fangs poking out of her mouth, and laid her talons on Sir Arthur's lapels. She crooned to him, a sibilant susurrus of fascination. In the movements of her hips and shoulders and the arch of her eyes, there was a cruel cunning that was beyond human. This was a creature that killed for the pleasure of it, and was glad of an audience.

Sir Arthur was backed against a mantelpiece. His hand reached out, and found a plain crucifix mounted between two candlesticks. The Reverend Mr Haskins had evidently not been very High Church, for there were few other obvious signs of his profession in the room.

Rose's black-red lips neared Sir Arthur's face, to administer a killing kiss. Her fork-tipped tongue darted out and slithered between his eyes and across his cheek, leaving a shining streak.

Sir Arthur took the cross and intersposed it between his face and hers. He pressed it to her forehead.

Rose reacted as if a drop of molten lead had been applied. She screeched inhumanly and turned away, crouching into a ball. The scales on her legs and back sizzled and disappeared, like butter pats on a hot griddle. Her body shrank again, with a cracking of bones.

'Oh my stars,' said someone from the doorway.

Two men, strangers, stood in the hall, amazed at the scene. The one who spoke was a prosperous-looking man, face seamed and clothes practical. Behind him was the silhouette of someone large, soft and practically hairless.

Rose looked up at the newcomers. Her eyes were round again, and full of puzzlement rather than malice. Catriona had a sense that the monster was forgotten.

The girl snatched up the dressing gown and slipped into it, modestly closing it over her body. Then she hurled herself at a window, and crashed through the panes into the gathering dusk outside.

She hit the ground running and was off, away over the fields.

'I knew that weren't Aunt Rose,' said the newcomer.

———

'Anti-Christine'

'The Great Beast is among you,' announced the fat bald man, referring to himself rather than the departed Rose.

Sir Arthur still clung to the cross that had seen off the Rose creature.

'Of all things, I thought of *Dracula*,' he said, wondering at his survival. 'Bram Stoker's novel.'

Winthrop was familiar with the book.

'The cross had exactly the effect on that creature as upon the vampires in *Dracula*.'

'Ugh,' said the bald man, 'what a horrid thing. Put it away, Sir Arthur.'

Farrar had noticed the rector's body, and was sunk into a couch with his head in his hands. This was too weird for most people. The honest farmer would have to leave these matters for the experts in the uncanny.

The man who had arrived with Farrar wore a once-expensive coat. The astrakhan collar was a little ragged and his pinstripe trousers shiny at the knees. A great deal of this fellow's time was spent on his knees, for one reason or other. His face was fleshy, great lips hanging loose. Even his hands were plump, slug-white flippers. His great dome shone and his eyes glinted with unhealthy fire.

Winthrop recognised the controversial figure of Aleister Crowley, self-styled 'wickedest man in England'. Quite apart from his well-known advocacy of black magic, sexual promiscuity and drug use, the brewery heir — perhaps from a spirit of ingrained contrariness — had blotted his copybook in loudly advocating the Kaiser's cause during the War. In his younger days, he was reckoned a daring mountaineer, but his vices had transformed him into a flabby remnant who looked as though he would find a steep staircase an insurmountable obstacle.

'Aren't you supposed to be skulking in Paris?' Winthrop asked.

'Evidently, sir, you have the advantage of me,' Crowley admitted.

'Edwin Winthrop, of the Diogenes Club.'

The black magician smiled, almost genuinely.

'Charles Beauregard's bright little boy. I have heard of you, and of your exploits among the shadows. And this charming *fille de l'occasion* must be Miss Catriona Kaye, celebrated exposer of charlatans. I believe you know that dreadful poseur A.E. Waite. Is it not well past time you showed him up for the faker he is, dear lady?'

Crowley loomed over Catriona. Winthrop remembered with alarm that he was famous for bestowing 'the serpent's kiss', a mouth-to-mouth greeting reckoned dangerous to the receiving party. He contented himself with kissing her knuckles, like a gourmand licking the skin off a well-roasted chicken leg.

'And Sir Arthur Conan Doyle, whose fine yarns have given me and indeed all England such pleasure. This is a most distinguished company.'

Sir Arthur, who could hardly fail to know who Crowley was, looked at his crucifix, perhaps imagining it might have an efficacy against the Great Beast.

If so, Crowley read his mind. 'That bauble holds no terror for a magus of my exalted standing, Sir Arthur. It symbolises an era which is dead and gone, but rotting all around us. I have written to Mr Trotsky in Moscow, offering to place my services at his disposal if he would charge me with the responsibility of eradicating Christianity from the planet.'

'And has he written back?' Catriona asked, archly.

'Actually, no.'

'*Quelle surprise!*'

Crowley flapped his sausage-fingers at her.

'Naughty, naughty. Such cynicism in one so young. You would make a fine Scarlet Woman, my dear. You have all the proper attributes.'

'My sins are scarlet enough already, Mr Crowley,' Catriona replied. 'And, to put it somewhat bluntly, I doubt from your general appearance that you would be up to matching them these days.'

The magus looked like a hurt little boy. For an instant, Winthrop had a flash of the power this man had over his followers. He was such an obvious buffoon one might feel him so pathetic that to contradict his constant declamations of his own genius would be cruel. He had seriously harmed many people, and sponged unmercifully off many others. The Waite he had mentioned was, like the poet Yeats, another supposed initiate of a mystic order, with whom he had been conducting an ill-tempered feud over the decades.

'The time for the Scarlet Woman is ended,' Crowley continued, back in flight. 'Her purpose was always to birth the perfect being, and now that has been superseded. I hurried here on the boat train when news reached me that *she* had appeared on Earth. She who will truly bring to an end the stifling, milk-and-water age of the cloddish carpenter.'

'I find your tone objectionable, man,' Sir Arthur said. 'A clergyman is dead.'

'A modest achievement, I admit, but a good start.'

'The fellow's mad,' Sir Arthur blustered. 'Quite cuckoo.'

Winthrop tended to agree but wanted to hear Crowley out.

He nodded towards the smashed window. 'What do you think she is, Crowley? The creature you saw attacking us?'

'I suppose Anti-Christ is too masculine a term. We shall have to get used to calling her the Anti-Christine.'

Catriona, perhaps unwisely, giggled. She was rewarded with a lightning-look from the magus.

'She was brought to us by demons, in the centre of a circle of ancient sacrifice, enlivened by blood offerings. I have been working for many years to prepare the Earth for her coming, and to open the way for her appearance upon the great stage of magickal history. She has begun her reign. She has many faces. She is the get of the Whore of Babylon and the Goat of Mendes. She will cut a swathe through human society, mark my words. I shall be her tutor in sublime wicked-ness. There will be blood-letting and licence.'

'For such a committed foe of Christianity, you talk a lot of Bible phrases,' Winthrop said. 'Your parents were Plymouth Brethren, were they not?'

'I sprang whole from the earth of Warwickshire. Is it not strange that such a small county could sire both of England's greatest poets?'

Everyone looked at him in utter amazement.

'Shakespeare was the other,' he explained. 'You know, the *Hamlet* fellow.'

Sir Arthur was impatient and Catriona amused, but Winthrop was alert. This man could still be dangerous.

'"The Great God Pan",' Catriona said.

Crowley beamed, assuming she was describing him.

'It's a short story,' she said. 'By Arthur Machen. That's where he's getting all this nonsense. He's casting Rose in the role of the anti-hero-ine of that fiction.'

'Truths are revealed to us in fictions,' Crowley said. 'Sir Arthur, who has so skilfully blended the real and the imagined throughout his career, will agree. And so would Mr Stoker, whom you mentioned. There are many, indeed, who believe your employers, Mr Winthrop, are but the inventions of this literary knight.'

Sir Arthur grumbled.

'At any rate, since the object of my quest is no longer here, I shall depart. It has been an unalloyed pleasure to meet you at such an exhilarating juncture.'

Crowley gave a grunting little bow, and withdrew.

———————

'A Living Looking-Glass'

'Well,' said Catriona, hardly needing to elaborate on the syllable.

'He's an experience, and no mistake,' Edwin admitted.

Having been yanked from horror into comedy, she was light-headed. It seemed absurd now, but she had been near death when the Rose Thing was closing on her throat.

'I see it,' said Sir Arthur, suddenly.

He lifted the blanket from the rector's head and pointed to the ghastly wound with the crucifix. Despite everything else, Sir Arthur was pleased with himself, and amazed.

'I've made a *deduction*,' he announced. 'I've written too often of them, but never until now truly understood. It's like little wheels in your head, coming into alignment. Truly, a marvellous thing.'

Sam Farrar looked up from his hands. He was glumly drained of all emotion, a common fellow unable to keep up with the high-flown characters, human and otherwise, who had descended into his life.

'The creature we saw had extended eye-teeth,' Sir Arthur lectured. 'Like a snake's fangs. Perhaps they were what put me in mind of Bram Stoker's vampires. Yet this wound, in the unfortunate Reverend Mr Haskins's throat, suggests a single stabbing implement. It is larger, rounder, more of a gouge than a bite. The thing we saw would have left two small puckered holes. Haskins was attacked by something different.'

'Or something differently shaped,' Edwin suggested.

'Yes, indeed. We have seen how the Changeling can alter her form. Evidently, she has a large repertoire.'

Catriona tried to imagine what might have made the wound.

'It looks like an insect bite, Sir Arthur,' she said, shuddering, 'made by . . . good lord . . . a *gigantic mosquito*.'

'Bart hated insects,' Farrar put in, blankly. 'Had a bad experience years ago. Never did get the whole story of it. If a wasp came in the room, he was froze up with fear.'

An idea began to shape in her mind.

The Reverend Mr Haskins hated insects. And she had a horror of snakes. Earlier, she had thought Rose was the sort of child who presented herself to suit who she was with. That had been a real insight.

'She's who we think she is,' she said.

Sir Arthur shook his head, not catching her drift.

'She is who we want her to be, or what we're afraid she is,' she continued. 'Sir Arthur wished to think her a friend to the fairies, and so she seemed to be. Edwin, for you it would be most convenient if she were a fraud; when you thought that most strongly, she made the slip about the telephone. The Reverend Mr Haskins was in terror of insects, and she became one; I am not best partial to crawling reptiles, and so she took the form of a snake woman. Every little thing, she reacts to. When I asked her what her name was, she quoted mine back to me. Sir Arthur, you thought of a scene in a novel, and she played it out. She's like a living looking-glass, taking whatever we think of her and becoming exactly that thing.'

Sir Arthur nodded, convinced at once. She was not a little flattered to detect admiration in his eyes. She had made a deduction too.

Edwin was more concerned.

'We've got to stop Crowley,' he said.

'*Crowley?*' she questioned.

'If he gets hold of her, she'll become what *he* thinks she is. And he thinks she's the end the world.'

'The Altar of Sex Magick'

There was only one place the Anti-Christine could have flown to: Angel Field, where once had stood a stone circle. Crowley knew

Farrar Farm, since he had called there first, assuming the divine creature would be in the care of her supposed nephew. But Angel Field was a mystery, and there were no street-lights out here in the wilds of Sussex to guide the way.

Before departing, penniless, for England, he had telegraphed several of his few remaining disciples, beseeching funds and the loan of a car and driver. He was an international fugitive, driven from his Abbey of Thelema in Sicily at the express order of the odious Mussolini, and reduced to grubbing a living in Paris, with the aid of a former Scarlet Woman who was willing to sell her body on the streets to keep the magus in something approaching comfort.

He had left these damp, dreary islands for ever, he had hoped. He was no longer welcome in magical circles in London, brought low by the conspirings of lesser men who failed stubbornly to appreciate his genius.

No chauffeured car awaited him at Victoria, so he had hired one, trusting his manner and force of personality to convince one Alfred Jenkinsop, Esq, that he was good for the fee once the new age had dawned. As it happened, he expected the concept of money to be wiped away with all the other detritus of the dead past.

He found Jenkinsop in his car, outside Farrar Farm, reading *The Sporting Life* by torchlight. The fellow perked up to see him, and stuck his head out of the window.

'Have you seen a female pass this way?' Crowley asked.

Jenkinsop was remarkably obtuse on the point. It took him some moments to remember that he had, in fact, happened to see a girl, clad only in a dressing gown, running down the road from the rectory and onto the farm.

'Which way did she go?'

Jenkinsop shrugged. Crowley made a mental note to erase his somewhat comical name from the record of this evening when he came to write the official history of how the Anti-Christine was brought to London as a protegé of the Great Beast.

'Come, man,' he said, 'follow me.'

The driver showed no willingness to get out of the car.

'It's a cold night, guv,' he said, as if that explained all.

Crowley left him to 'the pink 'un', and trudged through Farrar's open front gate. His once-expensive shoes sank in mud and he felt icy moisture seep in through their somewhat strained seams. Nothing to one who had survived the treacherous glacial slopes of Chogo-Ri, but still a damned nuisance.

If Farrar's vandal of a grandfather hadn't smashed the stones, it would have been easier to find Angel Field. It was a cloudless night, but the moon was just a shining rind. He could make out the shapes of hedgerows, but little more.

He had an alarming encounter with a startled cow.

'Mistress Perfection,' he called out.

Only mooing came back.

Finally, he discerned a fire in the night and made his way towards it. He knew his feet stood upon the sod of Angel Field. For the Anti-Christine was at the centre of the light, surrounded by her impish acolytes.

They were attendant demons, Crowley knew. Naked, hairless and without genitals. They had smooth, grey, dwarf bodies and large black insect eyes. Some held peculiar implements with lights at their extremities. They all turned, with one fluid movement, to look at him.

She was magnificent. Having shed her snakeskin, she had become the essence of voluptuous harlotry, masses of electric gorgon-hair confined by a shining circlet of silver, robe gaping open immodestly over her gently swelling belly, wicked green eyes darting like flames. Her teeth were still sharp. She looked from side to side, smile twisted off-centre.

This was the rapturous creature who would degrade the world.

Crowley worshipped her.

The occasion of their meeting called for a ceremony. The imps gathered around him, heads bobbing about his waist-height. Some extended spindle-fingered hands, tipped with sucker-like appendages, and touched him.

He unloosed his belt and dropped his trousers and drawers. He knelt, knees well-spaced, and touched his forehead to the cold, wet ground.

One of the imps took its implement and inserted it into Crowley's rectum. He bit a mouthful of grassy sod as the implement expanded inside him.

Crowley's body was the altar of sex magick.

The commingling of pain and pleasure was not new to him. This was quite consistent with the theory and practice of magick he had devised over many years of unparalleled scholarship. As the metallic probe pulsed inside him like living flesh, he was thrust forward into his new golden dawn.

The imp's implement was withdrawn.

Hands took Crowley's head and lifted it from the dirt. The Anti-Christine looked at him with loathing and love. Their mouths opened, and they pounced. Crowley trapped her lower lip between his teeth and bit until his mouth was full of her blood. He broke the serpent's kiss, and she returned in kind, nipping and nibbling at his nose and dewlaps.

Her lips were rouged with her own blood, and marked with his teeth.

Oh joy!

'Infernal epitome,' he addressed her, 'we must get you quickly to London, where you can spread your leathery wings, open your scaled legs and begin to exert a real influence. We shall start with a few seductions, of men and women naturally, petty and great persons, reprobates and saints. Each shall spread your glorious taint, which will flash through society like a new tonic.'

She looked pleased by the prospect.

'There will be fire and pestilence,' he continued. 'Duels and murders and many, many suicides. Piccadilly Circus will burn like Nero's Rome. Pall Mall will fall to the barbarians. The Thames will run red and brown with the blood and ordure of the King and his courtiers. We shall dig up the mouldy skeletons of Victoria and Albert and revivify them with demon spells, to set them copulating like mindless mink in Horseguard's Parade. St Paul's shall be turned into a brothel of Italianate vileness, and Westminster Abbey made an adjunct to the London Zoological Gardens, turned over to obscene apes who will defecate and fornicate where the foolishly pious once sat. *The London Times* will publish blasphemies and pornography, illustrated only by the greatest artists of the age. The Lord Mayor's head will be used as a ball in the Association Football Cup Final. Cocaine, heroin and the services of child prostitutes will be advertised in posters plastered to the sides of all omnibuses. Willie Blasted Yeats shall be burned in effigy in place of Saint Guy Fawkes on every November 5th, and all the other usurpers of the Golden Dawn laid low in their own filth. All governments, all moralities, all churches, will collapse. The City will burn, must burn. Only we Secret Chiefs will retain our authority. You shall beget many children, homunculi. It will be a magnificent age, extending for a thousand times a thousand years.'

In her shining, darting eyes, he saw it was all true. He buttoned up his trousers and spirited her away to where Jenkinsop waited with the car, unwitting herald of welcome apocalypse.

'The Fire-Wheel'

Winthrop held *Katie's* stick back, flying at an angle, nose into the wind, so the dark, shadowed quilt of Sussex filled his view. The dawnlight just pricked at the East, flashing off ponds and streams. Night-flying was tricky in a country dotted with telegraph poles and tall trees, but at least there wasn't some Fokker stalking him. He tried to keep the Camel level with the tiny light funnels that were the headlamps of what must be Crowley's car.

They had got to Farrar Farm just after Crowley's departure, with Rose or Christine or whatever the girl chose to be called. He had set Catriona and Sir Arthur on their tail in the Bentley, and borrowed Sir Arthur's surprisingly sprightly runabout to make his way to the airfield at Falmer, where his aeroplane was hangared. It was like the War again, rousing a tired ground staff to get him into the air within minutes of his strapping on helmet and boots.

He had assumed few automobiles would be on the roads of Sussex at this hour of the morning, but had homed in on a couple of trundling milk trucks before picking up the two vehicles he assumed were Crowley's car and his own Bentley. He trusted Catriona at the wheel, though Sir Arthur had seemed as startled at the prospect of being driven by a woman as he had when confronted by the girl's monstrous snake-shape. When Winthrop had last seen them, Sir Arthur was still clutching his crucifix and Catriona was tucking stray hair under her sweet little hat.

He wished he had time to savour the thrill of being in the air again. He also regretted not storing ammunition and even a couple of bombs with *Katie*. Her twin machine-guns were still in working order, synchronised to fire through the prop blades, but he had nothing to fire out of them. His revolver was under his jacket, but would be almost useless: it was hard to give accurate fire while flying one-handed, with one's gun-arm flapping about in sixty-mile-an-hour airwash.

Suddenly, the sun rose. In the West.

A blast of daylight fell on one side of Winthrop's face. He felt a tingle as if he were being sun-burned. For a moment, the air currents were all wrong, and he nearly lost control of *Katie*.

The landscape below was bleached by light. The two cars were quite distinct on the road. They were travelling between harvested wheat-fields. There were circles and triangles etched into the stubble, shapes that reminded Winthrop of those on Rose's silver ribbon.

Winthrop looked at the new sun.

It was a wheel of fire, travelling in parallel with *Katie*. He pushed the stick forward and climbed up into the sky, and the fire-shape climbed with him. Then it whizzed underneath the Camel and came up on his right side.

He looped up, back and below, feeling the tug of gravity in his head and the safety harness cutting into his shoulders. It would take a demon from hell to outfly a Sopwith Camel in anger, as the fire-wheel recognised instantly by shooting off like a Guy Fawkes rocket, whooshing up in a train of sparks.

Katie was now flying even, and sparks fell fizzing all around. Winthrop was afraid they were incendiaries of unknown design, but they passed *through* his fuselage and wings, dispersing across the fields.

His eyes were blotched with light-bursts. It was dark again and the fire-wheel gone. Winthrop recalled the stories of the signs in the sky at the time of Rose Farrar's disappearance. He assumed he had just had personal experience of them. He would make sure they went into the report.

Proper dawn was upon them.

A long straight stretch of road extended ahead of Crowley's car. They were nearing the outskirts of the city. Crowley's driver must be a good man, or possessed of magical skills, since the Bentley was lagging behind.

He knew he had to pull a reckless stunt.

Throttling *Katie* generously, he swooped low over the car and headed off to the left, getting as far ahead of Crowley as possible, then swung round in a tight semi-circle, getting his nose in alignment with the oncoming vehicle. He would only get one pass at this run.

He took her down, praying the road had been maintained recently.

Katie's wheels touched ground, lifted off for a moment, and touched ground again.

Through the whirling prop, Winthrop saw Crowley's car. They were on a collision course.

The car would be built more sturdily than the canvas and wood plane. But *Katie* had whirling twin blades in her nose, all the better to scythe through the car's bonnet and windshield, and severely inconvenience anyone in the front seat.

Crowley might think himself untouchable. But he wouldn't be doing his own driving.

Winthrop hoped a rational man was behind the wheel of Crowley's car.

The distance between the two speeding vehicles narrowed.

Winthrop was oddly relaxed, as always in combat. A certain fatalism possessed him. If it was the final prang, so be it. He whistled under his breath.

It had been a good life. He was grateful to have known Cat, and the Old Man. He had done his bit, and a bit more besides. And he was with *Katie* at the last.

Crowley's car swerved, plunging through a hedgerow. Winthrop whooped in triumph, exultant to be alive. He cut the motors and upturned the flaps. Wind tore at the wings as *Katie* slowed.

Another car was up ahead.

The Bentley.

———

"'I believe . . .'"

Catriona pressed down on the foot-brake with all her strength. She was not encouraged by Sir Arthur's loud prayer. The aeroplane loomed large in the windshield, prop blades slowing but still deadly. She couldn't remember whether they were wood or metal, but guessed it wouldn't make much difference.

The Bentley and the Camel came to a halt, one screeching and the other purring, within a yard of each other. She recommenced breathing and unclenched her stomach. That was not an experience she would care to repeat.

Somewhat shaken, she and Sir Arthur climbed out of the car. Edwin was already on the ground, pulling off his flying helmet. He had his revolver.

'Come on, you fellows,' he said. 'The enemy's downed.'

She helped Sir Arthur along the road. The car they had been pursuing had jumped the verge and crashed into a hedge. Crowley was extricating himself from the front seat with some difficulty. A stunned driver sat in the long grass, thrown clear of his car, shaking his head.

The rear door of the car was kicked open and a female fury exploded from it.

Rose was in mostly human shape, but Catriona could tell from her blazing snake-eyes she had been filled with Crowley's cracked fancies. She was transformed into a species of demonic Zuleika Dobson, set to enslave and conquer and destroy London and then the world. As the dawnlight shone in the Anti-Christine's frizzy halo of hair, Catriona believed this creature was capable of fulfilling Crowley's mad prophecies. She was a young woman now, still recognisably the child she had been, but with a cast of feature that suggested monumental cruelty and desperate vice. Her hands were tipped with claw-nails.

Her inky eyes radiated something. Hypnotic black swirls wound in her pupils. She was humming, almost sub-audially, radiating malicious female energy. Sir Arthur gasped. And Edwin skidded to a halt. The revolver fell from his hand.

Catriona was appalled. Even these men, whom she respected, were struck by Rose. Then, she was fascinated. It was alien to her, but she saw what magnificence this creature represented. This was not madness, but . . .

No, she decided. It was madness.

'You are powerless to stop her,' Crowley yelled. 'Bow down and worship her filthiness!'

Catriona fixed Rose's eyes with her own.

She took Sir Arthur's hand and reached out for Edwin's. He hesitated, eyes on Rose's body, then clutched. Catriona held these men fast.

It was Sir Arthur who gave her the idea. And, perhaps, another distinguished author-knight, J.M. Barrie.

'Do you believe in fairies?' she asked.

Crowley looked aghast.

Sir Arthur and Edwin understood.

With all her heart, she imagined benevolence, worshipped purity, conceived of goodness, was enchanted by kindly magic. As a child, she had loved indiscriminately, finding transcendent wonders in sparkling dew on spun webs, in fallen leaves become galleons on still ponds.

'I believe in fairies,' she declared.

She recognised her kinship with the kindly knight. She was a sceptic about many things, but there was real magic. She could catch it in her hand and shape it.

The English countryside opened up for her.

She truly believed.

Rose was transfixed. She dwindled inside her dressing gown, became a girl again. Dragonfly wings sprouted from her back, and delicate feelers extended from her eyebrows. She hovered a few inches above the grass. Flowers wound around her brow. She shone with clean light.

Sir Arthur was tearful with joy, transported by the sight. Edwin squeezed her hand.

Spring flowers sprouted in the autumn hedgerow.

Crowley was bewildered.

'No,' he said, 'you are scarlet, not watercolour.'

He was cracked and had lost.

'Come here,' Catriona said, to the girl.

Rose, eight years old again and human, skipped across the road and flew into her arms, hugging her innocently. Catriona passed her on to Sir Arthur, who swept her up and held her fiercely to him.

'I think your new age has been postponed,' Edwin told Crowley.

'Curse you,' Crowley swore, shaking his fist like the melodrama villain he wished he was.

'You're going to pay for the car, sir,' said the driver. 'Within the hour.'

Crowley was cowed. He looked like a big baby in daylight. His bald head was smudged and his trousers were badly ripped and stained.

There were new people on the scene. She supposed it was inevitable. You couldn't land a biplane and crash a car without attracting attention.

Two men stood on the other side of the road. Catriona didn't know where they could have come from. She had heard no vehicle and there were no dwellings in sight.

Rose twisted in Sir Arthur's hug to look at the men.

Catriona remembered what the girl had said about the friends of the Little People. Undertakers in smoked glasses.

The two men were the same height, tall even without their black top hats. They wore black frock coats, black trousers, black cravats, black gloves. Even black spats and black-tinted glasses that seemed too large for human eyes. Their faces were ghost-white, with thin lips.

'They've come for me,' Rose said. 'I must go away with them.'

Gently, Sir Arthur set her down. She kissed him, then kissed Catriona and Edwin, even Crowley.

'Don't worry about me,' she said, sounding grown-up, and went to the undertakers. They each took one of her hands and walked her down the road, towards a shimmering light. For a while, the three figures were silhouetted. They they were gone, and so was the light.

Edwin turned to look at her, and shrugged.

'The Vicinity of the Inexplicable'

The Old Man nodded sagely when Winthrop concluded his narrative. He did not seem surprised by even the most unusual details.

'We've come across these undertakers before,' Beauregard said. 'All in black, with hidden eyes. They appear often in the vicinity of the inexplicable. Like the Little Grey People.'

They were back in the Strangers Room.

'I suppose we should worry about Rose,' Winthrop mused, 'but she told us not to. Considering that she seems to be whatever we think she is, she might have meant that it would be helpful if we thought of her as safe and well since she would then, in fact, be so. It was Cat who saw through it all, and hit upon the answer.'

Catriona was thoughtful.

'I don't know, Edwin,' she said. 'I don't think we saw a quarter of the real picture. The Little Grey People, the fire-wheel in the skies, the Changeling, the undertakers. All this has been going on for a long time, since well before the original Rose was taken away. We were caught between the interpretations put on the phenomena in the last few days by Sir Arthur and Crowley, fairies and the Anti-Christine. In the last century, it was angels and demons. Who knows what light future researchers will shine upon the business?'

Withrop sipped his excellent brandy.

'I shouldn't bother yourself too much about that, old thing. We

stand at the dawn of a new era, not the apocalypse Crowley was prat-
tling about but an age of scientific enlightenment. Mysteries will be
penetrated by rational inquiry. We shall no longer need to whip up
fairy tales to cope with the fantastical. Mark my words, Catty-Kit. The
next time anything like this happens, we shall get to the bottom of it
without panic or hysteria.'

*Here is a story featuring the agents of the Diogenes Club in an earlier era:
Edwin Winthrop, Catriona Kaye and Charles Beauregard (like Richard
and Vanessa from 'Tomorrow Town') are all characters I created in my first
stabs at writing, either at school (that stuff is destroyed, mercifully) or as a
playwright in the early 1980s. I played Edwin myself in the 1982
performance of* My One Little Murder Can't Do Any Harm *at the
Bridgwater Arts Centre, and he popped up in tiny moments in my novels*
Jago *and* Demon Download *(written as Jack Yeovil) before getting a lead
role (in the* Anno Dracula *timeline) in* The Bloody Red Baron.

*Whenever the subject of belief in UFOs comes up, I have an impres-
sion that people never take the trouble to deconstruct the term. The U
stands for 'unidentified'; so, of course, there are unidentified flying objects.
That doesn't mean they are alien spacecraft. When 'flying saucers' were first
sighted in the late 1940s, the general assumption was that they were
advanced aircraft made by Western governments (who had kept the
Manhattan Project secret, so were known to do this sort of thing without
telling the public) or the Other Side. Throughout history, there have been
rashes of sightings of angels, saints, fairies, etc. UFO abduction stories –
which I take about as seriously as the poodle in the microwave or the
hairy-handed hitch-hiker – have many similarities with older legends about
children taken by the fairies and changelings left in their cribs. Some people
misinterpreted 'Angel Down' (and the thematically-related 'Residuals', a
piece co-written with Paul McAuley) as reductive — suggesting aliens were
behind all these phenomena. Actually, in the world of this story, the whole
modern myth paraphenalia of alien abduction/visitation is just another
attempt to explain away the truly inexplicable. Those objects remain
unidentified.*

DEAD
TRAVEL
FAST

In the great shed, a waterfall of molten iron poured into a long mould. Today, the undercarriage of a new engine was being cast, for the Great Western Railway, the Plymouth-to-Penzance line.

Massingham was confused for moments by the infernal glow, the terrific roar and the insufferable heat. No matter how many times he might be brought to the foundry, it was not an environment a man could become accustomed to. Those who worked here often ended up deaf or blind or prostrate with nervous disorder.

He looked around for the Count de Ville, and saw the foreign visitor standing much too close to the mould, in danger of being struck by spatters of liquid metal. The soft red drops were like acid bullets. They would eat through a man's chest or head in a second. In twenty years' service with the firm, Massingham had seen too many such accidents.

Whoever had let the visitor venture so close would answer for it. It was bad enough when one of the workers got careless and was maimed or killed, but to let an outsider, who had pulled strings to get a tour of the works, suffer such a fate would bring unpleasant publicity. The Board of Directors would most certainly hold Massingham responsible for such a catastrophe.

De Ville was a black silhouette, fringed with bitter crimson. He seemed to look directly at the white hot iron, unaffected by the harsh glow that ruined others' eyes. All Massingham knew about the Count was that he was a foreign gentleman, with a great interest in railways. The Board scented an opportunity, assuming this toff was well enough connected in his own country to put in a word when it came to the purchase of rolling-stock. Two-thirds of the world ran on rails cast in this shed, riding in carriages made in the factory, pulled by engines manufactured by the firm.

'Count de Ville,' Massingham coughed.

He had spoken too softly, above the tinkle of teacups in a drawing-room not the roaring din of the casting shed, but the Count's ears were as sharp as his eyes were hardy. He turned round, eyes reflecting the burning red of the furnaces, and bowed slightly from the waist.

'I'm Henry Massingham, the under-manager. I'm to show you round.'

'Excellent,' said the Count. 'I am certain to find the tour most enlightening. My own country is sadly backward by comparison with your great empire. I am anxious to be introduced to all the marvels of the age.'

He made no especial effort to raise his voice over the racket, but was heard clearly. His elongated vowels gave him away as someone whose first language was not English, but he had no trouble with his consonants save perhaps for a little hiss in his sibilants.

With no little relief, Massingham left the casting-shed, followed by the tall, thin foreigner. The noise resounded in his ears for a few moments after they were out in the open. Though it was a breezy day, he could still feel the intense heat of the foundry on his cheeks.

Out in daylight, under thick clouds that obscured the sun, the Count was a less infernal figure. He was dressed entirely in black, like a Roman Catholic priest, with a long coat over tight swathes of material that bespoke no London tailoring, and heavy boots suitable for harsh mountains. Oddly, he topped off his ensemble with a cheap straw hat of the type one buys at the sea-side to use for a day and lose by nightfall. Massingham had an idea the Count was inordinately and strangely fond of the hat; his first English-bought item of clothing.

It occurred to Massingham that he didn't know which country the Count was from. The name de Ville sounded French, but a rasp in his voice suggested somewhere in Central Europe, deep in that ever-changing patch of the map caught between the Russias and the Austro-Hungarian Empire. Running rails up and down mountains was an expensive business, and a solid contract to provide a railway system for such an area could be a long-term high-earner for the firm.

Massingham escorted the Count about the factory, following the creation of an engine by visiting all the stages of the manufacture, from the primal business of casting through to the fine detail-work on the boilerplate and the polishing of the brass finishings. The Count was especially delighted, like a little boy, with the steam whistle. The fore-man fired up an engine on the test-bed, purely so de Ville might have the childish joy of pulling the chain and making the shrill toot-toot that would announce the coming of an iron giant to some out-of-the-way halt.

The Count de Ville was a railway enthusiast of great passion, who had from afar memorised his Bradshaw's guide to timetables and was merely seeing for the first time processes he had read of and imagined for many years. He probably knew more about trains than did Massingham, whose responsibilities were mostly in overseeing the book-keeping, and who wound up delivering more lectures than he received.

'What a world it shall be, when the globe is encircled round about by steel rails,' enthused the Count. 'Men and matériel shall be trans-ported in darkness, in sealed carriages, while the world sleeps. Borders shall become meaningless, distances will be an irrelevance and a new civilisation rise to the sound of the train whistle.'

'Ahem,' said Massingham, 'indeed.'

'I came to this land by sea,' de Ville said sadly. 'I am irretrievably a creature of the past. But I shall conquer this new world, Mr Massingham. It is my dearest ambition to become a railwayman.'

There was something strange in his conviction.

The tour concluded, Massingham hoped to steer de Ville to the board-room, where several directors would be waiting, hiding behind genial offers of port and biscuits, ready to make casual suggestions as to possible business arrangments and privately determined not to let the Count escape without signing up for a substantial commitment. Massingham's presence would not be required at the meeting, but if a contract were signed, his part in it would be remembered.

'What is that building?' de Ville asked, indicating a barn-like structure he had not been shown. It stood in a neglected corner of the works, beyond a pile of rejected, rusting rails.

'Nothing important, Count,' said Massingham. 'It's for tinkering, not real work.'

The word 'tinkering' appealed to de Ville.

'It sounds most fascinating, Mr Massingham. I should be most interested to be allowed inside.'

There was the question of secrecy. It was unlikely that the Count was a spy from another company, but nevertheless it was not wise to let it be known what the firm was working on. Massingham chewed his moustache for a moment, unsure. Then he recalled that the only tinkerer in residence at the moment was George Foley, of the improbable contraption. There was no real harm in showing the Count that white elephant, though he feared a potential customer might conclude the firm was foolhardy indeed to throw away money on such an obvious non-starter and might take his business elsewhere.

'We have been allowing space to an inventor,' said Massingham. 'I fear we have become a safe harbour for an arrant crackpot, but you might find some amusement at the bizarre results of his efforts.'

He lead the Count through the double doors.

Several shots sounded, rattling the tin roof of the shed. Bursts of fire lit the gloom.

Immediately, Massingham was afraid that de Ville was the victim of an assassination plot. Everyone knew these Balkan nobs were pursued by anarchists eager to pot them with revolvers in revenge for injustices committed down through the centuries by barbarous ancestors.

A stench of sulphur stung his nostrils. Clouds of foul smoke were wafting up to the roof. There was a slosh and a hiss as a bucket of water was emptied on a small fire.

The reports had been not shots but small explosions. It was just Foley's folly, again. Massingham was relieved, but then annoyed when he wiped his brow with his cuff to find his face coated with a gritty, oily discharge.

Through smoke and steam, he saw Foley and his familiar, the boy Gerald, fussing about a machine, faces and hands black as Zulus', overalls ragged as tramps'. George Foley was a young man, whose undeniable technical skills were tragically allied to a butterfly mind that constantly alighted upon the most impractical and useless concepts.

'My apologies, Count,' said Massingham. 'I am afraid that this is what one must expect when one devotes oneself to the fantastic idea of an engine worked by explosion. Things will inevitably blow up.'

'Combustion,' snapped Foley. 'Not explosion.'

'I crave your pardon, Foley,' said Massingham. 'Infernal combustion.'

Foley's written proposals were often passed round the under-managers for humorous relief.

'Internal,' squeaked Gerald, an eleven-year-old always so thickly greased and blackened that it was impossible to tell what the colour of his hair or complexion might be. 'Internal combustion, not infernal.'

'I believe my initial choice of word was apt.'

'That's as may be, Massingham, but look . . .'

The device that had exploded was shaking now, emitting a grumble of noise and spurts of noxious smoke. A crank was turning a belt, which was turning a wheel. Massingham had seen such toys before.

'Five times more efficient than steam,' Foley said. 'Maybe ten, a dozen . . .'

'And five times more likely to kill you.'

'In the early days of steam, many were killed,' said the Count. He gazed into Foley's engine, admiring the way the moving parts meshed. It was a satisfyingly complicated toy, with oiled pistons and levers and cogs. A child's idea of a wonderful machine.

'I'm sorry, sir,' said Foley, 'and you are . . .'

'This is the Count de Ville,' explained Massingham. 'An important connection of the firm, from overseas. He is interested in railways.'

'Travel,' said the Count. 'I am interested in travel. In the transport of the future.'

'You have then chanced upon the right place, Count,' said Foley. He did not offer a dirty hand, but nodded a greeting, almost clicking his heels. 'For in this workshop is being sounded the death-knell of the whole of the rest of the factory. My transport, my horseless carriage, will make the steam engine as obsolete as the train made the stagecoach.'

'Horseless carriage?' said the Count, drawing out the words, rolling the idea around his mind.

'It's a wonder, sir,' said Gerald, eyes shining. Foley tousled the boy's already-greasy bird's nest of hair, proud of his loyal lackey.

Massingham suppressed a bitter laugh.

Foley led them past the still-shaking engine on its fixed trestle, to a dust-sheeted object about the size of a small hay-cart. The inventor and the nimble Gerald lifted off the canvas sheet and threw it aside.

'This is my combustion carriage,' said Foley, with pride. 'I shall have to change the name, of course. It might be called a petroleum caleche, or an auto-mobile.'

The invention sat squarely on four thick-rimmed wheels, with a small carriage-seat suspended above them to the rear of one of Foley's combustion engines.

'There will be a housing on the finished model, to keep the elements out of the engine and cut down the noise. The smoke will be discharged through these pipes.'

'The flat wheel-rims suggest this will not run on rails,' said the Count.

'Rails,' Foley fairly spat. 'No, sir. Indeed not. This will run on roads. Or, if there are no roads, on any reasonably level surface. Trains are limited, as you know. They cannot venture where rail-layers have not been first, at great expense. My carriage will be free, eventually, to go everywhere.'

'Always in a straight line?'

'By means of a steering apparatus, the front wheels can be turned like a ship's rudder.'

Massingham was impatient with such foolishness.

'My dear Count,' said Foley, 'I foresee that this device, of which Mr Massingham is so leery, will change the world as we know it, and greatly for the better. The streets of our cities will no longer be clogged with the excrement of horses. No more fatalities or injuries will be caused by animals bolting or throwing their riders. And there will be no more great collisions, for these carriages are steerable and can thus avoid each other. Unlike horses, they do not panic; and, unlike trains, they do not run on fixed courses. Derailments, obviously, are out of the question. The first and foremost attribute of the combustion carriage is its safety.'

The Count walked round the carriage, eyeing its every detail, smiling with his sharp teeth. There was something animal-like about de Ville, a single-mindedness at once childish and frightening.

'May I?' The Count indicated the seat.

Foley hesitated but, sensing a potential sponsor, shrugged.

De Ville climbed up into the seat. The carriage settled under his weight. The axles were on suspension springs, like a hansom cab. The Count ran his hands around the great steering-wheel, which was as unwieldy and stiff as those that worked the locks on a canal. There were levers to the side of the seat, the purpose of which was unknown to Massingham, though he assumed one must be a braking-mechanism.

Beside the wheel was a rubber-bulbed horn. The Count squeezed it experimentally.

Poop-poop!

'To alert pedestrians,' explained Foley. 'The engine runs so quietly that the horn will be necessary.'

The Count smiled, eyes rimmed with red delight. He poop-pooped again, evidently in love. His craze for trains was quite forgotten. Poop-poop had trumped toot-toot.

Foreigners were a lot like children.

'How does it start?'

'With a crank.'

'Show me,' de Ville ordered.

Foley nodded to Gerald, who darted to the front of the contraption with a lever and fitted it into the engine. He gave it a turn, and nothing happened. Massingham had seen this before. Usually, the dignitaries summoned to witness the great breakthrough had retreated by the time the engine caught. Then it would only sputter a few moments, allowing the carriage to lurch forward a yard or two before at best stalling and at worst exploding.

If Foley's folly blew up and killed the Count, Massingham would have to answer for it. The man clearly had an impulse towards death.

Gerald cranked the engine again, and again, and . . .

. . . nipped out of the way sharpish. Small flames burst in the guts of the machine, and the pistons began to pump.

The carriage moved forward, and the Count poop-pooped the blasted horn again. He would have been as happy with the noise-maker alone as the whole vehicle.

Slowly, the carriage trundled towards the open doors of the workshop. Foley looked alarmed, but didn't protest. Picking up more speed than usual, the carriage disappeared out of the doors. The Count's straw hat blew off and was wafted up towards the roof by the black smoke that poured thickly from the pipes at the rear of the machine.

Massingham, Foley and Gerald followed the carriage to the doorway. Astonished, they saw the Count piloting the machine, with growing expertise, yanking hard on the steering-wheel and turning in ever tighter circles, circumnavigating the pile of rails, weaving in and out between sheds and buildings.

A cat shot out of the way, its tail flat. Workmen passing by stopped to stare. A small crowd gathered, of idle hands distracted from their appointed tasks. Some of the directors poked their heads out, silk hats held to their heads.

It was a ridiculous sight, but somehow stirring. The Count was very intent, very serious. But the machine just looked silly, not majestic like a steam engine. Still, Massingham had a glimpse of what Foley saw in the thing.

The Count poop-pooped the horn. Someone cheered.

Gerald, delighted, danced in the wake of the carriage.

The Count made a hard turn and suddenly the boy's legs were under the front wheels. Bright blood spurted up into the oily engine, as if it were Moloch demanding sacrifice.

Foley shouted. Massingham felt a hammer-blow to his heart.

The Count seemed not to have realised what he had done, and drove on, grinding the boy under the carriage, merrily poop-pooping the damnable horn. The wheel-rims were reddened, and left twin tracks of blood for twenty feet in the rutted earth. Workmen rushed to help the boy, who was yelling in pain, legs quite crushed, face white under the dirt.

De Ville found the brake and brought the carriage to a halt.

Foley was too shocked to speak.

The Count stepped down, exhilarated.

'What a marvellous transport,' he declared. 'It will indeed be the machine of the future. I share your vision, Mr Foley. You will make the world a swifter, purer place. These vehicles will be armoured, making each driver a warrior apart from others, a knight whose mind is one with that of his steed. You have invented a movable castle, one which can be equipped for assault and defence. The carriage can serve as refuge, land-ironclad, vehicle of exploration and finally casket or tomb. I shall be among the first purchasers of your wonderful carriage. You may number me as a sponsor of its manufacture. I shall not rest until the whole world runs on infernal combustion.'

He reached up into the air, and his straw hat was returned to his long fingers the swirling smoke. The quality of Gerald's screaming changed, to a low, whimpering sob. The Count appeared not to notice the noise, though Massingham remembered the sharpness of his ears.

The Count de Ville tapped his hat on to his head at a jaunty angle, gave the bulb-horn a final, fond poop-poop and walked into the black clouds of smoke, which seemed to part for him and then closed around him like a cloak.

Massingham thought about the future. There was probably money in it.

A risk of theme anthologies is that if you write a story for one and don't get in, you're stuck with a very specific piece which won't suit other markets. This was solicited by P.N. Elrod for a collection of stories which purport to fill in the gaps in Bram Stoker's Dracula by showing what the Count was doing on his trip to London when he is only glimpsed by the novel's many narrators. She never rejected the piece or acknowledged receipt, but it's not in the book (Dracula in London) – so draw your own conclusions. When he heard about this premise, Steve Baxter quite rightly suggested that he was probably taking in the shows, visiting the tourist spots and asking for directions like any other foreigner in London. Another risk of theme anthologies is that everyone has the same idea and you get a clutch of stories which read very similarly: so I resolved to do a Dracula story in which he didn't bite anyone, and which focused on an aspect of the character Stoker gave him other than bloodlust.

Though the primary purpose of 'Dead Travel Fast' was to fit in with Stoker's text, there is nothing here that contradicts the timeline I have established in the Anno Dracula *novels.*

AMERIKANSKI DEAD
AT THE
MOSCOW MORGUE;

OR:
CHILDREN OF MARX
AND COCA-COLA

At the Railway Station in Borodino, Yevgeny Chirkov was separated from his unit. As the locomotive slowed, he hopped from their carriage to the platform, under orders to secure, at any price, cigarettes and chocolate. Another unknown crisis intervened and the steam-driven antique never truly stopped. Tripping over his rifle, he was unable to reach the outstretched hands of his comrades. The rest of the unit, jammed half-way through windows or hanging out of doors, laughed and waved. A jet of steam from a train passing the other way put salt on his tail and he dodged, tripping again. Sergeant Trauberg found the pratfall hilarious, forgetting he had pressed a thousand roubles on the private. Chirkov ran and ran but the locomotive gained speed. When he emerged from the canopied platform, seconds after the last carriage, white sky poured down. Looking at the black-shingled track-bed, he saw a flattened outline in what had once been a uniform, wrists and ankles wired together, neck against a gleaming rail, head long gone under sharp wheels. The method, known as 'making sleepers', was favoured along railway lines. Away from stations, twenty or thirty were dealt with at one time. Without heads, Amerikans did no harm.

Legs boiled from steam, face and hands frozen from winter, he wandered through the station. The cavernous space was sub-divided by sandbags. Families huddled like pioneers expecting an attack by Red Indians, luggage drawn about in a circle, last bullets saved for women and children. Chirkov spat mentally; Amerika had invaded his imagination, just as his political officers warned. Some refugees were coming from Moscow, others fleeing to the city. There was no rule. A wall-sized poster of the New First Secretary was disfigured with a blotch, red gone to black. The splash of dried blood suggested something had been finished against the wall. There were Amerikans in Borodino. Seventy miles from Moscow, the station was a museum to resisted invasions. Plaques, statues and paintings honoured the victories of 1812 and 1944. A poster listed those local officials executed after being implicated in the latest counter-revolution. The air was tangy with ash, a reminder of past scorched earth policies. There were big fires nearby. An army unit was on duty, but no one knew anything about a time-table. An officer told him to queue and wait. More trains were coming from Moscow than going to, which meant the capital would eventually have none left.

He ventured out of the station. The snow cleared from the fore-court was banked a dozen yards away. Sunlight glared off muddy white. It was colder and brighter than he was used to in the Ukraine. A trio of Chinese-featured soldiers, a continent away from home, offered to share cigarettes and tried to practise Russian on him. He understood they were from Amgu; from the highest point in that port, you could see Japan. He asked if they knew where he could find an official. As they chirruped among themselves in an alien tongue, Chirkov saw his first Amerikan. Emerging from between snowbanks and limping towards the guard-post, the dead man looked as if he might actually be an American. Barefoot, he waded spastically through slush, jeans-legs shredded over thin shins. His shirt was a bright picture of a parrot in a jungle. Sunglasses hung round his neck on a thin string. Chirkov made the Amerikan's presence known to the guards. Fascinated, he watched the dead man walk. With every step, the Amerikan crackled: there were deep, ice-threaded rifts in his skin. He was slow and brittle and blind, crystal eyes frozen open, arms stiff by his sides.

Cautiously, the Corporal circled round and rammed his rifle-butt into a knee. The guards were under orders not to waste ammunition; there was a shortage. Bone cracked and the Amerikan went down like a devotee before an icon. The Corporal prodded a colourful back with his boot-toe and pushed the Amerikan on to his face. As he wriggled, ice-shards worked through his flesh. Chirkov had assumed the dead would stink but this one was frozen and odourless. The skin was pink and unperished, the rips in it red and glittery. An arm reached out for the corporal and something snapped in the shoulder. The corporal's boot pinned the Amerikan to the concrete. One of his comrades produced a foot-long spike and worked the point into the back of the dead man's skull. Scalp flaked around the dimple. The other guard took an iron mallet from his belt and struck a professional blow.

It was important, apparently, that the spike should entirely trans-fix the skull and break ground, binding the dead to the earth, allowing the last of the spirit to leave the carcass. Not official knowl-edge: this was something every soldier was told at some point by a comrade. Always, the tale-teller was from Moldavia or had learned from someone who was. Moldavians claimed to be used to the dead. The Amerikan's head came apart like a rock split along fault lines. Five solid chunks rolled away from the spike. Diamond-sparkles of ice glinted in reddish-grey inner surfaces. The thing stopped moving at once. The hammerer began to unbutton the gaudy shirt and detach it from the sunken chest, careful as a butcher skinning a horse. The jeans were too deeply melded with meat to remove, which was a shame; with the ragged legs cut away, they would have made fine shorts for a pretty girl at the beach. The Corporal wanted Chirkov to have the sunglasses. One lens was gone or he might not have been so generous with a stranger. In the end, Chirkov accepted out of courtesy, resolving to throw away the trophy as soon as he was out of Borodino.

Three days later, when Chirkov reached Moscow, locating his unit was not possible. A despatcher at the central station thought his comrades might have been reassigned to Orekhovo Zuyevo, but her superior was of the opinion the unit had been disbanded nine months earlier. Because the despatcher was not disposed to contradict an eminent Party member, Chirkov was forced to accept the ruling that he was without a unit. As such, he was detailed to the Spa. They had in a permanent request for personnel and always took precedence. The posting involved light guard duties and manual labour; there was little fight left in Amerikans who ended up at the Spa. The despatcher gave Chirkov a sheaf of papers the size of a Frenchman's sandwich and complicated travel directions. By then, the rest of the queue was getting testy and he was obliged to venture out on his own. He remembered to fix his mobility permit, a blue luggage-tag with a smudged stamp, on the outside of his uniform. Technically, failure to display the permit was punishable by summary execution.

Streetcars ran intermittently; after waiting an hour in the street outside central station, he decided to walk to the Spa. It was a ques-tion of negotiating dunes of uncleared snow and straggles of undisciplined queue. Teams of firemen dug methodically through depths of snow, side-by-side with teams of soldiers who were burning down buildings. Areas were cleared and raked, ground still warm enough to melt snow that drifted onto it. Everywhere, posters warned of the Amerikans. The Party line was still that the United States was responsible. It was air-carried biological warfare, the Ministry announced with authority, originated by a secret laboratory and disseminated in the Soviet Union by suicidal infectees posing as tourists. The germ galvanised the nervous systems of the recently-deceased, triggering the lizard stems of their brains, inculcat-ing in the Amerikans a disgusting hunger for human meat. The 'news' footage the Voice of America put out of their own dead was staged and doctored, footage from the sadistic motion pictures that were a symptom of the West's utter decadence. But everyone had a different line: it was . . . creeping radiation from Chernobyl . . . a judgment from a bitter and long-ignored God . . . a project Stalin abandoned during the Great Patriotic War . . . brought back from Novy Mir by cosmonauts . . . a plot by the fomenters of the Counter-Revolution . . . a curse the Moldavians had always known.

Fortunately, the Spa was off Red Square. Even a Ukrainian sapling like Yevgeny Chirkov had an idea how to get to Red Square. He had carried his rifle for so long that the strap had worn through his epaulette. He imagined the outline of the buckle was stamped into his collar bone. His single round of ammunition was in his inside breast pocket, wrapped in newspaper. They said Moscow was the most exciting city in the world, but it was not at its best under twin siege from winter and the Amerikans. Helicopters swooped overhead, broadcasting official warnings and announcements: comrades were advised to stay at their workplaces and continue with their duly-delegated tasks; victory in the struggle against the American octopus was inevitable; the crisis was nearly at an end and the master strategists would soon announce a devastating counter-attack; the dead were to be disabled and placed in the proper collection points; another exposed pocket of traitors would go on trial tomorrow.

In an onion-domed church, soldiers dealt with Amerikans. Brought in covered lorries, the shuffling dead were shifted inside in ragged coffles. As Chirkov passed, a dead woman, bear-like in a fur coat over forbidden undergarments, broke the line. Soldiers efficiently cornered her and stuck a bayonet into her head. The remains were hauled into the church. When the building was full, it would be burned: an offering. In Red Square, loudspeakers shouted martial music at the queues, *John Reed at the Barricades*. Lenin's tomb was no longer open for tourists. Sergeant Trauberg was fond of telling the story about what had happened in the tomb when the Amerikans started to rise. Everyone guessed it was true. The Spa was off the

Square. Before the Revolution of 1918, it had been an exclusive health club for the Royal Family. Now it was a morgue.

———————

He presented his papers to a thin officer he met on the broad steps of the Spa, and stood frozen in stiff-backed salute while the man looked over the wedge of documentation. He was told to wander inside smartly and look out Lyubachevsky. The officer proceeded, step by step, down to the square. Under the dusting of snow, the stone steps were gilded with ice: a natural defence. Chirkov understood Amerikans were forever slipping and falling on ice; many were so damaged they couldn't regain their footing, and were consequently easy to deal with. The doors of the Spa, three times a man's height, were pocked with bullet-holes new and old. Unlocked and unoiled, they creaked alarmingly as he pushed inside. The foyer boasted marble floors, and ceilings painted with classical scenes of romping nymphs and athletes. Busts of Marx and Lenin flanked the main staircase; a portrait of the New First Secretary, significantly less faded than neighbouring pictures, was proudly displayed behind the main desk.

A civilian he took to be Lyubachevsky squatted by the desk reading a pamphlet. A half-empty vodka bottle was nestled like a baby in the crook of his arm. He looked up awkwardly at the new arrival and explained that last week all the chairs in the building had been taken away by the Health Committee. Chirkov presented papers and admitted he had been sent by the despatcher at the railway station, which elicited a shrug. The civilian mused that the central station was always sending stray soldiers for an unknown reason. Lyubachevsky had three days' of stubble and mismatched eyes. He offered Chirkov a swallow of vodka—pure and strong, not diluted with melted snow like the rat poison he had been sold in Borodino—and opened up the lump of papers, searching for a particular signature. In the end, he decided it best Chirkov stay at the Spa. Unlocking a cabinet, he found a long white coat, muddied at the bottom. Chirkov was reluctant to exchange his heavy greatcoat for the flimsy garment but Lyubachevsky assured

him there was very little pilferage from the Spa. People, even parasites, tended to avoid visiting the place unless there was a pressing reason for their presence. Before relinquishing his coat, Chirkov remembered to retain his mobility permit, pinning it to the breast of the laboratory coat. After taking Chirkov's rifle, complimenting him on its cleanliness and stowing it in the cabinet, Lyubachevsky issued him with a revolver. It was dusty and the metal was cold enough to stick to his skin. Breaking the gun open, Chirkov noted three cartridges. In Russian roulette, he would have an even chance. Without a holster, he dropped it into the pocket of his coat; the barrel poked out of a torn corner. He had to sign for the weapon.

Lyubachevsky told him to go down into the Pool and report to Director Kozintsev. Chirkov descended in a hand-cranked cage lift and stepped out into a ballroom-sized space. The Pool was what people who worked in the Spa called the basement where the dead were kept. It had been a swimming bath before the Revolution; there, weary generations of Romanovs had plunged through slow waters, the tides of history slowly pulling them under. Supposedly dry since 1916, the Pool was so cold that condensation on the marble floors turned to ice-patches. The outer walls were still decorated with gilted plaster friezes and his bootfalls echoed on the solid floors. He walked round the edge of the pit, looking down at the white-coated toilers and their unmoving clients. The Pool was divided into separate work cubicles and narrow corridors by flimsy wooden partitions that rose above the old water level. A girl caught his eye, blonde hair tightly gathered at the back of her neck. She had red lipstick and her coat sleeves were rolled up on slender arms as she probed the chest cavity of a corpse, a girl who might once have been her slightly older sister. The dead girl had a neat, round hole in her forehead and her hair was fanned over a sludgy discharge Chirkov took to be abandoned brains. He coughed to get the live girl's attention and inquired as to where he could find the Director. She told him to make his way to the Deep End and climb in, then penetrate the warren of partitions. He couldn't miss Kozintsev; the Director was dead centre.

At the Deep End, he found a ladder into the pool. It was guarded by a soldier who sat cross-legged, a revolver in his lap, twanging on a jew's harp. He stopped and told Chirkov the tune was a traditional American folk song about a cowboy killed by a lawyer, 'The Man Who Shot Liberty Valance'. The guard introduced himself as Corporal Tulbeyev and asked if Chirkov was interested in purchasing tape cassettes of the music of Mr Edward Cochran or Robert Dylan. Chirkov had no cassette player but Tulbeyev said that for five thousand roubles he could secure one. To be polite, Chirkov said he would consider the acquisition: evidently a great bargain. Tulbeyev further insinuated he could supply other requisites: contraceptive sheaths, chocolate bars, toothpaste, fresh socks, scented soap, suppressed reading matter. Every unit in the Soviet Union had a Tulbeyev, Chirkov knew. There was probably a secretary on the First Committee of the Communist Party who dealt disco records and mint-flavoured chewing gum to the High and Mighty. After a decent period of mourning, Chirkov might consider spending some of Sergeant Trauberg's roubles on underwear and soap.

Having clambered into the Pool, Chirkov lost the perspective on the layout of the work-spaces he had from above. It was a labyrinth and he zigzagged between partitions, asking directions from the occasional absorbed forensic worker. Typically, a shrug would prompt him to a new pathway. Each of the specialists was absorbed in dissection, wielding whiny and smoky saws or sharp and shiny scalpels. He passed by the girl he had seen from above—her name-tag identified her as Technician Sverdlova, and she introduced herself as Valentina—and found she had entirely exposed the rib-cage of her corpse. She was the epitome of sophisticated Moscow girl, Chirkov thought: imperturbable and immaculate even with human remains streaked up to her elbows. A straggle of hair whisped across her face, and she blew it out of the way. She dictated notes into a wire recorder, commenting on certain physiological anomalies of the dead girl. There was a rubbery resilience in the undecayed muscle tissue. He would have liked to stay, but had to report to Kozintsev. Bidding her goodbye, he left her cubicle, thumping a boot against a tin bucket full of watches, wedding-rings and eyeglasses. She said he could take anything he wanted but he declined. Remembering, he found the bent and broken sunglasses in his trousers pocket and added them to the contents of the bucket. It was like throwing a kopeck in a wishing-well, so he made a wish. As if she were telepathic, Valentina giggled. Blushing, Chirkov continued.

————

He finally came to a makeshift door with a plaque that read 'V.A. Kozintsev, Director'. Chirkov knocked and, hearing a grunt from beyond, pushed through. It was as if he had left the morgue for a sculptor's studio. On one table were moist bags of variously coloured clays, lined up next to a steaming samovar. In the centre of the space, in the light cast by a chandelier that hung over the whole Pool, a man in a smock worked on a bust of a bald-headed man. Kozintsev had a neatly-trimmed beard and round spectacles. He was working one-handed; long fingers delicately pressing hollows into cheeks; a glass of tea in his other hand. He stood back, gulped tea and tutted, extremely dissatisfied with his efforts. Instantly accepting the newcomer, Kozintsev asked Chirkov for help in going back to the beginning. He set his glass down and rolled up his sleeves. They both put their hands in the soft face and pulled. Clays came away in self-contained lumps: some stranded like muscles, others bunched like pockets of fat. A bare skull, blotched with clay, was revealed. Glass eyes stared hypnotically, wedged into sockets with twists of newspaper. Chirkov realised he had heard of the Director: V.A. Kozintsev was one of leading reconstruction pathologists in the Soviet Union. He had, layering in musculature and covering the results with skin, worked on the skulls tentatively identified as those of the Former Royal Family. He had recreated the heads of palaeolithic men, murder victims and Ivan the Terrible.

Chirkov reported for duty and the Director told him to find something useful to do. Kozintsev was depressed to lose three days' work and explained in technical detail that the skull wasn't enough.

There had to be some indication of the disposition of muscle and flesh. As he talked, he rolled a cigarette and stuck it in the corner of his mouth, patting his smock pockets for matches. Chirkov understood this was one of Kozintsev's historical projects: high profile work sanctioned by the Ministry of Culture, unconnected to the main purpose of the Spa—which, just now, was to determine the origins and capabilities of the Amerikans—but useful in attracting attention and funds. While the Director looked over charts of facial anatomy, puffing furiously on his cigarette, Chirkov picked up the discarded clays and piled them on the table. On a separate stand was a wigmaker's dummy head under a glass dome: it wore a long but neat black wig and facsimile wisps of eyebrows, moustache and beard. Once the skull was covered and painted to the correct skin tone, hair would be applied. He asked Kozintsev to whom the skull belonged, and, off-handedly, the Director told him it was Grigory Rasputin. There had been trouble getting glass eyes with the right quality. Contemporary memoirs described the originals as steely blue, with pupils that contracted to pinpoints when their owner was concentrating on exerting his influence. Chirkov looked again at the skull and couldn't see anything special. It was just bare bone.

———

Each evening at nine, the Director presided over meetings. Attendance was mandatory for the entire staff, down to Chirkov. He was billeted in the Spa itself, in a small room on the top floor where he slept on what had once been a masseur's table. Since food was provided (albeit irregularly) by a cafeteria, there was scarce reason to venture outside. At meetings, Chirkov learned who everyone was: the ranking officer was Captain Zharov, who would rather be out in the streets fighting but suffered from a gimpy knee; under Kozintsev, the chief coroner was Dr Fyodor Dudnikov, a famous forensic scientist often consulted by the police in political murder cases but plainly out of his depth with the Spa's recent change of purpose. The Director affected a lofty disinterest in the current emergency, which left the morgue actually to be run by a conspiracy between Lyubachevsky, an administrator seconded from the Ministry of Agriculture, and Tulbeyev, who was far more capable than Captain Zharov of keeping greased the wheels of the military machine.

Chirkov's girl Valentina turned out to be very eminent for her years, a specialist in the study of Amerikans; at each meeting, she reported the findings of the day. Her discoveries were frankly incomprehensible, even to her colleagues, but she seemed to believe the Amerikans were not simple reanimated dead bodies. Her dissections and probings demonstrated that the Amerikans functioned in many ways like living beings; in particular, their musculature adapted slowly to their new state even as surplus flesh and skin sloughed off. Those portions of their bodies that rotted away were irrelevant to the functioning of the creatures. She likened the ungainly and stumbling dead creatures to a pupal stage, and expressed a belief that the Amerikans were becoming stronger. Her argument was that they should be categorised not as former human beings but as an entirely new species, with its own strengths and capabilities. At every meeting, Valentina complained she could only manage so much by examining doubly-dead bodies and that the best hope of making progress would be to secure 'live' specimens and observe their natural progress. She had sketched her impressions of what the Amerikans would eventually evolve into: thickly-muscled skeletons like old anatomical drawings.

Valentina's leading rival, A. Tarkhanov, countered that her theories were a blind alley. In his opinion, the Spa should concentrate on the isolation of the bacteriological agent responsible for the reanimations, with a view to the development of a serum cure. Tarkhanov, a Party member, also insisted the phenomenon had been created artificially by American genetic engineers. He complained the monster-makers of the United States were so heavily financed by capitalist cartels that this state-backed bureaucracy could hardly compete. The one common ground Valentina held with Tarkhanov was that the Spa was desperately under-funded. Since everyone at the meetings had to sit on the floor, while Director Kozintsev was elevated cross-legged on a desk, the procurement of chairs was deemed a priority, though all the scientists also had long lists of medical supplies and instruments without which they could not continue their vital researches. Lyubachevsky always countered these complaints by detailing his repeated requests to appropriate departments, often with precise accounts of the elapsed time since the request had been submitted. At Chirkov's third meeting, there was much excitement when Lyubachevsky announced that the Spa had received from the Civil Defence Committee fifty-five child-sized blankets. This was unrelated to any request that had been put in, but Tulbeyev offered to arrange a trade with the Children's Hospital, exchanging the blankets for either vegetables or medical instruments.

At the same meeting, Captain Zharov reported that his men had successfully dealt with an attempted invasion. Two Amerikans had been found at dawn, having negotiated the slippery steps, standing outside the main doors, apparently waiting. One stood exactly outside the doors, the other a step down. They might have been forming a primitive queue. Zharov personally disposed of them both, expending cartridges into their skulls, and arranged for the removal of the remains to a collection point, from which they might well be returned as specimens. Valentina moaned that it would have been better to capture and pen the Amerikans in a secure area—she specified the former steam bath—where they could be observed. Zharov cited standing orders. Kozintsev concluded with a lengthy lecture on Rasputin, elaborating his own theory that the late Tsarina's spiritual adviser was less mad than popularly supposed and that his influence with the Royal Family was ultimately instrumental in bringing about the Revolution. He spoke with especial interest and enthusiasm of the so-called Mad Monk's powers of healing, the famously ameliorative hands that could ease the symptoms of the Tsarevich's haemophilia. It was his contention that Rasputin had been possessed of a genuine paranormal talent. Even Chirkov thought this beside the point, especially when the Director wound down by admitting another failure in his reconstruction project.

With Tulbeyev, he drew last guard of the night; on duty at three a.m., expected to remain at the post in the foyer until the nine o'clock relief. Captain Zharov and Lyubachevsky could not decide whether Chirkov counted as a soldier or an experimental assistant; so he found himself called on to fulfil both functions, occasionally simultaneously. As a soldier, he would be able to sleep away the morning after night duty, but as an experimental assistant, he was required to report to Director Kozintsev at nine sharp. Chirkov didn't mind overmuch; once you got used to corpses, the Spa was a cushy detail. At least corpses here *were* corpses. Although, for personal reasons, he always voted, along with two other scientists and a cook, in support of Technician Sverdlova's request to bring in Amerikans, he was privately grateful she always lost by a wide margin. No matter how secure the steam bath might be, Chirkov was not enthused by the idea of Amerikans inside the building. Tulbeyev, whose grandmother was Moldavian, told stories of *wurdalaks* and *vryolakas* and always had new anecdotes. In life, according to Tulbeyev, Amerikans had all been Party members: that was why so many had good clothes and consumer goods. The latest craze among the dead was for cassette players with attached headphones; not American manufacture, but Japanese. Tulbeyev had a collection of the contraptions, harvested from Amerikans whose heads were so messed up that soldiers were squeamish about borrowing from them. It was a shame, said Tulbeyev, that the dead were disinclined to cart video players on their backs. If they picked up that habit, everyone in the Spa would be a millionaire; not a rouble millionaire, a dollar millionaire. Many of the dead had foreign currency. Tarkhanov's pet theory was that the Americans impregnated money with a bacteriological agent, the condition spreading through contact with cash. Tulbeyev, who always wore gloves, did not seem unduly disturbed by the thought.

Just as Tulbeyev was elaborating upon the empire he could build with a plague of video-players, a knock came at the doors. Not a sustained pounding like someone petitioning for entry, but a thud as if something had accidentally been bumped against the other side of the oak. They both shut up and listened. One of Tulbeyev's tape machines was playing Creedence Clearwater Revival's 'It Came Out of the Sky' at a variable speed; he turned off the tape, which scrunched inside the machine as the wheels ground, and swore. Cassettes were harder to come by than players. There was a four-thirty-in-the-morning Moscow quiet. Lots of little noises; wind whining round the slightly-warped door, someone having a coughing-fit many floors above, distant shots. Chirkov cocked his revolver, hoping there was a round under the hammer, further hoping the round wasn't a dud. There was another knock, like the first. Not purposeful, just a blunder. Tulbeyev ordered Chirkov to take a look through the spy-hole. The brass cap was stiff but he managed to work it aside and look through the glass lens.

A dead face was close to the spy-hole. For the first time, it occurred to Chirkov that Amerikans were scary. In the dark, this one had empty eye-sockets and a constantly-chewing mouth. Around its ragged neck were hung several cameras and a knotted scarf with a naked woman painted on it. Chirkov told Tulbeyev, who showed interest at the mention of photographic equipment and crammed around the spy-hole. He proposed that they open the doors and Chirkov put a bullet into the Amerikan's head. With cameras, Tulbeyev was certain he could secure chairs. With chairs, they would be the heroes of the Spa, entitled to untold privileges. Unsure of his courage, Chirkov agreed to the scheme and Tulbeyev struggled with the several bolts. Finally, the doors were loose, held shut only by Tulbeyev's fists on the handles. Chirkov nodded; his comrade pulled the doors open and stood back. Chirkov advanced, pistol held out and pointed at the Amerikan's forehead.

The dead man was not alone. Tulbeyev cursed and ran for his rifle. Chirkov did not fire, just looked from one dead face to the others. Four were lined in a crocodile, each on a different step. One wore an officer's uniform, complete with medals; another, a woman, had a severe pinstripe suit and a rakish gangster hat; at the back of the queue was a dead child, a golden-haired, green-faced girl in a baseball cap, trailing a doll. None moved much. Tulbeyev returned, levering a cartridge into the breech, and skidded on the marble floor as he brought his rifle to bear. Taken aback by the apparently unthreatening dead, he didn't fire either. Cold wind wafted in, which explained Chirkov's chill. His understanding was that Amerikans always attacked; these stood as if dozing upright, swaying slightly. The little girl's eyes moved mechanically back and forth. Chirkov told Tulbeyev to fetch a scientist, preferably Valentina. As his comrade scurried upstairs, he remembered he had only three rounds to deal with four Amerikans. He retreated into the doorway, eyes fixed on the dead, and slammed shut the doors. With the heel of his fist, he rammed a couple of the bolts home. Looking through the spy-hole, he saw nothing had changed. The dead still queued.

Valentina wore a floor-length dressing-gown over cotton pyjamas. Her bare feet must be frozen on the marble. Tulbeyev had explained about the night visitors and she was reminding him of Captain Zharov's report. These Amerikans repeated what the Captain had observed: the queuing behaviour pattern. She brushed her hair out of the way and got an eye to the spy-hole. With an odd squeal of delight, she summoned Chirkov to take a look, telling him to angle his eye so he could look beyond the queue. A figure struggled out of the dark, feet flapping like beached fish. It went down on its face and crawled up the steps, then stood. It took a place behind the little girl. This one was naked, so rotted that even its sex was lost, a skeleton held together by strips of muscle that looked like wet leather. Valentina said she wanted that Amerikan for observation, but one of the others was necessary as well. She still thought of capturing and observing specimens. Tulbeyev reminded her of the strangeness of the situation and asked why the dead were just standing in line, stretching down the steps away from the Spa. She said something about residual instinct, the time a citizen must spend in queues, the dead's inbuilt need to mimic the living, to recreate from trace memories the lives they had once had. Tulbeyev agreed to help her capture the specimens but insisted they be careful not to damage the cameras. He told her they could all be millionaires.

Valentina held Tulbeyev's rifle as a soldier would, stock close to her cheek, barrel straight. She stood by the doorway covering them as they

ventured out on her mission. Tulbeyev assigned himself to the first in
the queue, the dead man with the cameras. That left Chirkov to deal
with the walking skeleton, even if it was last in line and, in Moscow,
queue-jumping was considered a worse crime than matricide. From
somewhere, Tulbeyev had found a supply of canvas post-bags. The idea
was to pop a bag over an Amerikan's head like a hood, then lead the
dead thing indoors. Tulbeyev managed with one deft manoeuvre to
drop his bag over the photographer's head, and whipped round behind
the Amerikan, unravelling twine from a ball. As Tulbeyev bound dead
wrists together, the twine cut through grey skin and greenish-red fluid
leaked over his gloves. The rest of the queue stood impassive, ignoring
the treatment the photographer was getting. When Tulbeyev had wres-
tled his catch inside and trussed him like a pig, Chirkov was ready to
go for the skeleton.

He stepped lightly down to the skeleton's level, post-bag open as
if he were a poacher after rabbit. The Amerikans all swivelled their eyes
as he passed and, with a testicles-retracting spasm of panic, he missed
his footing. His boot slipped on icy stone and he fell badly, his hip
slamming a hard edge. He sledged down the steps, yelping as he went.
A shot cracked and the little girl, who had stepped out of the queue
and scrambled towards him, became a limp doll, a chunk of her head
dryly gone. Tulbeyev had got her. At the bottom of the steps, Chirkov
stood. Hot pain spilled from his hip and his side was numb. His lungs
hurt from the frozen air, and he coughed steam. He still held his bag
and gun; luckily, the revolver had not discharged. He looked around:
there were human shapes in the square, shambling towards the Spa.
Darting up the steps, unmindful of the dangers of ice, he made for the
light of the doorway. He paused to grab the skeleton by the elbow and
haul it to the entrance. It didn't resist him. The muscles felt like snakes
stretched over a bony frame. He shoved the skeleton into the foyer and
Tulbeyev was there with his ball of twine. Chirkov turned as Valentina
shut the doors. More Amerikans had come: the skeleton's place was
taken and the little girl's, and two or three more steps were occupied.
Before bolting the doors, Valentina opened them a crack and consid-

ered the queue. Again, the dead were still, unexcited. Then, like a drill team, they all moved up a step. The photographer's place was taken by the officer, and the rest of the line similarly advanced. Valentina pushed the doors together and Chirkov shut the bolts. Without pausing for breath, she ordered the specimens to be taken to the steam baths.

———————

Breakfast was a half-turnip, surprisingly fresh if riddled with ice-chips. Chirkov took it away from the cafeteria to chew and descended to the Pool to report to the Director. He assumed Valentina would make mention at the evening meeting of her unauthorised acquisition of specimens. It was not his place to spread gossip. Arriving at the cubicle before the Director, his first duty was to get the samovar going: Kozintsev survived on constant infusions of smoky tea. As Chirkov lit the charcoal, he heard a click, like saluting heels. He looked around the cubicle and saw no-one. All was as usual: clays, wig, shaping-tools, skull, samovar, boxes piled to make a stool. There was another click. He looked up at the chandelier and saw nothing unusual. The tea began to bubble and he chewed a mouthful of cold turnip, trying not to think about sleep, or Amerikans.

Kozintsev had begun again on the reconstruction. The skull of Grigory Yefimovich Rasputin was almost buried in clay strips. It looked very much like the head of the Amerikan Chirkov had secured for Valentina: flattened reddish ropes bound the jaws together, winding up into the cavities under the cheek-bones; enamel chips replaced the many missing teeth, standing out white against grey-yellow; delicate filaments swarmed round the glass eyes. It was an intriguing process and Chirkov had come to enjoy watching the Director at work. There was a sheaf of photographs of the monk on one stand but Kozintsev disliked consulting them. His process depended on extrapolating from the contours of the bone, not modelling from likenesses. Rasputin's potato-like peasant nose was a knotty problem. The cartilage was long-gone, and Kozintsev obsessively built and abandoned noses. Several were trodden flat into the sloping tile floor. After the

Revolution, the faith healer had been exhumed by zealots from his tomb in the Imperial Park and, reportedly, burned; there was doubt, fiercely resisted by the Director, as to the provenance of the skull.

As Chirkov looked, Rasputin's jaw sagged, clay muscles stretching; then, suddenly, it clamped shut, teeth clicking. Chirkov jumped, and spat out a shocked laugh. Kozintsev arrived, performing a dozen actions at once, removing his frock-coat and reaching for his smock, bidding a good morning and calling for his tea. Chirkov was bemused and afraid, questioning what he had seen. The skull bit once more. Kozintsev saw the movement at once, and asked again for tea. Chirkov, snapping out of it, provided a cupful and took one for himself. Kozintsev did not comment on the appropriation. He was very interested and peered close at the barely animated skull. The jaw moved slowly from side to side, as if masticating. Chirkov wondered if Grigory Yefimovich were imitating him and stopped chewing his turnip. Kozintsev pointed out that the eyes were trying to move, but the clay hadn't the strength of real muscle. He wondered aloud if he should work in strands of string to simulate the texture of human tissue. It might not be cosmetically correct. Rasputin's mouth gaped open, as if in a silent scream. The Director prodded the air near the skull's mouth with his finger and withdrew sharply as the jaws snapped shut. He laughed merrily, and called the monk a cunning fellow.

The queue was still on the steps. Everyone had taken turns at the spy-hole. Now the line stretched down into the square and along the pavement, curving around the building. Tulbeyev had hourly updates on the riches borne by the Amerikans. He was sure one of the queue harboured a precious video-player: Tulbeyev had cassettes of *101 Dalmatians* and *New Wave Hookers* but no way of playing them. Captain Zharov favoured dealing harshly with the dead, but Kozintsev, still excited by the skull activity, would issue no orders and the officer was not about to take action without a direct instruction, preferably in writing. As an experiment, he went out and, half-way down the steps, selected an Amerikan at random. He shot it in the head and the finally dead bag of bones tumbled out of the queue. Zharov kicked the remains, and, coming apart, they rolled down the steps into a snow-drift. After a pause, all the dead behind Zharov's kill took a step up. Valentina was in the steam baths with her specimens: news of her acquisitions had spread through the Spa, inciting vigorous debate. Tarkhanov complained to the Director about his colleague's usurpation of authority, but was brushed off with an invitation to examine the miraculous skull. Dr Dudnikov placed several phone calls to the Kremlin, relaying matters of interest to a junior functionary, who promised imminent decisions. It was Dudnikov's hope that the developments could be used as a lever to unloose vital supplies from other institutions. As ever, the rallying cry was *chairs for the Spa!*

In the afternoon, Chirkov napped standing up as he watched Kozintsev at work. Although the jaw continually made small movements, the skull was cooperative and did not try to nip the Director. He had requisitioned Tulbeyev's jew's harp and was implanting it among thick neck muscles, hoping it would function as a crude voice-box. To Chirkov's disgust, Rasputin was becoming expert in the movement of its unseeing eyes. He could suck the glass orbs so the painted pupils disappeared in the tops of the sockets, showing only milky white marbles. This was a man who had been hard to kill: his murderers gave him poison enough to fell an elephant, shot him in the back and chest with revolvers, kicked him in the head, battered him with a club and lowered him into the River Neva, bound in a curtain, through a hole in the ice. The skull bore an indentation which Kozintsev traced to an aristocrat's boot. In the end, men hadn't killed the seer; the cause of his death was drowning. As he worked, the Director hummed cheerful snatches of Prokofiev. To give the mouth something to do, Kozintsev stuck a cigarette between the teeth. He promised Grigory Yefimovich lips would come soon, but there was nothing yet he could do about lungs. His secret dream, which he shared with the skull (and, perforce, Chirkov), was to apply his process to a complete skeleton. Regrettably, and as he had himself predicted while alive, most of the monk had been scattered on the wind.

Lyubachevsky barged into the cubicle, bearing a telephone whose cord unreeled through the maze of the Pool like Ariadne's thread. There was a call from the Kremlin, which Kozintsev was required to take. While Chirkov and Lyubachevsky stood, unconsciously at attention, the Director chatted with the New First Secretary. Either Dr Dudnikov had tapped into the proper channels or Tarkhanov was the spy everyone took him for and had reported on the sly to his KGB superior. The First Secretary was briefed about what was going on at the Spa. He handed out a commendation to Kozintsev and insisted extra resources would be channelled to the morgue. Chirkov got the impression the First Secretary was mixing up the projects: Kozintsev was being praised for Valentina's studies. The Director would be only too delighted to employ any funds or supplies in furthering his work with the skull.

Following the telephone call, the Director was in excellent spirits. He told the skull a breakthrough was at hand, and insisted to Lyubachevsky that he could hear a faint twang from the jew's harp. Grigory Yefimovich was trying to communicate, the Director claimed. He asked if he remembered eating the poisoned chocolates? After the jaw first moved, Kozintsev had constructed rudimentary clay ears, exaggerated cartoon curls which stuck out ridiculously. Having abandoned any attempt to simulate the appearance in life of the monk, he was attempting instead to provide working features. Since Rasputin's brains must have rotted or burned years ago, it was hard to imagine what the Director aspired to communicate with. Then, over the loudspeaker, Dr Dudnikov reported that there were soldiers outside the Spa, setting up explosives and declaring an intention to dynamite the building. Grigory Yefimovich's glass eyes rolled again.

———

Engineers were packing charges around the foyer. Entering the Spa through the kitchens, they had avoided the Amerikan-infested steps. It appeared a second queue was forming, stretching off in a different direction, still leading to the front doors. The officer in command, a fat man with a facial birthmark that made him look like a spaniel, introduced himself as Major Andrey Kobylinsky. He strode about, inspecting the work, expressing pride in his unit's ability to demolish a building with the minimum of explosive matter. As he surveyed, Kobylinsky noted points at which surplus charges should be placed. To Chirkov's unschooled eye, the Major appeared to contradict himself: his men were plastering the walls with semtex. Kozintsev and Captain Zharov were absorbed in a reading of a twelve-page document which authorised the demolition of the Spa. Dr Dudnikov protested that the First Secretary himself had, within the last minute, commended the Spa and that important work to do with the Amerikan invasion was being carried out in the Pool, but Kobylinsky was far more interested in which pillars should be knocked out to bring down the decadent painted roof. As they worked, the engineers whistled 'Girls Just Want to Have Fun'.

Satisfied that the charges were laid correctly, Major Kobylinsky could not resist the temptation to lecture the assembled company on the progress and achievements of his campaign. A three-yard square map of Moscow was unfolded on the floor. It was marked with patches of red as if it were a chessboard pulled out of shape. The red areas signified buildings and constructions Kobylinsky had blown up. Chirkov understood the Major would not be happy until the entire map was shaded in red; then, Kobylinsky believed the crisis would be at an end. He proclaimed that this should have been done immediately the crisis begun, and that the Amerikans were to be thanked for prompting such a visionary enterprise. As the Major lectured, Chirkov noticed Tulbeyev at the main desk with Lyubachevsky, apparently trying to find a pen that worked. They sorted through a pot of pencils and chalks and markers, drawing streaks on a piece of blotting paper. Under the desk were packages wired to detonators. Kobylinsky checked his watch and mused that he was ahead of his schedule; the demolition would take place in one half an hour. Lyubachevsky raised a hand and ventured the opinion that the explosives placed under the main staircase were insufficient for the task of bringing down such a solidly-constructed structure. Barking disagreement, Kobylinsky strutted over and examined the charges in question, finally agreeing that safe was better than sorry and ordering the application of more explosives.

While Kobylinsky was distracted, Tulbeyev crept to the map and knelt over Red Square, scribbling furiously with a precious red felt-tip. He blotched over the Spa, extending an area of devastation to cover half the Square. When Kobylinsky revisited his map, Tulbeyev was unsuspiciously on the other side of the room. One of the engineers, a new set of headphones slung round his neck, piped up with an observation of a cartographical anomaly. Kobylinsky applied his concentration to the map and gurgled to himself. According to this chart, the Spa had already been dealt with by his unit: it was not a building but a raked-over patch of rubble. Another engineer, a baseball cap in his back pocket, volunteered a convincing memory of the destruction, three days ago, of the Spa. Kobylinsky looked again at the map, getting down on his hands and knees and crawling along the most famous thoroughfares of the city. He scratched his head and blinked in his birthmark. Director Kozintsev, arms folded and head high, said that so far as he was concerned the matter was at an end; he requested the engineers to remove their infernal devices from the premises. Kobylinsky had authorisation to destroy the Spa but once, and had demonstrably already acted on that authorisation. The operation could not be repeated without further orders, and, if further orders were requested, questions would be asked as to whether the engineers were as efficient as Kobylinsky would like to claim: most units needed to destroy a building only once for it to remain destroyed. Almost in tears, the bewildered Major finally commanded the removal of the explosives and, with parental tenderness, folded up his map into its case. With no apologies, the engineers withdrew.

————

That night, Valentina's Amerikans got out of the steam bath and everyone spent a merry three hours hunting them down. Chirkov and

Tulbeyev drew the Pool. The power had failed again and they had to fall back on oil lamps, which made the business all the more unnerving. Irregular and active shadows were all around, whispering in Moldavian of hungry, unquiet creatures. Their progress was a slow spiral; first, they circled the Pool from above, casting light over the complex, but that left too many darks unprobed; then they went in at the Deep End and moved methodically through the labyrinth, weaving between the partitions, stumbling against dissected bodies, ready to shoot hatstands in the brain. Under his breath, Tulbeyev recited a litany he claimed was a Japanese prayer against the dead: *sanyo, sony, seiko, mitsubishi, panasonic, toshiba* . . .

They had to penetrate the dead centre of the Pool. The Amerikans were in Kozintsev's cubicle: staring at the bone-and-clay head as if it were a colour television set. Rasputin was on his stand under a black protective cloth which hung like long hair. Chirkov found the combination of the Amerikans and Rasputin unnerving and, almost as a reflex, shot the skeleton in the skull. The report was loud and echoing. The skeleton came apart on the floor and, before Chirkov's ears stopped hurting, others had come to investigate. Director Kozintsev was concerned for his precious monk and probed urgently under the cloth for damage. Valentina was annoyed by the loss of her specimen but kept her tongue still, especially when her surviving Amerikan turned nasty. The dead man barged out of the cubicle, shouldering partitions apart, wading through gurneys and tables, roaring and slavering. Tarkhanov, incongruous in a silk dressing gown, got in the way and sustained a nasty bite. Tulbeyev dealt with the Amerikan, tripping him with an axe-handle, then straddling his chest and pounding a chisel into the bridge of his nose. He had not done anything to prove Valentina's theories; after a spell in captivity, he simply seemed more decayed, not evolved. Valentina claimed the thing Chirkov had finished had been a model of biological efficiency, stripped down to essentials, potentially immortal. Now, it looked like a stack of bones.

———

Even Kozintsev, occupied in the construction of a set of wooden arms for his reanimated favourite, was alarmed by the size of the queue. There were four distinct lines. The Amerikans shuffled constantly, stamping nerveless feet as if to keep warm. Captain Zharov set up a machine-gun emplacement in the foyer, covering the now-barred front doors, although it was strictly for show until he could be supplied with ammunition of the same gauge as the gun. Chirkov and Tulbeyev watched the Amerikans from the balcony. The queue was orderly; when, as occasionally happened, a too-far-gone Amerikan collapsed, it was trampled under by the great moving-up as those behind advanced. Tulbeyev sighted on individual dead with binoculars and listed the treasures he could distinguish. Mobile telephones, digital watches, blue jeans, leather jackets, gold bracelets, gold teeth, ball-point pens. The Square was a paradise for pickpockets. As night fell, it was notable that no lights burned even in the Kremlin.

When the power came back, the emergency radio frequencies broadcast only soothing music. The meeting was more sparsely attended than usual, and Chirkov realised faces had been disappearing steadily, lost to desertion or wastage. Dr Dudnikov announced that he had been unable to reach anyone on the telephone. Lyubachevsky reported that the threat of demolition had been lifted from the Spa and was unlikely to recur, though there might now prove to be unfortunate official side effects if the institution was formally believed to be a stretch of warm rubble. The kitchens had received a delivery of fresh fish, which was cause for celebration, though the head cook noted as strange the fact that many of the shipment were still flapping and even decapitation seemed not to still them. Valentina, for the hundredth time, requested specimens be secured for study and, after a vote— closer than usual, but still decisive—was disappointed. Tarkhanov's suicide was entered into the record and the scientists paid tribute to the colleague they fervently believed had repeatedly informed on them, reciting his achievements and honours. Tulbeyev suggested a raiding party to relieve the queuing Amerikans of those goods which could be used for barter, but no one was willing to second the proposal, which sent him into a notable sulk. Finally, as was expected, Kozintsev gave an account of his day's progress with Grigory Yefimovich. He had achieved a certain success with the arms: constructing elementary shoulder joints and nailing them to Rasputin's stand, then layering rope-and-clay muscles which interleaved with the neck he had fashioned. The head was able to control its arms to the extent of stretching out and bunching up muscle strands in the wrists as if clenching fists which did not, as yet, exist. The Director was also pleased to report that the head almost constantly made sounds with the jew's harp, approximating either speech or music. As if to demonstrate the monk's healing powers, Kozintsev's sinus trouble had cleared up almost entirely.

Two days later, Tulbeyev let the Amerikans in. Chirkov did not know where the Corporal got the idea; he just got up from the gun emplacement, walked across the foyer, and unbarred the doors. Chirkov did not try to stop him, distracted by efforts to jam the wrong type of belt into the machine gun. When all the bolts were loose, Tulbeyev flung the doors back and stood aside. At the front of the queue, ever since the night they had brought in Valentina's specimens, was the officer. As he waited, his face had run, flesh slipping from his cheeks to form jowly bags around his jaw. He stepped forwards smartly, entering the foyer. Lyubachevsky woke up from his cot behind the desk and wondered aloud what was going on. Tulbeyev took a fistful of medals from the officer, and tossed them to the floor after a shrewd assessment. The officer walked purposefully, with a broken-ankled limp, towards the lifts. Next in was the woman in the pinstripe suit. Tulbeyev took her hat and perched it on his head. From the next few, the Corporal harvested a silver chain identity bracelet, a woven leather belt, a pocket calculator, an old brooch. He piled the tokens behind him. Amerikans filled the foyer, wedging through the doorway in a triangle behind the officer.

Chirkov assumed the dead would eat him and wished he had

seriously tried to go to bed with Technician Sverdlova. He still had two rounds left in his revolver, which meant he could deal with an Amerikan before ensuring his own everlasting peace. There were so many to choose from and none seemed interested in him. The lift was descending and those who couldn't get into it discovered the stairs. They were all drawn to the basement, to the Pool. Tulbeyev chortled and gasped at each new treasure, sometimes clapping the dead on the shoulders as they yielded their riches, hugging one or two of the more harmless creatures. Lyubachevsky was appalled, but did nothing. Finally, the administrator got together the gumption to issue an order: he told Chirkov to inform the Director of this development. Chirkov assumed that since Kozintsev was, as ever, working in the Pool, he would very soon be extremely aware of this development, but he snapped to and barged through the crowd anyway, choking back the instinct to apologise. The Amerikans mainly got out of his way, and he pushed to the front of the wave shuffling down the basement steps. He broke out of the pack and clattered into the Pool, yelling that the Amerikans were coming. Researchers looked up—he saw Valentina's eyes flashing annoyance and wondered if it was not too late to ask her for sex—and the crowd edged behind Chirkov, approaching the lip of the Pool.

He vaulted in and sloshed through the mess towards Kozintsev's cubicle. Many partitions were down already and there was a clear path to the Director's work-space. Valentina pouted at him, then her eyes widened as she saw the assembled legs surrounding the Pool. The Amerikans began to topple in, crushing furniture and corpses beneath them, many unable to stand once they had fallen. The hardiest of them kept on walking, swarming round and overwhelming the technicians. Cries were strangled and blood ran on the bed of the Pool. Chirkov fired wildly, winging an ear off a bearded dead man in a shabby suit, and pushed on towards Kozintsev. When he reached the centre, his first thought was that the cubicle was empty, then he saw what the Director had managed. Combining himself with his work, V.A. Kozintsev had constructed a wooden half-skeleton which fitted over his shoulders, making his own head the heart of the new body he had fashioned for Grigory Yefimovich Rasputin. The head, built out to giant size with exaggerated clay and rubber muscles, wore its black wig and beard, and even had lips and patches of sprayed-on skin. The upper body was wooden and intricate, the torso of a colossus with arms to match, but sticking out at the bottom were the Director's stick-insect legs. Chirkov thought the body would not be able to support itself but, as he looked, the assemblage stood. He looked up at the caricature of Rasputin's face. Blue eyes shone, not glass but living.

Valentina was by his side, gasping. He put an arm round her and vowed to himself that if it were necessary she would have the bullet he had saved for himself. He smelled her perfumed hair. Together, they looked up at the holy maniac who had controlled a woman and, through her, an empire, ultimately destroying both. Rasputin looked down on them, then turned away to look at the Amerikans. They crowded round in an orderly fashion, limping pilgrims approaching a shrine. A terrible smile disfigured the crude face. An arm extended, the paddle-sized hand stretching out fingers constructed from surgical implements. The hand fell onto the forehead of the first of the Amerikans, the officer. It covered the dead face completely, fingers curling round the head. Grigory Yefimovich seemed powerful enough to crush the Amerikan's skull, but instead he just held firm. His eyes rolled up to the chandelier, and a twanging came from inside the wood-and-clay neck, a vibrating monotone that might have been a hymn. As the noise resounded, the gripped Amerikan shook, slabs of putrid meat falling away like layers of onionskin. At last, Rasputin pushed the creature away. The uniform gone with its flesh, it was like Valentina's skeleton, but leaner, moister, stronger. It stood up and stretched, its infirmities gone, its ankle whole. It clenched and unclenched teeth in a joke-shop grin and leaped away, eager for meat. The next Amerikan took its place under Rasputin's hand, and was healed too. And the next.

Once, long ago and far away, John Skipp and Craig Spector edited an anthology called The Book of the Dead, *of mostly fine stories set more or less in the world of George A. Romero's 'Living Dead' films. It was so well-received that the editors produced a further volume,* Still Dead. *Then, remembering that there were three Romero dead movies, they set out to do a third volume, which may well have been called* Deader *Than Ever* or Deadest Yet. *Since, in my other life as a movie critic, I had written extensively about Romero in my book* Nightmare Movies, *I was pleased to be asked by John to come up with something for this third book. I did a little rewriting at Craig's suggestion, got paid (as I remember it) and waited for the story to appear.*

Years passed. I'm not really privy to what happened, but various publishers and editors fell out with each other and, though the third dead book nearly happened at least twice (I once received page proofs) it never managed to stumble into print. If you've been picking up anthologies of original horror stories, you've already read quite a few ship-jumping tales from the collection (Douglas E. Winter's wonderful 'The Zombies of Madison County' is one). For a while, 'Amerikanski Dead' was due to come out as a chap-book — but that never quite happened either. Then, with the bogus millennium looming, I was asked by Al Sarrantonio if I had anything he might look at for what was then called 999: The Last Horror Anthology, *intended to be one of those genre-summing, über-collection doorstops that the field needs every so often to stay alive. I dug out this, and it wound up as the lead-off story in the somewhat more modestly-titled* 999: New Stories of Horror and Suspense. *For that appearance, the story lost its sub-title (a quote from Jean-Luc Godard) to keep the list of contents tidy, but I'm restoring it here.*

Though the rising of the dead is supposed to be a global phenomenon, Romero's movies — Night of the Living Dead *(1968),* Dawn of the Dead *(1979) and* Day of the Dead *(1984) — are all about America. One or two of the stories in the dead collections are about foreign parts (Poppy Z. Brite's 'Calcutta, Lord of Nerves') and Clive Barker was connected with a comic book spin-off that had dead folks (including the Royal Family) in London. But Romero's films belong now to the era of the superpower face-off, and I thought it would be interesting to see what might be happening in the then-Soviet Union during the time between* Dawn *and* Day *and, more importantly, what it might mean. The title is a riff on* The Living Dead at the Manchester Morgue, *the British release title of the Spanish-Italian movie* No profanar el sueño de los muertos *(1974) — known in America as* Don't Open the Window *or* Let Sleeping Corpses Lie *(rarely has one film had so many great titles).*

The business about reconstructing faces from skulls is mentioned in Martin Cruz Smith's Gorky Park, *but I remembered it from a 1960s BBC science documentary (*Tomorrow's World?*) in which the skull of Ivan the Terrible was used as a template to recreate his head. For Rasputin details, I drew on Robert K. Massie's* Nicholas and Alexandra, *Sir David Napley's* Rasputin in Hollywood *and various unreliable movie and TV performances by whiskery scenery-chewers like Lionel Barrymore, Boris Karloff, Tom Baker and Christopher Lee.*

THE

BIG FISH

The Bay City cops were rousting enemy aliens. As I drove through the nasty coast town, uniforms hauled an old couple out of a grocery store. The Taraki family's neighbours huddled in thin rain howling asthmatically for bloody revenge. Pearl Harbor had struck a lot of people that way. With the Tarakis on the bus for Manzanar, neighbours descended on the store like bedraggled vultures. Produce vanished instantly, then destruction started. Caught at a sleepy stop light, I got a good look. The Tarakis had lived over the store; now, their furniture was thrown out of the second-storey window. Fine china shattered on the sidewalk, spilling white chips like teeth into the gutter. It was inspirational, the forces of democracy rallying round to protect the United States from vicious oriental grocers, fiendishly intent on selling eggplant to a hapless civilian population.

Meanwhile my appointment was with a gent who kept three pictures on his mantelpiece, grouped in a triangle around a statue of the Virgin Mary. At the apex was his white-haired mama, to the left Charles Luciano, and to the right, Benito Mussolini. The Tarakis, American-born and registered Democrats, were headed to a dustbowl concentration camp for the duration, while Gianni Pastore, Sicilian-born and highly unregistered *capo* of the Family Business, would spend his war in a marble-fronted mansion paid for by nickels and dimes dropped on the numbers game, into slot machines, or exchanged for the favours of nice girls from the old country. I'd seen his mansion before and so far been able to resist the temptation to bean one of his twelve muse statues with a bourbon bottle.

Money can buy you love but can't even put down a deposit on good taste.

The palace was up in the hills, a little way down the boulevard from Tyrone Power. But now, Pastore was hanging his mink-banded fedora in a Bay City beachfront motel complex, which was a real estate agent's term for a bunch of horrible shacks shoved together for the convenience of people who like sand on their carpets.

I always take a lungful of fresh air before entering a confined space with someone in Pastore's business, so I parked the Chrysler a few blocks from the Seaview Inn and walked the rest of the way, sucking on a Camel to keep warm in the wet. They say it doesn't rain in Southern California, but they also say the U.S. Navy could never be taken by surprise. This February, three months into a war the rest of the world had been fighting since 1936 or 1939 depending on whether you were Chinese or Polish, it was raining almost constantly, varying between a light fall of misty drizzle in the dreary daytimes to spectacular storms, complete with DeMille lighting effects, in our fear-filled nights. Those trusty Boy Scouts scanning the horizons for Jap subs and Nazi U-Boats were filling up influenza wards and manu-facturers of raincoats and umbrellas who'd not yet converted their plants to defense production were making a killing. I didn't mind the rain. At least rainwater is clean, unlike most other things in Bay City.

A small boy with a wooden gun leaped out of a bush and sprayed me with sound effects, interrupting his onomatopoeic chirruping with a shout of 'die you slant-eyed Jap!' I clutched my heart, staggered back, and he finished me off with a quick burst. I died for the Emperor and tipped the kid a dime to go away. If this went on long enough, maybe little Johnny would get a chance to march off and do real killing, then maybe come home in a box or with the shakes or a taste for blood. Meanwhile, especially since someone spotted a Jap submarine off Santa Barbara, California was gearing up for the War Effort. Aside from interning grocers, our best brains were writing songs like 'To Be

Specific, It's Our Pacific', 'So Long Momma, I'm Off to Yokahama', 'We're Gonna Slap the Jap Right Off the Map' and 'When Those Little Yellow Bellies Meet the Cohens and the Kellys'. Zanuck had donated his string of Argentine polo ponies to West Point and got himself measured for a comic opera Colonel's uniform so he could join the Signal Corps and defeat the Axis by posing for publicity photographs.

I'd tried to join up two days after Pearl Harbor but they kicked me back onto the streets. Too many concussions. Apparently, I get hit on the head too often and have a tendency to black out. When they came to mention it, they were right.

The Seaview Inn was shuttered, one of the first casualties of war. It had its own jetty, and by it were a few canvas-covered motor launches shifting with the waves. In late afternoon gloom, I saw the silhouette of the *Montecito*, anchored strategically outside the three-mile limit. That was one good thing about the Japanese; on the downside, they might have sunk most of the U.S. fleet, but on the up, they'd put Laird Brunette's gambling ship out of business. Nobody was enthusiastic about losing their shirt-buttons on a rigged roulette wheel if they imagined they were going to be torpedoed any moment. I'd have thought that would add an extra thrill to the whole gay, delirious business of giving Brunette money, but I'm just a poor, twenty-five-dollars-a-day detective.

The Seaview Inn was supposed to be a stopping-off point on the way to the *Monty* and now its trade was stopped off. The main building was sculpted out of dusty ice cream and looked like a three-storey radiogram with wave-scallop friezes. I pushed through double-doors and entered the lobby. The floor was decorated with a mosaic in which Neptune, looking like an angry Santa Claus in a swimsuit, was sticking it to a sea-nymph who shared a hairdresser with Hedy Lamarr. The nymph was naked except for some strategic shells. It was very artistic.

There was nobody at the desk and thumping the bell didn't improve matters. Water ran down the outside of the green-tinted windows. There were a few steady drips somewhere. I lit up another Camel and went exploring. The office was locked and the desk register didn't have any entries after December 7, 1941. My raincoat dripped and began to dry out, sticking my jacket and shirt to my shoulders. I shrugged, trying to get some air into my clothes. I noticed Neptune's face quivering. A thin layer of water had pooled over the mosaic and various anenome-like fronds attached to the sea god were apparently getting excited. Looking at the nymph, I could understand that. Actually, I realised, only the hair was from Hedy. The face and the body were strictly Janey Wilde.

I go to the movies a lot but I'd missed most of Janey's credits: *She-Strangler of Shanghai, Tarzan and the Tiger Girl, Perils of Jungle Jillian.* I'd seen her in the newspapers though, often in unnervingly close proximity with Pastore or Brunette. She'd started as an Olympic swimmer, picking up medals in Berlin, then followed Weissmuller and Crabbe to Hollywood. She would never get an Academy Award but her legs were in a lot of cheesecake stills publicising no particular movie. Air-brushed and made-up like a good-looking corpse, she was a fine commercial for sex. In person she was as bubbly as domestic champagne, though now running to flat. Things were slow in the detecting business, since people were more worried about imminent invasion than missing daughters or misplaced love letters. So when Janey Wilde called on me in my office in the Cahuenga Building and asked me to look up one of her ill-chosen men friends, I checked the pile of old envelopes I use as a desk diary and informed her that I was available to make inquiries into the current whereabouts of a certain big fish.

Wherever Laird Brunette was, he wasn't here. I was beginning to figure Gianni Pastore, the gambler's partner, wasn't here either. Which meant I'd wasted an afternoon. Outside it rained harder, driving against the walls with a drumlike tattoo. Either there were hailstones mixed in with the water or the Jap air force was hurling fistfuls of pebbles at Bay City to demoralise the population. I don't know why they bothered. All Hirohito had to do was slip a thick envelope to the Bay City cops and the city's finest would hand over the whole community to the Japanese Empire with a ribbon around it and a bow on top.

There were more puddles in the lobby, little streams running from one to the other. I was reminded of the episode of *The Perils of Jungle Jillian* I had seen while tailing a child molester to a Saturday matinee. At the end, Janey Wilde had been caught by the Panther Princess and trapped in a room which slowly filled with water. That room had been a lot smaller than the lobby of the Seaview Inn and the water had come in a lot faster.

Behind the desk were framed photographs of pretty people in pretty clothes having a pretty time. Pastore was there, and Brunette, grinning like tiger cats, mingling with showfolk: Xavier Cugat, Janey Wilde, Charles Coburn. Janice Marsh, the pop-eyed beauty rumoured to have replaced Jungle Jillian in Brunette's affections, was well represented in artistic poses.

On the phone, Pastore had promised faithfully to be here. He hadn't wanted to bother with a small-timer like me but Janey Wilde's name opened a door. I had a feeling Papa Pastore was relieved to be shaken down about Brunette, as if he wanted to talk about something. He must be busy because there were several wars on. The big one overseas and a few little ones at home. Maxie Rothko, bar owner and junior partner in the *Monty*, had been found drifting in the seaweed around the Santa Monica pier without much of a head to speak of. And Phil Isinglass, man-about-town lawyer and Brunette frontman, had turned up in the storm drains, lungs full of sandy mud. Disappearing was the latest craze in Brunette's organisation. That didn't sound good for Janey Wilde, though Pastore had talked about the Laird as if he knew Brunette was alive. But now Papa wasn't around. I was getting annoyed with someone it wasn't sensible to be annoyed with.

Pastore wouldn't be in any of the beach shacks but there should be an apartment for his convenience in the main building. I decided to explore further. Jungle Jillian would expect no less. She'd hired me for five days in advance, a good thing since I'm unduly reliant on eating and drinking and other expensive diversions of the monied and idle.

The corridor that led past the office ended in a walk-up staircase. As soon as I put my size nines on the first step, it squelched. I realised something was more than usually wrong. The steps were a quiet little waterfall, seeping rather than cascading. It wasn't just water, there was unpleasant, slimy stuff mixed in. Someone had left the bath running. My first thought was that Pastore had been distracted by a bullet. I was wrong. In the long run, he might have been happier if I'd been right.

I climbed the soggy stairs and found the the apartment door unlocked but shut. Bracing myself, I pushed the door in. It encountered resistance but then sliced open, allowing a gush of water to shoot around my ankles, soaking my dark blue socks. Along with water was a three-weeks-dead-in-the-water-with-rotten-fish smell that wrapped around me like a blanket. Holding my breath, I stepped into the room. The waterfall flowed faster now. I heard a faucet running. A radio played, with funny little gurgles mixed in. A crooner was doing his best with 'Life is Just a Bowl of Cherries', but he sounded as if he were drowned full fathom five. I followed the music and found the bathroom.

Pastore was face down in the overflowing tub, the song coming from under him. He wore a silk lounging robe that had been pulled away from his back, his wrists tied behind him with the robe's cord. In the end he'd been drowned. But before that hands had been laid on him, either in anger or with cold, professional skill. I'm not a coroner, so I couldn't tell how long the Family Man had been in the water. The radio still playing and the water still running suggested Gianni had met his end recently but the stench felt older than sin.

I have a bad habit of finding bodies in Bay City and the most profit-minded police force in the country have a bad habit of trying to make connections between me and a wide variety of deceased persons. The obvious solution in this case was to make a friendly phone call, absent-mindedly forgetting to mention my name while giving the flatfeet directions to the late Mr Pastore. Who knows, I might accidentally talk to someone honest.

That is exactly what I would have done if, just then, the man with the gun hadn't come through the door . . .

———

I had Janey Wilde to blame. She'd arrived without an appointment, having picked me on a recommendation. Oddly, Laird Brunette had once said something not entirely uncomplimentary about me. We'd met. We hadn't seriously tried to kill each other in a while. That was as good a basis for a relationship as any.

Out of her sarong, Jungle Jillian favoured sharp shoulders and a veiled pill-box. The kiddies at the matinee had liked her fine, especially when she was wrestling stuffed snakes, and dutiful Daddies took no exception to her either, especially when she was tied down and her sarong rode up a few inches. Her lips were four red grapes plumped together. When she crossed her legs you saw swimmer's smooth muscle under her hose.

'He's very sweet, really,' she explained, meaning Mr Brunette never killed anyone within ten miles of her without apologising afterwards, 'not at all like they say in those dreadful scandal sheets.'

The gambler had been strange recently, especially since the war shut him down. Actually the *Montecito* had been out of commission for nearly a year, supposedly for a refit although as far as Janey Wilde knew no workmen had been sent out to the ship. At about the time Brunette suspended his crooked wheels, he came down with a common California complaint, a dose of crackpot religion. He'd been tangentally mixed up a few years ago with a psychic racket run by a bird named Amthor, but had apparently shifted from the mostly harmless bunco cults onto the hard stuff. Spiritualism, orgiastic rites, chanting, incense, the whole deal.

Janey blamed this sudden interest in matters occult on Janice Marsh, who had coincidentally made her name as the Panther Princess in *The Perils of Jungle Jillian*, a role which required her to torture Janey Wilde at least once every chapter. My employer didn't mention that her own career had hardly soared between Jungle Jillian and *She-Strangler of Shanghai*, while the erstwhile Panther Princess had gone from Republic to Metro and was being built up as an exotic in the Dietrich-Garbo vein. Say what you like about Janice Marsh's

Nefertiti, she still looked like Peter Lorre to me. And according to Janey, the star had more peculiar tastes than a seafood buffet.

Brunette had apparently joined a series of fringe organisations and become quite involved, to the extent of neglecting his business and thereby irking his long-time partner, Gianni Pastore. Perhaps that was why person or persons unknown had decided the Laird wouldn't mind if his associates died one by one. I couldn't figure it out. The cults I'd come across mostly stayed in business by selling sex, drugs, power or reassurance to rich, stupid people. The Laird hardly fell into the category. He was too big a fish for that particular bowl.

———

The man with the gun was English, with a Ronald Colman accent and a white aviator's scarf. He was not alone. The quiet, truck-sized bruiser I made as a fed went through my wallet while the dapper foreigner kept his automatic pointed casually at my middle.

'Peeper,' the fed snarled, showing the photostat of my license and my supposedly impressive deputy's badge.

'Interesting,' said the Britisher, slipping his gun into the pocket of his camel coat. Immaculate, he must have been umbrella-protected between car and building because there wasn't a spot of rain on him. 'I'm Winthrop. Edwin Winthrop.'

We shook hands. His other companion, the interesting one, was going through the deceased's papers. She looked up, smiled with sharp white teeth, and got back to work.

'This is Mademoiselle Dieudonné.'

'Geneviève,' she said. She pronounced it 'Zhe-ne-vyev', suggesting Paris, France. She was wearing something white with silver in it and had quantities of pale blonde hair.

'And the gentleman from your Federal Bureau of Investigation is Finlay.'

The fed grunted. He looked as if he'd been brought to life by Willis H. O'Brien.

'You are interested in a Mr Brunette,' Winthrop said. It was not a question, so there was no point in answering him. 'So are we.'

'Call in a Russian and we could be the Allies,' I said.

Winthrop laughed. He was sharp. 'True. I am here at the request of my government and working with the full co-operation of yours.'

One of the small detective-type details I noticed was that no one even suggested informing the police about Gianni Pastore was a good idea.

'Have you ever heard of a place called Innsmouth, Massachusetts?'

It didn't mean anything to me and I said so.

'Count yourself lucky. Special Agent Finlay's associates were called upon to dynamite certain unsafe structures in the sea off Innsmouth back in the twenties. It was a bad business.'

Geneviève said something sharp in French that sounded like swearing. She held up a photograph of Brunette dancing cheek to cheek with Janice Marsh.

'Do you know the lady?' Winthrop asked.

'Only in the movies. Some go for her in a big way but I think she looks like Mr Moto.'

'Very true. Does the Esoteric Order of Dagon mean anything to you?'

'Sounds like a Church-of-the-Month alternate. Otherwise, no.'

'Captain Obed Marsh?'

'Uh-huh.'

'The Deep Ones?'

'Are they those coloured singers?'

'What about Cthulhu, Y'ha-nthlei, R'lyeh?'

'*Gesundheit.*'

Winthrop grinned, sharp moustache pointing. 'No, not easy to say at all. Hard to fit into human mouths, you know.'

'He's just a bedroom creeper,' Finlay said, 'he don't know nothing.'

'His grammar could be better. Doesn't J. Edgar pay for elocution lessons?'

Finlay's big hands opened and closed as if he were rather there were a throat in them.

'Gené?' Winthrop said.

The woman looked up, red tongue absently flicking across her red lips, and thought a moment. She said something in a foreign language that I did understand.

'There's no need to kill him,' she said in French. Thank you very much, I thought.

Winthrop shrugged and said 'fine by me.' Finlay looked disappointed.

'You're free to go,' the Britisher told me. 'We shall take care of everything. I see no point in your continuing your current line of inquiry. Send in a chit to this address,' he handed me a card, 'and you'll be reimbursed for your expenses so far. Don't worry. We'll carry on until this is seen through. By the way, you might care not to discuss with anyone what you've seen here or anything I may have said. There's a War on, you know. Loose lips sink ships.'

I had a few clever answers but I swallowed them and left. Anyone who thought there was no need to kill me was all right in my book and I wasn't using my razored tongue on them. As I walked to the Chrysler, several ostentatiously unofficial cars cruised past me, headed for the Seaview Inn.

It was getting dark and lighting was striking down out at sea. A flash lit up the *Montecito* and I counted five seconds before the thunder boomed. I had the feeling there was something out there beyond the three-mile limit besides the floating former casino, and that it was angry.

I slipped into the Chrysler and drove away from Bay City, feeling better the further inland I got.

————

I take *Black Mask*. It's a long time since Hammett and the fellow who wrote the Ted Carmady stories were in it, but you occasionally get a good Cornell Woolrich or Erle Stanley Gardner. Back at my office, I saw the newsboy had been by and dropped off the *Times* and next month's pulp. But there'd been a mix-up. Instead of the *Mask*, there was something inside the folded newspaper called *Weird Tales*. On the cover, a man was being attacked by two green demons and a stereotype vampire with a widow's peak. '"Hell on Earth", a Novelette of Satan in a Tuxedo by Robert Bloch' was blazed above the title. Also promised were 'A new Lovecraft series, "Herbert West—Re-Animator"' and '"The Rat Master" by Greye la Spina'. All for fifteen cents, kids. If I were a different type of detective, the brand who said *nom de* something and waxed a moustache whenever he found a mutilated corpse, I might have thought the substitution an omen.

In my office, I've always had five filing cabinets, three empty. I also had two bottles, only one empty. In a few hours, the situation would have changed by one bottle.

I found a glass without too much dust and wiped it with my clean handkerchief. I poured myself a generous slug and hit the back of my throat with it.

The radio didn't work but I could hear Glenn Miller from somewhere. I found my glass empty and dealt with that. Sitting behind my desk, I looked at the patterns in rain on the window. If I craned I could see traffic on Hollywood Boulevard. People who didn't spend their working days finding bodies in bathtubs were going home not to spend their evenings emptying a bottle.

After a day, I'd had some excitement but I hadn't done much for Janey Wilde. I was no nearer being able to explain the absence of Mr Brunette from his usual haunts than I had been when she left my office, leaving behind a tantalising whiff of *essence de chine*.

She'd given me some literature pertaining to Brunette's cult involvement. Now, the third slug warming me up inside, I looked over it, waiting for inspiration to strike. Interesting echoes came up in relation to Winthrop's shopping list of subjects of peculiar interest. I had no luck with the alphabet soup syllables he'd spat at me, mainly because 'Cthulhu' sounds more like a cough than a word. But the Esoteric Order of Dagon was a group Brunette had joined, and Innsmouth, Massachusetts, was the East Coast town where the organisation was registered. The Esoteric Order had a temple on the beach front in Venice, and its mumbo-jumbo hand-outs promised 'ancient and intriguing rites to probe the mysteries of the Deep.' Slipped in with the recruitment bills was a studio biography of Janice Marsh, which helpfully revealed the movie star's place of birth as Innsmouth, Massachusetts, and that she could trace her family back to Captain Obed Marsh, the famous early 19th Century explorer of whom I'd never heard. Obviously Winthrop, Geneviève and the FBI were well ahead of me in making connections. And I didn't really know who the Englishman and the French girl were.

I wondered if I wouldn't have been better off reading *Weird Tales*. I liked the sound of Satan in a Tuxedo. It wasn't Ted Carmady with an automatic and a dame, but it would do. There was a lot more thunder and lightning and I finished the bottle. I suppose I could have gone home to sleep but the chair was no more uncomfortable than my Murphy bed.

The empty bottle rolled and I settled down, tie loose, to forget the cares of the day.

———

Thanks to the War, Pastore only made Page 3 of the *Times*. Apparently the noted gambler-entrepreneur had been shot to death. If that was true, it happened after I'd left. Then, he'd only been tortured and drowned. Police Chief John Wax dished out his usual 'over by Christmas' quote about the investigation. There was no mention of the FBI, or of our allies, John Bull in a tux and Mademoiselle la Guillotine. In prison, you get papers with neat oblongs cut out to remove articles the censor feels provocative. They don't make any difference: all newspapers have invisible oblongs. Pastore's sterling work with underprivileged kids was mentioned but someone forgot to write about the junk he sold them when they grew into underpivileged adults. The obit photograph found him with Janey Wilde and Janice Marsh at the premiere of a George Raft movie. The phantom Jap sub off Santa Barbara got more column inches. General John L. DeWitt, head of the Western Defense Command, called for more troops to guard the coastline, prophesying 'death and destruction are likely to come at any moment'. Everyone in California was looking out to sea.

After my regular morning conference with Mr Huggins and Mr Young, I placed a call to Janey Wilde's Malibu residence. Most screen idols are either at the studio or asleep if you telephone before ten o'clock in the morning, but Janey, with weeks to go before shooting started on *Bowery to Bataan*, was at home and awake, having done her thirty lengths. Unlike almost everyone else in the industry, she thought a swimming pool was for swimming in rather than lounging beside.

She remembered instantly who I was and asked for news. I gave her a precis.

'I've been politely asked to refrain from further investigations,' I explained. 'By some heavy hitters.'

'So you're quitting?'

I should have said yes, but 'Miss Wilde, only you can require me to quit. I thought you should know how the federal government feels.'

There was a pause.

'There's something I didn't tell you,' she told me. It was an expression common among my clients. 'Something important.'

I let dead air hang on the line.

'It's not so much Laird that I'm concerned about. It's that he has Franklin.'

'Franklin?'

'The baby,' she said. 'Our baby. My baby.'

'Laird Brunette has disappeared, taking a baby with him?'

'Yes.'

'Kidnapping is a crime. You might consider calling the cops.'

'A lot of things are crimes. Laird has done many of them and never spent a day in prison.'

That was true, which was why this development was strange. Kidnapping, whether personal or for profit, is the riskiest of crimes. As a rule, it's the province only of the stupidest criminals. Laird Brunette was not a stupid criminal.

'I can't afford bad publicity. Not when I'm so near to the roles I need.'

Bowery to Bataan was going to put her among the screen immortals.

'Franklin is supposed to be Esther's boy. In a few years, I'll adopt him legally. Esther is my house-keeper. It'll work out. But I must have him back.'

'Laird is the father. He will have some rights.'

'He said he wasn't interested. He . . . um, moved on . . . to Janice Marsh while I was . . . before Franklin was born.'

'He's had a sudden attack of fatherhood and you're not convinced?'

'I'm worried to distraction. It's not Laird, it's her. Janice Marsh wants my baby for something vile. I want you to get Franklin back.'

'As I mentioned, kidnapping is a crime.'

'If there's a danger to the child, surely . . .'

'Do you have any proof that there is danger?'

'Well, no.'

'Have Laird Brunette or Janice Marsh ever given you reason to believe they have ill-will for the baby?'

'Not exactly.'

I considered things.

'I'll continue with the job you hired me for, but you understand that's all I can do. If I find Brunette, I'll pass your worries on. Then it's between the two of you.'

She thanked me in a flood and I got off the phone feeling I'd taken a couple of strides further into the LaBrea tar pits and could feel sucking stickiness well above my knees.

I should have stayed out of the rain and concentrated on chess problems but I had another four days' worth of Jungle Jillian's retainer in my pocket and an address for the Esoteric Order of Dagon in a clipping from a lunatic scientific journal. So I drove out to Venice, reminding myself all the way that my wipers needed fixing.

Venice, California, is a fascinating idea that didn't work. Someone named Abbot Kinney had the notion of artificially creating a city like Venice, Italy, with canals and architecture. The canals mostly ran dry and the architecture never really caught on in a town where, in the twenties, Gloria Swanson's bathroom was considered an aesthetic triumph. All that was left was the beach and piles of rotting fish. Venice, Italy, is the Plague Capital of Europe, so Venice, California, got one thing right.

The Esoteric Order was up the coast from Muscle Beach, housed in a discreet yacht club building with its own small marina. From the exterior, I guessed the cult business had seen better days. Seaweed had tracked up the beach, swarmed around the jetty, and was licking the lower edges of the front wall. Everything had gone green: wood, plaster, copper ornaments. And it smelled like Pastore's bathroom, only worse. This kind of place made you wonder why the Japs were so keen on invading.

I looked at myself in the mirror and rolled my eyes. I tried to get that slap-happy, let-me-give-you-all-my-worldly-goods, gimme-some-mysteries-of-the-orient look I imagined typical of a comunicant at one of these bughouse congregations. After I'd stopped laughing, I remembered the marks on Pastore and tried to take detecting seriously. Taking in my unshaven, slept-upright-in-his-clothes, two-bottles-a-day lost soul look, I congratulated myself on my foresight in spending fifteen years developing the ideal cover for a job like this.

To get in the building, I had to go down to the marina and come at it from the beach-side. There were green pillars of what looked like fungus-eaten cardboard either side of the impressive front door, which held a stained glass picture in shades of green and blue of a man with the head of a squid in a natty monk's number, waving his eyes for the artist. Dagon, I happened to know, was half-man, half-fish, and God of the Philistines. In this town, I guess a Philistine God blended in well. It's a great country: if you're half-fish, pay most of your taxes, eat babies and aren't Japanese, you have a wonderful future.

I rapped on the squid's head but nothing happened. I looked the squid in several of his eyes and felt squirmy inside. Somehow, up close, cephalopod-face didn't look that silly.

I pushed the door and found myself in a temple's waiting room. It was what I'd expected: subdued lighting, old but bad paintings, a few semi-pornographic statuettes, a strong smell of last night's incense to cover up the fish stink. It had as much religious atmosphere as a two-dollar bordello.

'Yoo-hoo,' I said, 'Dagon calling . . .'

My voice sounded less funny echoed back at me.

I prowled, sniffing for clues. I tried saying nom de something and twiddling a non-existant moustache but nothing came to me. Perhaps I ought to switch to a meerschaum of cocaine and a deerstalker, or maybe a monocle and an interest in incunabula.

Where you'd expect a portrait of George Washington or Jean Harlow's Mother, the Order had hung up an impressively ugly picture of 'Our Founder'. Capt. Obed Marsh, dressed up like Admiral Butler, stood on the shore of a Polynesian paradise, his good ship painted with no sense of perspective on the horizon as if it were about three feet tall. The Capt., surrounded by adoring if funny-faced native tomatoes, looked about as unhappy as Errol Flynn at a Girl Scout meeting. The painter had taken a lot of trouble with the native nudes. One of the dusky lovelies had hips that would make Lombard green and a face that put me in mind of Janice Marsh. She was probably the Panther Princess's great-great-great grandmother. In the background, just in front of the ship, was something like a squid emerging from the sea. Fumble-fingers with a brush had tripped up again. It looked as if the tentacle-waving creature were about twice the size of Obed's clipper. The most upsetting detail was a robed and masked figure standing on the deck with a baby's ankle in each fist. He had apparently just wrenched the child apart like a wishbone and was emptying blood into the squid's eyes.

'Excuse me,' gargled a voice, 'can I help you?'

I turned around and got a noseful of the stooped and ancient Guardian of the Cult. His robe matched the ones worn by squid-features on the door and baby-ripper in the portrait. He kept his face shadowed, his voice sounded about as good as the radio in Pastore's bath and his breath smelled worse than Pastore after a week and a half of putrefaction.

'Good morning,' I said, letting a bird flutter in the higher ranges of my voice, 'my name is, er . . .'

I put together the first things that came to mind.

'My name is Herbert West Lovecraft. Uh, H.W. Lovecraft the Third. I'm simply fascinated by matters Ancient and Esoteric, don't ch'know.'

'Don't ch'know' I picked up from the fellow with the monocle and the old books.

'You wouldn't happen to have an entry blank, would you? Or any incunabula?'

'Incunabula?' He wheezed.

'Books. Old books. Print books, published before 1500 *anno domini*, old sport.' See, I have a dictionary too.

'Books . . .'

The man was a monotonous conversationalist. He also moved like Laughton in *The Hunchback of Notre Dame* and the front of his robe, where the squidhead was embroidered, was wet with what I was disgusted to deduce was drool.

'Old books. Arcane mysteries, don't ch'know. Anything cyclopaean and doom-haunted is just up my old alley.'

'The *Necronomicon*?' He pronounced it with great respect, and great difficulty.

'Sounds just the ticket.'

Quasimodo shook his head under his hood and it lolled. I glimpsed greenish skin and large, moist eyes.

'I was recommended to come here by an old pal,' I said. 'Spiffing fellow. Laird Brunette. Ever hear of him?'

I'd pushed the wrong button. Quasi straightened out and grew about two feet. Those moist eyes flashed like razors.

'You'll have to see the Cap'n's Daughter.'

I didn't like the sound of that and stepped backwards, towards the door. Quasi laid a hand on my shoulder and held it fast. He was wearing mittens and I felt he had too many fingers inside them. His grip was like a gila monster's jaw.

'That will be fine,' I said, dropping the flutter.

As if arranged, curtains parted, and I was shoved through a door. Cracking my head on the low lintel, I could see why Quasi spent most of his time hunched over. I had to bend at the neck and knees to go down the corridor. The exterior might be rotten old wood but the heart of the place was solid stone. The walls were damp, bare and covered in suggestive carvings that gave primitive art a bad name. You'd have thought I'd be getting used to the smell by now, but nothing doing. I nearly gagged.

Quasi pushed me through another door. I was in a meeting room no larger than Union Station, with a stage, rows of comfortable armchairs and lots more squid-person statues. The centrepiece was very like the mosaic at the Seaview Inn, only the nymph had less shells and Neptune more tentacles.

Quasi vanished, slamming the door behind him. I strolled over to the stage and looked at a huge book perched on a straining lectern. The fellow with the monocle would have salivated, because this looked a lot older than 1500. It wasn't a Bible and didn't smell healthy. It was open to an illustration of something with tentacles and slime, facing a page written in several deservedly dead languages.

'The *Necronomicon*,' said a throaty female voice, 'of the mad Arab, Abdul Al-Hazred.'

'Mad, huh?' I turned to the speaker. 'Is he not getting his royalties?'

I recognised Janice Marsh straight away. The Panther Princess wore a turban and green silk lounging pajamas, with a floorlength housecoat that cost more than I make in a year. She had on jade earrings, a pearl cluster pendant and a ruby-eyed silver squid brooch. The lighting made her face look green and her round eyes shone. She still looked like Peter Lorre, but maybe if Lorre put his face on a body like Janice Marsh's, he'd be up for sex goddess roles too. Her silk thighs purred against each other as she walked down the temple aisle.

'Mr Lovecraft, isn't it?'

'Call me H. W. Everyone does.'

'Have I heard of you?'

'I doubt it.'

She was close now. A tall girl, she could look me in the eye. I had the feeling the eye-jewel in her turban was looking me in the brain. She let her fingers fall on the tentacle picture for a moment, allowed them to play around like a fun-loving spider, then removed them to my upper arm, delicately tugging me away from the book. I wasn't unhappy about that. Maybe I'm allergic to incunabula or perhaps an undiscovered prejudice against tentacled creatures, but I didn't like being near the *Necronomicon* one bit. Certainly the experience didn't compare with being near Janice Marsh.

'You're the Cap'n's Daughter?' I said.

'It's a honorific title. Obed Marsh was my ancestor. In the Esoteric Order, there is always a Cap'n's Daughter. Right now, I am she.'

'What exactly is this Dagon business about?'

She smiled, showing a row of little pearls. 'It's an alternative form of worship. It's not a racket, honestly.'

'I never said it was.'

She shrugged.

'Many people get the wrong idea.'

Outside, the wind was rising, driving rain against the Temple. The sound effects were weird, like sickening whales calling out in the Bay.

'You were asking about Laird? Did Miss Wilde send you?'

It was my turn to shrug.

'Janey is what they call a sore loser, Mr Lovecraft. It comes from taking all those bronze medals. Never the gold.'

'I don't think she wants him back,' I said, 'just to know where he is. He seems to have disappeared.'

'He's often out of town on business. He likes to be mysterious. I'm sure you understand.'

My eyes kept going to the squid-face brooch. As Janice Marsh breathed, it rose and fell and rubies winked at me.

'It's Polynesian,' she said, tapping the brooch. 'The Cap'n brought it back with him to Innsmouth.'

'Ah yes, your home town.'

'It's just a place by the sea. Like Los Angeles.'

I decided to go fishing, and hooked up some of the bait Winthrop had given me. 'Were you there when J. Edgar Hoover staged his fireworks display in the twenties?'

'Yes, I was a child. Something to do with rum-runners, I think. That was during Prohibition.'

'Good years for the Laird.'

'I suppose so. He's legitimate these days.'

'Yes. Although if he were as Scotch as he likes to pretend he is, you can be sure he'd have been deported by now.'

Janice Marsh's eyes were sea-green. Round or not, they were fascinating. 'Let me put your mind at rest, Mr Lovecraft or whatever your name is,' she said, 'the Esoteric Order of Dagon was never a front for boot-legging. In fact it has never been a front for anything. It is not a racket for duping rich widows out of inheritances. It is not an excuse for motion picture executives to gain carnal knowledge of teenage drug addicts. It is exactly what it claims to be, a church.'

'Father, Son and Holy Squid, eh?'

'I did not say we were a Christian church.'

Janice Marsh had been creeping up on me and was close enough to bite. Her active hands went to the back of my neck and angled my head down like an adjustable lamp. She put her lips on mine and squashed her face into me. I tasted lipstick, salt and caviar. Her fingers writhed up into my hair and pushed my hat off. She shut her eyes. After an hour or two of suffering in the line of duty, I put my hands on her hips and detached her body from mine. I had a fish taste in my mouth.

'That was interesting,' I said.

'An experiment,' she replied. 'Your name has such a ring to it. Love . . . craft. It suggests expertise in a certain direction.'

'Disappointed?'

She smiled. I wondered if she had several rows of teeth, like a shark.

'Anything but.'

'So do I get an invite to the back-row during your next Dagon hoe-down?'

She was businesslike again. 'I think you'd better report back to Janey. Tell her I'll have Laird call her when he's in town and put her mind at rest. She should pay you off. What with the War, it's a waste of manpower to have you spend your time looking for someone who isn't missing when you could be defending Lockheed from Fifth Columnists.'

'What about Franklin?'

'Franklin the President?'

'Franklin the baby.'

Her round eyes tried to widen. She was playing this scene innocent. The Panther Princess had been the same when telling the white hunter that Jungle Jillian had left the Tomb of the Jaguar hours ago.

'Miss Wilde seems to think Laird has borrowed a child of hers that she carelessly left in his care. She'd like Franklin back.'

'Janey hasn't got a baby. She can't have babies. It's why she's such a psycho-neurotic case. Her analyst is getting rich on her bewildering fantasies. She can't tell reality from the movies. She once accused me of human sacrifice.'

'Sounds like a square rap.'

'That was in a film, Mr Lovecraft. Cardboard knives and catsup blood.'

Usually at this stage in an investigation, I call my friend Bernie at the District Attorney's office and put out a few fishing lines. This time, he phoned me. When I got into my office, I had the feeling my telephone had been ringing for a long time.

'Don't make waves,' Bernie said.

'Pardon,' I snapped back, with my usual lightning-fast wit.

'Just don't. It's too cold to go for a swim this time of year.'

'Even in a bathtub.'

'Especially in a bathtub.'

'Does Mr District Attorney send his regards?'

Bernie laughed. I had been an investigator with the DA's office a few years back, but we'd been forced to part company.

'Forget him. I have some more impressive names on my list.'

'Let me guess. Howard Hughes?'

'Close.'

'General Stillwell?'

'Getting warmer. Try Mayor Fletcher Bowron, Governor Culbert Olson, and State Attorney General Earl Warren. Oh, and Wax, of course.'

I whistled. 'All interested in little me. Who'd 'a thunk it?'

'Look, I don't know much about this myself. They just gave me a message to pass on. In the building, they apparently think of me as your keeper.'

'Do a British gentleman, a French lady and a fed the size of Mount Rushmore have anything to do with this?'

'I'll take the money I've won so far and you can pass that question on to the next sucker.'

'Fine, Bernie. Tell me, just how popular am I?'

'Tojo rates worse than you, and maybe Judas Iscariot.'

'Feels comfy. Any idea where Laird Brunette is these days?'

I heard a pause and some rumbling. Bernie was making sure his office was empty of all ears. I imagined him bringing the receiver up close and dropping his voice to a whisper.

'No one's seen him in three months. Confidentially, I don't miss him at all. But there are others . . .' Bernie coughed, a door opened, and he started talking normally or louder. '. . . of course, honey, I'll be home in time for Jack Benny.'

'See you later, sweetheart,' I said, 'your dinner is in the sink and I'm off to Tijuana with a professional pool player.'

'Love you,' he said, and hung up.

I'd picked up a coating of green slime on the soles of my shoes. I tried scraping them off on the edge of the desk and then used yesterday's *Times* to get the stuff off the desk. The gloop looked damned esoteric to me.

I poured myself a shot from the bottle I had picked up across the street and washed the taste of Janice Marsh off my teeth.

I thought of Polynesia in the early 19th Century and of those fish-eyed native girls clustering around Capt. Marsh. Somehow, tentacles kept getting in the way of my thoughts. In theory, the Capt. should have been an ideal subject for a Dorothy Lamour movie, perhaps with Janice Marsh in the role of her great-great-great and Jon Hall or Ray Milland as girl-chasing Obed. But I was picking up Bela Lugosi vibrations from the set-up. I couldn't help but think of bisected babies.

So far none of this running around had got me any closer to the Laird and his heir. In my mind, I drew up a list of Brunette's known associates. Then, I mentally crossed off all the ones who were dead. That brought me up short. When people in Brunette's business die, nobody really takes much notice except maybe to join in a few drunken choruses of 'Ding-Dong, the Wicked Witch is Dead' before remembering there are plenty of other Wicked Witches in the sea. I'm just like everybody else: I don't keep a score of dead gambler-entrepreneurs. But, thinking of it, there'd been an awful lot recently, up to and including Gianni Pastore. Apart from Rothko and Isinglass, there'd been at least three other closed casket funerals in the profession. Obviously you couldn't blame that on the Japs. I wondered how many of the casualties had met their ends in bathtubs. The whole thing kept coming back to water. I decided I hated the stuff and swore not to let my bourbon get polluted with it.

Back out in the rain, I started hitting the bars. Brunette had a lot of friends. Maybe someone would know something.

By early evening, I'd propped up a succession of bars and leaned on a succession of losers. The only thing I'd come up with was the blatantly obvious information that everyone in town was scared. Most were wet, but all were scared.

Everyone was scared of two or three things at once. The Japs were high on everyone's list. You'd be surprised to discover the number of shaky citizens who'd turned overnight from chisellers who'd barely recognise the flag into true red, white and blue patriots prepared to shed their last drop of alcoholic blood for their country. Everywhere you went, someone sounded off against Hirohito, Tojo, the Mikado, *kabuki* and *origami*. The current rash of accidental deaths in the Pastore-Brunette circle were a much less popular subject for discussion and tended to turn loudmouths into closemouths at the drop of a question.

'Something fishy,' everyone said, before changing the subject.

I was beginning to wonder whether Janey Wilde wouldn't have done better spending her money on a radio commercial asking the Laird to give her a call. Then I found Curtis the Croupier in Maxie's. He usually wore the full soup and fish, as if borrowed from Astaire. Now he'd exchanged his carnation, starched shirtfront and pop-up top hat for an outfit in olive drab with bars on the shoulder and a cap under one epaulette.

'Heard the bugle call, Curtis?' I asked, pushing through a crowd of patriotic admirers who had been buying the soldier boy drinks.

Curtis grinned before he recognised me, then produced a supercilious sneer. We'd met before, on the *Monteáto*. There was a rumour going around that during Prohibition he'd once got involved in an honest card game, but if pressed he'd energetically refute it.

'Hey cheapie,' he said.

I bought myself a drink but didn't offer him one. He had three or four lined up.

'This racket must pay,' I said. 'How much did the uniform cost? You rent it from Paramount?'

The croupier was offended. 'It's real,' he said. 'I've enlisted. I hope to be sent overseas.'

'Yeah, we ought to parachute you into Tokyo to introduce loaded dice and rickety roulette wheels.'

'You're cynical, cheapie.' He tossed back a drink.

'No, just a realist. How come you quit the Monty?'

'Poking around in the Laird's business?'

I raised my shoulders and dropped them again.

'Gambling has fallen off recently, along with leading figures in the industry. The original owner of this place, for instance. I bet paying for wreaths has thinned your bankroll.'

Curtis took two more drinks, quickly, and called for more. When I'd come in, there'd been a couple of chippies climbing into his hip pockets. Now he was on his own with me. He didn't appreciate the change of scenery and I can't say I blamed him.

'Look cheapie,' he said, his voice suddenly low, 'for your own good, just drop it. There are more important things now.'

'Like democracy?'

'You can call it that.'

'How far overseas do you want to be sent, Curtis?'

He looked at the door as if expecting five guys with tommy guns to come out of the rain for him. Then he gripped the bar to stop his hands shaking.

'As far as I can get, cheapie. The Philippines, Europe, Australia. I don't care.'

'Going to war is a hell of a way to escape.'

'Isn't it just? But wouldn't Papa Gianni have been safer on Wake Island than in the tub?'

'You heard the bathtime story, then?'

Curtis nodded and took another gulp. The juke box played 'Doodly-Acky-Sacky, Want Some Seafood, Mama' and it was scary. Nonsense, but scary.

'They all die in water. That's what I've heard. Sometimes, on the *Monty*, Laird would go up on deck and just look at the sea for hours. He was crazy, since he took up with that Marsh popsicle.'

'The Panther Princess?'

'You saw that one? Yeah, Janice Marsh. Pretty girl if you like clams. Laird claimed there was a sunken town in the bay. He used a lot of weird words, darkie bop or something. Jitterbug stuff. Cthul-whatever, Yog-Gimme-a-Break. He said things were going to come out of the water and sweep over the land, and he didn't mean U-Boats.'

Curtis was uncomfortable in his uniform. There were dark patches where the rain had soaked. He'd been drinking like W.C. Fields on a bender but he wasn't getting tight. Whatever was troubling him was too much even for Jack Daniel's.

I thought of the Laird of the *Monty*. And I thought of the painting of Capt. Marsh's clipper, with that out-of-proportion squid surfacing near it.

'He's on the boat, isn't he?'

Curtis didn't say anything.

'Alone,' I thought aloud. 'He's out there alone.'

I pushed my hat to the back of my head and tried to shake booze out of my mind. It was crazy. Nobody bobs up and down in the water with a sign round their neck saying 'Hey Tojo, Torpedo Me!' The *Monty* was a floating target.

'No,' Curtis said, grabbing my arm, jarring drink out of my glass.

'He's not out there?'

He shook his head.

'No, cheapie. He's not out there alone.'

All the water taxis were in dock, securely moored and covered until the storms settled. I'd never find a boatman to take me out to the *Montecito* tonight. Why, everyone knew the waters were infested with Japanese subs. But I knew someone who wouldn't care any more whether or not his boats were being treated properly. He was even past bothering if they were borrowed without his permission.

The Seaview Inn was still deserted, although there were police notices warning people away from the scene of the crime. It was dark, cold and wet, and nobody bothered me as I broke into the boathouse to find a ring of keys.

I took my pick of the taxis moored to the Seaview's jetty and gassed her up for a short voyage. I also got my .38 Colt Super Match out from the glove compartment of the Chrysler and slung it under my armpit. During all this, I got a thorough soaking and picked up the beginnings of influenza. I hoped Jungle Jillian would appreciate the effort.

The sea was swelling under the launch and making a lot of noise. I was grateful for the noise when it came to shooting the padlock off the mooring chain but the swell soon had my stomach sloshing about in my lower abdomen. I am not an especially competent seaman.

The *Monty* was out there on the horizon, still visible whenever the lightning lanced. It was hardly difficult to keep the small boat aimed at the bigger one.

Getting out on the water makes you feel small. Especially when the lights of Bay City are just a scatter in the dark behind you. I got the impression of large things moving just beyond my field of perception. The chill soaked through my clothes. My hat was a felt sponge, dripping down my neck. As the launch cut towards the *Monty*, rain and spray needled my face. I saw my hands white and bath-wrinkled on the wheel and wished I'd brought a bottle. Come to that, I wished I was at home in bed with a mug of cocoa and Claudette Colbert. Some things in life don't turn out the way you plan.

Three miles out, I felt the law change in my stomach. Gambling was legal and I emptied my belly over the side into the water. I stared at the remains of my toasted cheese sandwich as they floated off. I thought I saw the moon reflected greenly in the depths, but there was no moon that night.

I killed the engine and let waves wash the taxi against the side of the *Monty*. The small boat scraped along the hull of the gambling ship and I caught hold of a weed-furred rope ladder as it passed. I tethered the taxi and took a deep breath.

The ship sat low in the water, as if its lower cabins were flooded. Too much seaweed climbed up towards the decks. It'd never reopen for business, even if the War were over tomorrow.

I climbed the ladder, fighting the water-weight in my clothes, and heaved myself up on deck. It was good to have something more solid than a tiny boat under me but the deck pitched like an airplane wing. I grabbed a rail and hoped my internal organs would arrange themselves back into their familiar grouping.

'Brunette,' I shouted, my voice lost in the wind.

There was nothing. I'd have to go belowdecks.

A sheet flying flags of all nations had come loose, and was whipped around with the storm. Japan, Italy and Germany were still tactlessly represented, along with several European states that weren't really nations any more. The deck was covered in familiar slime.

I made my way around towards the ballroom doors. They'd blown in and rain splattered against the polished wood floors. I got inside and pulled the .38. It felt better in my hand than digging into my ribs.

Lightning struck nearby and I got a flash image of the abandoned ballroom, orchestra stands at one end painted with the name of a disbanded combo.

The casino was one deck down. It should be dark but I saw a glow under a walkway door. I pushed through and cautiously descended. It wasn't wet here but it was cold. The fish smell was strong.

'Brunette,' I shouted again.

I imagined something heavy shuffling nearby and slipped a few steps, banging my hip and arm against a bolted-down table. I kept hold of my gun, but only through superhuman strength.

The ship wasn't deserted. That much was obvious.

I could hear music. It wasn't Cab Calloway or Benny Goodman. There was a Hawaiian guitar in there but mainly it was a crazy choir of keening voices. I wasn't convinced the performers were human and wondered whether Brunette was working up some kind of act with singing seals. I couldn't make out the words but the familiar hawk-and-spit syllables of 'Cthulhu' cropped up a couple of times.

I wanted to get out and go back to nasty Bay City and forget all about this. But Jungle Jillian was counting on me.

I made my way along the passage, working towards the music. A hand fell on my shoulder and my heart banged against the backsides of my eyeballs.

A twisted face stared at me out of the gloom, thickly-bearded, crater-cheeked. Laird Brunette was made up as Ben Gunn, skin shrunk onto his skull, eyes large as hen's eggs.

His hand went over my mouth.

'Do Not Disturb,' he said, voice high and cracked.

This wasn't the suave criminal I knew, the man with tartan

cummerbunds and patent leather hair. This was some other Brunette, in the grips of a tough bout with dope or madness.

'The Deep Ones,' he said.

He let me go and I backed away.

'It is the time of the Surfacing.'

My case was over. I knew where the Laird was. All I had to do was tell Janey Wilde and give her her refund.

'There's very little time.'

The music was louder. I heard a great number of bodies shuffling around in the casino. They couldn't have been very agile, because they kept clumping into things and each other.

'They must be stopped. Dynamite, depth charges, torpedoes . . .'

'Who?' I asked. 'The Japs?'

'The Deep Ones. The Dwellers in the Sister City.'

He had lost me.

A nasty thought occurred to me. As a detective, I can't avoid making deductions. There were obviously a lot of people aboard the *Monty*, but mine was the only small boat in evidence. How had everyone else got out here? Surely they couldn't have swam?

'It's a war,' Brunette ranted, 'us and them. It's always been a war.'

I made a decision. I'd get the Laird off his boat and turn him over to Jungle Jillian. She could sort things out with the Panther Princess and her Esoteric Order. In his current state, Brunette would hand over any baby if you gave him a blanket.

I took Brunette's thin wrist and tugged him towards the staircase. But a hatch clanged down and I knew we were stuck.

A door opened and perfume drifted through the fish stink.

'Mr Lovecraft, wasn't it?' a silk-scaled voice said.

———

Janice Marsh was wearing pendant squid earrings and a lady-sized gun. And nothing else.

That wasn't quite as nice as it sounds. The Panther Princess had no nipples, no navel and no pubic hair. She was lightly scaled between the legs and her wet skin shone like a shark's. I imagined that if you stroked her, your palm would come away bloody. She was wearing neither the turban she'd affected earlier nor the dark wig of her pictures. Her head was completely bald, skull swelling unnaturally. She didn't even have her eyebrows pencilled in.

'You evidently can't take good advice.'

As mermaids go, she was scarier than cute. In the crook of her left arm, she held a bundle from which a white baby face peered with unblinking eyes. Franklin looked more like Janice Marsh than his parents.

'A pity, really,' said a tiny ventriloquist voice through Franklin's mouth, 'but there are always complications.'

Brunette gibbered with fear, chewing his beard and huddling against me.

Janice Marsh set Franklin down and he sat up, an adult struggling with a baby's body.

'The Cap'n has come back,' she explained.

'Every generation must have a Cap'n,' said the thing in Franklin's mind. Dribble got in the way and he wiped his angel-mouth with a fold of swaddle.

Janice Marsh clucked and pulled Laird away from me, stroking his face.

'Poor dear,' she said, flicking his chin with a long tongue. 'He got out of his depth.'

She put her hands either side of Brunette's head, pressing the butt of her gun into his cheek.

'He was talking about a Sister City,' I prompted.

She twisted the gambler's head around and dropped him on the floor. His tongue poked out and his eyes showed only white.

'Of course,' the baby said. 'The Cap'n founded two settlements. One beyond Devil Reef, off Massachusetts. And one here, under the sands of the Bay.'

We both had guns. I'd let her kill Brunette without trying to shoot her. It was the detective's fatal flaw, curiosity. Besides the Laird was dead inside his head long before Janice snapped his neck.

'You can still join us,' she said, hips working like a snake in time to the chanting. 'There are raptures in the deeps.'

'Sister,' I said, 'you're not my type.'

Her nostrils flared in anger and slits opened in her neck, flashing liverish red lines in her white skin.

Her gun was pointed at me, safety off. Her long nails were lacquered green.

I thought I could shoot her before she shot me. But I didn't. Something about a naked woman, no matter how strange, prevents you from killing them. Her whole body was moving with the music. I'd been wrong. Despite everything, she was beautiful.

I put my gun down and waited for her to murder me. It never happened.

———

I don't really know the order things worked out. But first there was lightning, then, an instant later, thunder.

Light filled the passageway, hurting my eyes. Then, a rumble of noise which grew in a crescendo. The chanting was drowned.

Through the thunder cut a screech. It was a baby's cry. Franklin's eyes were screwed up and he was shrieking. I had a sense of the Cap'n drowning in the baby's mind, his purchase on the purloined body relaxing as the child cried out.

The floor beneath me shook and buckled and I heard a great straining of abused metal. A belch of hot wind surrounded me. A hole appeared. Janice Marsh moved fast and I think she fired her gun, but whether at me on purpose or at random in reflex I couldn't say. Her body sliced towards me and I ducked.

There was another explosion, not of thunder, and thick smoke billowed through a rupture in the floor. I was on the floor, hugging the tilting deck. Franklin slid towards me and bumped, screaming, into my head. A half-ton of water fell on us and I knew the ship was breached. My guess was that the Japs had just saved my life with a torpedo. I was waist deep in saltwater. Janice Marsh darted away in a sinuous fish motion.

Then there were heavy bodies around me, pushing me against a bulkhead. In the darkness, I was scraped by something heavy, cold-skinned and foul-smelling. There were barks and cries, some of which might have come from human throats.

Fires went out and hissed as the water rose. I had Franklin in my hands and tried to hold him above water. I remembered the peril of Jungle Jillian again and found my head floating against the hard ceiling.

The Cap'n cursed in vivid 18th Century language, Franklin's little body squirming in my grasp. A toothless mouth tried to get a biter's grip on my chin·but slipped off. My feet slid and I was off-balance, pulling the baby briefly underwater. I saw his startled eyes through a wobbling film. When I pulled him out again, the Cap'n was gone and Franklin was screaming on his own. Taking a double gulp of air, I plunged under the water and struggled towards the nearest door, a hand closed over the baby's face to keep water out of his mouth and nose.

The *Monteaito* was going down fast enough to suggest there were plenty of holes in it. I had to make it a priority to find one. I jammed my knee at a door and it flew open. I was poured, along with several hundred gallons of water, into a large room full of stored gambling equipment. Red and white chips floated like confetti.

I got my footing and waded towards a ladder. Something large reared out of the water and shambled at me, screeching like a seabird. I didn't get a good look at it. Which was a mercy. Heavy arms lashed me, flopping boneless against my face. With my free hand, I pushed back at the thing, fingers slipping against cold slime. Whatever it was was in a panic and squashed through the door.

There was another explosion and everything shook. Water splashed upwards and I fell over. I got upright and managed to get a

one-handed grip on the ladder. Franklin was still struggling and bawl-
ing, which I took to be a good sign. Somewhere near, there was a lot
of shouting.

I dragged us up rung by rung and slammed my head against a
hatch. If it had been battened, I'd have smashed my skull and spilled
my brains. It flipped upwards and a push of water from below shoved
us through the hole like a ping-pong ball in a fountain.

The *Monty* was on fire and there were things in the water around
it. I heard the drone of airplane engines and glimpsed nearby launches.
Gunfire fought with the wind. It was a full-scale attack. I made it to
the deck-rail and saw a boat fifty feet away. Men in yellow slickers
angled tommy guns down and spraying the water with bullets.

The gunfire whipped up the sea into a foam. Kicking things died
in the water. Someone brought up his gun and fired at me. I pushed
myself aside, arching my body over Franklin and bullets spanged
against the deck.

My borrowed taxi must have been dragged under by the bulk of
the ship.

There were definitely lights in the sea. And the sky. Over the city,
in the distance, I saw firecracker bursts. Something exploded a
hundred yards away and a tower of water rose, bursting like a puffball.
A depth charge.

The deck was angled down and water was creeping up at us. I held
on to a rope webbing, wondering whether the gambling ship still had
any lifeboats. Franklin spluttered and bawled.

A white body slid by, heading for the water. I instinctively grabbed
at it. Hands took hold of me and I was looking into Janice Marsh's
face. Her eyes blinked, membranes coming round from the sides, and
she kissed me again. Her long tongue probed my mouth like an eel,
then withdrew. She stood up, one leg bent so she was still vertical on
the sloping deck. She drew air into her lungs—if she had lungs—and
expelled it through her gills with a musical cry. She was slim and white
in the darkness, water running off her body. Someone fired in her

direction and she dived into the waves, knifing through the surface and disappearing towards the submarine lights. Bullets rippled the spot where she'd gone under.

I let go of the ropes and kicked at the deck, pushing myself away from the sinking ship. I held Franklin above the water and splashed with my legs and elbows. The *Monty* was dragging a lot of things under with it, and I fought against the pull so I wouldn't be one of them. My shoulders ached and my clothes got in the way, but I kicked against the current.

The ship went down screaming, a chorus of bending steel and dying creatures. I had to make for a launch and hope not to be shot. I was lucky. Someone got a polehook into my jacket and landed us like fish. I lay on the deck, water running out of my clothes, swallowing as much air as I could breathe.

I heard Franklin yelling. His lungs were still in working order.

Someone big in a voluminous slicker, a sou'wester tied to his head, knelt by me, and slapped me in the face.

'Peeper,' he said.

———

'They're calling it the Great Los Angeles Air Raid,' Winthrop told me as he poured a mug of British tea. 'Some time last night a panic started, and everyone in Bay City shot at the sky for hours.'

'The Japs?' I said, taking a mouthful of welcome hot liquid.

'In theory. Actually, I doubt it. It'll be recorded as a fiasco, a lot of jumpy characters with guns. While it was all going on, we engaged the enemy and emerged victorious.'

He was still dressed up for an embassy ball and didn't look as if he'd been on deck all evening. Geneviève Dieudonné wore a fisherman's sweater and fatigue pants, her hair up in a scarf. She was looking at a lot of sounding equipment and noting down readings.

'You're not fighting the Japs, are you?'

Winthrop pursed his lips. 'An older war, my friend. We can't be distracted. After last night's action, our Deep Ones won't poke their scaly noses out for a while. Now I can do something to lick Hitler.'

'What really happened?'

'There was something dangerous in the sea, under Mr Brunette's boat. We have destroyed it and routed the . . . uh, the hostile forces. They wanted the boat as a surface station. That's why Mr Brunette's associates were eliminated.'

Geneviève gave a report in French, so fast that I couldn't follow.

'Total destruction,' Winthrop explained, 'a dreadful set-back for them. It'll put them in their place for years. Forever would be too much to hope for, but a few years will help.'

I lay back on the bunk, feeling my wounds. Already choking on phlegm, I would be lucky to escape pneumonia.

'And the little fellow is a decided dividend.'

Finlay glumly poked around, suggesting another dose of depth charges. He was cradling a mercifully sleep-struck Franklin, but didn't look terribly maternal.

'He seems quite unaffected by it all.'

'His name is Franklin,' I told Winthrop. 'On the boat, he was . . .'

'Not himself? I'm familiar with the condition. It's a filthy business, you understand.'

'He'll be all right,' Geneviève put in.

I wasn't sure whether the rest of the slicker crew were feds or servicemen and I wasn't sure whether I wanted to know. I could tell a Clandestine Operation when I landed in the middle of one.

'Who knows about this?' I asked. 'Hoover? Roosevelt?'

Winthrop didn't answer.

'Someone must know,' I said.

'Yes,' the Englishman said, 'someone must. But this is a war the public would never believe exists. In the Bureau, Finlay's outfit are known as "the Unnameables", never mentioned by the press, never honoured or censured by the government, victories and defeats never recorded in the official history.'

The launch shifted with the waves, and I hugged myself, hoping for some warmth to creep over me. Finlay had promised to break out a bottle later but that made me resolve to stick to tea as a point of honour. I hated to fulfil his expectations.

'And America is a young country,' Winthrop explained. 'In Europe, we've known things a lot longer.'

On shore, I'd have to tell Janey Wilde about Brunette and hand over Franklin. Some flack at Metro would be thinking of an excuse for the Panther Princess's disappearance. Everything else—the depth charges, the sea battle, the sinking ship—would be swallowed up by the War.

All that would be left would be tales. Weird tales.

It occurred to me that Raymond Chandler and H.P. Lovecraft had a lot in common. Born in 1888 and 1890, they lived unhappily in America but dreamed of a lost and imaginary England. Awkward outsiders, they were often beset with financial troubles and began their writing careers in pulp magazines. Their visionary, challenging work was first presented alongside lurid dross, though they later came to be recognised as central to separate movements within their chosen genres, hard-boiled crime and weird horror. Married strangely to older wives, they distrusted and feared women, often presenting cruel, almost inhuman female characters. Some of their greatest work is set in seaside towns whose physical corruption has an almost philosophical dimension, and they used despised genres to make a genuine contribution to English and American letters. Since their deaths, they have become the most imitated and influential writers in their fields and are capable of inspiring entire collections devoted to their characters and themes. Personally, I found the love of Chandler's prose which I developed in my late teens helped cure habits I'd picked up through an earlier interest in Lovecraft; which is not to denigrate HPL, whom I still admire and enjoy.

Here, I wanted to bring a touch of Lovecraft's Innsmouth to Chandler's Bay City, fusing elements from 'The Shadow Over Innsmouth' and Farewell, My Lovely. *If its narrator isn't quite Philip Marlowe, he certainly would like to be. I see him as more like Dick Powell than*

Bogart. The stylistic tangle the story can't resolve has something to do with the disparity between a Lovecraft protagonist, who is always overhwelmed by his hostile world, and a Chandler hero, who somehow shrugs it off. The other set of cross-generic twins of the period are Robert E. Howard and Cornell Woolrich, a pair of mother-dominated paranoid miseries whose vision of a hostile universe makes Lovecraft's cosmic horror seem quite sunny, but I can't envision a story called 'Conan Wears Black', though a chance meeting in a diner with Bob and Cornell comparing photographs of their mothers has some horrific possibility.